Hello there!

Thank you so much for choosing to read *The Sixpenny Orphan*. It's a story of two orphaned sisters, torn apart in tragic events.

When I was writing this book, the power of emotions I went through had me in tears! The book begins with the orphans as children, then jumps ten years ahead when they are reunited, but their lives have drastically changed and nothing is as it seems. It's a powerful read, with some wonderful characters, not all of whom are as nice as they may first seem.

The book is set in the northeast village of Ryhope where I grew up. This time the story unfolds in the farming community. I hope that I've done justice to the village in bringing the setting alive.

Please follow me on social media to keep up to date with all news, competitions and giveaways from my author page on Facebook **/GlendaYoungAuthor** and Twitter **@flaming_nora** – do come and say hello!

I really hope you enjoy this book.

Glenda Young

Praise for Glenda Young:

'Real sagas with female characters right at the heart' *Woman's Hour*

'The feel of the story is totally authentic . . . Her heroine
in the grand Cookson tradition . . . Inspirationally delightful'
Peterborough Evening Telegraph

'In the world of historical saga writers, there's a brand new
voice – welcome, Glenda Young, who brings a freshness
to the genre' *My Weekly*

'Will resonate with saga readers everywhere . . .
a wonderful, uplifting story' Nancy Revell

'I really enjoyed . . . It's well researched and well written and
I found myself caring about her characters' Rosie Goodwin

'Glenda has an exceptionally keen eye for domestic detail
which brings this local community to vivid, colourful life'
Jenny Holmes

'I found it extremely well written, and having always loved sagas,
one of the best I've read' Margaret Kaine

'All the ingredients for a perfect saga' Emma Hornby

'Her descriptions of both character and setting are wonderful . . .
there is a warmth and humour in bucket loads' *Frost Magazine*

'A gripping saga' *People's Friend*

By Glenda Young

Saga Novels
Belle of the Back Streets
The Tuppenny Child
Pearl of Pit Lane
The Girl with the Scarlet Ribbon
The Paper Mill Girl
The Miner's Lass
A Mother's Christmas Wish
The Sixpenny Orphan

Helen Dexter Cosy Crime Mysteries
Murder at the Seaview Hotel
Curtain Call at the Seaview Hotel

GLENDA YOUNG

The Sixpenny Orphan

HEADLINE

First published in 2023 by
HEADLINE PUBLISHING GROUP

First published in paperback in 2023 by
HEADLINE PUBLISHING GROUP

1

Cataloguing in Publication Data is available from the British Library

ISBN 978 1 4722 8328 3

Typeset in Garamond by Avon DataSet Ltd, Alcester, Warwickshire

Printed and bound in Great Britain by Clays Ltd, Elcograf S.p.A.

HEADLINE PUBLISHING GROUP
An Hachette UK Company
Carmelite House
50 Victoria Embankment
London EC4Y 0DZ

www.headline.co.uk
www.hachette.co.uk

For Ryhope

Acknowledgements

My thanks go to Brian Ibinson and Peter Hedley of Ryhope Heritage Society; Sunderland Antiquarian Society; Sharon Vincent for her knowledge of women's social history in Sunderland; Rob Shepherd; John Wilson and staff at Fulwell Post Office; Hayley and the team at Sunderland Waterstones; Katy Wheeler at the *Sunderland Echo*; Claire Pickersgill of Hype That PR; Simon Grundy of Sun FM 103.4; Gilly Hope and Anna Foster at BBC Radio Newcastle; Beverley Ann Hopper; Tony Kerr; Izzy McDonald-Booth and the team in the shop at the beautiful National Glass Centre, Sunderland; Pauline Martin at The Word / National Centre for the Written Word in South Shields (one of my favourite places in the north-east); Michelle Watson of Culture, Heritage & Libraries at Northumberland County Council.

Special thanks to Kate Byrne, my editor at Headline, and to my agent, Caroline Sheldon. And to my husband, Barry, for his love and support and all the frothy coffees he brings me when I lock myself away to write.

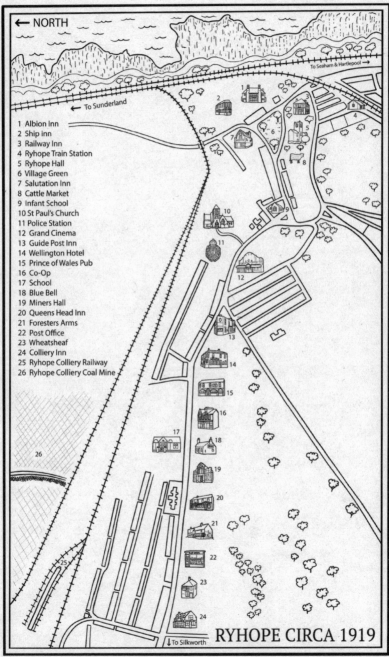

← NORTH

To Seaham & Hartlepool →

← To Sunderland

1 Albion Inn
2 Ship inn
3 Railway Inn
4 Ryhope Train Station
5 Ryhope Hall
6 Village Green
7 Salutation Inn
8 Cattle Market
9 Infant School
10 St Paul's Church
11 Police Station
12 Grand Cinema
13 Guide Post Inn
14 Wellington Hotel
15 Prince of Wales Pub
16 Co-Op
17 School
18 Blue Bell
19 Miners Hall
20 Queens Head Inn
21 Foresters Arms
22 Post Office
23 Wheatsheaf
24 Colliery Inn
25 Ryhope Colliery Railway
26 Ryhope Colliery Coal Mine

↓ To Silkworth

RYHOPE CIRCA 1919

Illustration by Jo Blakeley

www.glendayoungbooks.com

Chapter One

Autumn 1909

'Poppy, are you awake? I need to tell you a secret,' Rose whispered.

Poppy turned on the straw mattress, which was itching her arms and legs. 'What is it?' she replied, taking care not to let Nellie hear.

'Nellie got another letter today.'

Poppy reached for her sister's hand. 'Where is it?'

'I saw her put it in her pocket. It was another big envelope with fancy writing on the front.'

On the floor beneath them in the barn at the back of the cattle market, Nellie began to snore. Slowly Poppy raised herself off the mattress and peered down to look at her.

'She's fast asleep. We could creep down the ladder and steal the letter from her pocket,' she said.

Rose gripped her hand. 'No. What if she wakes up? Our lives won't be worth living if she catches us. Anyway, what would we do with it?'

'I'd take it to Sid. He can read,' Poppy said decisively.

'Poppy, please don't do it,' Rose begged. 'You've been stealing too much lately. Ambrose Trewhitt almost caught you taking stuff from his shop again yesterday.'

'How are we supposed to eat if I don't steal food?' Poppy lay down again. Her leg began to itch and she scratched her knee. 'The straw's full of fleas, they're biting me,' she moaned. 'They never bite you. It's not fair.'

'Shush, Nellie will hear.'

The sisters lay in silence, still holding hands. Below them, Nellie's rattling snores were getting louder and stronger. Each time she exhaled, it sounded to Poppy as if the barn roof would blow off. The thought of this made her giggle.

'Stop it,' Rose urged. 'Don't wake her. She'll be furious.'

Poppy stuffed her hand into her mouth to quell her laughter. She wasn't as frightened of Nellie as her younger sister was. But she knew that if the woman woke from her precious sleep before she was ready, she would take her anger out on them both. She snuggled down and pulled the coarse, rough blanket up to her chin. It had once been used to cover horses, and stank of farmyard dirt.

'I'm scared, Poppy,' Rose said.

'Of Nellie? Don't be. Leave her to me, I can handle her,' Poppy said, more assertively than she felt.

At just ten years old, Poppy was a year older than Rose, and she thought herself very grown up. Their parents had died two years ago, and the sisters had moved into the barn to live with Nellie Harper. They had done a lot of growing up since. They'd also done a lot of crying, trying to come to terms with their lives as unloved, unwanted orphans. Their dad had died at the pit, and three months later, their mam was found drowned on the beach. The talk in the village was that she had thrown herself from the cliffs after her beloved husband passed away, and died suffering a broken heart. More cruel gossip suggested that she'd been bad with her nerves and unstable in her mind, for why else would a mother leave two little girls alone? With no relatives in the village, it was widow woman Nellie Harper who offered to take Poppy and Rose. However, she didn't do so out of the goodness of her heart. She had her own reasons, and they all involved cold, hard cash.

Nellie worked as a knocker-upper. It was her job to wake coal miners from their sleep so they'd be at work in time for their shift. She carried a long stick that she tapped against the window until the miner inside called out to let her know he was up. Job done, she moved to the next house, then the next. If any miner didn't wake at her insistent rapping, she'd throw stones at his bedroom window until he flung it open. No miner was left in bed, for if he was late for work, there'd be no money coming into the house and no food for his bairns. Worse, Nellie's reputation as a reliable knocker-upper would be at stake, and she wouldn't get paid.

She knew how crucial her role was, and she took her work seriously. In the small village of Ryhope, on the north-east coast, she walked the pit lanes day and night to coincide with the miners' shifts. Sometimes she worked as many as four shifts in the day. When she returned home, ready to settle in her chair for a snooze, it was often time for her to set out again. However, in order for her to get out of bed on time to start work, she needed someone to wake *her*. This was where Poppy and Rose came in, the only reason Nellie had taken them in after their mam died.

'Rose, remember it's your turn to wake Nellie in the morning,' Poppy whispered. 'You mustn't go to sleep. You've got to stay awake and listen for the three bells.'

The bells were the chimes from St Paul's church, close to the farm where they lived.

'It's my turn to go to school tomorrow,' she added sleepily.

The sisters had to take turns to go to school as they only had one pair of boots between them. The village school had high standards and wouldn't allow any child inside with bare feet. Attending school on alternate days was better than nothing, but it meant that both girls were far behind when it came to reading and writing. Poppy in particular struggled to learn. Words seemed to change in front of her eyes, and attempting to read confused her.

As she turned on the straw, she saw her sister's pretty face lit by moonlight streaming through holes in the roof. She took in Rose's pale skin and her fluttering eyelids. She wondered if she was asleep and dreaming about something nice. Something from the days before their dad died at the pit, before their mam drowned on the beach and before Nellie Harper came into their lives.

She sighed, staring up at the slats of rotten wood above her. On bitterly cold days, when Poppy complained about the sleet and snow coming in, Nellie reminded her where she and Rose might have ended up if she hadn't taken them in. A shiver ran down Poppy's back when Nellie threatened her like that. She'd heard rumours of dark, forbidding institutions where unwanted orphans were left at the gates, taken in by stern-faced harridans and never seen again. She'd also heard of a house in Ryhope run by a woman called Miss Gilbey, who took in destitute girls. But whenever she'd spotted Miss Gilbey walking by on the street, the woman's long black skirts and pinched face scared the living daylights out of her.

Their home with Nellie, such as it was, was at the back of the farm owned by Nellie's brother, Norman. It had once been a cow barn, before the animals were moved to a different barn that Nellie complained offered better accommodation than the one she lived in with the orphans. And on top of that, she added bitterly, Norman had the effrontery to demand rent for the squalid space, and even charged her for coal for the fire.

The barn was big and airy, with a ladder leading up to the hayloft where Poppy and Rose slept. Downstairs, where Nellie lived, there was a coal fire against a stone wall and a big stuffed armchair that had seen better days. The chair was where Nellie sat, slept and ate. It was where she barked out instructions to Poppy and Rose as she taught them how to cook what little food she could afford. Poppy boiled cabbages to make soup, or did her best to bake bread whenever Nellie could afford to buy flour. Norman sometimes brought dead chickens and chucked these at Nellie, imploring his sister to feed the orphans, who were all skin and bone. Sometimes he brought turnips and potatoes, and Nellie would command Poppy to make stew. She gave no love to the two girls and showed little kindness. Instead, she treated them as a nuisance to be endured for the sake of waking her up for her work.

Rose yawned and turned on her side. When her eyes opened, Poppy realised her sister was awake and hadn't been dreaming at all.

'I know it's my turn to wake Nellie up. I'll listen for the bells. Go to sleep, Poppy,' Rose mumbled.

'I don't think I can. I'm worried about Nellie's letter. I think something's wrong. You've seen the way she's been lately, acting strange. When I fetched water from the yard for our bath last week, she told me to make sure I washed behind my ears. Then she told me to brush my hair a hundred times before I went to bed.'

'A hundred times?' Rose cried. 'But she knows you can't count past twelve.' Poppy could only count as far as the number of bells she heard chiming from St Paul's church.

'Shush,' Poppy said, worried about waking Nellie.

The sisters stiffened in bed, waiting to hear the reassuring noise of Nellie snoring, proof that she was still asleep, before they continued.

'Why's she so bothered about how I look? She's never taken an interest before. She's even started checking my head for nits, and that hasn't happened since she took us in.'

'She hasn't done anything like that to me,' Rose said.

'That's because you're so pretty,' Poppy said. 'You don't need anyone to remind you to brush your hair or wash your face. I need a bit more telling.'

'You're pretty too,' Rose said.

'I'm not and you know it.' Poppy sighed. 'You don't have to tell lies.'

'I'm not telling lies,' Rose said with a catch in her voice. 'I love you, Poppy. You're the prettiest girl I know.'

6

'You're prettier than me, Mam always said so. That's why she called you Rose, because roses were her favourite flowers. You're delicate and sweet, just like a beautiful rose. Whereas I'm named after poppies, and they grow like weeds. They put down stubborn roots and some people don't like them. And my hair's not as nice as yours. Yours is lovely and straight, while mine's curly and I hate it.'

'Dad had curly hair. You must take after him.'

The girls were silent for a moment, as they always were when talk turned to their parents.

'Do you remember Dad?' Poppy asked eventually.

'Sometimes,' Rose replied sadly. 'I remember his voice, the way it used to make me feel safe and warm. And I remember the way Mam tucked us into bed at night and kissed us to send us to sleep.'

Poppy shifted on the straw. 'Another family lives in the house we used to live in. I sometimes look in through the windows and I see a little boy with his mam. There's often a pram in the garden by the front door. I hope that family are as happy as we were once.' She crossed her fingers.

'Mam always said you were pretty,' Rose said sleepily.

Poppy touched her nose. 'I've got too many freckles. Even Sid says he's never seen anyone with freckles like mine. Mam used to say that putting mustard paste on your face takes the freckles away. I might try it one day.'

'You'll smell of mustard for ever,' Rose said. 'Then Sid won't want to kiss you.'

'Eew . . . who says I want to kiss Sid? I don't want to kiss anyone, and certainly not a boy.'

'Do you really think Sid would read the letter for us if you stole it from Nellie?' Rose asked.

'I'm sure he would,' Poppy replied. 'There's not much he wouldn't do for me. I'm his best friend. I'm certain something's up with Nellie. She keeps looking at me really odd when she thinks I don't see her.'

'It does sound strange,' Rose said. She propped herself up in bed. 'How many letters do you think she's received?'

'I've seen three arrive lately, and if you saw one today, that makes four. Did it have the same writing on the front as the others?'

Rose nodded in the darkness, then sank back on to the straw. 'Maybe she's got a boyfriend and he's writing her love letters,' she said.

'You're such a soppy little sister at times,' Poppy chided. 'Who'd want smelly Nellie as his sweetheart? No, I don't think you're right. I think there's something else going on. It's more than a coincidence that her telling me how to dress and wash started when the letters first arrived. I've got to find out.'

'Be careful. If she knows you're on to her, she could put us out on the streets, and we'd be sent to the workhouse or to live with Miss Gilbey, that strange woman who takes in unwanted girls. This place is horrible, but it's all we've got.'

Poppy reached for Rose's hand again. 'We've got each other. I'll look after you. First thing tomorrow after Nellie leaves for work, I'm going to find the letter.'

Chapter Two

When the three bells chimed from the tower at St Paul's, Poppy stirred in her bed. She heard the bells clearly, but Rose was still asleep. She gently nudged her sister. 'Rose, it's time for you to wake Nellie.'

Rose stirred, yawned loudly, then stepped out of bed. When her bare feet hit the cold wooden floor, she winced with pain. She tiptoed across the room to the ladder and carefully climbed down to where Nellie was snoring. She walked across the barn to Nellie's chair and gently touched her shoulder. Nellie was a chubby woman, and her shoulder felt fleshy and meaty under Rose's small hand.

'It's time to go to work, Nellie,' Rose said quietly – too quietly, for Nellie didn't stir. She tried again, louder this time, and shook her shoulder hard. This time Nellie woke with a start.

'Yes, girl, I'm awake,' she said grumpily. 'Get me my stick.'

Nellie's knocking-up stick was always kept in the corner of the room, and Rose fetched it quickly. She handed it to Nellie, who snatched it from her.

'Oh, it's you,' groaned the woman, squinting at Rose in the darkness. 'I thought it was your sister's turn to wake me this morning.'

'No, it's Poppy's turn to go to school.'

'Aye, well, make sure she does go. I want her head full of learning – tell her it's important.'

'Is it important for me to learn too?' Rose asked.

Nellie shot her a look. 'No one needs to be clever when they're as pretty as you. You'll do as you are.'

Poppy listened to the sounds from below. She heard Nellie's chair creak as she stood. She heard her cough and splutter as she cleared her chest, then she heard her boots clatter on the floor as she got ready to go out.

'Set the fire, girl, I want it ready for when I return,' Nellie ordered. 'I've got another two shifts to work yet.'

Rose was already ahead of Nellie's command, rolling pages of newspaper and tying them into knots. These went to build the fire first, followed by sticks of wood that Nellie forced Rose and Poppy to chop each night. Finally a shovelful of coal went on top. The sisters took pride in setting the fire each day, as its warmth was their only comfort.

'Help me, girl. Get my coat,' Nellie demanded.

Rose walked across the dark room, finding her way instinctively. The only light coming in was through the holes in the roof, but it was enough for her to see Nellie's distinctive outline. She was a short woman, with no consideration for how she looked. Her clothes were dirty, unwashed, and she never took pride in her appearance – not like the orphans' mam had once done. Nellie never smelled good, even after her weekly bath. She was old, and her face was heavy with a permanent scowl.

Her eyes were dark and beady, like pieces of coal. She wore a heavy brown skirt that reached to the ground. Each time she walked across the farmyard, the skirt trailed in the cow muck and dirt. It had deep pockets on either side of her big hips. She wore the same black boots every day and never took them off, not even while sleeping. Over her skirt she wore a long-sleeved black woollen cardigan pulled tight across her ample chest. Some of the buttons were missing and others were fastened in the wrong holes. This all added to the impression that she didn't care how she looked or what others thought about her.

'Now, girl! Are you deaf? I asked you to fetch my coat!' she yelled.

Poppy looked down from the hayloft. She didn't like the way Nellie was speaking to her sister.

Rose quickly pulled Nellie's jacket from a metal hook by the door. 'Sorry, Nellie,' she said, handing the garment over.

Nellie held her stick in one hand and reached for the jacket with the other. 'I'll give you sorry!' she snarled, and as she spoke, she brought the stick down sharply.

In the dim light of the barn, Poppy watched in horror. Without thinking, she leapt out of bed, not feeling the ice-cold floor under her bare feet, ignoring the autumn chill coming through the holes in the roof. She flew down the ladder, her feet barely touching the rungs. Rose was in tears, and Nellie was furious with her for reasons Poppy couldn't understand. But one thing she was sure about was that Rose had done nothing wrong. She stormed up to Nellie. The stench coming off the woman was almost overpowering.

11

'Leave her alone, you big bully!' she screamed into Nellie's face.

Nellie tried to bring the stick down again, this time on Poppy, but Poppy was ready for it. With all the strength she had in her, she pushed both hands against Nellie's chest, toppling her back into her chair. The stick clattered to the ground. Poppy stood still, her heart pounding, then she ran to Rose and put her arm protectively around her shoulders.

'Leave her alone,' she said, more measured this time.

Nellie looked as if she didn't know what had hit her. She glanced from Poppy to Rose and back again. 'You're nothing more than a wild animal, girl,' she spat.

Poppy tightened her grip on Rose's shoulders. 'No one hurts my sister. No one. Especially you, Nellie Harper. We might be forced to live with you in this hovel, but it doesn't give you the right to beat us. I'll tell Norman if you do it again.'

'Leave my brother out of this,' Nellie hissed. 'He doesn't need to know what goes on back here.'

Poppy stepped forward, shielding Rose. 'Why did you try to hit her?'

'She deserved it, she's slovenly.' Nellie pressed both hands against the arms of her chair and slowly raised herself up. Poppy and Rose took a step backwards, afraid that she might lunge for them. Poppy had never seen her in such a bad mood, and she was determined to protect her sister. Nellie pointed a chubby finger at the girls. 'Rose, get my stick, now!'

Rose picked up the knocking-up stick.

'As for you . . .' Nellie snarled, taking a step closer to Poppy.

But Poppy was determined not to let the woman get the better of her. She crossed her arms and tilted her chin defiantly. 'What about me?'

'Oh, don't get cocky, lass. Remember, I can have you thrown out of here any time.' Nellie waved a hand in the air, pointing up to the hayloft. 'Think this place is bad, do you? Think I do wrong by you and your sister?'

That was exactly what Poppy thought, but she knew better than to reply. Instead, she bit her tongue and waited for Nellie to get to the point.

'Well, things might be changing soon,' Nellie said darkly.

Rose looked at Poppy and opened her mouth in shock. Poppy shook her head, warning her sister to keep quiet.

Nellie grabbed the stick from Rose and picked up her jacket. 'Set the fire good and high,' she ordered Rose, then she turned and pointed at Poppy. 'And you, get yourself back to bed, get some sleep. You need to be alert for school. Learn all you can, it'll stand you in good stead.'

'What for?' Poppy asked. 'Why are you so keen for me to learn all of a sudden?'

Nellie thrust her arms into her jacket and walked to the door without replying. She slid it open and stepped out of the barn into the yard.

As soon as the door shut, Rose ran straight into Poppy's arms.

'Did she hurt you?' Poppy asked.

Rose shook her head. 'I moved just in time. The stick hit the chair, but the noise scared me.'

'Something's rattled her,' Poppy said, trying to work things out. 'It's got to be connected to the letters. Maybe Norman knows what's going on.'

'We can't ask him,' Rose said quickly. 'He doesn't like us.'

'He brings us chickens sometimes, doesn't he? He might know something.' Poppy glanced around the dim room. 'Let's look for the letter. It might be here.'

She dropped her arm from Rose's shoulders and hurried to Nellie's chair. She lifted the cushion and shook it, then ran to the fireplace, where a pile of newspapers waited to be rolled into knots for the fire. She lifted each sheet, shaking them all, hoping an envelope would fall out, then picked up the mat from the hearth, but there was nothing underneath. Meanwhile Rose was on her hands and knees looking under the table and the two spindly chairs, but there was nothing there either, and the cupboard that Nellie used as a pantry was empty apart from mouldy cheese and a box of tea.

Chapter Three

'The letter's not here, she must still have it in her pocket,' Poppy sighed.

Rose was dragging the mat from the hearth, ready to start beating dirt from it in the yard.

'Let me help you,' Poppy offered.

Rose shook her head. 'I can manage. You should go back to bed.'

But Poppy had already lifted one end of the mat. 'I'm not tired any more. Anyway, you're only little, I want to help.' She was always reluctant to leave Rose to her chores. Her sister seemed too young and too small to do the work on her own.

Between them they carried the mat outside and threw it on to the flagstones. Two chickens walked by, hoping for crumbs.

'Not today, chickens. We've no food for ourselves, never mind for sharing.'

Out in the farmyard, moonlight shone on a barn where pigs snuffled in straw. The air was filled with a dull, earthy aroma. When the girls had first arrived to live here, the stench used to make them gag, but they barely noticed the horrid smell now. The air was crisp and cold as autumn turned into winter. Poppy shivered in the chilly air and put her arms around herself, hugging her thin cotton nightdress to her skinny frame.

'What'll we eat today, Poppy?' Rose asked.

Poppy thought for a moment. 'I'll find us something, don't worry. Norman might feed us if he's in a good mood. There's no harm in asking him, is there?'

'Be careful when you speak to him,' Rose warned. 'Don't upset him, especially if you decide to ask him about Nellie's letter. And please go back to bed. It's your turn to sleep in. I don't mind cleaning the mat. Nellie says you have to learn, it's important.'

'Yes, but who's it important to? Not me, that's for sure. I don't care if I learn things or not. I'd be happy never to see school again.'

Rose raised her eyebrows. 'Ah, but if you never saw school again, you'd never see Sid. I think that'd make you sad.'

Poppy shrugged, then reluctantly went back indoors. She climbed the ladder to the hayloft and crawled under the blanket. Although her legs were still itching from insects crawling in the straw, and a mouse was nibbling her toe, she soon drifted off to sleep.

At daybreak, she was woken by a scratching noise by her head. She swiped her hand against the creature that was trying to snuggle under the blanket.

'Flaming mice!' she yelled. She stretched her arms, yawned loudly, then scratched her itching head before leaning across the bed to look downstairs. There was no sign of Nellie. Rose was setting the coal fire alight ready for Nellie's return. The warmth from the fire soon spread up to the hayloft and warmed Poppy's bones. Her stomach rumbled with hunger. It had been a long time since their last meal, of thin soup that Poppy had cooked from cabbage.

Just as she was about to climb out of bed, there was a banging at the barn door. She knew it'd be Norman; he was the only person who called, and he'd be expecting to see Nellie. No one ever called to see the girls. Even Sid stayed away, as he was scared of Nellie – and he wasn't usually scared of anything.

'Nellie!' Norman called.

Poppy leapt out of bed, pulled on her dress and boots and raced downstairs. She crossed her fingers and hoped the farmer had brought them some food. Norman was a big, strong man, with hands like shovels. He looked like Nellie in every way, unwashed and taking no account of his appearance. His face was weathered and worn, mired in farm muck and shaped by a lifetime of demanding work. However, his expression was less harsh than his sister's, and he didn't scowl as much. Whenever Poppy came across him tending his animals – his cows and his pigs, even the chickens in the yard – she saw a tender side to him that she never saw in Nellie. He treated the animals well, even better than he treated his sister. He spoke gently to the cows, called each one by name; asked his pigs how they were when he fed them. Poppy had even seen tears in his eyes on the day he said goodbye to his favourite sow when she was sold.

As she ran towards him, she glanced at his hands to see if he'd brought them anything. She was disappointed to see nothing there. She stopped by the coal fire, letting the heat warm the back of her legs.

'Morning, Norman. How are you?' she said politely, exactly as their mam had taught her.

'Our Nellie not back from work yet?' he said gruffly.

Poppy shook her head.

'Tell her I want a word with her the minute she gets back.'

He turned to walk away, but Poppy wasn't going to miss her chance to ask him what was burning in her mind. 'Norman?' she called.

He turned and glared at her. 'What, girl?'

She stepped forward to the barn door. The words were stuck in her throat, but she knew she couldn't throw this chance away. She didn't know when she might get to speak to him again without Nellie about. From the corner of her eye, she saw Rose edging towards her. Wanting to protect her little sister made her even more determined to get to the bottom of what was going on.

'Well, spit it out, girl,' Norman said. 'I'm a busy man, I can't stand here all day waiting for you to speak. Cat got your tongue?'

'It's about the letters,' Poppy blurted, and once the first words had left her lips, she couldn't stop the rest tumbling out. 'I wondered if there was another letter for Nellie. You could leave it with me, I'll give it to her, I swear.' She hoped that if her mam could see her from heaven above, she would forgive her for lying, again. 'I'll look after it. I'll put it on her chair by the fire so she won't miss it when she comes back from work. She can read it when she has her cup of tea, there should be enough light by the fire for her to see it. So . . .' she paused and took a deep breath, 'is there a letter? Can I take it?'

She held her hand out, but it was shaking so much she dropped it to her side hoping to disguise how nervous she felt. All the while she kept her gaze fixed on Norman's stern face.

'A letter?' he growled. 'So early in the day? Don't be daft, lass. The post boy isn't due for hours. Anyway, what do you know about Nellie's letters? They're no concern of yours. If you take my advice, you'll stop sticking your nose into matters that don't concern you. What Nellie gets up to is her business.'

He walked away just as Nellie appeared at the farm gate. Rose headed back indoors, but Poppy stayed by the door and peeked out to watch him talking to his sister. She felt certain he was telling her what had just happened. Then Nellie turned towards the barn, and Poppy jumped back.

'She's coming!'

Rose went back to her chores, swilling the floor and sweeping the dirt from the barn to the yard. No matter how often the girls did this job, the muck came straight back in. When Nellie entered the barn, a chicken followed her, and Rose shooed it away with the brush. Nellie put her knocking-up stick back in its usual place. She peeled off her jacket and sank into her chair, rubbing her hands in front of the fire.

'Make a pot of tea, girl,' she ordered Rose.

'We've got no milk,' Rose replied.

'Norman's got plenty. Go and get some. Tell him I'll pay for it at the end of the week, when I give him my rent and coal money.'

Rose scurried off towards the farmhouse. Meanwhile Nellie settled into her chair, laid her head back, letting her eyes close, and began gently snoring.

Poppy watched her carefully, wondering about the letter and if she still had it. That was when she saw the tip of the envelope poking from Nellie's skirt pocket. She took a step forward, but her boots tapped the ground noisily and she was afraid the old woman would wake. She bent down and slid her boots off, first one foot, then the other. Nellie's eyes were still closed. Her breathing was getting slower; she was fast asleep now. Poppy crept closer, quietly, carefully, and with each step she took she could see the envelope more clearly in Nellie's pocket. She took another step and reached her hand out, hardly daring to breathe. Just one more step and she'd have the letter. She'd take it to Sid; he'd read it to her, tell her what it said.

It was right in front of her now, hers for the taking, her fingers inches away. She looked at Nellie's face; her eyes were still closed. Poppy's breath caught in her throat. She didn't dare move, but she had to get the letter. It wasn't as if she hadn't stolen before. In order to feed her and Rose, she'd become adept at taking things she shouldn't from Ambrose and Ella Trewhitt, who ran the village shop. It was either that or starve. She leaned forward and touched the envelope. She had it between her finger and thumb and she began to pull it from Nellie's pocket—

'Got the milk!' Rose cried from the doorway.

Nellie's eyes shot open and Poppy jumped back in fright. The letter remained in Nellie's pocket, but to Poppy's relief, the woman seemed unaware of what had just happened. She turned away, her heart racing. If Nellie had caught her, she might have made good on her threat to turn her and Rose out. She knew she'd had a lucky escape.

'Make enough tea for the three of us. You two might as well have a hot drink,' Nellie said. 'And you, Poppy . . .'

Poppy turned. 'Yes?' she said, as innocently as she could.

'You'll need a slice of bread before you go to school. Toast it on the fire.'

'Thanks, Nellie,' she said.

Poppy drank her hot tea by the fire with Nellie and Rose, then slipped her boots back on and climbed up to the hayloft. Taking the horse blanket from the bed, she wrapped it around her shoulders. It was all she had to protect her from the bitterly cold day. She never knew what had happened to the clothes she and Rose had brought to the barn when Nellie took them in, but she suspected that Nellie had sold them. Their parents' belongings and the furniture from their house had been taken by their landlord as payment for rent owed. All the orphans now had in the world were the clothes they stood up in and their shared pair of boots.

Poppy and Rose walked together to the barn door and Poppy stepped outside. Rose stayed where she was, watching as her sister headed away.

'Poppy!' she called. She raised her hand in a wave, and then clenched her fist.

Poppy knew exactly what it meant. It was their special wave; their secret, wordless way of telling each other not to worry. Rose opened and closed her fist three times, as if her hand was a flower, blooming in sunshine. Poppy did the same in return, then set off across the farmyard.

Two chickens followed her as far as the farm gate. From there it was a short walk to school, and she smiled as she thought about seeing Sid on the way. She met him on the village green each morning when it was her turn to wear the boots and go to school. She pushed a matted curl from her eyes, and her fingers stuck on a piece of straw caught in her hair. She plucked it out and threw it on the ground. As she walked past the farmhouse, Norman was watching from a window. Poppy caught his eye and raised her hand in a wave, hoping she could atone for being so forward earlier, but he scowled and turned away.

Chapter Four

———————

Poppy walked to the village green, where magnificent oak trees stood next to wooden benches on which old men from the village gathered each afternoon to pass the time of day. Next to one of the benches was a horse trough; this was the spot where she always met Sid. She heard him whistling as he walked towards her, and saw his round, mucky face topped by messy brown hair. He had his hands in his pockets as he kicked his way through fallen leaves, causing them to fly in the air.

'Morning, Sid,' she called. She shivered and pulled the blanket tight. It was icy cold, and her face was red raw.

'Morning, Pops!' he called cheerily, giving her a toothy grin. Sid was always smiling, always happy, whistling or singing as he walked. Nothing ever got him down, and Poppy enjoyed being with him. He was her only friend. When he reached her, she threaded her arm through his and they walked in step towards the school.

'How's your mam?' Poppy asked.

Sid shrugged. 'She's all right, getting better. At least she's out of bed now. The new baby's a little smasher, another one for me to look after. I'm the best biggest brother in the world.'

'I wish you were my big brother,' Poppy said.

He looked at her. 'But if I was your brother, then I couldn't be your friend.'

'Why not?'

'Stands to reason, doesn't it?' he replied, and the matter was closed, although Poppy wasn't sure what he meant.

'Does your mam's new baby cry a lot?' she asked.

'Crikey, yes. He's got a good pair of lungs on him. He keeps me awake at night. But Mam says it's a good thing to have a noisy bairn. She doesn't like it when new ones are quiet. The last one was quiet and it didn't live long.'

Poppy cuddled into Sid's side as they walked.

'Sid?'

'What, Pops?'

'Where do you think they come from?'

'Who?'

'Babies.'

'Why, Dr Anderson brings them in his black bag, everyone knows that,' he said matter-of-factly. 'Fancy you not knowing.'

Poppy felt hurt. Sid was right, she really should have known.

'What's Rose doing today?' he asked.

'Oh, the usual. Cleaning the barn, cooking for Nellie, chasing mice. One of them bit me in the night, right on the end of my toe.'

'You're lucky you've only got mice. We've got rats in our yard. You should see their big eyes; they glow red in the dark.'

Poppy dropped her arm from his. 'Stop it, Sid, that's scary,' but he wasn't about to give up.

'And you should see their teeth,' he said, baring his own. 'They can bite through chair legs, and even people's fingers.'

She put her hands over her ears. 'I'm not listening.'

But Sid carried on regardless. 'They scratch at the doors in the dead of night until you let them in,' he said, curling his fingers into claws, 'and then they—'

Poppy ran ahead. 'Stop it!'

He hurried to catch up with her and beamed an apologetic smile. 'Sorry, Pops. I was only teasing.' He offered his arm again, and after a moment's hesitation, she took it.

'Friends again?' he asked.

'All right, but don't scare me like that.'

They walked on arm in arm.

'Sid?'

'Yes, Pops?'

'Do you think I'm pretty? I mean, even with my freckles and all?'

He gave her a cheeky wink. 'Yes, I think you're pretty. I love your curly hair and I love your crazy freckles.'

'I wish *I* loved my freckles,' she muttered.

Suddenly he stopped walking and rummaged in his jacket pocket. 'Almost forgot, I brought this for you.' He offered her a slice of stale bread. 'Took it from the pantry this morning. Mam said you could have it.'

Poppy took the bread gratefully and tucked it under the blanket. 'I'll keep it for later, when I get hungry. I don't need it right now, as Nellie toasted bread for me this morning.'

'She fed you?' Sid said, surprised. 'She must be going soft in her old age.'

'I think she's up to something,' Poppy said, but as they

were now entering the schoolyard, she decided to say no more.

'See you at home time,' Sid said, then he ran off to join his friends, who were playing football in the yard.

The pavement outside the school was full of children, crowding through the iron gates towards the sturdy stone building with a bell tower on the roof next to four tall chimneys. Until the bell rang to allow the children indoors, everyone had to stand out in the cold. Poppy shrank back against the wall and dropped her gaze to the ground. She was the only child wrapped in a blanket. She wasn't invited to join the others skipping and jumping, and she was never included in secret conversations when girls huddled in groups. Straw was always caught in her hair, and her hands and face were dirty. No matter how many times she washed them, she couldn't get them clean. She shivered again and pulled the blanket tighter.

Relieved when the bell finally rang, she rushed to get inside. In the schoolroom, a coal fire burned at the front, and children jostled for the seats closest to it. However, as cold as she was, Poppy headed to the back, as far away as possible from Mr Hylton, the teacher. Sid was sitting a few rows ahead of her, next to his good friend Dan. She sank low in her seat, dreading the day ahead. The schoolwork always proved impossible for her to understand, as letters and numbers turned into sticks and curls. She didn't know how to read or write, and learning seemed beyond her. She hoped the teacher wouldn't pick her to read. She needed to hear what the other children said first, and then she'd copy them. It was what she'd always done, how she'd got by so far.

Her stomach rumbled, and she carefully placed the slice of bread from Sid in her lap and tore a tiny piece off with her dirty nails. Mr Hylton was looking down at the register as he called out the children's names. Certain she couldn't be seen, she stuck the piece of bread into her mouth.

'Here, sir!' the children chanted as their names were called out.

'Marion Gregory?'

'Here, sir!'

'Poppy Harper?'

Poppy hated being given Nellie's surname. It had happened as soon as Nellie had taken her and Rose in, and she vowed that she'd never get used to it . . . never. To call herself Harper was to erase her mam and dad from her life. She was determined to remember her parents every way she could. In her heart, she and Rose would always be the Thomas girls.

'Poppy Harper?' Mr Hylton called again, looking up from his list.

'Here, sir,' Poppy said quietly.

'Rose Harper?'

'She's not well again, sir.' It was the standard excuse.

Mr Hylton shot her a dark look. 'Again?' he barked. 'It seems to me that it's either you or your sister sitting in my classroom, never both of you at the same time.'

Poppy shifted in her seat, kicking her boots against the chair legs. She wished with all her heart that she and Rose had a pair each so they could come to school together.

Mr Hylton returned his attention to calling out the register and Poppy sank lower into her seat, relieved not to be the focus of attention for a while. As he worked his way through the list – George Hibbert, Fred Jackson,

Sidney Lawson, Edie Lyme – she broke off more bread and put it in her mouth.

'Sir! Poppy Harper's eating in class!'

Poppy glared at the girl sitting by her side. 'Edie Lyme, you've got a big mouth,' she hissed.

'At least I don't stink of cow poo,' Edie replied.

Poppy felt herself redden. 'I don't smell,' she said under her breath.

Edie stuck her tongue out. 'You stink.'

Mr Hylton banged a wooden cane against the side of his desk.

'Poppy Harper. Come here, now,' he said sternly.

Poppy's heart sank. She grabbed the piece of bread and closed her fist around it. All eyes in the room turned towards her, and she heard Edie Lyme whispering as she made her way to the front. When she reached Mr Hylton, she knew what to do. She'd been there many times before. She held her right hand out, ready for the cane. In her left hand she held tight to the bread. But instead of striking her, Mr Hylton simply glared at her.

'What am I to do with you and your sister?' he sighed.

Poppy felt herself being appraised, all the way up from the boots she shared with Rose to her curls and her freckles and the straw that was still stuck in her hair.

'Were you eating in class?' Mr Hylton asked.

She shook her head. 'No, sir.'

'Then what's that in your hand?' he demanded.

She made a show of extending her empty right hand further. She even turned it over, as if looking for something. 'Nothing, sir.' She heard sniggering behind her.

'Quiet!' Mr Hylton yelled, and the noise stopped immediately. He took a step forward. 'What's in your other hand?'

Poppy pulled her fist away and hid it behind her back. 'I demand you show me what you're hiding.'

She shook her head. 'It's nothing.'

Mr Hylton raised the cane. 'Nothing?' he said darkly.

There was silence in the room as the children waited anxiously, each one of them relieved that they weren't in Poppy's position. Poppy kept her gaze on the floor, concentrating on Mr Hylton's black shoes.

'It's bread, sir,' she said.

'Oh, so one minute you say there's nothing in your hand, and the next you're telling me there's bread. That makes you a liar as well as a thief!'

Her head jerked up. 'I didn't steal it!' she cried.

Behind her she heard the sound of a chair being scraped back.

'I gave it to her,' said a voice.

She turned to look at Sid. He had his hands in his pockets, and his normally cheerful expression had been replaced by a look of concern.

'Sidney Lawson, come here,' Mr Hylton demanded.

Sid shuffled along the row and walked to the front to stand beside Poppy. Mr Hylton took the bread from Poppy's hand and laid it on his desk. As he shook his head and tutted out loud, her stomach churned with hunger.

'You two, stand over there,' he said.

The children knew what to do. Together they walked to the corner of the room and turned their backs to their classmates.

'You'll both stay there until I tell you to turn around.'

As Mr Hylton carried on taking the register, Sid and Poppy stood side by side, holding hands, staring silently at the wall.

Chapter Five

At the end of the day, when the bell rang, Poppy was last out of the school. Because she sat at the back of the class, she had to wait until everyone else had left the room. When she eventually made her way to the yard, she was heartened to find Sid waiting.

'You all right, Pops?' he said.

She knew what he was really trying to ask, as he was well aware how she struggled with schoolwork.

'I can give you a hand if you'd like?' he offered as they walked from the yard, arm in arm. 'I could come to the barn and help you to learn words and numbers.'

'I thought you were too scared of Nellie to come?'

He shrugged. 'If it'll help you learn to read and write, I'll try hard not to be scared.'

But Poppy knew that Nellie wouldn't welcome Sid – or indeed any visitor – to the barn. She'd never seen the old woman talk to anyone apart from Norman, not even the farmhands. She kept herself to herself, and the only friends she had were the other knocker-uppers who walked the streets with her.

Poppy sighed and pulled the blanket more tightly

around her shoulders. It was only mid-afternoon, but already the sky was dark with heavy clouds, and the air was icy cold.

'Come on, Pops, let me help you,' Sid persisted. 'Don't you want to learn to read? It's fun, you know, once you get used to it. You can even read comics.'

'Where do you get the money for comics from?' she asked, intrigued.

He gave a big smile and stuck his chest out. 'I've got a job,' he said proudly.

'Where?'

He pointed to the bottom of the village green, to a large, grand house. To one side of it was a tall tower with windows looking out over the oak trees and the horse trough. Poppy's eyes widened.

'You're working at Ryhope Hall?' she cried. She dropped her hand from his arm. 'Oh my word, you'll be turning all la-di-da. You'll be too posh to be friends with me.'

'Don't be like that, Pops,' Sid sulked. 'I'm helping Dad in the garden, that's all. It's not as if I'm working indoors like one of the serving staff. Now that *would* be la-di-da.'

He smiled, and Poppy's heart went out to him.

'I could buy you things when I get paid,' he said, sliding his arm through hers, and she snuggled up to him gratefully.

'I mean things to eat, you know,' he said sheepishly. 'I don't like to see you and Rose going without. Nellie should be ashamed of herself, the way she treats you. That's what my mam says, anyway.'

Right on cue, Poppy's stomach rumbled. All she'd eaten all day was the toasted bread Nellie had given her that morning, and the tiny bite of stale crust from Sid.

31

Mr Hylton had confiscated the remains of it. She knew
Rose wouldn't have eaten anything either, and she'd been
working all day doing chores.

Ahead of them on the village green was the Trewhitts'
shop, and another pang of hunger hit her as she and Sid
neared it. She peered inside. Through the small black-
leaded panes she saw an array of pies and pastries displayed
on patterned plates. Small, round tarts with ruby-red
centres where jam oozed through the pastry made her feel
so hungry she was afraid she might faint. The recipe for
the tarts was a family secret Ambrose Trewhitt guarded
with his life. Many had asked him for it; some had even
offered to pay him for it, but Ambrose wouldn't sell. He
swore he'd take it to his grave.

Poppy stood a moment longer gazing in. The shop
looked empty inside. Neither Ambrose nor his wife Ella
was anywhere to be seen.

'Seen enough, Pops? Come on, I need to get home,'
Sid said.

'You go, Sid. I want to stay here for a while.'

He gave her a strange look. 'Okay, if you're sure. Tell
Rose I'll meet her by the horse trough in the morning.
And speaking of Rose, are we walking up Tunstall Hill
for her birthday? Say yes, Pops. I love going up there
every year, it's our tradition.'

'I don't know, Sid,' Poppy sighed. 'I'll have to see what
Nellie says. She might expect us to work in the barn.'

Sid nodded sympathetically, then turned to make his
way home, whistling as he went.

Once he'd gone, Poppy looked left and right along the
street, relieved to see no one about. Then she pressed her
face to the cold window and looked at the jam tarts again.

Suddenly an idea came to her. All she had to do was run inside the shop as quickly as she could, take the tarts and run out. She weighed up the situation. What was the worst that could happen if she was caught? Ambrose would scold her and Ella would ban her from returning, again. Poppy had already been barred from the shop for stealing, and she figured she had nothing to lose. It wasn't as if the Trewhitts could tell her parents, was it? And even if word reached Nellie, there was little she could do to make Poppy's life worse than it already was.

She glanced around again, making sure she couldn't be seen, then walked to the shop door. She knew she'd have to be quick once she was inside. There was a bell above the door that tinkled to announce anyone walking in. The noise would summon Ambrose and Ella to the counter at the same time; they always did everything together and were rarely apart. She took a deep breath, and for good measure pulled the blanket up to hide her face. Then, with a trembling hand, she pushed at the door.

The sound of the doorbell rang loud in her ears, and her heart pounded as she hurried inside. Something on a shelf to her right caught her eye; she recognised the shape and colour of the tin, though it wasn't something she'd seen from the window. Her hand shot out to take it and she stuffed it in her pocket. Then she went to the window and lifted the plate of jam tarts. In her rush, two of the tarts spilled to the floor. All she had to do now was run out. She tilted the plate to her chest so no more tarts could slide off. She had to keep hold of as many as she could.

She was certain she'd got away with her crime. But just as she was about to head to the door, ready to run like the clappers all the way to the barn, she was stopped in her tracks by the tinkle of the bell. A man had entered the shop. It was Reverend Daye, vicar of St Paul's church. Her heart dropped when she saw him, and she gasped. She was so shocked to see him there that her hands trembled violently and she dropped the plate. It smashed, the noise cutting right through her, and the jam tarts landed on the Trewhitts' pristine floor.

'Poppy?' Reverend Daye said kindly.

She tried to push past him, she dodged this way and that, but he was a big man, and he filled the doorway with his bulky frame. Then a noise from behind her caused her to spin round.

'What's going on here?' Ambrose Trewhitt demanded. 'Oh, good afternoon, Vicar,' he said when he noticed who had entered his shop. He stood ramrod straight behind his counter, wearing a shirt and tie under a brown overall. His silver hair was swept to one side.

'What the devil has happened?' cried Ella Trewhitt. She was a thin woman with a mass of brown hair piled on top of her head. Her overall, which matched her husband's, was worn over a pale blue jumper and a long black skirt. Ambrose and Ella put their heart and soul into their shop, and it was always as neat as a pin. She started when she saw the vicar. 'Sorry, Reverend, I didn't mean to invoke the devil,' she said, but then her eyes fell on Poppy and the jam tarts. 'Though as we're speaking of him, I feel he's arrived.'

'Now, now, Ella,' Reverend Daye said soothingly. 'I'm sure young Miss Harper has a perfectly innocent explanation.' He rocked back on his heels and beamed at Poppy, waiting for her to explain. She felt Ambrose and Ella staring at her too. How on earth would she get out of this?

Ella put her hands on her hips. 'What are you doing in

here, girl? I told you never to return after I caught you stealing last time.'

Poppy felt her face and neck redden and burn. She couldn't speak, knowing that nothing she could say would make the situation better. She might as well keep quiet and let events take their course. She girded herself, ready to have Ambrose scold her, ready to have Ella chase her out. She was mortified that this was happening, and the fact that it was unfolding in front of the vicar made things even worse. Her mam would have had strong words to say. She felt tears prick her eyes and dropped her gaze. At her feet were the tarts, crumbs everywhere, jam smeared on the floor.

'I'm sorry,' she whispered.

'Louder, girl!' Ambrose demanded.

She raised her gaze to meet his stern look. 'I said I'm sorry. Me and my sister don't eat. Nellie doesn't feed us. We need food, Mr Trewhitt.' She looked at Ella. 'Mrs Trewhitt, we're hungry.'

But any thoughts she might have had of Ella Trewhitt's heart melting came to nothing. Ella picked up a broom – the one she used for chasing rats from the yard – then lifted the edge of the counter and advanced into the shop.

Reverend Daye stepped forward and held up his hands. 'Now, Ella, there's no need for that. Let us have mercy on those less fortunate than ourselves.'

Ella reluctantly propped the broom against the wall.

'Perhaps there is some way Poppy can pay for the tarts?' the vicar offered.

Poppy's heart sank. 'I can't, sir, I have no money.'

He shook his head. 'No, I wasn't expecting you to hand over money.' He looked at Ambrose and Ella.

'Surely there must be work you can give the girl to pay for the food she has spoiled.' He raised his eyebrows expectantly.

A heavy silence hung in the shop. Poppy kept looking at the jam tarts. As squashed as they were now, she wanted nothing more than to scoop them off the floor and stuff them in her mouth.

Ella sighed heavily. 'Well, Vicar. We don't want to go against what the good Lord would want. I suppose we can find something to keep the devil from the girl's thieving hands. There are boxes to stack in the yard. Ambrose has moved a lot of them already, but she can finish doing that. Once the job is done to my satisfaction, I'll allow her to take the tarts. I'll not be able to sell them as they are now – they're ruined.'

'Thank you,' Poppy said, then she turned to smile gratefully at Reverend Daye.

'This way,' Ella said, indicating to Poppy to follow her. 'Ambrose, could you pick the jam tarts up once you've served the vicar?'

'Of course, dear,' Ambrose said. 'Now then, Reverend Daye, what can I get for you?'

'Well, my housekeeper is in the middle of making a beef stew for dinner, and she asked me to pick up a tin of mustard powder for her on my way home from my walk,' he replied.

Ambrose looked at the shelf where he kept tinned goods, but was surprised to see no mustard. He scratched his head. 'That's odd, I'm certain we had one tin left,' he muttered.

As Poppy walked past him, she patted her skirt, where the mustard tin nestled in her pocket.

Chapter Six

In the yard at the Trewhitts' shop, Poppy's arms began to ache as she moved the heavy wooden boxes. She knew Rose would be worried about where she'd got to and wondering why she hadn't returned yet from school. When at last she was finished and the boxes stacked, she brushed muck from her hands and walked into the shop.

She was relieved to see that the vicar had left. Ambrose and Ella stood together behind the counter. In front of them were the squashed jam tarts. Poppy didn't care that they had been on the floor. All she could think about was taking them back to the barn and sharing them with Rose. Her mouth began to water, thinking of eating the crisp golden pastry and the sweet, sticky jam. Ambrose and Ella had their arms crossed as they watched her. They never said a word, but she felt their disapproval. All she wanted was to pick up the tarts and run out, but she knew she'd have to say something first. Should she give another apology? Say thank you? She wondered what her mam would have told her to do.

She walked to the counter and stood opposite the

Trewhitts. The tarts were lying between them on a square of greased paper.

'May I take them?' she asked. She looked at the couple's stern faces. Neither of them spoke for a few moments.

'Just be grateful that Reverend Daye was here when we caught you, otherwise I'd have chased you out with the broom,' Ella said eventually.

Ambrose shuffled his feet and laid his hands on the counter top. 'Don't let us catch you stealing from us again, Poppy Thomas.'

Poppy started at the use of her real name. 'You called me Thomas, not Harper.'

Ambrose and Ella shared a look, then Ambrose cleared his throat. 'We knew your mam, God rest her soul.'

Ella nodded towards the tarts. 'Take them,' she said softly.

Poppy carefully folded the greased paper round the tarts and picked them up. 'Thank you,' she said, then turned to leave. The bell above the door tinkled as she stepped into the cold air.

In the shop, Ambrose and Ella turned to one another. 'Those poor orphan girls,' Ambrose sighed.

Outside, it had started to rain, and Poppy held the tarts to her under her blanket. She put her nose to the greased paper and breathed in the tempting scents of pastry and jam. She couldn't wait to show Rose what she'd got. They would share a feast and a half, the sweetest food they'd eaten in months. She had to hurry, for the bitterly cold rain threatened sleet on the way. With her free hand, she pulled the blanket over her head, careful to keep hold of the tarts.

As she stepped into the road to cross to the green, she lost her footing on the wet path and went down like a bag of spuds. She landed with a thud, face down, her hands scraped by stones where she'd tried to save herself from falling. The tarts flew from her grasp and fell into a puddle of water. She was back on her feet in seconds. Her hands hurt, her knees were sore, but she paid no mind to the pain. All that mattered was the food.

Frantically she scraped the tarts off the road. They were in a sorry state, soaking wet and covered in muck. Anyone else, anyone who wasn't starving, would have left them alone. But Poppy had worked hard stacking boxes to earn them, and she wasn't prepared to leave them now. She patted her pocket, relieved that the tin of mustard had survived. Ice-cold rain belted down on her, hitting her face and arms hard. She quickly bundled the sodden pastries under her blanket and ran as fast as she could through the cattle market into the barn.

The door was closed against the rain when she arrived, and she heaved at it with all her strength. It didn't slide easily, and she struggled using one hand, but she was determined not to lose the tarts again. She tumbled inside, soaked through, and shook the water from her hair. The coal fire was roaring, and she ran to it to get warm. Nellie was asleep in her chair, and Rose was up in the hayloft, darning Nellie's socks.

'Where have you been?' she called.

The noise woke Nellie, who moaned and groaned, muttering something under her breath about Norman treating his pigs better than he treated his sister. When she opened her eyes, she focused on Poppy.

'What have you got there?' she demanded, looking at

the mess of wet pastry and jam in Poppy's hands.

'Jam tarts,' Poppy replied. 'They got wet in the rain.' She kept quiet about them falling in the muddy puddle. 'They just need drying out on the hearth and they'll be as good as new.'

Nellie pushed herself out of her chair and walked to the fire, where Poppy was spreading out the remains of the tarts. 'They look dreadful,' she complained.

Poppy agreed, but she was so hungry, she wouldn't be dissuaded from her task. 'They'll be all right,' she said, trying to convince herself.

Behind her, Rose appeared and stood beside Nellie, looking at the pastry and jam. 'What happened to them?' she asked.

'They got wet in the rain,' Poppy said quickly, then stood, putting an end to their questions. 'Nellie, is there any food today?'

Nellie nodded at the pantry door. 'There are eggs, and there's bread you can toast on the fire. But make it quick. I have to leave soon, to call the next shift of miners out of bed for work. Where have you been anyway, girl? You're late. And where did you get those tarts from?'

Poppy stood up straight. 'I did some work for the Trewhitts and they paid me with pastries,' she said. She noticed Rose shoot her a quizzical look. She'd explain everything to her later, after Nellie had left. She wanted to savour the moment when she told Rose that the Trewhitts had known their mam, and that they'd called her by their real name. She'd tell her about the vicar too, but decided she'd keep quiet about dropping the tarts in the muck. A little bit of dirt on their food hadn't hurt them before, but Rose was more sensitive than Poppy, and she was worried that if she told her the truth, her sister wouldn't eat. She'd also ask Rose if she'd like to walk to the top of Tunstall Hill for her birthday, with Sid. She'd offer her the boots for the walk. It only seemed fair, seeing as it was Rose's birthday.

Once she'd warmed up a little, Poppy cut bread into slices while Rose put a pan of water to heat on the fire. When it was boiling, Poppy took three eggs from a box that Norman had left and placed them in the pan. She glanced at the jam tarts. They had dried out and started to crisp up. What little jam they'd had inside had almost disappeared, but that didn't matter to her. She longed to taste the crisp pastry in her mouth, and the remains of the sweet tang of jam.

The sisters worked quickly and efficiently preparing the meal. When it was ready, they ate in silence. Nellie sat in her chair and the girls on the floor. Poppy's blanket was laid out in front of the fire, drying from the rain, with steam rising from it. Each mouthful of food was like heaven. They hadn't eaten so well in a long time. Norman sold his eggs in the village and never offered Nellie any for free. However, Poppy knew better than to question Nellie and Norman's relationship, though she didn't understand it one bit. The only time Nellie spoke about her brother was to complain about him. There wasn't room in his small farmhouse for Nellie to live, but Poppy often wondered why she had been banished to the barn. Poppy would never force Rose to live in a barn if she had the chance for both of them to live in a house, no matter how small it was. She'd do anything to protect her sister.

She looked up and smiled at Rose, and saw a streak of

egg on her chin. The eggs and bread filled their stomachs. She knew they'd both sleep well that night.

'Make a pot of tea, girl, before I go to work,' Nellie ordered.

Poppy busied herself at the hearth with the kettle and teapot, doing as Nellie had ordered. While the tea was brewing, a companionable silence fell. Poppy licked her lips, looking forward to finally tasting the tarts. She poured the tea, added a dash of milk to each and handed mugs to Nellie and Rose. Then she took the pastries from the hearth. Stones, grit and dirt were stuck to the bottom of them, and she ran her fingers over them to remove the worst. Not once did she feel guilty for serving the tarts after what had happened to them. She was hungry, Rose was hungry, and they needed all the food they could get.

'Where do you say you got these from?' Nellie asked, inspecting her tart.

'Trewhitts,' Poppy said.

'Hmm . . . Ambrose is slipping on quality these days,' Nellie commented, but that didn't stop her from putting the whole thing in her mouth.

Rose took a tiny bite from hers before nibbling around the edge, picking dirt off as she went. Poppy snapped hers in half and bit into the pastry. It was tough and chewy. The dried-up jam left a ghost of a sweet taste on her tongue. But each mouthful was delicious, and she savoured every bite.

'We'll keep the others for breakfast tomorrow,' she said, wrapping the tarts in a cloth.

After the tea was drunk and the plates washed in hot water boiled on the fire, Nellie took her knocking-up stick and left. Alone in the barn, Poppy had a burning question for Rose.

'Did Nellie try to hit you again?'

Rose shook her head. 'I kept out of her way in the hayloft. You know she's too fat to climb the ladder. It's safe up there.'

'Did she receive another letter?'

'No, Norman didn't bring one. He hasn't been all day. Nellie's been sleeping mostly, and grumbling, as usual.'

Poppy told Rose about her day at school. And then slowly, carefully, her hand delved into her pocket.

'What have you got there?' Rose asked.

Poppy brought out the mustard tin.

Chapter Seven

'What's that?' Rose asked.

'Mustard powder.'

Rose took the tin from Poppy's hands, curious. 'How do you know when you can't read the label?'

'Because I remember the colour and shape of the tin from when Mam used to buy it. I'm going to make a paste to get rid of my freckles. Mam always said it worked as a cure.'

'Mam used to say a lot of strange things,' Rose warned. 'She got all her odd sayings from Granny Thomas. Do you remember when Granny was determined to find a donkey, because she said walking around it three times would cure Grandad's hiccups?'

Poppy laughed at the memory. 'Poor Grandad tried to stop her. He told her it was an old wives' tale, but she was sure she was right. I remember everyone laughing at her and saying she was wrong.'

'See!' Rose exclaimed. 'If Granny Thomas was wrong about the donkey and the hiccups, Mam might have been wrong about the mustard.'

'But what if she was right? What if mustard really will

get rid of my freckles? It's got to be worth a try. Will you help me while Nellie's out?'

Rose shrank against the wall and put her hands behind her back. 'I don't want to. I like you the way you are. I don't want your freckles to go.'

'Well, I do,' Poppy said firmly. 'I hate them, and my curly hair.'

With the tin in her hand, she went outside to fill a cup with water from the trough. Carefully she prised the lid off the tin and shook mustard powder into the cup.

'Pass me a spoon,' she said.

Rose found a spoon by the hearth and handed it to Poppy, who stirred the mixture. Rose pinched her nose. 'Eew, it smells awful.'

The girls watched the mustard powder dissolve as Poppy swirled the liquid.

'What do you do now? Do you drink it?' Rose asked.

'No, silly. You put it on your face, like this.' Poppy dipped her fingers in the cup and smeared the vile-smelling concoction over her cheeks and nose. Cold water dripped down her face, into her mouth and down her neck. 'I'm going to leave it on overnight,' she decided. 'And when I wake up in the morning, my freckles will have gone. Here, take the tin and hide it in the hayloft. We don't want Nellie finding it.'

Rose took the tin, but didn't move. She stared hard at Poppy. 'How did you get it? Did you steal it?'

Poppy couldn't fail to notice the accusing tone of her sister's voice. 'How else are we supposed to get things?' she fired back.

'Oh Poppy! One of these days your stealing will get us into so much trouble. You'll get caught, and then we'll be taken away. It's bad enough living here with Nellie, but you know there are worse places out there. Why do you keep doing it? The police will take you and . . .' Rose sank into Nellie's chair.

Poppy wiped at drips of mustard to stop them rolling down her neck. She walked towards Rose and sat on the arm of the chair. 'I'm sorry.'

'Did you steal the jam tarts too? Did you really work for the Trewhitts?'

Poppy didn't want to upset Rose any more than she already had. 'I worked in the yard at the shop, moving boxes for Ambrose,' she said. 'Oh, and you'll never guess what happened.'

Rose looked up. 'What?'

'Ambrose called me Poppy Thomas. He said he knew our mam.'

Her eyes widened. 'Really? What else did he say? Did our mam used to shop there? What did she buy?'

Poppy stroked Rose's cheek. 'He didn't say anything else, but it was lovely to be called by our real name.'

Rose looked into the hearth, at the dancing flames of the fire. 'Do you think he might tell us more about her if we asked him?'

'I think we should leave the Trewhitts to their business,' Poppy said. She was afraid that if Rose spoke to Ambrose, she'd find out she'd been caught stealing again, and that this time, the vicar had been there too.

'What do you remember most about Mam?' Rose asked.

'I remember that she smelled nice, of the rose water she used,' Poppy replied. 'And the gentle, loving way she tucked us into bed at night, all warm and cosy. And the way she sang us to sleep.' Her voice caught in her throat. Rose shifted in the seat, and Poppy fell into the chair to sit at her sister's side. Tears streamed down Rose's face.

'I miss her so much,' she said. 'We've only got each other now. That's why I worry about you being caught stealing and being taken away. You're the only person in my life. I couldn't bear to lose you.'

Poppy snuggled into Rose's side. 'I'm going nowhere. I'll never leave you, Rose. Never.' She laid her head on Rose's shoulder. Warmed by the coal fire, and feeling full and happy after the meal and her jam tart, she felt her eyes begin to close. Within minutes, the sisters were sleeping soundly, curled up together in Nellie's chair.

Hours later, they were woken by the scraping of the barn door being pulled open. Poppy jumped out of the chair and dragged Rose up by her arm just seconds before Nellie entered. The girls stood blinking, trying to pull themselves together. If they'd been caught in Nellie's chair, she wouldn't have been happy. She eyed them keenly as she walked to the fire to warm her backside.

'What are you two up to? You look sheepish.'

'Nothing, Nellie,' they chorused.

Nellie looked from Poppy to Rose. 'There's a funny smell in here. Smells like . . .' she sniffed the air, 'mustard.'

'It's the blanket,' Poppy said, thinking quickly. 'It got wet in the rain, and when it dried in front of the fire, it started to smell bad.' She was pleased that her answer seemed to satisfy Nellie.

'Get yourselves up to bed,' the old woman ordered.

The girls scarpered up the ladder, relieved to be out of her way.

* * *

47

In the days that followed, Poppy and Rose took their turns at school, walking from the horse trough each morning with Sid. Poppy searched for Nellie's letters, before finally deciding that the woman must have burned them, as they were nowhere to be found. As for Poppy's freckles, they remained stubbornly in place. She tried the mustard cure three more times, only stopping when she woke up one night, horrified to find a mouse licking mustard paste from her nose.

The weather in the coming weeks took a turn for the worse, but still the girls talked excitedly about Rose's birthday and their walk to Tunstall Hill. The walk was something they'd done since before they could remember. Their parents used to take them, with a picnic of sandwiches and boiled eggs with salt. They'd watch birds flying, spot squirrels in the trees and marvel at the view of their small village from the top of the hill. And although the weather at that time of year was never good, it had become a family tradition that Poppy and Rose carried on.

In mid December, on the morning of Rose's tenth birthday, Poppy and Rose set off for the village green as soon as Nellie left for work. It was Rose's turn to go to school that day, but instead they planned to walk out of the village, through the fields and up the hill. Sid was waiting at the horse trough when they arrived.

'Morning, girls. Happy birthday, Rose,' he said. He held out his hand, and the girls saw that he was holding a brown paper bag.

'Is that for me?' Rose cried excitedly. She took the bag and peered inside.

'What is it?' Poppy asked, trying to see.

The bag contained two slices of bread.

'There's one each for you, from Mam,' Sid said.

Rose took the bread out and handed one slice to Poppy.

'I think you should have both of them, as it's your birthday,' Poppy said, but Rose insisted she take one. Poppy ate it greedily as she walked across the village green, being careful where she placed her bare feet.

'You can wear my socks if you'd like,' Sid offered.

'You've got socks?' Poppy cried. 'Yes, please, Sid!'

'We could wear one of Sid's socks each and one boot each,' Rose said earnestly.

'It's your birthday, you keep the boots,' Poppy replied.

Sid sank to the grass, pulled his boots off and peeled off his socks.

'Here you go,' he said, handing the socks to Poppy, who pulled them on over her toes, which were red raw with cold.

'Oh Sid, they're lovely and warm.'

Sid stood and laced his boots up. When they were ready to start walking again, Poppy positioned herself between Rose and Sid. She held Rose's hand with her left hand and linked her right arm through Sid's.

'Won't your mam mind that you aren't at school today?' she asked.

'She won't mind what she doesn't know, and I won't tell her if you won't,' Sid said, giving a cheeky smile.

The three children walked in step, heading away from the school so that they wouldn't be seen, then rounding the corner by the Uplands, one of Ryhope's grandest homes. Poppy peeked around the wall, looking left and right to ensure that no one spotted them.

'Come on, the coast's clear,' she said, urging Rose and Sid to follow.

They hurried past St Paul's church, keeping their heads down, in case Reverend Daye should be looking out of the vicarage and catch them sneaking by. Once clear of the church, they crossed the road to avoid the police station, then ran as fast as they could to the coal mine on the colliery bank. From there they could see Tunstall Hill, just a short walk away.

'I always want to do this walk on my birthday,' Rose declared. 'Even when I'm as old as Nellie, I want to come every year with you both. It's my favourite place in the world. I can't think of a more perfect way to spend the day.'

Poppy squeezed her hand. 'Then we'll do it. Every year, no matter how old we get, even if we're old ladies, we'll walk here for your birthday.' She turned to Sid. 'And you'll come too, won't you?'

He gave her a cheeky wink. 'Just try and stop me.'

Chapter Eight

Poppy, Rose and Sid clambered up the hill. Poppy's feet were soaked through, as Sid's socks offered little protection, but when he urged her to take his boots, she declined. She knew they were too big for her, as she'd tried them on once before on a day when they'd walked down the mud track to the beach. Besides, her toes were so cold now that she could barely feel them, and she didn't think boots would be much use. She didn't care where she stood or what might be underfoot. There could be nettles that might sting, but she paid them no heed. She remembered how her mam used to say that nettles were good for the skin when used the right way.

She held tight to Sid's hand as they climbed to the top. Once there, she stood next to Rose, getting her breath back. Her cheeks were flushed red from exertion and her heart beat wildly as the wind whipped her hair into her eyes. She pushed her curls behind her ears so that she could see ahead, wanting to drink in the view. After a while, she sank to the damp grass, and Rose flopped down beside her, then Sid. They sat in a row looking out across rooftops and chimney pots. Poppy marvelled at the view.

Below them was Ryhope, the only place in the world that she knew. The small pit village was edged by high cliffs that towered over the menacing sea under a leaden sky.

'That's a snow cloud,' Sid said as he pointed out to sea.

'How do you know?' Poppy asked.

'Dad tells me all kinds of things about clouds and the weather,' he replied matter-of-factly. And in that moment, Poppy wished more than anything that she had someone to tell her such things. She had no one but Rose and Sid, although Sid was the most knowledgeable person she knew. He knew the names of the stars in the night sky, and the wild flowers that grew on the green. She saw his excited face light up as he pointed out landmarks between the hill and the sea.

'Look, there's St Paul's church!' he cried. 'I can see Reverend Daye walking up the path.'

'There's the coal mine,' Rose said. 'Look, here comes a train!' Smoke and steam rose as the train snaked its way below them, taking coal from the mine to the docks.

'There's the colliery bank with its shops and pubs. There's the Co-op!' Sid cried.

'There's the cattle market and the farm,' Poppy said. 'But I can't see anyone walking through the yard. Norman and the farmhands must be inside with the animals.'

The bells of St Paul's chimed.

'School will have started by now,' Sid said, biting his lip.

'Don't tell me you feel bad for taking a day off?' Poppy said. 'I'm disappointed in you, Sid Lawson. I thought you enjoyed coming up the hill for Rose's birthday.'

He shrugged. 'I do. It's just . . . I like learning things, Poppy. I like being at school. Mr Hylton says my reading is coming on a treat.'

'Then if you're so clever, sneaking off for one day won't harm you, will it?' she said. She slid her arm through his and pulled him close, then pointed south. 'Come on, Sid, tell us what's over there.'

He began to reel off everything he knew about the mining and fishing village of Seaham. Poppy and Rose listened intently. Afterwards, they sat in silence, listening to the wind as it blew, watching the sea as it crashed to the shore. Below them, people walked the streets, a horse and cart moved along a narrow lane, and thick, dark smoke from the mine blew out to sea.

'I love it up here,' Rose said.

'Me too,' Poppy agreed.

As they gazed at the view, they heard the bells of St Paul's chime another hour. Poppy sat between Rose and Sid and held hands with them both. She leaned towards her sister and whispered in her ear. 'I'm going to ask Sid if he'll read Nellie's letter if I find it.'

'No, Poppy, don't,' Rose hissed urgently. But Poppy had made up her mind.

'Sid?' she asked.

'What is it, Pops?'

'Would you read something for me if I gave it to you?'

'Course I would. Well, I'd try to. I'm not so clever with the big words, but I can try my best with the small ones. What is it? Do you want me to read it now? Have you got it in your pocket?'

'No . . . it's something that's in the barn. I just need to find it first.'

'When you get it, I'll read it. You know I'd do anything for you.'

Poppy laid her head on his shoulder. 'Thanks, Sid,' she said.

She looked again at the view, saw the village green and the house where she and Rose had lived before their parents died. If she tried really hard, she could even focus on the window of the bedroom they'd shared. But such memories were too painful to recall, and she forced her gaze away, back to the farm. Something moving in the farmyard caught her eye, and she leaned forward to take a better look.

'Look!' she cried. 'There's Nellie, walking through the yard. She shouldn't have finished knocking-up yet, unless she's taken on another shift we don't know about. And who's that man with her? It doesn't look like Norman.'

'That's definitely not Norman, he's too short,' Rose said, straining her eyes to see.

'He's wearing a top hat,' Sid added. 'He must be important if he's wearing a top hat.'

The girls stood, and Sid scrambled up after them. All three of them looked down, trying to work out who the man was.

'I've never seen Nellie with anyone before,' Rose said.

Poppy didn't like what she saw. She'd been feeling uneasy about the letters that Nellie had been receiving, and now there was a stranger at the farm.

'Something's up,' she said. She gathered her skirt in her hand and began to run down the hill. 'Come on,' she yelled. 'We've got to find out what's going on.'

They ran back to the village, taking care to stay away from the school. Sid hung back as Poppy stormed her way towards the cattle market.

'Come on, Sid,' she urged.

He shook his head. 'I think you should leave Nellie to her business. You shouldn't go poking your nose in where it's not wanted. That's what my mam says.'

Poppy's shoulders dropped and she tutted loudly. 'I thought you were my friend,' she said.

Rose stepped forward. 'Don't you want to know who Nellie was talking to?'

'I don't want to get caught at the farm,' he said. 'If Norman catches me, he'll tell my mam, and she'll find out I wasn't at school. Then Mam will tell Dad, and there'll be holy war at home.'

Poppy sank to the grass and pulled off his socks. 'You're too soft, Sid. Have these back,' she said. She flung the socks at him, but Sid picked them up and handed them back.

'Keep them. Dry them on the fire and they'll keep your feet warm at night,' he said.

She stuffed the socks into her pockets. 'Please come with us,' she said. 'Norman won't see you, he's always busy with his cows. And even if he does, he won't care. No one cares about us. Come on, Sid.'

Poppy took Rose's hand, and together they walked into the cattle market with Sid lagging reluctantly behind. It was busy inside, with men milling around inspecting sheep and pigs. Others were haggling over the price of Norman's cows. Norman was in the thick of it, calling out prices, extolling the virtues of his heaviest cow or the amount of meat that his sheep could provide. The men were so engrossed in their business, they didn't notice the children creeping along the edge of the yard, moving quickly and quietly with Poppy leading the way. However, there was no sign of Nellie or the man she'd been talking to.

When Poppy reached the barn at the back of the yard,

she paused. The door was closed, and she laid her ear against it. There was silence. She slid the door open, and she and Rose stepped inside. Sid hung back, unsure. Nellie wasn't there, but her stick was propped up in the corner of the room.

'She can't be at work; she never goes without her stick. Where's she gone?' Rose asked.

Poppy stood in the middle of the room with her hands on her hips. She looked around, hoping to find a clue that might reveal what had happened. In the time she'd lived with Nellie, she'd learned many things about her. She knew the woman didn't have a sense of humour, for she never cracked a smile. She knew she didn't get on with her brother, that he made her pay rent and buy coal for her fire, and never helped with the cost of her food. Plus, he forced her to live in the barn while he lived in the house. She knew that Nellie always took the biggest portion of food instead of sharing it equally with her and Rose. And she knew that Nellie was a creature of habit. She liked to be woken for work and then snooze in her chair when she came home. Work and sleep were all she did. She never saw friends that Poppy was aware of. And no one ever came to the barn. So where was she now if not at work? And who was the man they'd seen her walking in the yard with as they watched from the top of the hill?

Poppy was trying to make sense of it all when her eyes fell on something poking out from under Nellie's chair. She fell to her knees, reached under the chair and pulled the item towards her. Her heart leapt. She stood and held it up so that Rose could see it too. She could hardly believe what she'd found.

'It's Nellie's letter,' she gasped.

Chapter Nine

'Put it back!' Rose cried.

Poppy didn't move. Her hand trembled as she held the envelope. It was heavy paper, and on the front was spidery writing with looping letters in black ink.

'Sid! Tell her to put it back!' Rose cried, but when she spun around, Sid wasn't there. She hurried to the barn door to find him in the yard, keeping a watchful eye on Norman at the other end of the farm. 'Get inside,' she hissed, yanking him by his shoulder, and he almost fell into the barn.

'I wanted to make sure Norman wasn't on his way, I was only trying to protect you both,' he explained.

Rose pointed at her sister. 'Poppy's stealing things. Tell her to stop. Make her put it back. You're the only one she'll listen to.'

Sid stepped towards Poppy, who held out the envelope.

'Will you read it, Sid? Please?'

He hesitated a moment, and she wondered if he was having a change of heart now that the letter was in front of him.

'What is it, Sid? Are you frightened we'll get caught?' she asked.

Sid nodded. 'Rose is right, I think you should put it back. What if Nellie comes back? We'll be for it if she finds out.'

But Poppy stood firm. 'I need to know what's going on. There's something odd happening. Nellie's been treating me differently lately. I can't explain it, but I can feel it in here.' She laid a hand on her heart. 'I think something's going on that me and Rose need to know.'

Sid shook his head. 'Put it back.'

'Please, Sid,' Poppy begged. 'You said you would read it.'

He peered at the envelope. 'It looks really posh,' he said warily. 'Who would be writing to Nellie? Maybe it's from a man, courting her. That's what grown-ups do, you know, they write to each other and say soppy things about hearts and love and flowers. I know because Dad told me, he used to write letters to Mam when they were courting.'

Poppy inched the envelope further towards him. 'If it's a love letter, we'll know straight away, and we won't read it. I swear. I'll put it back in the envelope as soon as we know what it is.'

Finally Sid reached for the envelope, and Poppy was about to hand it to him when a figure appeared at the door.

'Nellie!' gasped Rose.

Poppy stuffed the letter in her pocket just as Nellie stepped into the barn.

'What are you doing here?' she barked to Sid, and he almost jumped out of his skin.

'Nothing,' he said. 'I mean, I was just—'

'You should be at school,' Nellie said, then she turned her attention to the girls. 'I don't know what's going on here, but I hope you're not up to no good.'

Poppy's mind whirled with a thousand lies, ready to defend Rose and Sid. She glanced at Rose, saw her sister's worried face and the tears in her eyes. She glanced at the knocking-up stick in the corner of the room, then moved to stand between Nellie and the stick so that she couldn't reach it. She was scared in case she tried to beat Rose. She squared her shoulders and forced her bare feet against the stone floor.

'It's my fault they aren't at school, Nellie,' she said quickly, thinking fast.

Rose and Sid turned to look at her as she carried on.

'I wasn't feeling well, so I . . . er, I had to get Rose from school to help me. I was being sick, see, and I didn't know what to do, so I . . . er . . .'

'She was really poorly, Nellie,' Sid chipped in, putting his hand to his head. 'She was bad in the head . . .'

'Stomach,' Poppy said at the same time.

Nellie narrowed her eyes and glared at both of them. 'I hope you two aren't telling lies.'

They shook their heads.

'No, Nellie.'

Nellie spun around to face Rose. 'And what have you got to say about this?'

To Poppy's surprise, Rose remained calm. 'It's just as Poppy says.'

Poppy felt a swell of pride. Rose wasn't given to telling lies – that was Poppy's domain – and she was grateful for her sister's support.

59

Rose's answer seemed to satisfy Nellie, for she walked to her chair and sat down.

'Get the fire going, girl,' she ordered Poppy. 'And see that Norman gives you a cabbage – he promised me one this morning. You'll make soup and bread and we'll eat when I wake. But for now, I need to sleep. It's been a busy morning and I've still got two shifts of miners to wake up from their beds. Some days I don't know whether I'm coming or going.' As she settled in her chair, she turned around to face Sid. 'As for you, lad, don't let me catch you in here again, you hear?'

'Yes, Nellie,' Sid replied.

Poppy watched as Nellie's eyes began to close. She nudged Sid with her elbow, nodded at Rose then pointed at the barn door.

'Run!' she whispered.

The children raced from the barn, Poppy's bare feet slapping against cobbles and stones. She pressed her hand to her pocket, terrified in case the letter flew out and got lost. In the cattle market, Norman was still engrossed with his buyers, and no one noticed Poppy, Rose and Sid as they ran to the village green.

'Where will we go to read it?' Rose asked.

Poppy looked around wildly. 'We need somewhere no one will see us. Come on, let's go to the beach. We can hide inside Old Man's Cave.'

She kept her hand on her pocket to protect the letter as she ran on. The road turned into a long, winding mud track that ran under the railway before finally ending at Ryhope beach. The beach was fringed with high, menacing cliffs all the way to Seaham in the south and Hendon in the north. No one ever walked there for the beauty of it.

Its sand was blackened by coal that washed up in drifts. Many villagers picked coal off the beach to burn on their fires. Even on a summer's day, when the sea was still and the sky blue, it was a forbidding place, full of dangerous rocks. Today, the sea ahead of them was grey and dark under a heavy sky. It churned and crashed to the shore. Two men were fishing from a large rock, their backs turned to the children.

Poppy made her way over stones and pebbles, each step painful in bare feet, until she reached a cave in the cliffs that was nicknamed Old Man's Cave. Rumour in the village was that a hermit had once lived there. Inside the damp cave, the roar of the sea echoed. Poppy settled on a rock, with Sid sitting on one side and Rose on the other. She pulled the letter from her pocket and smoothed the envelope against her skirt.

'I don't think this is a good idea,' Sid said, worried.

'I need to know what it says, Sid. I promise you, if you do this for me, I won't ask you for anything again.'

Sid looked at the sea. 'It's not the letter, Pops, it's the tide. Look, you can see it reaching further up the beach since we arrived.'

'We've got plenty of time,' Poppy said, fully focused on the envelope.

'Sid's right. We need to be quick. Open it,' Rose said, keeping one eye on the encroaching water.

Poppy took a deep breath and ran her finger along the flap of the envelope, then slowly pulled the letter out. There were two pages, folded together. She flattened them out before handing them to Sid. She could feel her heart beating.

'What does it say?'

He looked at the letter and shook his head. 'It's really hard, Pops. It's not like the writing we learn at school. It's grown-up writing, joined together. I don't think I can read it.'

'Try, Sid, please. It's our only chance.'

He returned to the letter, concentrating hard. He moved his finger slowly along the lines, pausing when he recognised a letter or a word that he knew.

'Does it say "To my darling Nellie" at the start? Is it a love letter? Because if it is, we won't read it,' Poppy said.

Sid concentrated hard on the words at the beginning of the letter. 'No . . . it starts by saying . . . "Dear Miss Ellen Harper".'

'Ellen?' Rose said.

Poppy shrugged. 'It must be Nellie's real name.'

Sid carried on reading. 'I know these two words, they say "Albion Inn",' he said confidently. 'I recognise them because I've walked past that pub every day of my life and seen its name on the sign. That's definitely what it says.'

'What business could Nellie have with the Albion Inn?' Poppy wondered. She pointed to a line in the middle of the page. 'What about those ones?'

He pulled the letter close to his eyes, squinting to see better. 'It's hard, Pops, really hard.' But then his face lit up. 'I know what this bit says, it's a number. There's a two and a four and there's a month of the year. We've been learning about months at school. It says "December", that's this month. So I think this is the twenty-fourth of December.'

'Does it mention my name, or Rose's?'

Sid scanned the letter, looking for their names. 'I don't think so,' he said.

'Can you tell who the letter is from?'

'Yes, who sent it?' Rose chimed. 'But be quick, Sid, the tide . . .'

Sid lifted the second sheet of paper and ran his finger all the way to the end. 'There's a name here, but it might take me a while to figure it out.'

'Take your time, Sid,' Poppy said.

Rose cast an anxious glance at the sea, which had started to lap around the cave entrance. 'No, he can't take his time. He needs to be quick,' she said, but Poppy and Sid were so engrossed in the letter, they didn't hear her warning.

'I think the first name starts with the letter M,' he said. 'I know that letter. And then there's a small a, or it might be an o – it's hard to tell, the letters aren't straight. There's definitely a big letter S at the start of the second word, I recognise that as it's the same as my name. I think, Pops, I think . . . the first name might be Malcolm. Yes, I'm sure it is Malcolm . . . and the second name is . . .'

Rose stood. 'We need to go – look, the tide's coming into the cave.'

'It's Scurrfield. Malcolm Scurrfield,' Sid said with a sigh of relief.

'Poppy! Sid! Come on!' Rose screamed.

Poppy gasped when she looked up. They'd been sitting in the cave for so long that the tide was at the cliffs now, pushing against the rocks. Seawater was pouring into the cave.

'Come on, we'll have to wade back to the track,' she said, taking Rose's hand.

'No, Pops, we can't,' Sid said. 'It's too dangerous. If we go out there, the waves will crush us against the cliffs.'

'But we can't stay in here – we'll die!' Poppy yelled.

Pulling Rose by the hand, she ventured out of the cave. It wasn't too bad at first; her feet found the sand and rocks, and with her free hand she steadied herself against the cliff. But then a wave lashed against her and she lost her grip. Behind her, Rose fell and was thrashed around in the choppy water like a rag doll.

'Rose!' Poppy cried. She reached and grabbed hold of her sister. 'Sid, come and help!' she shouted.

Sid was already fighting his way to the girls through water that was up to his waist. In all the commotion, no one saw Nellie's letter wash out to sea.

'Hold on tight,' Poppy shouted as she took Sid's hand. The children pushed against the surging sea, tripping over rocks and stones, keeping their focus on the track ahead. They had no choice but to reach it. To return to the cave would mean certain death, and the cliffs were too steep to climb.

'It's my fault, I'm sorry!' Poppy said.

'Stop talking, Pops. Swim!' Sid begged.

'I can't swim!' she cried back, but her thin voice was lost as a powerful wave surged over her and Rose.

Chapter Ten

Poppy couldn't breathe. Her mouth filled with seawater, and pain shot through her as she was crashed against the rocks. The water was up to her shoulders and already above Rose's head. Sid was hanging on to the cliff with one hand and holding out his other to Poppy.

'Grab my hand, Pops!' he ordered.

But Poppy couldn't let go of Rose; she wouldn't, she had to keep her sister afloat. The track was ahead of her – just a few more steps over the rocks and she'd reach it. She was almost there, and Sid was behind her, urging her and Rose on, when another wave crashed against them. She stumbled and lost her footing.

'Rose!'

Suddenly she felt herself being lifted up and out of the water. She couldn't fathom it at first, and had no idea what was happening.

'Stay calm,' a deep voice said, then she felt her body connect with something hard, and realised she'd been dropped on to the track.

'Rose! Save Rose, please!' she pleaded to the man who'd rescued her. She lay sobbing, watching as he waded back to drag her sister from the sea.

When at last Rose was lying next to her, gasping for air, Poppy whispered a thank you to the heavens for saving their lives. Then she turned to thank the man, and was shocked to see that it was Ambrose Trewhitt.

He was already heading back into the water, with his son Michael at his side. The sea reached their chests, but they waded confidently to where Sid was clinging to the cliff. She saw Sid jump on to Michael's back, and the man carried him to the track. Sid fell into the mud next to Poppy.

'Thank you,' she said, overcome with relief.

Water streamed from Ambrose and Michael's faces and arms. Ambrose stood over the children, shaking his head.

'You stupid bairns, you could have been killed! Don't you know how dangerous Old Man's Cave is when the tide's coming in?'

'We were just playing, sir,' Sid said, trembling with fear and shock.

'Playing?' Ambrose roared. 'Old Man's Cave isn't a playground. Men have been killed when the tide has caught them unawares! You were lucky me and Michael were fishing and saw you when we did. I dread to think what might have happened if we hadn't. Now get yourselves home and don't let me catch you here again.'

Poppy slowly rose and helped her sister to stand too. Sid got to his feet, and together, soaking wet and shivering, they began to walk back towards the village. Poppy turned to see Ambrose standing at the end of the track. He was bent double as if catching his breath.

'Ambrose!' she called. 'Are you all right?'

He turned and waved a dismissive hand.

'Scram, the lot of you,' Michael yelled.

The children quickly walked away.

'Mam's going to kill me when she sees the state I'm in,' Sid said. 'My arm's bleeding where it was gashed on the rocks.'

'My leg hurts,' Poppy sighed.

'At least we'll have Nellie's fire to dry us at the barn,' Rose said.

Poppy slapped her hand against her forehead. 'We won't, you know. I was supposed to set the fire before we ran out. Nellie won't be in a good mood when we get back.'

'What'll we tell her about where we've been and how we ended up getting wet?' Rose asked.

'Leave that to me, I'll think of something,' Poppy replied. 'And not a word about her letter, all right?'

'I knew this was a bad idea,' Rose muttered darkly.

'Have you still got the letter, Sid?' Poppy asked, but she knew before he replied what must have happened.

'Sorry, Pops, I reckon it floated away.'

When they reached the village green, the girls left Sid and headed through the cattle market. They huddled together, soaking wet, holding hands, and what a sorry sight they made. They reached the barn with water dripping from them.

'Remember, leave Nellie to me. I'll do all the talking,' Poppy said.

She slid the door to one side. Inside, the coal fire was burning, and Nellie was in her chair, reading from a sheet of thick, creamy white paper. Poppy gasped. Another letter had arrived.

At the sound of the door, Nellie stood, slowly folded the letter and put it in her pocket. Poppy noticed something odd: the knocking-up stick wasn't where it should be in the corner of the room. Her heart dropped to the floor when she saw it at Nellie's feet. Nellie bent down to pick it up, and quick as a flash, Poppy moved to shield Rose. She knew the old woman was displeased with them for running out earlier, and for bringing Sid to the barn. She'd expected a tongue-lashing, but the sight of the stick made her fear the worst. She stood completely still as Nellie turned towards her, gripping it with both hands. Poppy knew better than to speak first.

'Trying to protect your little sister again,' Nellie hissed. 'Rose, come out from behind Poppy.'

Rose shifted slightly so that she was only half shielded. She dropped her gaze to the floor, while Poppy kept her eyes on Nellie, ready to run if need be. Where they would go to, she had no idea. Maybe Sid's mam would offer them shelter. But she dismissed the thought immediately, for Sid's mam had enough on her plate with the new baby, as well as all her other children.

Nellie stepped towards them, her face twisted with hate. Poppy saw that her fingers were gripping the stick so tightly her knuckles had turned white.

'What the devil happened to you?' she snarled. 'Look at you both! You're soaking wet.' She took another step forward. 'Well? Anyone want to tell me what you've been up to?'

'We fell in the sea,' Poppy said quickly.

Nellie rocked back on her heels. 'Oh? And what were you doing at the beach?' She brought the stick down and whacked it hard against the floor before Poppy could reply. 'You should have been here, working for me. And Rose should've been at school. I had to light my own fire. What's the point of having you here if I have to do things myself?'

'Sorry, Nellie,' Poppy said, hoping the apology would be enough to appease the woman. But Nellie only whacked the stick against the floor again. Each time she brought it down, Poppy and Rose shook with fright.

'Sit by the fire and get dry,' she ordered at last.

Poppy was surprised at this. She'd expected Nellie to tell her to start cooking dinner on the hearth, or send them up to bed without food. It wouldn't have been the first time she'd done so. She took Rose's hand and, keeping a keen eye on Nellie in case she struck out with her stick, the girls walked to the fire. As they sat by the hearth, they turned their faces to the flames and rubbed their hands to get warm. Poppy's leg was sore, and Rose was complaining about her arm hurting, injuries caused from being crashed against the rocks, but Nellie paid their complaints little heed. Poppy stretched her legs out in the hope that her feet would thaw out and warm up. Slowly Nellie sat down in her armchair, but she still held her stick in her hand. Aware that the danger wasn't yet over, Poppy kept alert to every movement the woman made.

'You look like drowned rats,' Nellie moaned. 'It'll be pneumonia next for the pair of you. You'll be no good to me if you catch flu and can't wake me up for my work.'

Poppy felt troubled by her words. 'We'll be fine. We're strong, me and Rose,' she said defiantly.

As if to prove her point, Rose sat up straight and looked at Nellie. Nellie lifted her chin, then narrowed her eyes. 'Care to tell me what happened at the beach? And what you were doing there? This afternoon when I caught you in here with that boy, you told me you weren't feeling well, and then you disappeared. Something's not right. Old Nellie's never wrong.'

Poppy gulped, and her mind whirled with the lies she'd tried to get straight on their walk home from the beach. 'We . . .' she faltered. 'We . . . went fishing for food. I couldn't find a cabbage and we were hungry,' she said at last, and once the first lies left her lips, the rest tumbled out. 'But we got the tide wrong. There were no fish, just dangerous waves, and we got caught in a cave and a fisherman rescued us. We might have drowned if he hadn't seen us.'

'Who was he, this fisherman?' Nellie demanded.

'He didn't give his name,' Poppy replied. She didn't want to mention Ambrose and his son in case she got into more trouble.

As she spoke, she glanced under Nellie's chair, wondering how long it would be before the woman realised one of her precious letters was missing. Nellie caught her looking, and an evil grin spread across her face. Poppy took a deep breath and readied herself, going over her prepared lies. But Nellie never said a word. Instead, she laid her stick on the floor, reached into her pocket and pulled out the letter she'd been reading when the girls had returned to the barn.

'See this?' she said, waving it in the air.

Poppy's heart skipped a beat. Was she finally about to find out what was going on? Was this letter from Malcolm Scurrfield, the same man who'd sent the letter that Sid had tried to read? Whatever it said must have something to do with her and Rose. Otherwise why would Nellie be taunting them with it? She kept her eyes firmly on it.

'This is my ticket to freedom,' Nellie said.

Poppy was puzzled. What did a ticket have to do with her and Rose?

Nellie looked around the barn. 'I've lived too long in this dump. Norman stuck me in here thinking he was giving me charity, but this place isn't fit for pigs, never mind someone like me. I'm not getting any younger, I need to look after myself. I'm getting out of here the minute I receive what I'm due. I'll find somewhere with a roof that doesn't leak, somewhere with a garden. Somewhere I can live on my own, in peace and quiet. I'll have my own money, enough to give up the knocking-up.'

She leaned forward and bared her blackened teeth at the sisters. 'You're not stupid girls. I'm sure you don't need me to tell you that once I leave here, you'll need to find somewhere else to live.'

Poppy felt the ground shift beneath her. She knew exactly what it meant. If Nellie didn't need her and Rose to knock her up for work, then she didn't need them at all.

'But . . . where will we go if you throw us out?' she said. Her words left her in a whisper.

Nellie snapped the letter against her palm. 'You'll find out soon enough.'

Poppy had never felt so scared. She knew that whatever was coming, she had to be strong, not just for herself but also for her little sister. She grabbed Rose's hand and squeezed it tight, then gave her a smile of reassurance, while inside she was shaking like a leaf.

Chapter Eleven

In the chilly days that followed, Poppy watched Nellie like a hawk, hoping for a clue as to what was going on. One day in the farmyard she even followed Norman, asking him if he knew anything about Nellie's plans, but he shouted at her to leave him alone.

'I'm busy, girl. Haven't you got work to do or school to go to?' he yelled, and so Poppy slunk away.

On Christmas Eve morning, while Rose was at school and Nellie was asleep in her chair by the fire, Poppy decided to head to the Trewhitts' shop to say thank you to Ambrose for saving them at the beach. There was snow on the ground, but as it was Rose's turn to wear the boots, she had no choice but to go out with nothing on her feet but Sid's socks. She glanced at Nellie again to ensure she was asleep, then slipped quietly from the barn into the yard.

The ice-cold air pricked her skin. She shivered under her blanket, then pulled it tight around her shoulders, but it offered little protection. She ran quickly across the green to where the Trewhitts' shop stood in the middle of a row of terraced houses. When she reached it, she stared in through the window. The display was decorated for Christmas with a plate of coloured marzipan shaped into perfect tiny apples, strawberries and pears. A plate of mince pies dusted with sugar made her drool. She put her hand to the glass and peered further inside. Ella and Ambrose were sitting on stools behind the counter, each cradling a mug in their hands. There were no customers inside, just the Trewhitts enjoying their hot drinks, deep in conversation with each other.

Poppy turned her back to the window and leaned against it as she tried to gather the courage to enter. Ella wouldn't welcome her, not after she'd been caught stealing last time. But if she didn't go inside, how was she to thank Ambrose and tell him how grateful she was? She crossed her arms under her blanket and hugged herself to keep warm. She tried to think of the right words to say once she walked through the door, but as she was thinking, she heard snippets of conversation coming from inside, the Trewhitts' voices carrying to the window where she stood. She wouldn't have listened, really she wouldn't, but she heard them mention her name. And then Rose's name too. She stiffened. Had they spotted her? She spun around, expecting to see Ella scowling through the window, shooing her away. But Ella was still behind the counter with Ambrose. Poppy leaned back a little so that her ear was close to the glass, all the better to hear more clearly.

'You've seen him? When?' Ella exclaimed.

'Last night at the Albion Inn, when I called in for a pint. He's a big fella, tall, strong. In his thirties, I'd say. Well dressed he was, too, in a top hat.'

Poppy wondered who they were talking about.

'Is he married?'

'Now how am I to know?' Ambrose laughed. 'Only a woman would ask such a question. I tried to engage him in conversation, but he wasn't much for talking, so I just watched him for a while. He read his newspaper, had two pints of stout, then disappeared up the stairs to the room that Hetty and Jack Burdon rent out at the Albion. And that's all I know.'

'How long's he staying?' Ella asked.

'I heard him mention that he's taking the girls today,' Ambrose said.

'Fancy taking them on Christmas Eve, of all days,' Ella sighed. 'Those poor little things.'

Poppy's blood turned cold in her veins. Her heart began to hammer, and her breath quickened, but she was determined to find out more. She needed to know what was going on. Her bottom lip trembled. Behind her, the conversation continued, and she heard her name and Rose's again. She took a deep breath, then pushed the door open. The tinkle of the bell made Ella and Ambrose turn.

'Where's he taking us?' she demanded.

'Poppy Thomas, I told you never to come back here!' Ella said harshly.

Ambrose laid his hand on his wife's arm. 'Leave her to me, love. Let her be, under the circumstances.'

Poppy searched Ambrose and Ella's faces. 'Please, tell me what's happening. Who's the man you were talking about? Is it Malcolm Scurrfield?'

Ella set her mug on the counter as Ambrose raised himself out of his chair.

'Now, Poppy, don't get yourself upset,' he said kindly.

'Ambrose, please tell me. You knew our mam; she'd want you to tell me.'

'I suppose the lass has got a point,' Ella said quietly.

Poppy tried to stay calm, but inside she was shaking. Ambrose beckoned her forward and she took a hesitant step to the counter.

'You need to speak to Nellie,' he said softly, then glanced at Ella. 'It's not our business what goes on at the farm.'

'Yes, talk to Nellie, love,' Ella advised.

Poppy didn't know what to do. She wanted to run from the shop straight to Nellie to demand to know the truth, but the shock of what she'd heard pinned her to the spot. Her legs didn't seem to work. Finally she found the strength to turn and walk out, the bell jangling as the door slammed behind her.

At first she walked, then she began to run as fast as she could, panting, almost out of breath, red in the face, her heart pounding. She ran through the cattle market, into the yard, ready to slide the barn door open and confront Nellie with all that she knew. But the door was already open, and she stopped in her tracks. Nellie was up and about, which was unusual for her at that time of day and wasn't part of her current routine.

Poppy walked into the barn and glared at Nellie. 'I demand to know what's going on,' she said. She was surprised at the strength of the words that left her, for she was shaking inside.

'Sit down, girl,' Nellie ordered, but Poppy didn't move. 'I said, sit down!' she said, more firmly.

Poppy reluctantly sat by the fire as Nellie settled into her chair. She was raging inside, furious, but she knew enough not to act up. She had to stay calm and focused and listen to what the woman had to say.

'You and your sister are leaving today,' Nellie said quickly. Poppy's heart skipped a beat.

'Leaving? Where are we going?'

'You will be taken by Mr Scurrfield . . .'

Sid had read the name right after all.

'. . . to live with him in Sunderland.'

Poppy's mouth opened and closed. She couldn't find the words. 'Away from Ryhope?' she said at last, trying to understand the enormity of leaving the village. 'Away from Sid?'

'It'll be a better life for you both. The Scurrfields are important people, they'll teach you some manners. Heaven knows you need them.'

'But why, Nellie? Why?'

Nellie's face softened for a second. 'Mr Scurrfield read my advertisement in the *Sunderland Echo* offering two orphans for sale and he decided to buy you. It's as simple as that, a business transaction.'

Poppy was aghast. 'You're selling us in the same way that Norman sells pigs?'

Nellie's face hardened again. 'You should think yourself lucky. Scurrfield will arrive to collect you in two hours' time. You need to go to the school now to fetch Rose. When Mr Scurrfield arrives, I want you and your sister scrubbed and washed, wearing your best clothes, with your hair brushed and your eyes bright.'

'But what about . . .'

Sid, she thought. *What about Sid?* When would she tell him she was leaving? She crossed her fingers and hoped he was at school so she could speak to him when she collected Rose. Then something occurred to her. 'You want us to wear our best clothes when he comes for us?' she said. 'We don't have any best clothes.' She looked down at her torn skirt and pulled the horse blanket around her. 'You know we've only got what we're wearing now.'

'Aye, well, that'll have to do. At least we can do something about your hair. You need to look presentable when he collects you. Now go to the school and bring Rose as fast as you can.'

Poppy was stunned as she walked to the school, and anxious thoughts whirled through her mind. Could it really be true what Nellie had said? Was Scurrfield the reason she had been taking an interest in Poppy looking smart and being clean behind her ears? She must have been trying to prepare her for meeting the man. The thought of leaving Ryhope was terrifying, and yet ... there was something exciting too. They were leaving for a better life, Nellie had said, and Poppy had no choice but to believe her. If it was true, they'd no longer have to live in the barn with the stench of cows and pigs. And no matter what Scurrfield and his missus were like, she and Rose would always have each other. But what was life like outside of Ryhope? She didn't have a clue.

When she reached the school, she didn't even knock at the door; she just barged in and took Rose by the arm.

'Poppy Harper! What on earth do you think you're doing?' Mr Hylton exclaimed, but Poppy paid him no heed.

'We have to go, Rose, it's important,' she said.

'Where are you going, Pops?' Sid called across the schoolroom.

'We're leaving, Sid, Nellie's sending us away.'

He leapt from his seat and ran towards the door.

'Sidney Lawson, get back here this instant!' the teacher yelled, but Sid had already left the room.

'You were right, Sid, the name in the letter *was* Malcolm Scurrfield,' Poppy said as they walked. 'He's an important man and he's going to take me and Rose.'

'Where are we going?' asked Rose.

'Sunderland. We're going to live there with Mr Scurrfield and his wife.'

She kept quiet about the fact that Nellie had sold them; she didn't want Rose asking questions she couldn't answer. What if she asked her how much the woman had been paid? It must be quite a sum, for Nellie had mentioned being able to give up her job as a knocker-upper. Clearly they were of some value.

'Will you come back?' Sid asked, breaking into her troubled thoughts.

Poppy looked at her friend. 'Yes,' she said with a smile. She crossed her fingers and hoped she was right. She turned to Rose. 'Nellie says it'll be a better life, really it will.'

'Nothing could be as bad as living with her in that stinky old barn, that's what my mam says,' Sid said. 'But when are you leaving?'

'In two hours. Mr Scurrfield's coming to collect us. Nellie says we have to get washed and look smart.'

Sid put his hands in his pockets and kicked dirt on the ground. 'I don't want you to go,' he said.

Poppy felt tears prick her eyes. 'And I don't want to leave you, but Sunderland's not far away, Sid, we'll come and visit often, I promise. I can't turn down a better life for me and Rose.'

'You could run away. We'll all run away, and hide on Tunstall Hill,' Sid said, but Poppy shook her head.

'Will you come and see us off?'

He nodded sadly. 'I'll wait on the village green.'

She took his hands in hers, then leaned forward and kissed his cheek. Sid sniffed and wiped the back of his hand across his eyes.

'I'll miss you, Pops,' he said.

Poppy knew he was trying to be brave, but despite his efforts, a tear trickled down his cheek. She'd never seen him so upset, and in that instant, she felt as if her heart would break. Sid was her only friend and she'd miss him too.

'It'll be all right, you'll see,' she said, but she couldn't disguise the crack in her voice.

Chapter Twelve

In the barn, Nellie had pans of water boiling on the fire and the tin bath ready by the hearth. There was even a bar of carbolic soap. Poppy couldn't remember the last time she'd seen soap.

'Poppy, you get in first,' Nellie said. 'Don't forget to wash behind your ears and scrub your neck.'

'But no one ever sees behind my ears,' Poppy sulked.

'Just do it!' Nellie barked, then turned to Rose. 'You get in after your sister.'

Poppy washed herself thoroughly under Nellie's eagle eye. It felt strange knowing it would be the last time she'd use the tin bath.

'Where in Sunderland do the Scurrfields live?' she asked.

'Keep your mouth shut and don't ask questions,' Nellie barked.

When Poppy had finished and it was Rose's turn to bathe, Nellie took the blanket outside and shook dirt from it. Then the girls sat by the fire to dry their long hair. Poppy's hair sprang into curls as it dried.

'Have two hours passed yet?' she asked impatiently.

Part of her couldn't wait to get away. Whatever lay ahead for her and Rose couldn't be anywhere near as bad as the life they lived with Nellie. And yet there was another part of her that was scared of leaving Ryhope and Sid. What if the Scurrfields treated them even worse than Nellie did? But hadn't Nellie said that they were respectable, important people? Poppy crossed her fingers and hoped for kindness and love.

'Stand up, both of you, and let me inspect you,' Nellie said.

Poppy and Rose scrambled to their feet and stood together, holding hands. Nellie brushed their hair again, pulling at knots in Poppy's curls. Then she dusted down their skirts and ran a cloth around the boots, which Poppy was wearing. Rose's feet were bare. Just as she finished, the barn door scraped open. Poppy looked up. This was it, she thought. This must be Scurrfield. She stood straight and glanced at Rose.

'Give him a big smile when he comes in,' she whispered.

Both sisters plastered smiles on to their faces. Poppy had built up a picture in her mind of Mr Scurrfield as a round, chubby man with a pleasant face and a kind expression. She'd imagined someone she would feel comfortable with; someone who'd treat them well. But she was in for a nasty surprise when Malcolm Scurrfield walked in. He was a tall, thin man, who walked as if he had a stick down his coat to keep his back straight. He wore a black top hat and a long black coat with smart polished boots. She'd never seen such fine clothes. But his face didn't carry the kindly expression she'd hoped for. His skin was sallow, his cheeks sunken. His eyes were tired, watery and small and his nose was long and thin.

As soon as he saw the girls, he whipped his hat off to reveal cropped black hair. He walked straight to Poppy and looked her hard in the eye.

'Ah, we meet at last. You must be . . .'

'This one's Poppy Harper, sir. She's the eldest,' Nellie said quickly.

Scurrfield's face twisted into a grimace as he attempted a smile. Poppy took a step back, afraid. He turned his attention to Rose.

'And who is this little thing?' he said.

'She's the younger one, sir. She's called Rose,' Nellie replied.

Poppy watched in horror as Scurrfield lifted a gnarled hand and touched Rose's cheek, letting his finger trail down her face.

'You're a pretty girl, Rose Harper,' he said. 'My wife will enjoy meeting you, I'm sure.'

At the mention of his wife, Poppy thought it odd that Mrs Scurrfield hadn't come to meet her and Rose. Surely if she was taking them into her home she'd want to see them first? Well, maybe important people who lived in Sunderland did things differently. She looked at Scurrfield again, and there was something about the way he held on to Rose's face with his long, bony fingers that made her feel queasy. No one had ever touched either of the girls that way, prodding and stroking them as if they were animals, and she didn't like it one bit. She tugged at Rose, pulling her away from the man, and his hand dropped to his side.

'Our name isn't Harper,' she said defiantly. Her eyes flashed anger at Scurrfield. 'I'm Poppy Thomas and this is Rose Thomas.'

'How dare you speak to the gentleman like that!' Nellie cried, then she turned to Scurrfield. 'I'm ever so sorry, sir.'

Scurrfield began pacing the floor with his hands behind his back, all the while keeping his eyes on Poppy. Suddenly he came to a stop. 'I wasn't warned that you were insolent,' he said, looking straight at her.

Poppy felt her cheeks burn with anger, but she had to make a stand before he took them from the barn. Rose was young and innocent; she needed to be protected, and Poppy was the only one who could do it. 'Our name is Thomas,' she said firmly. 'And I'd be grateful, sir, if you didn't touch my sister in that way again.'

Scurrfield stood still for a long time, looking from Poppy to Rose. Behind him, Nellie waited with a sour expression on her face. Then he did something unexpected: he delved into his coat pocket and brought out a small, round purse. He held it in one hand and with the other rummaged inside it until he found what he was looking for, bringing out a silver coin. Poppy stood rigid, nervous. She could feel Rose trembling at her side and knew her sister was frightened too.

In the dim light of the barn, Scurrfield returned the purse to his pocket and held the silver coin aloft. 'This is a sixpence,' he said. 'Ever seen one before?'

Poppy had seen a sixpence many times while their parents were alive, but she was too scared to reply. Rose kept silent too as they watched the coin glinting in the light from the fire.

'On one side of the coin is the King's head and on the other a coat of arms. Now, I'm going to throw the sixpence into the air, and when it lands, it will determine which girl I take with me.'

'No, sir!' Nellie roared as she stepped forward to face him. 'That was not the deal we made. You either buy both girls or leave empty-handed.'

'He bought us? Nellie sold us?' Rose whispered, horrified.

'Sir, the older girl is clean and doesn't have nits. You can even check behind her ears, I made her scrub there every day,' Nellie urged, but Scurrfield seemed unmoved. 'You must take both of them, I insist. The advertisement I placed, and you responded to, was to buy both orphans.'

Poppy was horrified by what she was hearing, and she put her arm around Rose's shoulders. Her heart felt heavy and she wished she hadn't spoken so badly to Scurrfield. The thought of being apart from her sister was too much to bear.

'We won't be separated,' she said firmly, holding tight to Rose. 'Take us both.'

Scurrfield's upper lip twitched. 'Mrs Scurrfield will only allow well-behaved, obedient children into our home. And it seems to me, Poppy *Harper . . .*' he empha-sised the surname, which made Poppy's blood boil, 'that you need taking down a peg or two. If I take both of you, you'll be in cahoots, and one might lead the other astray. I won't risk upsetting my wife like that.' He turned to Nellie. 'Let me be clear, Miss Harper. I'll repeat what I've just said. I will take only one girl. As for which one, this sixpence will decide.' He pointed at Poppy. 'When the coin falls, if it shows the King's head, I'll take you.' He indicated Rose. 'And if it shows the coat of arms, I'll take you.'

'Please, sir! I need the money from the sale of both of them,' Nellie begged.

'I don't think you've got any choice, Miss Harper,' Scurrfield said. 'You've already told me I was the only person to come forward after reading your notice in the newspaper. What's it to be? Do I take one orphan and give you half the money, or take neither of them, which means you'll receive nothing at all?'

Nellie stepped back, giving Scurrfield his answer. He took the coin in his right hand and held his left hand out, palm up. Poppy shivered with fear as she watched him throw the sixpence in the air.

Chapter Thirteen

Poppy watched in horror as the sixpence spun in the air, glittering in the firelight. She felt sick to her stomach, blaming herself for forcing Mr Scurrfield to choose between her and Rose. She couldn't bear the thought of being separated from her sister. How would she cope without her? More importantly, how would Rose manage on her own? Oh, why couldn't she have kept her mouth shut? Her mam always used to call her a chatterbox who didn't know when to keep quiet.

She squeezed her eyes shut when the sixpence landed in Scurrfield's palm. He closed his right hand over his left, cupped his hands towards him and peered in through the gap. Poppy leaned forward on tiptoe, hoping to see the coin, but Scurrfield hid it completely. She wished with all her heart that it had landed on the floor and rolled out to the yard, never to be seen again. Her mouth turned dry and her legs began to shake, but she kept her eyes on Scurrfield's face. Was she mistaken, or was there a slight twitch around his mouth as he opened his hands and looked at the coin? Without showing it to Nellie or the girls, he placed it back in his purse.

There was silence, and the anticipation became too much for Poppy. 'Please, sir, take us both,' she urged. 'We only have each other. We don't know how to live apart.'

'Silence, girl!' Scurrfield said. He turned to Nellie. 'The coin fell on its tail. I'll take the younger, prettier girl.'

Nellie marched to Rose and pulled her sharply by the arm, moving her to stand next to Scurrfield. The shock of it was too much for Poppy. Her shaking legs gave way and she collapsed to the ground, crying and pleading. 'No!' she screamed. 'You can't take her. Please, sir, take me too. Don't separate us, I beg you.'

'Get up,' Scurrfield hissed. 'You're insolent and disobedient, and now you're acting as though you're a farm animal, writhing around on the ground.'

Poppy clambered to her knees, then slowly began to stand. She cast a quick glance at Scurrfield and Nellie, and then at Rose, who was mute with shock. As quickly as she could, she grabbed her sister and ran to the door. But Scurrfield reached it before them and blocked their way with his gangly frame. He pointed at Poppy.

'Take this disrespectful girl from my sight,' he ordered.

Nellie rushed forward and held tight to Poppy's arms, pinning them behind her back. Scurrfield laid his hand on Rose's shoulder and gave an evil grin. 'I will take her right now. There is no time to waste, I must get the child home. Mrs Scurrfield will be pleased with my Christmas gift to her this year.'

'No!' Poppy yelled.

Nellie slapped her across her face, which made her scream even more.

'I beg you, sir, please don't take my sister from me!'

But Scurrfield was already leading Rose to the door. There was no fight in Rose's body; her shoulders were slumped and tears streamed down her face.

'Don't go with him, Rose!' Poppy screamed.

'I think you've forgotten something, sir,' Nellie said, striding purposefully towards Scurrfield with her palm outstretched.

'Ah yes, the payment.' Scurrfield let go of Rose's shoulders so that he could pull his leather purse from his pocket, and Poppy saw her opportunity. She ran to her sister and threw her arms around her.

'I'll find you,' she whispered in Rose's ear. 'I'll look for you every day and I'll find you and we'll be together again.'

'Promise?' Rose said, her bottom lip trembling with fear.

Before Poppy could reply, Nellie was on her, pinning her arms behind her back.

'Here, half of the sum as agreed,' Scurrfield said, handing over the purse. Then he looked at Rose and handed her the sixpence that had just decided her fate. 'And this is for you, dear child. A sixpence to spend as you wish.'

Rose took the coin and held it awkwardly between finger and thumb. She stared at it for a long time, and Poppy wondered what was going through her mind.

'I can spend it on anything I please?' she asked eventually.

'Anything,' Scurrfield replied.

Rose held the sixpence out to Poppy. 'I want to buy my sister's boots.'

Scurrfield's gaze fell to Poppy's feet. 'Nonsense!' he

roared. 'Those boots aren't worth a ha'penny. Why, they're falling to pieces.'

Poppy watched Rose force a smile at the man. She'd seen that look on her sister's face before and knew that Rose was play-acting to cover her fears.

Rose straightened her spine a little as she continued. 'I am sure Mrs Scurrfield would not want me to enter her home in bare feet, no matter how bad the condition of the boots,' she said sweetly.

Scurrfield gave this a moment's thought. 'Yes, I expect you're right,' he said. 'I suppose you could take the boots, if that is really what you wish.'

'It is, sir,' Rose said.

She gave Poppy the sixpence. The sisters clasped each other's hands.

'Promise me that you'll come and find me,' Rose whispered.

'I promise,' Poppy whispered back.

She sank to the floor, pulled the boots off and handed them to Rose, who put them on. Behind them, Nellie was busy counting the coins that Scurrfield had paid her.

'Miss Harper, I am leaving now with the child,' Scurrfield said officiously. He draped his arm around Rose's shoulders and led her to the door.

Poppy wanted to run after her sister and never let her go. She wanted nothing more than to hug Rose and kiss her. But her legs felt like lead, and she stood rooted to the spot in front of the fire, too shocked to move. The last sound she heard was the scuffing of Rose's boots against the stones in the yard. And then there was silence, just the roaring fire and Nellie sliding coins along the tabletop, totting up her spoils.

Poppy still couldn't move. What had just happened seemed too big to understand, unreal, and she struggled to take it in. She needed someone to talk to, but who? That was when she remembered Sid, who was waiting on the village green. Sid, who thought she was leaving with Rose. She forced her feet forward slowly, trying to break her mind and body free from the shock of what had happened and the fear of what lay ahead. Step by careful step, as if in a trance, she walked to the barn door. She didn't feel the ice-cold air on her face as she stepped into the yard. She didn't care about the stones biting into the soles of her bare feet. She didn't hear Norman haggling over the price of a cow. She felt numb. It was as if her heart had been ripped from her body, leaving her wounded and raw.

Life without her sister was unthinkable. What would become of them both? She feared for herself, living with Nellie in the barn, but at least she knew what to expect. Above all, she feared for Rose and her unknown life with the Scurrfields. She crossed her fingers and sent a silent wish that Mrs Scurrfield was a good woman, kind and true. If she was, she might protect Rose from Mr Scurrfield's evil gaze and gnarled fingers.

Ahead of her on the green stood a smart carriage behind a muscled black horse. Inside the carriage she saw Rose's tiny face pressed up against the window. Sid was waiting as he'd promised, and Poppy walked up to him and slipped her hand into his. Her touch caught him by surprise, and when he turned to look at her, she saw that he'd been crying.

'Would you like me to help you climb up to sit beside Rose?' he offered, his voice shaking.

Poppy shook her head. 'No, I'm staying with Nellie. He's only taking Rose. He doesn't want me. I spoke against him in the barn, and he called me insolent and disrespectful.'

Sid's mouth opened in shock. 'But you belong together. He can't take Rose and leave you!'

'He is,' Poppy said sadly.

She reached her hand to the carriage window and laid it on the cold glass where Rose was gazing out. And then, with a lurch, the carriage began to move. Poppy and Sid ran alongside, and Poppy kept her eyes locked on her sister's ashen face. She saw Rose's hand at the window, saw her fist open and close three times, their secret sign, and she thought her heart would break.

At first they were able to keep up with the carriage as the horse walked across the green. But as soon as its hooves hit the road, it began to pick up its pace.

'Come on, Sid, run faster!' Poppy yelled.

And so they ran, as fast as they could, but they weren't fast enough. Poppy wouldn't give in, though, she wouldn't stop running even when Sid called to tell her that it was no good. She ran as tears flowed down her face. She ran until the carriage turned into a speck in the distance. Only when it disappeared from view did she stop. Exhausted and in turmoil, she passed out and fell to the ground.

It was Sid who came to her aid. He'd followed her all the way, calling out to her, begging her to turn around and come back. He lifted her in his arms, then laid her down on a grass verge, away from passing horses and carts. He saw the sixpence fall from her pocket and retrieved it from the road. Despite the bitter cold of the day, he took his jacket off and tucked it around her.

At last Poppy opened her eyes, and she and Sid sat together in tears. Later, as the day darkened, they made their way back to Ryhope. Nothing was said as they walked; no words could express the horror of what had happened. 'Lean on me, I'm strong. I'll look after you,' Sid told her. He handed her the sixpence, and Poppy put it in her pocket. Then she took his arm, and together they made their way back to the barn.

Chapter Fourteen

Ten Years Later, June 1919

Poppy stirred in bed when she heard the chimes of St Paul's bells. Her husband was fast asleep by her side, snoring as usual. She turned and gently nudged his shoulder, trying to wake him up.

'Sid. It's time to go to work.'

He moaned in his sleep, then turned over and started snoring again.

'Sid, it's time to get up,' she said, more firmly this time. When he still didn't move, she gently rocked his shoulder again, then leaned across to kiss him on the cheek. This time, he flung a leg out of bed and stumbled to the stairs that led down to the ground floor, heading out to the netty in the yard.

Poppy lay still for a moment, savouring her time alone. How she loved these silent moments in the dead of night. She'd get up soon enough to cook Sid's breakfast of fried bread and sausage. Then, once he'd left for work, she'd wake their sons, Harry and Sonny. The boys were now three years old, dark-haired, with fat little cheeks, and always smiling, just like their dad. After they'd been fed and were dressed, she would tend to baby Emily, who was just six months old. Emily always slept soundly, and for that Poppy counted her blessings, though recently she hadn't been eating as well as normal, and Poppy was becoming worried about her.

From the cot at the end of her bed, she could hear the baby's gentle snores. For five wonderful minutes, she had nothing to do, nowhere to be and no one relying on her to get them through the day. She closed her eyes and breathed deeply, enjoying the moment of stillness. And then her thoughts turned, as they did every day, to her sister.

After Rose was taken by Scurrfield on that cold Christmas Eve, Poppy had had no choice but to stay with Nellie. She never returned to school and never learned to read and write. She skivvied for the old woman, keeping the barn tidy and the coal fire burning. And she cried for Rose every day. There wasn't a day that went by when she didn't think about her sister and wonder where she was. Even now, ten years on, she still cried in her sleep and blamed herself for what had happened. If only she hadn't spoken badly to Mr Scurrfield that day. If only she had kept quiet, been less forward, not answering him back when he'd scraped his finger down Rose's cheek. If only she hadn't forced him to choose between her and Rose, they might still be together today. As for Nellie, the money she'd received from selling Rose hadn't been enough to follow her dream of giving up work and moving out of the barn. Her anger towards Norman became bitter and her mood darkened a great deal. She was also furious at Scurrfield for not taking both girls and paying her the money she felt was due to her. She often muttered his name darkly under her breath.

The years passed, and Nellie's health began to fail. Poppy awoke one winter morning to find her dead in her chair. A pauper's funeral was held at St Paul's church on a frosty December day, attended only by Poppy and Norman. When the funeral ended and they stepped from the church, Poppy came face to face with Miss Gilbey, who'd always scared her half to death when she'd passed her on the street. Norman seemed to have been expecting her, although the meeting came as a shock to Poppy. Miss Gilbey was a tall, thin woman with cropped dark hair. She wore a long black coat that hung on her skinny frame, and on her feet were pointed black boots. Her face was neither kind nor too stern, and her eyes were a piercing blue. Norman explained that she was going to take Poppy to live with her now that Nellie was dead.

'But I live in the barn,' Poppy said, confused.

'No. I won't take responsibility for you,' Norman said firmly.

'Come with me, Poppy,' Miss Gilbey ordered.

When Poppy didn't move, Miss Gilbey gently took her by the arm and walked her from the church to her home on St Paul's Terrace. And that was where Poppy lived from that day on, learning to cook, bake and clean. Her fears about Miss Gilbey and the harsh way she looked and dressed were unfounded, as the woman proved herself charitable and kind. Many times Poppy wished that she and Rose had been taken in by Miss Gilbey rather than Nellie after their parents had died. How differently their lives might have turned out.

Miss Gilbey's house was furnished sparsely, with no

luxuries inside, and Poppy was expected to work for her keep, but while she was there she made friends with the other girls and was grateful for their companionship. In the years she lived at Miss Gilbey's, she grew from a girl into a young woman. She worked as a cleaner at the Guide Post Inn under the supervision of the stern pub landlady, Mrs Pike. Then she and Sid began courting, as their friendship turned to romance. Sid worked at the pit hewing coal, a job he complained bitterly about, for it was hard, dangerous work.

When they were first married, they lived with Sid's parents, Maisie and Bill. But when their sons were born – twins, which took everyone by surprise, not least Poppy and Sid – they knew they had to find their own home, for there wasn't enough room in Maisie and Bill's house on Scotland Street to bring up their family. They could have moved into the pit house that was tied to Sid's job at the mine. But while they were considering whether the dirty pit lane was a suitable place to bring up two babies, Poppy heard the news that Norman was seeking a new tenant for the barn. If anyone had told her she'd be living back in the place she'd once shared with Nellie and Rose, she'd have laughed in their face. But when she and Sid visited the barn, it felt surprisingly like home and proved a strong reminder of Rose. Sid was also pleased at the amount of space and the fact that the barn was situated in such a pleasing location, being close to the green and the beach. With his dad's help and Norman's permission, the place was repaired and became Poppy and Sid's new home.

Poppy could hear Sid moving about downstairs, setting the fire, then filling the kettle with water from the farm trough. Light filled the barn once the fire was burning, and she opened her eyes and looked up at the roof. It no longer had holes in it after Sid and his dad had fixed the place up. Not only that, but the ladder that Poppy and Rose had once climbed was now a sturdy staircase with a handrail. Poppy and Sid slept upstairs, with the baby in a cot, while Harry and Sonny shared a bed under the stairs.

The first thing Poppy did when she climbed out of bed was to check on Emily, relieved to see that she was fast asleep. Pulling a wool blanket around her shoulders, she headed downstairs. Sid was sitting by the fire, already wearing his work clothes, moving coals with a poker. Poppy lifted the kettle and took a pan from the hearth. Working quickly and quietly so as not to wake the boys, she prepared Sid's breakfast, to feed him for his gruelling day ahead. They kept their voices low as they talked, for their boys in their bed were just a few feet away.

'Are you working with the Trewhitts today?' Sid asked.

'Yes, they've asked me to clean the shop. Ella can't manage it any more, the rheumatism in her hands is getting worse. She really should see the doctor, but she's as stubborn as the day's long.'

'Says the woman who isn't stubborn at all,' Sid smiled.

Poppy looked fondly at her husband. He seemed the same to her now as he'd done when he was a boy. His mop of brown hair, his round face and the mischievous glint in his eyes – none of it had changed. He was a good man, a loving husband and father, gentle and kind, and she counted her blessings each day.

She lifted the kettle and poured water into the teapot. 'I thought I'd go for a walk today,' she said. 'I'll take Emily with me; the fresh air might do her good and help build her appetite.'

'Is she still off her milk? We should take her to see Dr Anderson if she's not right in a day or two,' Sid said, sounding worried.

'And where are we going to get money to pay the doctor?' Poppy replied. 'You know how we're fixed. The Trewhitts don't pay me much, and we've got the boys to clothe and feed.' She looked around the old barn. 'I sometimes wonder if we made the wrong decision turning down the pit house. We wouldn't need to pay rent if we had a tied house. Maybe we should think about moving? It'd free up a few bob and we desperately need the money.'

'We're going nowhere, Pops. I've come to love this place – it's our home. Me and Dad worked on it long and hard, doing it up, and the farm's a wonderful place for the boys. If we lived on the colliery, they wouldn't have any freedom. You know what they're like with all that energy in them. If we lived in a pit house, all five of us, it'd be like a pressure cooker waiting for things to explode. Besides, you know how I'm fixed at the mine. Working underground is not a job I do willingly. It never gives me enough time to see my boys growing up. The only thing that keeps me going is knowing I'm coming home to the peace and quiet of the barn.'

Poppy poured strong tea and a splash of milk into mugs. She knew he was right. She handed him a mug, then used a fork to move the sausages around the frying pan.

'Where will you go for your walk?' Sid asked.

'I thought I'd visit the churchyard and tend Rose's grave,' she replied.

He laid his hand on her arm. 'I wish you wouldn't call it that, love.'

Poppy shook her head. 'Then what should I call it?

She's dead, Sid, she must be. After all these years, what else could have happened? There's been a war, for heaven's sake. A war that lasted four years. Ryhope escaped the damage, but bombs were dropped on Sunderland, and that's where she was taken. She must be dead. I can't allow myself to think that she's still out there and hasn't tried to come back.'

'But we've no proof of that, love. Why torture yourself by visiting the churchyard?'

Poppy pushed her curls behind her ears and shook the handle of the frying pan as the sausages sizzled. 'Because I have to, Sid. I don't know what else to do. You know how I've suffered since she was taken. I cried every day for a year.' She put her hand on her heart. 'Even now, it still hurts. And it makes me feel better to visit the church and sit by the stone I call her grave. It's somewhere I go to mourn my loss. I can't explain it better than that.'

'Don't we mourn her every year on her birthday?' Sid said. 'We always go to Tunstall Hill and remember her there. Besides, I'm surprised Reverend Daye hasn't chased you away. You need to be careful he doesn't think you've gone mad sitting at the back of the churchyard talking to yourself.'

Poppy slid two sausages from the pan on to a plate, then cut a chunk of bread and handed it to Sid. As he tucked into his breakfast in front of the fire, she sat opposite cradling her mug. Her stomach turned from the smell of the food, and she took a sip of tea, hoping to quell the nausea. It was the second morning in a row she'd felt sick at the smell of Sid's breakfast. She dreaded the truth of what it meant, as the last thing they needed was another mouth to feed. She kept quiet about it, though;

there was no point in telling Sid yet. She remembered that her mam used to say nettle tea was good for an upset stomach, and she decided to pick some leaves when she was out on her walk.

The boys were up and dressed, playing tag in the barn and running out to the yard. It was a beautiful June morning, sunny and warm with a cloudless blue sky. When Poppy and Rose had lived in the barn as children, the place had been lifeless and dull, with Nellie in her armchair and the girls upstairs sleeping on the straw. Now it was full of love, life, noise, boisterous boys, her baby and Sid.

She called her sons to order and made them sit at the table to eat their breakfast of oats. Getting them to stay still when they were a bundle of energy was always a challenge. They were at an age when they wanted to run around the farm and see the animals. She was looking forward to the autumn, when they would start at the village school and their days would take on a new routine.

When breakfast was over, the boys waited for her to give them the once-over. She and Sid prided themselves on keeping their children clean and tidy. While it was true that their clothes were worn and scuffed, ill-fitting, bought second-hand from the rag and bone cart, at least they had a pair of boots each, which was more than she and Rose ever had.

'Did you wash behind your ears this morning?' she asked Sonny.

'Why do I have to? No one ever looks behind my ears,' Sonny sulked.

Poppy picked up a damp cloth from the hearth and scrubbed the dirt from her son's ears.

'And what about you, Harry? I hope you had a proper wash,' she said.

Harry stuck his chest out and beamed with pride. 'I did, Mam,' he said.

Poppy kissed both boys on the cheek. 'Now go outside to play while I tend to your sister.'

The twins tumbled out of the barn, running and spinning, chasing each other, and Poppy watched them go. She knew that some folk in Ryhope pitied her and Sid for living at the back of the farm, but Poppy felt like she had everything she wanted. She had a husband who loved her, two wonderful, funny, smart boys and a baby girl she adored. While it was true that they didn't have much in a material sense, they had a solid roof over their heads and they shared a lot of love. However, Poppy's heart ached every day for her missing sister.

The sound of Emily crying pulled her from her reverie. She walked up the stairs and lifted her from her cot, and the baby immediately stopped crying.

'How are you this morning, my angel?' Poppy cooed. 'Shall we try to drink some milk today?'

She cradled the child in her arms as she carefully descended the stairs, then bathed her in the tin bath. Afterwards, she managed to get her to take some milk, but still not as much as she'd hoped.

Once the baby was fed, Poppy cut herself a slice of bread, which she toasted on the fire, then ate her own breakfast. She cleaned the dishes, then wrapped Emily in a blanket and stepped out into the yard with the child in her arms, calling the boys to her. They came running, excited to be heading to the village and the place that Poppy called Rose's grave.

Chapter Fifteen

Tucked away behind St Paul's church was a small piece of earth. Poppy took her blanket from around her shoulders and laid it on the dry grass next to a large honey-coloured stone. Gently and carefully she laid Emily down, then she called the boys to her.

'Sit down, Harry. Sonny, stop running around. Remember, we have to be quiet in the churchyard.'

They did as they were told and sat down at Poppy's side. Around the stone, tiny white daisies and bright yellow buttercups bloomed amongst the nettles. Poppy picked nettle leaves and put them in her pocket, hoping that the tea might ease her morning sickness. She pulled blades of grass from between the flowers, then ran her fingers gently over the stone.

'Mam, don't be sad,' Harry said, snuggling into her side.

She laid her arm around his shoulders. 'Oh, I'm not sad,' she said gently. 'I'm just remembering how things used to be and wishing your aunt Rose was with us.' She ruffled his hair and kissed him on the cheek. 'She would have loved you and Sonny and Emily. Aunt Rose was a beautiful girl, very pretty, everyone said so.'

Tears pricked the back of her eyes and she swallowed hard. She cuddled Sonny to her too, and for a few moments they all sat in silence. But then a noise behind her made her start. She turned to find out what it was, expecting a stray dog, and was horrified to see Reverend Daye. Immediately she jumped to her feet.

'I'm ever so sorry, I know I shouldn't be here,' she began, but the vicar smiled kindly. She noticed that he was holding something in his hand, but she was too distracted by pulling the boys to her and trying to pick up Emily that she didn't give it a second thought.

'My child, I haven't come to chase you. Far from it. I know what comfort it brings you to sit here and think about Rose.'

'You're not chasing me away?' Poppy said.

The vicar shook his head. 'No, I'm not. In fact . . .'

She watched, bemused, as he folded his tall figure to the ground and sat cross-legged. Harry and Sonny thought this was a wonderful game and plonked themselves down next to him. Reverend Daye patted a patch of grass by his side.

'Please, sit with me a while.'

Poppy looked left and right to see if anyone was passing by. The vicar sitting on the ground in the churchyard was a most unusual thing, and she didn't know quite what to think. But then Reverend Daye was a rather unusual man. He brought together the two different sides of Ryhope – the mining and farming communities – who rarely mixed anywhere else. Even when socialising, they kept apart. The miners drank in the pubs on the colliery bank, while the farmers favoured those around the green.

The vicar was respected by all, as he brought folk together to his church.

Poppy sat on the grass, holding Emily against her chest. She trusted that whatever Reverend Daye had to say, it was important for her to listen, for why else would he have made it his business to come and talk to her?

'I was just . . . I mean, I was . . . you know, thinking about Rose,' she explained. 'I didn't mean to trespass.'

Reverend Daye smiled kindly. 'It is never trespassing to use the church and its grounds to think about those we have loved.'

It was then that Poppy realised what he held in his hand. It was a slim white envelope with looping writing on the front. Probably some church business, she thought. But she was wrong, for he handed it to her.

'This was delivered by the post boy yesterday to the church,' he said as Poppy looked at the envelope, puzzled. 'I was going to walk to the farm today to deliver it to you, but then I saw you from the vicarage window. It's for you.'

She looked into his kind eyes. He was waiting for her to read it, she knew.

'For me?'

He pointed at the first line of the address. 'My child, yes. It has your name written on it, see? Miss Poppy Thomas.'

'But I'm Mrs Poppy Lawson now,' she said, turning the letter in her hand. There was no writing on the back of the envelope. 'Who would write a letter to me and send it to the church?' she asked, confused.

'There is only one way to find out,' the vicar replied. 'You must open it and read it.'

She felt herself blush with shame at being unable to read and write. She quickly stuffed the envelope in her pocket. 'I'll read it at home,' she said, getting to her feet.

Reverend Daye watched her keenly. 'If you'd like me to, I could read it for you,' he offered kindly, but Poppy shook her head. He stood too. 'There's no need to rush away,' he said. 'Please, stay as long as you wish. I could send my housekeeper out; she can bring some bread for your children.'

Poppy straightened her spine. 'Thank you, Vicar, but my bairns are well fed. I always see to that.'

He looked at her for a moment, and when he seemed satisfied that she didn't need his help, he wished her good day and walked away.

'Come on, boys, we're going home,' Poppy said as she marched down the church path. The twins followed, holding hands, Harry singing and Sonny doing his best to join in.

Poppy hurried from the churchyard, the letter burning a hole in her pocket. Sid was the only person she would trust to read it, but he wasn't due home from work for hours. He'd be weary when he got back, with his shoulders slumped and his spirit broken from working underground. He'd need a warm bath to scrub the coal dust from his skin. Then he'd need his dinner to replace the energy he'd spent during the day. She'd have to choose her moment carefully: when Sid was clean after she'd scrubbed his back in the tin bath by the fire, when his belly was full of potato pie and the bread she'd bake later that day, when his frown had disappeared into a smile as he hugged his boys and cradled Emily. Only then would she ask him to read the letter.

When they reached the barn, Norman was pottering in the yard. He scowled at the boys as they ran through the cattle market. 'Keep the bloody noise down!' he yelled.

Poppy shushed her sons and headed to the barn. Harry and Sonny stayed in the yard, running and chasing. She took the letter from her pocket and placed it on the mantelpiece, behind the china ornament in the shape of a sheepdog that had been a wedding present from Maisie and Bill. Then she pulled a chair to the barn door so that she could sit in the sunshine and watch her boys play. In her arms, Emily began to cry. She offered her milk, but Emily's eyes closed and her head fell to one side. Poppy ran her little finger across her baby's cheek.

'Come on, little one, please drink,' she whispered, but Emily steadfastly refused.

She looked at her baby's tiny round face and noticed how pale her skin was. If the child refused to eat, what could she do? She decided to ask Sid's mam. Maisie was a no-nonsense woman, and Poppy knew she could trust her advice. She had brought up Sid, his six sisters and three brothers, and if anyone could help, she could.

'Shall we go to see Granny Lawson, Emily?' Poppy cooed. 'We'll go tomorrow if you're still not going to eat. Come on, my darling girl, take some milk.'

But Emily's rosebud lips refused to suckle. Poppy raised her gaze to the yard, where Harry and Sonny were sitting on the ground, exhausted after chasing each other. Harry was happily chatting to the chickens that clucked around hoping for food. Poppy marvelled at her boys and her heart swelled with pride. Though they had been born just minutes apart, Harry had emerged as the slightly taller, less fearful boy. He was the leader where Sonny followed.

She closed her eyes and turned her face to the sun. She could feel Emily in her arms and hear the sounds of her sons calling to the chickens. She decided to enjoy the sunshine until the bells of St Paul's chimed eleven, when she would head to the Trewhitts' to work. Happiness rushed through her. How grateful she was for her life. But then, as it did each time she felt happy, her mind filled with guilt as her thoughts turned to Rose. If only her sister could see her now, she thought, and a tear made its way down her cheek.

Chapter Sixteen

When it was time for Poppy to head to work, she called the boys indoors. She wiped their hands with a cloth and gave them each a slice of dry bread. Before setting off on the short walk to the Trewhitts', she picked up the envelope from behind the china dog. She only had Reverend Daye's word that it was addressed to her, for she had no clue what it said. She traced the unfamiliar letters with her finger, and in that moment she vowed never to let her boys miss one day of school when they started in the autumn. She might not be able to read and write, but she was damned if her children would grow up the same way.

She placed the letter back, wondering again who it was from. Dread filled her stomach as she considered the possibilities. Was it a notice about the tenancy Sid had signed on the barn? No, surely not, for that would have been addressed to Sid and herself as Mr and Mrs Lawson. And why had it been sent to the church? Questions whirled in her mind that made her feel uneasy.

She realised that Harry was tugging at her arm. 'Mam,' he urged.

She pulled herself together and hoisted Emily into her arms, then Harry and Sonny followed her across the green to the shop.

She'd long ago been forgiven by Ambrose and Ella for stealing from them when she was younger. The Trewhitts were getting old now, and slow. Ella's rheumatism meant she couldn't hold items or deal with coins. But despite the pain she was in, she refused to miss a day's work. She sat on a stool at the end of the counter, chatting to customers, while Ambrose did much of the work. But Ambrose was slowing down too, his body old and his back stooped. When they'd offered Poppy a job cleaning the shop and the rooms where they lived above, she'd jumped at the chance. Ella remained proud of the place, and she expected Poppy to meet her exacting standards.

When Poppy reached the shop, she pushed the door open and the bell tinkled. Not that a bell was needed to announce her arrival when she was accompanied by two boisterous boys in high spirits. Behind the counter, Ambrose stood next to Ella, who was seated on her stool, both of them wearing their brown overalls. For as long as Poppy had known them, this was how she'd always seen them, working side by side.

'Harry! Sonny!' Ambrose called, happy to see the twins. He pulled the lid off a jar of boiled sweets, took out two hard sugared balls and handed one each to the boys.

'Morning, Ambrose, Ella,' Poppy said. 'How are you both today?'

'Ella's not so good,' Ambrose whispered. 'She's in a lot of pain.'

'It'd make me feel better to see the baby,' Ella said. 'And you can stop whispering about me, Ambrose. I'm not deaf, you know. I heard every word.'

Ambrose gave a wry smile. As Poppy moved Emily's blanket away from her face, the baby's eyes opened and latched on to Ella's face.

'My word, she's a beauty,' Ella said. 'She gets bonnier every day.'

'Is it all right if we head upstairs so I can start cleaning?' Poppy asked.

Ella nodded. 'Just watch those boys, and make sure they don't run around. I don't want anything broken.'

'I'll keep an eye on them, Ella, don't worry,' Poppy replied.

She was about to head behind the counter to go through to the back of the shop, where the stairs led up to where the Trewhitts lived, but the jingling bell above the door made her turn. She saw teenager Henry Donnelly, a lad always up to no good. Gossip in the village was that he spent more time being questioned by Ryhope police than at his job at the pit. Poppy brought Harry and Sonny to her and stood in front of them, shielding them from view. She didn't realise they were both peeping out from behind her skirt to see what was going on.

'Oh, it's you, is it? What do you want this time?' Ambrose said angrily.

Poppy had never heard him be so unfriendly to his customers, and she wondered what was going on. She stood her ground and waited to see how things would unfold.

Henry swaggered to the counter and Ambrose stepped back. 'I want the same as I had last time,' he sneered. He pointed to the jar of boiled sweets. 'I'll have some of them for a start.'

'You can have as many as you want, as long as you pay for them,' Ambrose said calmly.

Henry looked around the shop, as if deciding what he'd like next. He pointed to a large, flat glass dish that held golden jam tarts. 'I'll have them.'

'You're having nothing until I see your money,' Ambrose said.

'I'll pay you next year,' Henry sneered. He walked to the jam tarts and lifted the glass lid.

Poppy watched, waiting for Ambrose to remonstrate with the lad, but he seemed powerless to act. She couldn't understand what was going on.

'Ambrose, stop him!' she cried.

But Ambrose couldn't look her in the eye.

Henry took two jam tarts, one in each hand, then walked to the counter. 'I'll be back for more when I'm hungry,' he said, then he calmly walked out of the door.

Ambrose sighed heavily. 'That boy will be the death of me,' he moaned, shaking his head.

'Then why did you let him take the jam tarts without paying? He stole them from under your nose,' Poppy said.

Ella shifted in her seat. 'We've been having a few problems with Henry Donnelly. He comes in and steals things, and when we challenge him about it, he just laughs in our faces. There's not much we can do. We're too old and decrepit to chase him. Mind you, once upon a time I'd have set the broom on him.'

'I remember you used to chase *me* with the broom,' Poppy said.

'We turned a blind eye to a lot of the stuff you stole

from us in here,' Ella said. 'Because you and Rose were orphans, living from hand to mouth. Mind you, I never did understand why you took a tin of mustard . . .'

Poppy touched her freckled nose.

'. . . but Henry Donnelly should know better,' Ella continued. 'He doesn't need to steal food; he's got a job at the pit, his dad works there too and his mam works at the store. There's good money coming into his house.'

'There's nothing we can do, love,' Ambrose said, dejected.

Poppy looked at the Trewhitts' sad faces. 'Well, that's as may be. But there's something I can do. Harry, Sonny, stay here. I'll be straight back.'

With Emily in her arms, she stormed from the shop, setting the bell jingling off the hook as the door slammed behind her. Henry Donnelly was sitting on a bench on the green, stuffing his face with pastry and jam.

'Oi! You! I want a word with you,' she yelled.

He turned in surprise and stared at her as she strode to the bench. He rose, ready to run, but she put her hand on his shoulder and forced him back down.

'What do you think you're playing at? Ambrose and Ella are decent, hard-working people, they don't need to be upset by you. You should have more respect for your elders.'

Henry opened his mouth to say something, and pastry crumbs tumbled on to his chest.

'You know my husband, Sid, don't you?' Poppy said.

Henry nodded.

'And you know he's a strong fella, handy with his fists when he needs to be.' Sid had never hit anyone in his life, but there was no need for Henry to know that, so Poppy carried on. 'If I catch you stealing from the shop again, or if I hear from Ambrose and Ella that you've been taking things you haven't paid for, I won't be standing here having a word with you. Do you know what I'll be doing instead?'

Henry's eyes widened and he shook his head, causing crumbs to spray left and right.

'I'll be having a word with my husband, and I'll tell him all about you. He knows where you live.'

Henry gulped and swallowed the remaining tart. 'Sorry, missus,' he said.

'It's not me you should be apologising to,' Poppy said, nodding towards the shop. 'It's Mr and Mrs Trewhitt who need to hear those words.'

'Aw, no,' he moaned.

'Aw, yes, Henry. Otherwise I might have to have a word with my Sid tonight when he comes home from the pit.'

With her free hand, Poppy yanked Henry up from the bench by his jacket. She marched him to the shop, where she made him take his cap off, then she stood behind him while he apologised to the Trewhitts and promised he'd never steal again. After he'd left with his tail between his legs, Ambrose gave a sigh of relief.

'What on earth did you say to him to get him to apologise?' he said.

'It doesn't matter what I said, but if he ever comes back, let me know and I'll sort him out for you again.'

And with that, Poppy shooed the boys to the back of the shop so she could begin her work.

* * *

When the cleaning was done and the shop and living quarters were spick and span, Poppy said goodbye to the Trewhitts. However, Ambrose wasn't about to let her leave empty-handed, and he gave her the remaining jam tarts, patting her hand as he passed them over.

'Thanks, lass,' he said.

Poppy headed home with the boys, and as she neared the barn, her thoughts turned again to the letter. Sid would be home in a few hours' time, and then she'd find out what it said. Her stomach turned as she walked; she was feeling queasy again, and as soon as she reached the barn, she boiled hot water to make nettle tea.

The afternoon passed slowly, each hour marked by the chiming church bells. She kept glancing at the envelope. Harry and Sonny had their afternoon nap while Poppy tried to coax Emily to drink milk but failed once again. She boiled water for Sid's bath and chopped potatoes to make a pie. If there was one thing that life with Nellie and then Miss Gilbey had taught her, it was how to make hearty meals from paltry ingredients. She made sure she fed her family the best food she could afford. She wanted to protect her children in every way she could, and would never let them suffer hunger as she and Rose had.

Busy with her cooking, she heard the church bells chime seven and knew Sid would arrive home very soon. Her eyes flicked to the envelope again, and another wave of nausea hit her. It was still too soon to tell him, just in case she miscarried. It wouldn't be the first time she'd been through the agony of that, and she decided to keep her pregnancy to herself for now.

Chapter Seventeen

When Sid ambled into the barn, he was covered in coal dust and his face and hands were oily and black. His eyelids hung heavy and his body moved slowly. Poppy knew how tired he was, and her heart went out to him. She knew how much he detested working underground.

'Dad!' Harry cried.

'Shush,' Poppy warned him. 'Let your dad settle in and have his bath, and then you can talk to him.' She turned to Sid. 'The bath's ready for you, love,' she said.

And so their evening routine began. Sid bathed in the tin bath by the fire. Poppy scrubbed his back and massaged his weary shoulders as his head dipped forward. All the while she kept thinking of the letter on the mantelpiece. But she'd waited all day for Sid to come home, and she could wait another hour until he relaxed. The bathwater turned black as she washed the coal from his skin. When she was done, she handed him a cloth and he dried himself by the fire. Then he stepped into a fresh pair of trousers and a shirt that Poppy handed over. Only when he was clean and relaxed did he join his family at the table.

He kissed Harry and Sonny on the top of their heads

before he sat down, then chatted to them about their day, asking what they'd been up to, who they'd seen and where they'd been. The highlight had been the boiled sweets and jam tarts that Ambrose had given them.

Poppy smiled. 'Ambrose spoils those two, he adores them.'

'How's the baby?' Sid said, looking around. 'Where is she?'

'She's upstairs, asleep. She's still not taking much milk. I thought I'd visit your mam in the morning and ask for her advice.'

He gazed at her with concern. 'She's still not taking milk? Oh Pops, I'm worried sick about that bairn. But you're right about seeking Mam's help. She'll know what to do and will help us.' Poppy felt reassured by his words.

When their meal ended, she boiled the kettle to make tea. Meanwhile, Sid lifted his boys, one under each arm, as they kicked and screamed with laughter. He walked across the barn and dropped them giggling and laughing on to their bed. Then he tucked a blanket over them, stroked their hair, kissed them on the cheek and wished them a good night's sleep. Afterwards, he climbed the stairs to see Emily and sat with her a while, watching her in her cot.

When he returned downstairs, Poppy was pouring the tea. 'Here,' she said, handing him his mug.

They sat opposite each other by the hearth. Between them the coal fire roared.

'Any sugar?' Sid asked.

Poppy shook her head. 'I couldn't afford it, Sid. But there's a jam tart from Ambrose if you'd like one.' She handed it to him, then tried again to bring up the subject of moving to a pit house. 'You know, the rent we're paying on this place we could spend on food instead. Maybe it's time we thought seriously about moving on to the colliery?'

'I won't hear of it, Pops,' Sid said firmly. 'This old barn gives us space that we'd never have up there. The colliery's dirty, the air's filled with coal dust and smoke from the trains. Down here in the village, it's quiet and calm. Going without sugar in my tea is a small price to pay for such a tranquil life. At least we get our coal free – that's one perk of being a pitman, one advantage to working in that underground hell.'

He patted his stomach. 'That pie was filling, Pops. I enjoyed it.' He sipped his tea. 'How were Ambrose and Ella today?'

'Oh, same as ever,' Poppy replied. 'But they're getting old, Sid. Ella's in pain with her hands and Ambrose is slowing down. I had to have a word with Henry Donnelly while I was there. He came in and taunted Ambrose something terrible before stealing jam tarts. I made him apologise.'

Sid laughed aloud. 'Good on you, Pops. My word, this pastry is good. Didn't you tell me that you once stole some tarts from the Trewhitts?'

'Yes, but I was just a bairn, not Henry Donnelly's age. He should have more sense. Besides, his family can afford to buy food. When I used to steal, it was because Rose and I were starving.'

They drank their tea in companionable silence. The crackling of the fire and the ticking of the clock were the only sounds in the room. Tucked away in their bed under the stairs, their sons were soon fast asleep. Poppy noticed

Sid's eyes beginning to close and his head nodding forward. She gently shook him by the arm.

'Sid?'

'Eh? What?' he said, startled.

'You were falling asleep,' she said.

He gave a cheeky smile. 'Nah, I wasn't. I was just checking the inside of my eyelids.'

Poppy reached up and took the envelope from the mantelpiece. 'Sid, this came today. It was sent to the church. Reverend Daye gave it to me when he saw me tending Rose's grave. He said it's addressed to Miss Poppy Thomas on the front.'

Sid took the envelope and inspected it, turning it over in his hands.

'What is it?' he said, puzzled.

'Why, it's a letter.'

'I know it's a letter, but who's it from?'

'We'll have to open it and see,' she replied.

Sid got up to fetch a butter knife from the drawer and Poppy watched him slice the envelope open. Her heart began to race, and she took a deep breath and sat up straight in her seat. This was it; she was just moments away from finding out what the letter said. He brought the envelope back to his seat. Slowly and carefully, by the light from the fire, he reached inside and brought out a sheet of white paper.

'What does it say? Who's it from?' Poppy asked.

'Let me read it first, Pops,' he replied.

But she was desperate to know. She stood and walked to his side, looking at the letter, but all she could see were squiggles and lines.

'Read it to me, Sid, please,' she begged.

She sat on the floor at his feet and rested her chin on his knee. She heard him gasp.

'Is it bad news?' she said. 'Please, Sid, read it out. I can't bear it. I've waited all day for this.'

Sid laid his free hand on her shoulder.

'Who's it from?' she urged.

He took a deep breath and closed his eyes. When he opened them again, it was a moment before he could speak.

'Prepare yourself, Poppy,' he said gently.

Poppy looked into his big brown eyes. 'Prepare myself for what? What is it, Sid? I know that worried look on your face. What's wrong?'

'The letter . . .' he began. He stopped again, and Poppy knew he was struggling with the enormity of what it contained.

'Sid, for goodness' sake, tell me!' she cried, unable to take the suspense any longer.

Sid gulped. 'It's from Rose.'

Poppy's mouth opened, but no words came out. She was frozen to the spot. She looked at Sid's face and knew he was as shocked as her. 'Rose?' Her voice came out in a whisper at first, and then louder as his words sank in. 'Rose? The letter's from my sister?' Her hands flew to her heart. 'She's alive!' she gasped. 'Oh Sid, she's alive! All these years, all this time, and she wasn't killed in the war. Oh, what does she say? Will we ever see her again?'

Sid swallowed hard. 'It's not good news, love,' he said, his voice shaking. 'You might want to brace yourself for what you're about to hear.'

Poppy's face clouded over, and she balled her fists to steel herself. 'All right, I'm ready,' she said.

He lifted his arm from her shoulders and held the letter with both hands, his voice becoming serious as he read. Each word shot pain through Poppy's heart, for the letter was a cry for help.

My dear sister,

I think of you every day. I must be brief, in case I am discovered writing. I still live with the Scurrfields in Sunderland, on Gray Road by Mowbray Park. Malcolm Scurrfield has passed away and I live under the care of his son, James. He is a soldier returned from war and suffers greatly from all he has seen. He is consumed by anger, all of which is directed at me. I beg you, my sister, please do all you can to get me away from here. I have tried to write many times, but Malcolm Scurrfield destroyed my letters. He wanted me to lose all contact with you. Once I tried to escape, but he caught me and marched me from the tram.

I must go now, I hear footsteps. I do not know when, or even if, I will ever send this to you, but I know that I must. I miss you so much, my heart hurts every minute of each day.

Your loving sister,

Rose x

Poppy and Sid sat in silence.

'I wonder why she didn't try to escape when she posted this letter,' Poppy said after a while.

'Maybe she was accompanied by someone – a house-keeper, perhaps?' Sid suggested.

'And I wonder whether Mrs Scurrfield is still alive.'

'She makes no mention of her.'

'Does she mention bairns? Is she married?'

'No, Poppy, I read it all, every word. It sounds like she has a terrible life with James Scurrfield.'

Poppy's heart plummeted to the floor and tears began falling. 'She must be desperate, to write to us for help. We've got to do what we can.'

'Of course,' Sid replied quickly.

'We'll go to Gray Road, we have to. We've got to find her and bring her here,' she said, excited. 'She can live with us in the barn. We must help her.'

He folded the letter and placed it carefully back in the envelope. 'And we will, I promise,' he said.

'Tomorrow,' Poppy said, determined. 'Tomorrow I'm going to Gray Road. Now that I know she's alive, I've got to find her. I've got to see her again.'

'Poppy,' Sid said gently, stroking her curls. 'Don't go alone. Wait until my shifts at the pit change and I can come with you. I can't come tomorrow; it'd mean taking a day off work, and we can't afford to lose money. We're suffering enough as it is.'

Poppy struggled to her feet and began pacing in front of the fire.

'No, Sid, I need to see her as soon as I can. She needs my help. You read her words. Who knows what horrors she's living through with James Scurrfield.'

'But if you go on your own, you'll need to take the tram, and how will you know which one is the right one? How will you know how much to pay?'

'Someone will help if I ask them. I've got a tongue in my head, and you know I'm not backwards at coming forwards to ask. I'll give the coins to the conductor, he'll add them up for me. Don't try to dissuade me.'

'I'm not, love, honest,' Sid implored. 'All I'm asking is that you wait a few days until I can join you. It won't be easy on your own. James Scurrfield might be dangerous. And you've got Emily to think about. She isn't eating, and you said you'd take her to my mam tomorrow. Please, just wait a few days and let me come with you and help.'

But Poppy had made up her mind. 'No, Sid. I'll leave the bairns with your mam first thing in the morning, and then, no matter how hard it's going to be, I've got to go and find Rose.'

Chapter Eighteen

Poppy didn't sleep well that night, her mind churning constantly. Rose was alive. Alive! And each time she thought of that, relief swept through her. She had no clue where Gray Road was, but she was determined to find it. She'd ask and keep asking until she found her sister. She'd never been on a tram before and she wasn't sure what to do, but she'd watch what the other passengers did, listen to how they greeted the driver and conductor. She'd offer the same coins from her pocket as others did. She'd managed to get by in life so far by bluffing her way, and was resolute that nothing would stop her.

She tossed and turned through the night while Sid snored beside her, dead to the world. She wondered what Rose looked like now, and hoped she was as pretty as she'd been as a girl. But then she had to stop herself from getting carried away, for there was no guarantee that she would find her sister, even if she found Gray Road. Her thoughts turned to the Scurrfield men and her fists clenched with anger. She closed her eyes, blinking away tears that wouldn't stop falling. Eventually she heard the sound of St Paul's church bells. It was time to wake Sid up for work.

* * *

As Sid lit the fire and Poppy prepared breakfast, they barely spoke to one another. Poppy was feeling anxious about the day ahead, but she knew that if she mentioned it to Sid, he'd advise her again to wait. She knew he was being protective and wanted to help her, but she wasn't prepared to wait. They sat in silence in their chairs either side of the fire, eating their breakfast of bread and eggs. At last Sid picked up his jacket and cap. He hesitated by the fire and looked at Poppy.

'I know you, Pops. I know exactly what you'll be doing today, but as the man of this house, I'm going to have my say.'

'Sid, please—' she began, but he cut her short.

'I think what you're doing is wrong. You should wait until I can come with you. I want to help you, Pops, can't you see that? I'm not trying to stop you from finding your sister. I'd never do that. All I'm asking is that you wait a few days. And so I'll ask you again, for the final time: will you consider my request?'

Poppy looked into his big brown eyes. She couldn't give him the answer he wanted to hear, and so she said nothing at all. Sid put his cap on, thrust his arms into his jacket and leaned down to kiss her on the lips.

'You always were stubborn, even when we were bairns, and I don't think you'll change now. Just promise me you'll be careful, all right?'

'Promise,' she whispered.

He walked to the barn door and pulled it open, but before he stepped into the yard, he stopped dead in his tracks.

Poppy stood and walked towards him. 'What is it?'

She and Sid peered into the yard. There was just enough light for them to make out Norman walking towards them. They were puzzled to see him, as the only time they normally crossed paths was when Sid handed over their rent. The old man walked slowly these days, but it was the first time they'd seen him need the help of a stick. By the time he reached them, he was wheezing from exertion. He put both hands on top of the stick, leaned heavily on it and looked Sid square in the eye.

'I've got news for you, lad.'

'Oh aye? What's up, Norman?'

Norman looked around the yard, from the pig barns to the cow sheds, from the milking parlour to the cattle market. 'I've sold up.'

Poppy grabbed Sid's hand.

'Eh?' Sid said, trying to understand.

'I said I've sold up.'

'What? You've sold the farm?' Poppy said, reeling from shock. She and Sid shared a bewildered look.

'Aye, lass. I'm moving to my cousin John's place; he farms sheep in Weardale. Him and his family are taking me in. I can't run this place any more, even with the lads I've got working for me. I always knew there'd come a time when I'd have to give in, and this is it.'

'What does the sale mean for us, for the barn?' Poppy asked, worried.

Norman glanced through the open door.

'You'll have to deal with the new owner, lass. He might want to use it for livestock,' he said bluntly.

'But he can't throw us out of our home,' Poppy said, alarmed.

125

'He can do anything he wants, love, he owns it,' Sid warned. He looked at Norman. 'Who is the new owner? Anyone we know?'

'A chap called Amos Bird,' Norman said. 'I doubt you'll have heard of him, as he's not a Ryhope lad. Well, I thought I should tell you and give you fair warning that things will likely change in the coming weeks.'

And with that, he turned and walked slowly away, leaving Poppy and Sid dumbstruck.

'We'll talk tonight when I get home,' Sid said, squeezing Poppy's hand. 'Be careful, Pops, I'll be thinking of you all day, wondering if you're all right and hoping you find Rose. My heart won't rest until I know you're safely home. I'm scared for you, my love.'

'I'm scared too, Sid, but Rose needs me and I can't refuse her plea for help.'

He kissed her on the cheek, dug deep into his pocket and handed her enough coins to cover her tram fare, then reluctantly turned to walk away.

Poppy stood at the barn door, watching him leave. She pressed her back against the wall and forced herself not to cry. If the farm's new owner wanted them out, they'd have to find somewhere else to live. And at short notice too. It was too difficult to think about. The pit houses on the colliery bank went through her mind again. The air on the colliery was constantly filled with soot, smoke and noise from the trains taking coal from the mine. The houses were laid out in long, cramped rows, with families living cheek by jowl. The barn had many faults, but despite them all, she and Sid thought of it as home. It was where she and Rose had grown up. It was where she and Sid had brought their bairns up and where Emily had been born. It had come to be her sanctuary, the one place she felt safe. However, she knew she shouldn't let her heart rule her head on this. If they were living in a pit house, they'd have more money – not much, but a little. It'd be enough to clear their debts and feed the bairns. And yet although she'd already suggested to Sid that they should move to the colliery, being forced out of the barn was a different matter. She was starting to realise what a wrench it would be to leave.

She swallowed hard. There wasn't anything she could do now. She'd have to wait for Sid to come home and talk it through with him then. Until then, she had pressing business to attend to, for today was the day she was determined to find Rose.

Once the boys were up and dressed, Poppy gave them breakfast. Then she bathed the baby and tried to feed her again, but Emily suckled for just a short while. Poppy wrapped her in a blanket, called the boys to her and set off on the short walk to Scotland Street, where Sid's parents lived.

The boys walked behind her, holding hands, excited to be heading to Granny Lawson's house. Poppy had warned them to be on their best behaviour. Sid's mam was a formidable woman, and Poppy had to be on her mettle to deal with her. It wasn't that she didn't like Maisie – far from it, she relied on her for her wisdom and advice. But if Poppy ever needed a hug, or a kind word, Maisie was the wrong person for it. She was a no-nonsense woman, not given to showing emotion.

When they reached the terraced house at the end of Scotland Street, Poppy knocked hard at the door.

'Stand up straight,' she ordered the boys. Harry and Sonny stood to attention. 'And remember to smile at Granny Lawson when she answers the door.'

'Yes, Mam,' the boys chirped.

The door was flung open and Maisie stood in the doorway with her hands on her hips. She wore a pinny over a blue dress and her hands were covered in flour. Smudges of flour were on her face too. Her wavy brown hair was tied away from her face and she glared at Poppy with piercing blue eyes. But it wasn't Poppy she greeted first; it was her grandsons.

'Get inside, you two. Don't touch anything. Sit quietly and don't run about.'

'Morning, Maisie,' Poppy said.

'Morning, pet,' Maisie replied. 'Come on in. I'm in the middle of baking bread, so I can't stop to chat. But I'll put the kettle on once the bread's in the oven.'

'I can't stop to chat either,' Poppy tried to explain, as Maisie ushered her indoors. 'I've got to go out on business, and I was hoping you might be able to look after Emily and the boys while I'm gone.'

Maisie eyed her coolly. 'Business? Lasses shouldn't be going out on business. Lasses should be at home, looking after the house for their fellas.'

'It's important, Maisie. I wouldn't have asked otherwise,' Poppy pleaded. 'We received a letter yesterday . . .' She could hardly bring herself to say the words; it still didn't seem real. 'A letter from Rose.'

Maisie's mouth opened in shock, then she staggered backwards and placed her hand on the wall to keep herself from falling. 'No!' she cried in shock.

'That's why I need your help. I've got to go and find

her. Please, can you take the bairns? I'll be gone a few hours.'

'Of course, you know I'll look after my grandbairns.'

'Thank you,' Poppy said, relieved. 'But there's something else I wanted to ask you. It's Emily. She's not taking milk as she should, and I'm getting worried about her. Sid said we should take her to Dr Anderson, but you know how we're fixed; we can't afford the doctor. I was hoping you might be able to help, see if you can get her to take some warm milk.'

Maisie took the sleeping child. Then, with her free hand, she touched Poppy's shoulder in a rare moment of warmth.

'Just go. Scram. Find your sister,' she said kindly.

Poppy quickly kissed her on the cheek, stunning Maisie into silence with a show of affection she wasn't used to receiving. Then, with her heart going nineteen to the dozen, her nerves on edge about seeing Rose again, she left her mother-in-law's house and hurried towards the tram stop.

Chapter Nineteen

Poppy's stomach churned with anxiety over what lay ahead. And there was something else she was feeling too: her nausea had returned. She wondered again when the right time would be to tell Sid. Another baby on its way couldn't be happening at a worse time, for if the new farm owner wanted them out of the barn, what would happen to them all then?

She walked on, past the Railway Inn, towards the village green. She was aware that she didn't have the first clue about tram timetables and routes. She'd seen the double-decker trams trundling through Ryhope many times, but she'd never been outside the village, and the thought scared her. However, she had to do it. She had to find Rose. But how on earth would she find Gray Road? All she could do was ask the first person she saw when she got off the tram, and if they didn't know, she'd ask the next person, and the next, and keep on asking until she found it. The only thing that mattered was Rose.

As she walked, she worried about Emily again, and guilt over leaving her with Sid's mam stabbed her hard. She faltered a couple of times, ready to run back to her child, who was clearly unwell. She felt conflicted between caring for Emily and searching for Rose. And then ahead of her she saw the tram, travelling slowly from the village school, getting ready to stop.

'No!' she gasped. She wasn't ready for it yet; she'd expected a long wait at the stop, enough time to ask someone for help with the coins Sid had given her for her fare. She knew what a sacrifice he'd made giving her the money, for it was money they needed to pay Norman their rent.

She picked up the edge of her skirt and ran like the clappers, puffing and panting all the way. There she joined a queue. The woman in front of her was a short, bird-like woman wearing a green knitted hat despite the warmth of the midsummer day. Poppy recognised her as Lil Mahone, Ryhope's worst gossip, and so she kept her distance. If Lil turned and saw her, she'd fire questions, wanting to know where she was going and why. Well, it was none of Lil's business, and Poppy made sure she kept out of her sight.

She heard a noise behind her and turned to see a tall man in a dark coat and flat cap. 'Does this tram travel to Sunderland?' she asked.

The man gave her a piercing look. 'Of course it does. Where else do you expect it to go?' he said rudely. 'Can't you read the sign at the front?'

She turned away, her face turning red and hot. She'd never had her ignorance pointed out in such a blunt way before. She peered at the other people boarding the tram, watching carefully how they stepped up on to the platform, using the handrail for support. When it was her turn, she did the same. Some passengers walked upstairs to the top deck, while others settled into downstairs seats.

She glanced at the tram's lower deck, where all of the seats were taken apart from one – next to Lil Mahone. She decided to go upstairs instead to find an empty seat. As she stepped on to the spiral staircase, a bell rang behind her.

'Hold on tight, miss,' the conductor called.

She gripped the handrail as the tram jerked forward and made her way carefully up the stairs. She was relieved to see empty seats and headed straight to the front. As they trundled past the Trewhitts' shop, she could see in through the windows. She raised her hand to wave to Ella and Ambrose, but then stopped, feeling silly. Of course they couldn't see her, but she could see them, together behind their counter. She'd never experienced views like this before. The Albion Inn was ahead, and she could peer in through the top-floor windows to where Hetty and Jack Burdon lived. She looked down on gardens where pink hydrangeas frilled over walls, then settled back in her seat, taking in everything around her.

At the end of the village, the tram passed the forge before travelling under the railway bridge, where steam trains took coal from the mine to the docks. The bridge marked Ryhope's boundary. She gripped her seat, ready to see what lay beyond. To her right was the North Sea, where the tall chimneys of Hendon paper mill rose into the milky blue sky. To her left were fields, and if she turned her head, she could see the spire of St Paul's church as the tram left Ryhope behind. How thrilling it felt to be setting off on such an adventure.

The next stop was the Toll Bar Inn, where she leaned over to her left to watch passengers leave and new ones embark. She saw Lil Mahone step down on to the pavement, where she straightened her hat then bustled away with her handbag over her arm. Poppy watched her disappear, and then with another ding of the bell, the tram jerked forward again. She felt excited, nervous and scared about seeing Rose, and ran through a plan of what she would do. She would hug her sister and kiss her, then take her by the hand and leave the Scurrfields' house for good. Explanations would come later; they would have their whole life together to talk. Maybe she could even find Rose a job in the village, something to keep her close, for she was determined they'd never be separated again.

'Fares, please,' she heard from behind, and turned to see the conductor walking up the stairs. She had no clue how much the fare was, but she dug in her pocket and brought out her coins. The conductor was a young lad, his face smooth and unblemished; he looked as if he wasn't even old enough to shave. His youthfulness and look of innocence gave Poppy the confidence to speak up and ask for his help.

'Where to, miss?' he asked.

'Does the tram stop on Gray Road?'

'No, miss. The nearest stop to Gray Road is at the terminus in town. But you can walk to it from there. It shouldn't take you much longer than a quarter of an hour.'

She looked up into his friendly face. 'How do I walk there? What route should I take from the terminus?'

'Go straight up Toward Road past Victoria Hall and the gardens of Mowbray Park. Gray Road will be on your right. You can't miss it. Would you like one ticket to the terminus?'

Poppy couldn't believe her luck. She pressed the words

he'd said to her memory. Toward Road. Victoria Hall. Mowbray Park. Turn right.

'Yes, one ticket,' she replied.

He gave her the ticket, but she couldn't read what it said. She stared at it for a few moments, afraid to speak, then handed over her coins. The conductor looked at them, surprised.

'There's too much money here, miss. I need less than half of it. Here, let me . . .' He began picking out the correct coins and handed back those he didn't need.

Once he had moved on, Poppy put her ticket in her pocket and sat back in her seat for the rest of her ride. All she had to do when she reached the terminus was ask someone where Toward Road was. She could manage a fifteen-minute walk; she'd walk fifteen days to find Rose. The tram jerked and rumbled on, stopping en route to let passengers clamber aboard.

'Grangetown's the next stop!' she heard the conductor bellow downstairs. She'd never heard of the place but decided she liked what she saw. On her left was a huge park with mature trees and a stream. She turned her head to the right, where a stone wall rounded a corner, leading down a wide road to the sea.

When the tram reached the terminus, she held tight to the handrail as she climbed down the stairs. The conductor was waiting on the pavement, holding his hand out to help ladies step down from the platform.

'Thank you,' she said when he offered his arm. She looked around. There were trams going this way and that, and oh, the noise of it! People were rushing about, but these weren't people like those in Ryhope. These were well-dressed folk, not miners and farmers. They wore smart coats and hats, carried expensive-looking handbags over gloved hands; even the children were finely dressed. She gulped. 'Which way to Toward Road?' she asked the conductor.

He pointed in the direction of a large, ornate building built from big stone blocks. Poppy had never seen such a building before. The fanciest one she'd ever seen was the Co-op in Ryhope, but the building before her dwarfed that. It had sturdy domes on the top, and from one of them a large flag was flying.

'You need to walk past that building, miss, it's the museum and Winter Gardens,' he explained. 'Follow the path from the museum to Toward Road, walk past Victoria Hall and keep going until you reach a crossroads. From there, turn right on Gray Road.'

'Thank you,' Poppy said. He tipped his hat to her.

She walked slowly, tentatively, scared of the noise. There were so many people, and all of them seemed in a hurry to be somewhere else. She kept her head bowed, pulling her blanket around her, determined to reach the museum as quickly as she could and get away from the rumble of trams. She couldn't help noticing that there was a peculiar smell in the air, but she didn't know what it was or where it was coming from. In Ryhope, the air smelled of coal and smoke on the colliery, of the sea by the beach, and of pigs and cows at the barn. But there was a stench in the air here that she didn't like. She covered her hand with her nose and began to pick up her pace.

A woman smiled kindly as she approached. 'I'm no fan of the smell of hops either, dear. It's Vaux Brewery, they're brewing beer today,' she said before bustling away.

Poppy didn't know anything about beer, but at least the woman's words helped explain the odd smell. The museum loomed ahead, but first there was a busy road. She looked both ways before crossing, to ensure no trams were coming. Two horses trotted by, pulling a cart with two men atop. And then she was standing outside the magnificent building. She wondered what was inside, but couldn't stop to find out. She had something far more important to do.

Chapter Twenty

Poppy walked around the museum building. When she reached the back, she was astonished to see a lake with swans and ducks swimming by. In the middle of the lake was a fountain, spraying water high up in the air. She'd never seen anything so pretty. The lake was surrounded by trees and lawns, with an ornate iron bandstand behind rose bushes flowering in pink. And there was something else too, something so beautiful it almost took her breath away. There was a long, low building overlooking the lake. It seemed to be attached to the back of the museum, where the ornate stones gave way to a building made entirely of glass: glass domes and panels that fanned out like sunbeams. The sun glinted from the tallest dome, which had three glittering tiers.

A mother pushed a baby in a large black pram in front of this building, and another stab of guilt at leaving Emily behind pierced Poppy's heart. She hurried on past the lake, glancing around. Was she heading in the right direction? She ran through the words the conductor had given her. Toward Road. Victoria Hall. Mowbray Park. Turn right. The path ahead led past the lake and the fountain and wound its way into the park. She wondered if this was Mowbray Park, and if it was, should she keep on walking? She spun around, desperate to find someone to help. She didn't want to set off in the wrong direction in a place she didn't know.

She turned back to the museum, where the woman with the pram was now sitting on a bench, gazing out at the lake. Slowly Poppy walked up to her, then stopped, keeping a respectful distance. She stood tall and clasped her hands in front of her stomach.

'Excuse me,' she said, as politely as she could.

The woman snapped her gaze to her, then immediately, protectively, gripped the handle of her pram.

'Keep away from me, girl,' she hissed. 'What do you want? Money, is that it? You should be ashamed of yourself, begging in such a respectable place.'

Poppy was confused as to why the woman thought she was begging. But then she took in the smart shoes, tailored coat, perfectly curled hair and made-up face. In contrast, she knew she must look like an urchin. She wore her only pair of boots, which had gaping holes at the toes, and her skirt had seen better days. Suddenly things began to make sense. She dropped the blanket she was holding tight around her shoulders, exposing her good blouse, which she'd worn specially, then stuck her chest out and tried to explain.

'I'm not begging,' she implored. 'Please, I need your help, not your money.' She dug her hand into her pocket and pulled out her coins. 'I have my own money, look.'

The woman raised a perfectly manicured eyebrow, then looked her up and down. 'Then what is it you want? Speak up, girl, I haven't got all day.'

'Can you direct me to Toward Road?'

'That's all you want? You're not going to steal from me?'

Poppy was offended by the remark but knew better than to answer back. She was reliant on the woman's help to send her on her way to find Rose. 'I've never stolen anything in my life,' she said quickly, crossing her fingers against the lie.

The woman glared at her as if trying to decide whether to trust her or not. Finally she pointed a long, slim finger. 'That's Toward Road.'

Poppy saw an open gate leading from the park. 'Thank you,' she said, then she pulled the blanket around her shoulders and marched away, leaving the woman muttering darkly about urchins and thieves.

As she left the park, she saw a line of tall terraced houses. They were separated from the park by shrubs and trees, and as she walked along, she stared at them openmouthed. Most of the houses in Ryhope were made of limestone, cramped together in long rows. Around the village green, the houses were larger, built from brick, and many had magnificent gardens. But the houses that she saw now were tall and demanded attention. Some of them were four storeys high. She shuddered at the thought of all those stairs and windows. At home in the barn, she kept the place clean sweeping dust, straw and chickens away with her broom. In the Trewhitts' rooms above the shop, she used the lemon-scented polish that Ella gave her. She couldn't imagine the back-breaking work involved in keeping a four-storey home spick and span.

Soon she saw a large brick building that she thought at first was a church, though where were its spire and bells?

If it wasn't a church, was it the Victoria Hall the tram conductor had told her about? There was no one about for her to ask, and so she assumed that it was. She forced herself again to remember the route that he had given her. Toward Road. Victoria Hall. Mowbray Park. Turn right. Well, she was doing all right so far. She'd found her way to Toward Road, and now it looked as if she'd reached Victoria Hall. All she had to do was keep walking, for about a quarter of an hour, the conductor had said.

She marched on, past more houses to her left and more trees and roses to her right. She passed two gentlemen, and smiled at them as she walked by, but they recoiled in horror when they saw her. One of them even crossed the road as she approached, casting her a distasteful glance. Whatever reaction she'd expected from Sunderland folk, it certainly hadn't been this. Were these people afraid of her because of the way she looked? Yes, her clothes were worn, but her face was clean – she'd scrubbed it that morning with a damp cloth and had tied her curly hair back. She'd wanted to look as presentable as possible when she came face to face with Rose. And yet the woman in the park had assumed she was a beggar, while the look on the gentlemen's faces as she'd passed them suggested they found her unbecoming. Well, there wasn't anything she could do about that. She was Poppy Lawson, mother of three children, wife to Sid, and if the way she looked wasn't good enough for Sunderland folk, that was their problem, not hers.

After a while, she came to a crossroads. A road cut from north to south. Was this Gray Road? Should she turn right here? But it didn't yet feel as if she'd been walking for long enough. She looked at the street names etched into stones on each road, but she had no clue what they said. She was standing there scratching her head, wondering what to do, when a girl and boy ran past her, almost knocking into her as they went, as if they hadn't seen her.

'Hold on a moment!' Poppy cried.

The girl slowed down, laying a hand on her hat to stop it flying off. However, the boy pulled her forward, urging her on. 'She's just a street urchin, what are you bothering with her for?' he hissed.

The girl laughed and turned away, ready to run again.

'Is this Gray Road?' Poppy tried again.

The girl stopped fully this time.

'Don't speak to her, she'll steal your money if you're not careful,' the boy said, but the girl ignored him.

'No. Gray Road's the next street,' she replied. And with that, the pair ran off and their laughter disappeared on the breeze.

Poppy felt her mouth go dry and her legs begin to shake. She was just one street away from Rose. After ten years, they would finally be reunited. She began to feel dizzy and sick, and laid a hand against the wall to steady herself while she took long, deep breaths to calm her racing heart. When she was certain she no longer felt light-headed, she continued along Toward Road. With every step that she took, all she could think of was Rose. And then, finally, another crossroads lay ahead. This must be it, she thought, and with a pounding heart, she turned right on to Gray Road.

Chapter Twenty-One

When she rounded the corner, she looked left to right, desperately searching for houses. But all she could see was a high stone wall that ran either side of a long, wide road. Not for the first time, she cursed being unable to read. The street sign was behind her, etched into stone. She laid her fingers on the stone and welcomed its touch; it was warm from the sun. She ran her finger along the grooves of the first word, then the second. But she had no clue what they said. She inched forward, noting the trees behind the wall, remembering as much as she could in case she was on the wrong road and needed to turn around and head back. On her left, the wall turned to reveal a small church, and she noticed that its door was wide open. With no other option, she walked towards it, hoping there'd be someone inside who could confirm that she was on the right street. She peered around the door. 'Hello?' she called softly.

There was no reply, which meant there was only one thing for it, and so she tentatively entered, keeping as quiet as she could in case prayers were being said. Ahead of her she saw a woman sitting in a pew. She wore a blue velvet hat and had her head tilted forward. Poppy knew immediately that she was praying, so she waited a few moments until the woman raised her head, then walked forward until she was level with the end of the pew. She gave a little cough to politely announce her presence, and the woman turned to her with a friendly smile. She was an old lady, her face lined and her hair tucked neatly under her hat.

'Good morning,' she said. 'Welcome to St Michael's. I find the peace and quiet of the church helps to calm a busy mind.'

'I can't stay long, I'm afraid,' Poppy said.

'You have somewhere else to be, I understand. How may the church help you today?' The woman patted the pew next to her. 'Please sit for a few moments.'

Poppy slid on to the pew, unsure what to do. Should she pray too? she wondered. Although she and Sid didn't go to church regularly – just for weddings, christenings, funerals and the services at Easter and Christmas – she knew enough to know what to do. She closed her eyes and brought her hands together in prayer. But she wasn't giving thanks to the Lord; she was trying to work out how best to put her questions to the woman at her side, who might know where the Scurrfields lived. She opened her eyes, whispered *Amen* loud enough for the woman to hear, then turned towards her.

'Is this church . . . I mean, the road outside, is it Gray Road?' she asked.

'Why yes, child. That is Gray Road and this is St Michael's church. Couldn't you read the signs?'

Poppy dropped her gaze and shook her head.

'I see,' the woman said softly.

Poppy shifted in her seat. She had the information she needed and wanted nothing more than to run out of the church to start searching for Rose. However, she decided to press on with her questions to find out how much the woman might reveal.

'I'm looking for something,' she began.

The woman raised her eyes to the vaulted ceiling. 'And is this what brought you to our church? Well, everyone is searching for something, and many find what they are seeking right here.'

'No, I'm . . . well, the church is beautiful, yes, very restful and quiet, but I'm searching for someone I know. Someone who lives on Gray Road. But I can't seem to see any houses.'

The woman's eyes opened wide. 'My child, there is only one house on Gray Road. Are you sure you are searching in the right place?'

'Yes, I'm sure,' Poppy replied. 'There's just one house? Where might I find it? I couldn't see any houses from the road.'

'It's located a little further on, at the corner where Gray Road joins Belle Vue, which is a private terrace behind locked gates. The house at this end of Belle Vue has an address of Gray Road; it's the only house on the terrace that does. It's where James Scurrfield lives. But tell me, my child, what is a girl like you hoping to find there?'

At the mention of James Scurrfield, Poppy's heart skipped a beat. Rose was just along the road, only a few minutes away. She had to see her sister. But first she forced herself to find out more.

'Actually, it's the Scurrfield family I'm visiting. They're expecting me,' she lied. 'I understand they'll be home today. Perhaps you've seen them around?'

'Ah, the Scurrfields,' the woman said. She closed her eyes for a moment and pressed her palms together, and Poppy saw her lips moving silently as if delivering another prayer. Then she opened her eyes. 'The family used to come to church when Malcolm Scurrfield was alive. But he died not long after his son returned from war, and we don't see James in here. He tends to keep to himself.' She eyed Poppy closely. 'What is your business with James Scurrfield? Will you be taking up a position and working for him?'

Poppy's head spun as she tried to come up with a convincing lie. 'Yes . . . I'm . . . I'm going to be the new maid,' she said. She felt sure she'd be struck down at any moment. Telling lies was one thing, but doing so in church was even worse. She bit the inside of her cheek to stop herself from telling more.

'Then you must go there now and don't keep him waiting. I wouldn't want you to get into trouble for being late,' the woman replied.

'Do you know . . .' Poppy began, desperately wanting to find out if the woman could tell her anything about Rose. 'Do you know if there's a maid already in the house? A girl about my age, someone I could pal up with once I start work?'

The woman's face clouded over. 'Yes, I believe there is a girl who lives there,' she said cagily. 'Come to think of it, you remind me a little of her. You have similar eyes, I think. But it could be a trick of the light, it's quite dark in here.'

'Do you know her?' Poppy asked. 'Is she well?'

The woman brushed her hands against her skirt and

turned her face away. 'I'm led to understand that she doesn't often leave the house. I expect she's kept too busy with her chores.'

'Yes, I expect so,' Poppy said. It must be Rose, she thought. It had to be. She hoped the woman would reveal more, but their conversation seemed to have stalled. She pulled her blanket around her to keep off the chill – it really was cold in the church – then looked at the woman's kind, smiling face. But she didn't dare trust her, or anyone, with the truth of who she was seeking. Rose could be in danger, and she had to get her away. The thought of it propelled her to her feet.

'Thank you, I must go now,' she said.

The woman stood too and looked at her, all the way up from her boots with holes in to her skirt and blouse, the tattered blanket around her shoulders and her long curly hair.

'Forgive me if I go too far and say too much, dear, but there are societies in Sunderland who can help girls like you,' she said. 'I could give you directions to the nearest one, where you will be fed and they will give you new clothes. Perhaps boots without holes in, for surely they can't be comfortable on your poor feet.'

Poppy pulled her blanket tighter. 'I'm fine the way I am,' she said. 'I don't need charity.'

And with that she turned and walked out of the church. She was raging with indignation about being judged by her clothes and the way she looked. In Ryhope, people accepted her for who she was – a wife and mother, a close friend to the Trewhitts as well as a hard-working cleaner. But here in Sunderland, she was either pitied and offered charity or laughed at and scorned. She didn't like it one bit, and as soon as she found Rose, she was going to hurry home to Ryhope, where she felt safe.

When she emerged from the dark church, she was grateful to feel the warm sun on her face, and she blinked against the sunlight as she hurried away. And then she saw it, a little further along the road as the woman had said. It was a corner house, with an imposing side door opening on to Gray Road but the front tucked away on a private road. She crossed over and stood at the end of Belle Vue, peering in through a wrought-iron gate. She pushed the gate, but it wouldn't move, and she realised it was locked. As she peered along Belle Vue, she saw a pretty row of terraced houses with square gardens. In front of the gardens was a gravel drive that led to another set of gates at the end. She assumed those would be locked too, but she was determined not to leave without Rose. No locked gate could stop her now.

She looked up at the house. All was silent, and the windows and doors were closed. The house was three storeys high, with two bay windows on the ground floor looking out on the garden. On the floor above were four windows looking out to Belle Vue and another looking on to Gray Road. On the top floor, the windows were smaller – servants' rooms, she guessed. Was this where Rose lived? She peered up at the windows but couldn't see anything, as the sun was reflecting off the glass. She rattled the gates, hoping that if she rocked them back and forth enough, they'd somehow open and grant her access to the private road. But they stayed stubbornly locked.

She ran to the door that opened to Gray Road. She dared herself to push it, but it was locked and so she banged with her fists. When there was no response, she stepped back and looked up at a window above the door. She shielded her eyes from the sun but saw no movement at the window and heard no sound behind the door. She looked around for a stone, and found one that fitted snugly in her hand. Taking careful aim, she threw it. All she'd meant to do was tap on the window to bring someone to it, someone she could ask about Rose. But she flung the stone with more power than she'd expected, and it went sailing through. The window smashed, and she jumped back as a large shard of glass smashed at her feet.

As she stood open-mouthed, staring at the broken window, wondering what to do next, she heard a noise from behind the door. She swallowed hard and stood up straight, ready to apologise and explain that it had been an accident. But she never got a chance to speak. The door opened to reveal a hatchet-faced woman dressed in black. She wore a white pinny over her black skirt and her hair was scraped back harshly in a bun. She held a tin bucket in her hands. Poppy opened her mouth to ask for Rose, demand to see her, but before a word could leave her lips, the woman raised the bucket and threw its contents at her feet, as if sluicing away dirt on the road. Poppy gasped in shock as water soaked into her boots and drenched the bottom of her skirt.

'Get away from here! Scram!' the woman yelled. 'We don't want your sort hanging around like sewer rats. This is no place for girls like you. This is a respectable area. Now go, before I send for the police.'

Poppy found her breath. 'I need to see Rose,' she said.

The door was slammed in her face.

Chapter Twenty-Two

After the initial shock wore off, Poppy was fuming with anger. She'd been so excited about finding Rose that she hadn't slept all night. She'd been nervous about coming to Sunderland and taking the tram, scared of finding her way to Gray Road. Once she'd arrived, she'd suffered being sneered at by teenagers and ignored by a gentleman who'd crossed the road to avoid her. She'd even been accused of being a beggar by a woman in the park. Even the kindly woman in the church had assumed she was in need. Well, none of them knew the real Poppy Thomas, or Poppy Lawson as she was now. None of them knew how determined and stubborn she was.

She pushed her curls behind her ears and banged hard at the door. She waited, but there was silence. She banged again, but no one came, not even the hatchet-faced woman with her bucket this time. She stepped back and looked up at the smashed window. 'Rose!' she yelled. She waited to see if there would be any movement behind the window, but she was disappointed, even when she called again.

Around her, Gray Road was empty. There were no

horses and carts, or anyone walking. She was alone in the unfamiliar street, but not once did she think about leaving. Rose was inside this house, and the only things keeping them apart were bricks and stone. There had to be a way to get in, but how?

She ran back down Gray Road, along Toward Road then turned left, determined to reach the set of gates she'd spied at the other end of Belle Vue. But when she reached them, as she'd feared, they were locked too. She was clinging to them with both hands, trying to work out what to do, when the door of the house closest to her opened and a gentleman appeared wearing a striped waistcoat, a pressed shirt and smart trousers. He peered at her quizzically.

'Can I help you?' he asked, although his tone didn't sound helpful. Poppy had learned enough about Sunderland folk in the short time she'd spent there to know that she was being judged and found wanting. She stood up straight, pulled her blanket across her chest and smiled, ready to tell whatever lie she needed in order to get on to the private road.

'Yes, I'm here to see James Scurrfield,' she said. 'He promised the gate would be open for me, but it appears there's no one home and the gate at the other end is locked. I was hoping these ones might be open.'

The man walked towards her and stood behind the iron gates. He had dark bushy hair, a strong jaw and broad shoulders. He also wore a frown, and Poppy knew she'd need to do more to win him round.

'James Scurrfield, you say?' he said, scrutinising her. His gaze dropped to her skirt, which was wet around the edge, and her boots with the holes. 'What is your business?'

'I'm the new maid, sir,' Poppy replied. The lie tripped easily off her tongue. 'I'm starting work today. Mr Scurrfield sent me a letter and said the gate by Gray Road would be open for me, but it's not. I've knocked on the side door, sir, but no one came to answer.'

'May I see this letter he sent you?' the man asked.

Poppy floundered for a moment. She wanted more than anything to get beyond the gates, and this man was her only hope. She needed to find the right words to appease him.

'I lost it, sir, on my way from the tram. I'm ever so clumsy. I'm always losing things. I hope Mr Scurrfield forgives me. He seems like such a good man.'

'You've met him already?'

'Oh yes, sir. I was interviewed last week for the position of maid by Mr James Scurrfield himself. He appointed me to the role and asked me to start today.'

'James Scurrfield appointed you?' he asked.

'Yes, sir. However, I fear that if I don't report to the housekeeper within a few minutes, I may lose my job before I even begin. I need the work, sir, for my father is dying and I have to pay for the doctor.'

She paused, looking down at her boots where her toes poked through. She wriggled them for dramatic effect. 'You can see how I'm placed, sir. If I lose this job, my poor father won't get the help he so desperately needs.'

She hoped she wasn't going too far. She hadn't had to tell such bare-faced lies since the days when she stole food. However, she knew she'd tell a million lies to reach Rose. The thought of it brought tears to her eyes, and the man in front of her softened.

'Wait there,' he ordered.

Poppy's heart skipped a beat, and a smile began to play around her mouth. Had she done it? Would he let her in? She tried to force more tears from her eyes. It wasn't hard – she was feeling genuinely emotional about the thought of seeing Rose – and by the time the man returned with a large iron key, tears were streaming down her face. She watched as he turned the key in the lock. Oh, how she wanted to push him out of the way, barge past and run all the way. But she kept as still as she could, remembering to play her part and not give herself away. She wiped her hand across her eyes as the gate swung open.

'Thank you, sir. I'm sure Mr Scurrfield will be grateful for your help.'

The man stood back to allow her to enter Belle Vue. She thanked him again, and heard him turn the key behind her. This was it, she was in. In as ladylike a manner as she could manage, forcing herself not to run or scream with joy, she walked sedately along the gravel path. She wanted to turn around and check that the gentleman had disappeared into his home, but she knew better than to do that, as it might give the game away. She kept her gaze straight ahead while her heart pounded wildly. There were a dozen houses between one end of Belle Vue and the other. On she walked, past flowers in small gardens, past tall, imposing front doors and windows looking on to the drive. She didn't dare glance at them for fear of seeing someone who might take offence at how she looked and come out to challenge her. She couldn't risk being thrown out now she was so close. And then finally she was outside the last house on the road, the house with Rose inside.

From the private road, she was able to see the house in all its glory. Floral curtains hung at each window on the first two floors, but the windows on the top floor were bare. A tidy low privet hedge edged a small garden that was ordered and neat. A stone bird bath was placed in the middle of a lawn and two sparrows were splashing about. She didn't know what to do. If she banged on the door demanding to see Rose, she might be rewarded by having more dirty water thrown at her by the woman she assumed was the housekeeper. But what else could she do? The top windows were too high for her to throw a stone at to attract the attention of anyone up there.

She was looking from left to right, wondering what to do next, when a sound from above caught her attention. She looked up and was surprised to see a woman at a window on the top floor. She was gaunt, her cheekbones jutting from her thin face and the skin under her eyes dark. Her hair hung loose either side of her head and she was dressed in a heavy black gown. She looked like an old crone. She laid her bony fingers against the window and pressed her face to the glass.

Poppy stepped back and shielded her eyes to peer up at her. Was this one of the Scurrfields? But as she stared at her, trying to make sense of who she was, the woman smiled, stretching the skin on her face into a grotesque mask. And then she lifted her hand and waved, and the gesture took Poppy's breath away. For she didn't wave just once, she did it three times, opening her hand like a flower blooming in spring, just like Poppy and Rose had done as bairns.

At first Poppy didn't want to believe it. That couldn't be Rose . . . not her beautiful Rose, could it? But with a sickening lurch in the pit of her stomach, she realised that it was.

Suddenly the front door of the house was flung open and a man stood in the doorway. He had black hair, dark eyes and a long, stern face. He wore a smart grey coat that came to his knees, black trousers, sturdy shoes and a white shirt underneath a buttoned waistcoat.

'Who the devil are you? State your business,' he demanded.

Poppy snapped her gaze to him, her heart beating nineteen to the dozen. She wanted nothing more than to lift her eyes to the window to see Rose again. But she forced herself to address the man, deciding that there would be no more lies. She had to do everything she could to help Rose.

'I am Poppy Lawson, née Thomas,' she said, her voice quivering with shock and nerves. 'I've travelled from Ryhope to visit my sister Rose.'

The man stumbled backwards and gripped the side of the door to steady himself. 'Rose is my property,' he said calmly. Then he turned his head, calling into the dark hallway behind him. 'Mrs Hutchins! Come, help me remove this beggar.' He turned back to Poppy with an evil glint in his eye. 'You're persistent, I'll give you that. I thought my housekeeper had got rid of you, but like a bad smell you've returned. I will report you to the police for smashing my window. Make sure you don't return, if you know what's good for you.'

The hatchet-faced Mrs Hutchins barged out of the door. 'Don't worry, I'll get rid of her, Mr Scurrfield,' she said. She pushed past him and roughly grabbed Poppy's arm. James Scurrfield took her other arm, and together they frogmarched her to the iron gates. The housekeeper pulled a large key from her pocket, unlocked the gate and pushed Poppy through it. She stumbled and fell forward. When she pulled herself to her feet, Scurrfield had returned inside, but Mrs Hutchins was waiting with her hands on her hips, glaring.

'Get away, girl. And don't darken this door again,' she said, before she too went indoors.

Poppy stood at the gates, looking up to the window where she'd spotted her sister just moments before, but Rose was nowhere to be seen.

Chapter Twenty-Three

Poppy felt lost and didn't know what to do. She couldn't walk away now, not when Rose was so close. But what other choice did she have? She could bang and knock at the door until her knuckles bled, but she knew she wouldn't get inside. She rattled the gates in frustration and screamed her sister's name at the top of her voice. But none of it made any difference. No one came to the window and no one opened the door. She slumped to the ground and with tears in her eyes admitted defeat, for now.

After a few moments, she forced herself up and brushed dirt from her skirt. She knew she had no option but to head home. She retraced her steps to the terminus, but this time she didn't stop to look around at buildings and people. This time she kept her head down, her blanket tight around her, trying not to cry. Each time she thought of Rose, tears welled up inside her. How dreadful her sister had looked, how tired and thin. But she'd smiled and she'd waved and Poppy took heart from that.

As she walked, she thought about what to do next. She'd need to speak to Sid to ask for his help; they'd come up with a plan and return to Gray Road together.

When she reached the terminus, she had to ask for help to find the right tram. People gave her strange looks, and children sniggered when they thought she wasn't looking. She saw them whispering about her, caught their glances at her worn clothes, her wet skirt and broken-down boots, but she held her head high and marched on until she found a woman willing to point her in the right direction.

She stood in the queue with her hand holding tight to the coins in her pocket. Once aboard the tram, she didn't look at the view as she'd done earlier. Her mind was completely focused on Rose, on how she and Sid would free her from James Scurrfield. She wondered who else they could ask to help, but she only knew Ambrose and Ella, and they were too old and frail. Besides, they had their shop to run, and it would be wrong to expect them to give up their work. There was Sid's mam and dad, but they had barely a spare ha'penny between them to pay for the tram fare. And anyway, Poppy would need to rely on Maisie to look after the bairns when she and Sid tried to rescue Rose. Her mind went round in circles, and in the end she knew that only Sid could help.

She alighted from the tram at Ryhope village green feeling dejected and tired, emotionally wrung out after her visit to Gray Road. She'd been planning to head straight to Scotland Street to collect her bairns from Maisie, but instead she followed the path to St Paul's church, marching past lopsided gravestones sitting in the earth like rotting teeth. The church door was closed, and she was relieved to see it, for she didn't want to come across Reverend Daye. She didn't want anyone to see what she was going to do.

She followed the path around the back of the church to the familiar place where daisies and buttercups bloomed between nettles. Every week for ten years she'd visited that patch of earth. She'd pulled grass and weeds out with her fingers to keep it tidy and neat. She'd even placed tiny pebbles in rows as decoration. Whether in rain, snow, ice, autumn wind or spring sunshine, she'd come to the churchyard to sit and think about Rose. She'd brought her boys to see the stone when they were old enough and had told them all about their beautiful aunt. She'd been planning to tell Emily too, just as soon as she understood.

She looked down at the scrubbed earth and the stone. She'd called it Rose's grave, giving it a name, a status, in memory of her sister who she thought had died. But now she knew the truth. Rose was alive, she'd seen her with her own eyes. By the looks of her, she was ill – she'd appeared haggard, nothing more than skin and bones – and yet there had been her smile and their secret special wave. Poppy clung to the memory of Rose at the window; she'd see her again, of that she'd make sure.

She knelt down, gathered the pebbles in her hand and flung them angrily against the wall. She was angry at the Scurrfields for mistreating her sister, she was angry with Nellie Harper for selling her. She was angry with the world, even with God himself for allowing them to be separated, and she raised a clenched fist to the church spire. But most of all, she was angry with herself. She was angry for the words she'd flung at Malcolm Scurrfield on the day he'd taken Rose away all those years ago. They had caused him to label her as insolent and disobedient, and he'd refused to take them both. Instead, he'd used a sixpence to choose; a sixpence had decided their fate.

She'd wondered many times whether when Scurrfield had thrown the coin, it really had landed on the side he'd said it had, as no one had seen it but him. She stamped on the ground she'd tended lovingly for the last ten years. And then she turned and walked away, vowing never to return, never to call it Rose's grave. All that mattered now was getting her sister back.

She hurried from the church, past the village school and towards Scotland Street. Sid wasn't expected home until supper time, and she planned to bath the baby, feed the boys and then start cooking his dinner. She knew he'd have worried about her all day, and would be anxious to hear what had happened as soon as he returned home. She began to run. Ryhope East railway station came into view. Scotland Street stretched out in front of the station, and Maisie's house rumbled each time trains went by. When Poppy reached the house at the end, she knocked hard at the door. She hoped Maisie would answer with Emily in her arms and a smile on her face. She hoped there'd be good news, that Emily had taken milk, that she was brighter, more alert because of it. But when the door swung open, Maisie appeared looking flustered, red in the face, with no child in her arms. Poppy's heart sank.

'What's wrong?' she said, worried.

'It's the bairn, pet,' Maisie said, ushering her quickly indoors. 'The bairn's gone.'

Poppy looked at Maisie dumbstruck, then grabbed the woman's hands. 'No,' she breathed. 'No, please. Tell me it's not true. Not my baby, not my Emily. She can't be gone, please, Maisie, no.'

Maisie shook her head. 'It's not Emily, love. She's asleep by the fire.'

'Then what's happened?' Poppy demanded, squeezing Maisie's hands tight.

'It's Sonny, he's disappeared.'

Poppy ran along the hall and into the kitchen. Sure enough, Emily was sleeping by the fire, wrapped in a blanket in a wooden drawer that Maisie used as her cot. Harry was sitting on the floor playing with two pieces of coal, driving them into each other as if they were carts and smashing them against the hearth.

'Where is he?' Poppy demanded, looking around wildly. 'Where's he gone?' She flew to Harry's side and knelt down on the floor, placing both hands on his shoulders and looking him hard in the eye. 'Where's your brother?' she said firmly.

'It's not my fault,' he said, and his bottom lip began to quiver.

Poppy knew she'd have to keep her voice calm so as not to alarm him if she wanted the truth. 'What's not your fault?' she asked.

Harry turned his tearful eyes to her. 'He wanted to see the trains, Mam.'

Poppy stood and glared at Maisie. 'You let him go to see the trains? What were you thinking?'

Maisie sank into a chair at the kitchen table and put her head in her hands. 'I let them both out to play in the street for five minutes. Emily was crying and I was trying to feed her. I'd warmed milk on the fire, but she wouldn't take it. She started bawling and so I sent the lads outside. I told them, Poppy, I said not to go beyond the end of the street, but when I called them in for dinner, Sonny was nowhere to be seen. I've been out looking for him, we all have. I bundled Emily inside my coat and we went out, searched the streets and shouted for him.'

'And you searched the railway station?' Poppy demanded, her voice rising as panic set in. She felt herself getting too hot, and dropped the blanket from her shoulders.

Maisie raised her gaze. 'Yes, love. I'm sorry. We looked everywhere.'

Poppy felt sick. The ground moved beneath her, and she fell to the floor.

Chapter Twenty-Four

When Poppy opened her eyes, she was aware of someone looming over her.

'Sonny?' she whispered.

Maisie's face came closer. 'Poppy, can you hear me, love?'

Poppy blinked twice, trying to focus as she struggled to sit up.

'Here, have some of this.'

Maisie lifted a cup to Poppy's lips, and Poppy drank what was offered; it was something warm and sweet. She looked into Maisie's concerned face. 'What happened? Why I am on the floor?'

'You fainted, pet.'

The nightmare came rushing back. 'I need to find Sonny,' she said urgently. Harry was sitting on the floor by her side, gripping her skirt with both hands. Behind him, Emily was still asleep in the drawer.

'Don't try to stand,' Maisie warned. 'You might be dizzy. Sit for a while on the floor – here, drink more tea, the sugar in it will do you good.'

Poppy did as her mother-in-law instructed. Maisie crouched down beside her.

'It must have been the shock that made me pass out,' Poppy said.

'It must have been,' Maisie said, raising her eyebrow. 'Unless there's something else going on you want to tell me?'

'Something else?' Poppy said defensively. 'I don't know what you mean.'

Maisie laid her hand on Poppy's arm. 'Oh, I think you know all right. I've seen the way your face has been flushed lately, and the way your chest's filling out. I've had enough bairns of my own to know the signs when I see them. How far gone are you?'

Poppy scooted along the floor to rest her back against an armchair. Harry followed. 'I haven't bled for almost eight weeks,' she said.

'Does our Sid know?' Maisie asked.

Poppy shook her head. 'We've got enough on our plate without me springing this on him. We've barely got two ha'pennies to rub together, so how we'll afford to feed another bairn, I don't know. And I wanted to be sure, you know, after miscarrying before.'

'I understand, love. Your secret's safe with me, but I think you should tell him soon. He's got a right to know.'

Poppy put a hand on the chair behind her and pulled herself up to standing. 'I've got to go and find Sonny.'

'I'll come with you,' Maisie offered.

'No, you stay here with Emily and Harry. I know the sorts of places Sonny likes. He might be hiding in any one of them, thinking it's a game.' She hoped she was right.

'Sonny likes trains, Mam,' Harry piped up.

Poppy ruffled his hair. 'I know he likes trains, love. I'll find him, don't worry,' she said, though she sounded more certain than she felt.

'Are you sure you're feeling well enough to go out on your own?' Maisie asked, concerned. 'Have some more tea, or something to eat to build your strength up.'

'No, I've got to go and find my son,' Poppy said.

She walked slowly and carefully, forcing herself to take long, deep breaths, calling out for Sonny as she went. She headed straight to the railway station. Although Maisie had said she'd already checked there, it seemed to Poppy the most logical place for him to be. However, the station was deserted, and there was no one on the platform.

Thick black smoke billowed from the chimney of the stationmaster's house. The cloud of smoke caught in Poppy's throat, and she covered her mouth and nose. The little house needed its chimney cleaning, she thought, for chimney smoke should never be so black. If the stationmaster wasn't careful, there'd be sparks shooting out soon and his home could be in danger of fire.

She made her way to the station house and knocked at the door. She was greeted by a short, officious-looking man with a neat moustache, wearing trousers and a waistcoat in matching shades of blue.

'Excuse me, sir, I've lost a small boy, my son—'

'Mammy!' a child roared.

Poppy recognised her son's voice immediately, and with her heart beating wildly, she ran inside the cottage without waiting to be invited. Sonny flew into her arms and she squeezed him tight, relief rushing through her.

The stationmaster stepped aside as mother and son

were reunited. 'Oh, he's yours, is he?' he said. 'I found him wandering along the platform earlier; he said he was looking for trains. I asked him where he lived, as I was going to return him, but the poor lad kept gibbering on about chickens and a barn.'

'Thank you,' Poppy said. 'I'll always be grateful to you.'

The stationmaster scratched his head as she led Sonny away. She was about to step out of the cottage when she thought better of it and turned back.

'You need your chimney sweeping, by the way.'

When they returned to Maisie's house, Poppy gave both her sons a stern talking-to about never running away and always staying together.

'You must look after each other,' she said, and Harry slid his arm around Sonny's shoulders.

Maisie handed Poppy another mug of tea, and this time, it came with a slice of fruit cake on a plate. Slices of cake were also given to the boys.

'Speaking of looking after each other, how did you get on with finding Rose?' Maisie asked. 'I never had a chance to ask you before you collapsed, and then you went straight out to find him.' She nodded at Sonny.

Poppy took a deep breath. 'Well, I found her,' she said, 'but I didn't get to speak to her. She lives on a private road that's locked at both ends with iron gates. Too high to climb over.'

Maisie shot her a warning look. 'You shouldn't be thinking about climbing in your condition.'

'Oh, don't worry, I couldn't climb them whether pregnant or not. I really need to speak to Sid. He offered to come with me, and I should have listened. I'm sure together we'll come up with a plan.'

Maisie gave her a worried look. 'Just be careful, all right?'

That evening, back at the barn, Poppy fed the boys and sent them to bed with another stern lecture about never running off on their own. When she heard the bells of St Paul's chime the twilight hour, she prepared Sid's bath by the fire. Then she sat for a while with Emily in her arms, trying to get her to take milk, but once again Emily drank little and seemed listless. Concerned and worried, Poppy brought the baby's cot downstairs and laid it where she could keep a watchful eye on her. She heard the barn door slide open, then saw Sid's blackened face peek around it. When he spotted her, he broke into a smile of relief.

'You're home safe, thank goodness for that. I've been worried sick all day,' he said. He rushed to her and threw his arms around her, kissing her full on the lips.

'Oh Sid, you're going to get coal dust all over my face,' Poppy teased, brushing at her cheek when he finally stepped back.

'Did you see Rose? What happened?' he asked.

'I'll tell you all about it when you've had your bath and eaten your tea,' Poppy said.

Sid peeled his coal-blackened clothes off and slid into the warm bath. Poppy soaped his back and he dipped his neck forward, moving his head from side to side.

'Some of the fellas I work with won't let their wives wash their backs,' he said. 'They think it takes their strength away.'

'It takes the muck away, that's all,' Poppy tutted as she

scrubbed his blackened skin. 'Anyway, how's it been at work today?'

'Rotten,' Sid muttered. 'If I could give it up, Pops, I would. Working underground is no way to make a living. It's back-breaking work and I hate every stinking minute.'

Poppy kissed him gently on the top of his head.

Once he was clean, and the dirty water thrown into the yard, Sid checked on his sleeping sons and gave each one a kiss.

'Thank heavens I've got a day off this weekend,' he said as he sat by the fire. 'I haven't spent much time with the boys lately. I'll take them to play football on the green if it's nice.' Then he turned to Poppy, giving her his full attention. 'All right then, let's hear it. Did you find the house on Gray Road? Did you see Rose?'

Poppy described everything that had happened that day, leaving no stone unturned. When she'd finished, tears were streaming down her face. 'She looked awful, Sid, dreadful. She must be ill. I need to get her out of that house and bring her back here where she belongs. You offered to come with me and I should have listened. It'll take both of us, but together we'll get her away.'

Sid sank back in his chair. 'How are we going to do that?' he said. 'If Scurrfield and his housekeeper wouldn't allow you inside, what makes you think they'll let you in if we go together? They'll recognise you and chase you again. And they'll be after you for the money to pay for the window you broke.'

Poppy had already given this problem some thought. 'You're right, I can't show my face after what happened today. It's going to have to be you alone. I'll point out the house to you, and the window where I saw Rose. There's a church opposite; I'll wait there, out of sight, and once you've rescued her, we'll run back to the tram stop.' She leaned forward, a plan forming in her mind. 'But we'll need to spin a tale to whoever answers the door, whether it's the housekeeper or Scurrfield.'

Sid held his hands up to stop her saying more. 'I hope you're not expecting me to tell lies, Pops.'

That was exactly what she was planning. She knew she'd need to choose her words carefully in order to coax Sid into doing what was needed.

'Think of it less as a lie and more like telling a story. See, today I saw thick smoke coming from the station-master's chimney. It was black smoke – he really needs his chimney cleaned or he'll be having sparks shooting out soon.'

'What's that got to do with getting Rose back?'

'It gave me an idea. Would you pretend to be a chimney sweep, Sid?'

His mouth dropped open. 'What?' he said, incredulous. 'No, of course not, don't be so daft,' he said, shaking his head.

'Why not? Please, Sid, think about it. We can borrow poles and a brush from your mate Dan who cleans chimneys in the village. He'll not miss them for a few hours. All you'll have to do is turn up at the house on Gray Road, tell them you're the new chimney sweep doing the round because the regular fella is ill, and with any luck they'll let you inside. You'll get access to every room with a fireplace in it, and hopefully one of those rooms will have Rose inside. You can talk polite when you need to, you can fool the housekeeper. All you have to do is find Rose and bring her out, then cross the road to the church to collect me and together we'll bring her back here. Please, Sid, we have to rescue her.'

Sid sucked air through his teeth. 'I don't know, Pops, this doesn't sound good.'

A rush of nausea suddenly came upon her. She covered her mouth with her hands, then rushed out to the yard. Sid followed, concerned, asking if she was all right.

'Could you bring me a cup of water, Sid?'

He did as she asked. 'What's up, Pops? Have you eaten something that's disagreed with you?'

Poppy took a sip of water, and with her mother-in-law's words ringing in her head, she told him what she'd already told Maisie. Sid's mouth opened and closed, but no words came out.

'Are you telling me we're having another baby?' he said when he finally found the power of speech.

'Yes,' she said, taking another sip of water, all the while eyeing him carefully, for his face gave little away as her news sank in. 'Are you happy, Sid?' she asked.

'Happy?' he breathed. 'I'm dumbstruck. But . . . yes, I'm happy. Of course I'm happy. Another bairn on its way, who wouldn't want that? Still . . .'

Poppy nodded, only too aware of the problems a new child could bring.

'A baby!' Sid said, this time with a joyous smile. He rushed to Poppy and threw his arms around her, ready to lift her and twirl her around. But she pressed her feet to the ground and shook her head.

'No, Sid, I don't feel well enough, leave me be,' she said.

He placed his hands on her shoulders and looked her in the eye. 'Another baby on the way . . . My head's dizzy with the news, Pops. We've got our two beautiful boys, our gorgeous Emily . . .' he looked at Poppy's stomach, 'and now this little one too. It means our family is almost complete.'

'Almost?' Poppy said, puzzled.

'What I mean is . . .' Sid said, suddenly serious, 'all we need now is Rose.'

Poppy gasped. 'You'll help me rescue her? Really?'

Sid gently laid a hand on her stomach, then kissed her on her cheek.

'There's nothing I wouldn't do for you.'

Chapter Twenty-Five

On the morning of Sid's day off work, he was up early playing football on the green with Harry and Sonny. Once the boys were tired out, he took them back to the barn and enjoyed breakfast with Poppy. Poppy was excited to be heading to Gray Road again, this time with Sid. But she felt nervous too. It was obvious that Rose was living with bad people, and there was every chance that she and Sid might not be able to get her out of the Scurrfields' house, or even that they might be hurt in the process. As she fed the boys and nursed Emily, her stomach turned with anxiety over what lay ahead. However, she was determined to hide her feelings from the children. She didn't want them picking up on her worries. Fortunately, Harry and Sonny seemed oblivious, happy to be spending the day with Grandad Bill, who'd promised to take them fishing on the beach.

Despite Sid's offer to help her find Rose, he too was full of worry and doubt. 'I still don't understand why we can't go to the police and ask for their help,' he said.

'Oh Sid, we've been through this already,' Poppy replied. 'If we went to the police, what would we say?

171

The only crime that's been committed is James mistreating Rose, and I doubt very much that they'd be interested in something so trivial as a domestic event. Besides, Rose sent her plea for help to me. If she'd wanted the police involved, she would have written to them.'

Sid pulled his boots on and shot her a look, shaking his head. 'All I'm saying is—' he began, but Poppy held her hand up.

'No, Sid. We've got to do this ourselves. It's a family matter, nobody's business but ours.'

He walked to her and wrapped his arms around her, nuzzling his face in her neck. 'I love you, Mrs Lawson,' he said. He pulled his jacket on, then picked up the pole and brush he'd borrowed from Dan, his chimney sweep friend. 'Though I still think it's ridiculous for me to try to pass as a sweep. If Scurrfield discovers what I'm up to, we'll have the police involved whether we want it or not, and I'll become notorious as Ryhope's worst criminal!'

Poppy smiled, knowing she'd have to do her best to placate him. She wrapped her arms around his waist and brought him to her with a long, lingering kiss. 'Just think, Sid. By teatime tonight, we might have Rose here with us, home at last,' she breathed.

'Oh aye? And what are we going to feed her if she does come home?' he said softly.

Her smile dropped for a second. That was indeed a worry, for they couldn't afford to buy extra food. The money they were spending on tram fares was what they'd put aside to pay Norman their rent.

'We'll manage, Sid. Don't we always?' she murmured against his neck.

'We're going to have to, love, with another baby on the way.'

'Are you sure you're pleased, Sid, about the baby?'

'Course I am. I've said so, haven't I, and I'd never lie to you. You should know that much by now,' he said, kissing her on her cheek. But then his face clouded over. 'It's just, you know, with money being tight, things are going to be a struggle.'

He stepped back, holding the brush in his hand.

'How do I look? Think I'll pass as the town chimney sweep?'

Poppy looked him up and down, appraising him. 'Almost . . . but there's something missing,' she said.

She walked to the hearth, where the fireplace was filled with cold ash from last night's fire. She scooped up a handful and carefully dabbed it on his face, across his cheeks and brow, then stood back to admire her work. 'There, you look like you're covered in soot now, just like a chimney sweep should be.'

Sid rolled his eyes. 'I still can't believe we're mad enough to do this,' he sighed.

Poppy gathered the children to her and pulled her blanket around her shoulders. 'Come on, everyone. Let's go to Granny's house.'

Harry and Sonny ran ahead of their parents as the family made their way from the barn and through the yard. In the cattle market, Norman was resting on his walking stick, talking to a man neither Poppy nor Sid recognised.

'Morning, Norman!' Sid shouted.

Norman looked at him, taking in his soot-blackened face and the brush and pole in his hands, and gave him a quizzical look. Then he nudged the man at his side, who also turned to look.

'Sid, Poppy, I'd like you to meet Amos Bird,' Norman said.

Poppy gasped and cradled Emily tight. 'The man who's buying the farm,' she whispered to Sid.

'The least we can do is say hello to our new landlord,' he replied.

Poppy walked a step behind Sid, keeping her eyes on Amos Bird. She was trying to deduce what kind of man he was, but it was difficult to tell, for his countenance gave little away. He was a short, stocky man with a round, rugged face that was weathered from years of working the land. He was bald on top of his head, and wisps of brown hair fluttered around his ears. He had deep-set eyes, and she guessed he must be around the same age as Sid's dad. He wore a loose jacket with baggy trousers tucked into sturdy boots.

'Amos, this is the Lawson family, who live in the barn,' Norman said by way of introduction.

Sid stuck his free hand out towards Amos, who shook it heartily. 'Pleased to meet you, sir. This is my wife, Poppy and our bairns, Harry, Sonny and baby Emily.'

Amos beamed at the children and ruffled Harry's hair. 'What a pair of smashing lads you've got there. Twins, eh? Two peas in a pod,' he said.

Poppy took heart from the cheery way he greeted them, hoping he would look favourably on them staying in the barn. She felt her shoulders relax a little.

'It's good to meet you,' Amos continued. 'Actually, I'd been planning to call to see you today to introduce myself properly.'

Poppy and Sid looked at each other.

'Yes, of course, we should be back late afternoon,' Poppy said, feeling sure they'd have returned from Gray Road by then, if their plan worked as they hoped. 'I'll make some tea and have it ready for you.'

'Oh, don't go to any trouble, lass,' Amos said, his smile fading slightly. Poppy noticed that he looked briefly at Norman before returning his gaze to Sid. 'Now then, you all look like you're about to set off somewhere, so don't let me keep you.'

'Thank you, sir, we'll see you later,' Sid replied, and with that the family went on their way.

'What do you think he wants to see us about?' Poppy asked as they walked towards Scotland Street.

Sid shrugged. 'You heard him, he just wants to get to know us – we'll be his tenants, after all. Don't worry, Pops, it won't be anything more than that.'

A shiver ran down Poppy's spine. She looked at Emily's tiny face; her eyes were open and her rosebud mouth tightly closed.

'I hope you're right,' she replied.

Once the boys and Emily were settled with Maisie and Bill, Poppy and Sid walked to the tram stop.

'I feel a right bloody idiot with these poles and this muck on my face,' Sid hissed.

Poppy shushed him. 'If anyone says anything, just tell them you're working for Dan as a favour. This is our only chance to rescue Rose. Come on, Sid, we've got to stay focused.'

She threaded her arm through his, and when they reached the stop, they were first in line. By the time the tram arrived, the queue snaked all the way back to the school.

'Let's sit upstairs, Sid, it's fun, there's ever such a nice view,' Poppy said when they climbed aboard. But the conductor had other ideas and put his hand firmly on Sid's shoulder to stop him climbing the stairs.

'You're not going upstairs with those poles, lad. You can stay downstairs where I can keep my eye on them. They'll have someone's eye out if you're not careful. Anyway, why haven't you got yourself a cart?'

'He's doing his mate a favour,' Poppy quickly replied, ushering Sid to a double seat. 'And the cart's being used elsewhere.'

They slid into the seat with the pole and brush between them. Sid didn't say much as the tram set off, and Poppy knew that meant he was feeling anxious – and not just about their task once they reached Gray Road. This was the first time he had been outside of Ryhope or travelled on a tram. She was feeling it too, but just as she'd always been the strong one when she and Rose were children, she knew she had to be strong for her and Sid now. She chatted happily to help put them both at ease, pointing out landmarks that she'd passed the first time she'd taken the tram. And when they alighted at the terminus in Sunderland, she took him by the hand and led him to the museum.

'Have you ever seen such a thing, Sid? Isn't it beautiful?' she marvelled.

He could only agree that it was. Next she took him into Mowbray Park to show him the glass and iron building by the lake.

'Are those swans?' Sid said, hardly believing his eyes.

'And ducks, plenty of them,' Poppy replied.

As they walked on to Toward Road, she pointed out the tall, grand houses. At the first crossroads by the park, where she'd faltered last time, she marched bravely on. And then it was time to turn right on to Gray Road.

Rounding the corner, Poppy heard a peal of bells and sent silent thanks when she saw that the door of St Michael's church was open. Her plan was to sit inside near the door but out of sight of the Scurrfield house. If she chose her spot carefully, she'd be able to keep an eye on what was happening. And if she was challenged by anyone in the church or drawn into conversation again by the woman offering charity, she'd simply close her eyes, pretend to pray and hope to be left alone.

'This is it, Sid, the house is up here on the right,' she said as they drew near. 'The door you see there, the one you'll knock on, is the side door. But the front of the house looks on to the private road, Belle Vue. That's where I saw Rose at a window on the top floor, the one on the left-hand side.'

Sid took a deep breath. 'What'll I do if I find her?'

Poppy laid her hands on his shoulders. 'We've been through this umpteen times. You know the drill. If you find her, get her out of there as fast as you can. I'll see you as soon as you leave, I'll come running, and the three of us will escape down Toward Road to the tram stop.'

'But if Rose is as ill as you say, she might not be able to run,' Sid said. 'She might be too poorly, and what if—'

'Sid? Calm down,' Poppy said firmly.

He squared his shoulders. 'But what if I find her and she doesn't recognise me and refuses to leave?'

'If she doesn't know who you are, do this,' Poppy

said. She held her hand up, clenched her fist, then opened it three times like a flower blooming in the spring. She kissed him on the lips. 'Good luck.'

Crossing the road, she ducked into the church and slid on to the end of the pew closest to the door. Then, with her heart in her mouth, she watched Sid walk to the house and heard him knock three times on the door.

Chapter Twenty-Six

Poppy shivered under her blanket. She didn't know if it was due to the chilly air in the church or anticipation of what was about to happen. In the pews ahead, a handful of people sat with their heads bowed. She had entered the church unseen and was determined to stay as quiet as she could so as not to attract unwanted attention. She put her hands together, as if in prayer, in case anyone turned to see her, but kept her gaze on the house.

She saw Sid standing outside with his pole and brush. How proud she felt of him for doing this for her and Rose. And then she saw the door open, and her heart leapt. It was Mrs Hutchins, the housekeeper. She pressed her back against the hard wooden seat, afraid that the woman might notice her inside the church. Then she chided herself for being so daft – there was no way she could know she was there. She saw Sid shuffling from foot to foot, a sign that he was feeling nervous. She saw Mrs Hutchins' face cloud over, then she looked up and down the street. Poppy crossed her fingers and hoped Sid would stick to the words they'd prepared, and that his nerves wouldn't scupper their plan. But she needn't have worried, for the next thing she knew, he was stepping inside the house and Mrs Hutchins had closed the door. This was it; he was in! She breathed a sigh of relief. This time when she brought her hands together, she closed her eyes and prayed for real, for the safe release of her sister and to keep Sid safe too.

Time passed slowly. Some of the people in front of Poppy stood from their pews and left, while others came in to pray. She stayed where she was, her back aching from sitting on the hard seat. She craned her neck to see if she could spot any movement at a window in the house on Gray Road, but all was still. She worried for Sid, as he had no clue how to clean chimneys and she was concerned that Mrs Hutchins might be on to him. She hoped that his story would be enough to get him into the room where she'd seen Rose. If Scurrfield wasn't at home, if Sid only had the housekeeper to deal with, his task might be easier. However, there was no way of knowing who was at home, and there could be more members of the household they didn't know about.

'Come on, Sid,' she whispered under her breath as she kept watch.

And then, suddenly, the door was flung open. But it wasn't Sid who emerged, it was Rose.

Poppy leapt to her feet. 'Oh my God!' she cried.

Heads turned towards her.

'Amen, my child,' a man said before returning to his prayers.

'Hallelujah!' called another.

Poppy hurried to the church door. Rose was running down Gray Road, but Sid was nowhere to be seen. She didn't know what to do. Should she go after her sister or head to the house to help her husband? As she hovered by the door, her heart beating wildly, Sid appeared. He looked across the road to her and yelled, 'Run!'

She didn't waste any time. Sprinting from the church, she crossed the road towards Sid, who was holding his hand out to her. She was within inches of reaching him, their fingers almost touching, when she felt a stitch in her side, crippling her with pain. She stopped and doubled over. Sid glanced nervously behind him to make sure they weren't being followed, then crouched down beside her.

'Pops? Are you all right? Is it the baby?' he said, concerned.

Poppy put both hands to her side where the pain was. 'It's just a stitch, I'll be fine.' She straightened up. 'Come on, I need to see Rose,' she said.

They walked on quickly, Sid turning every few seconds to ensure they weren't being chased. When they were sure the coast was clear, Poppy leaned against a wall, breathing hard, pressing her hands to her side until she felt the pain fade. Sid stood next to her, getting his breath back, and she looked at his face, smudged with soot and streaked with sweat.

'You found Rose and I'll always be grateful,' she said. 'You're the best husband in the world, Sid Lawson.'

He beamed, then wrapped his arm around her waist to help her walk the rest of the way.

When they reached the crossroads where Toward Road met Mowbray Park, they saw Rose waiting by the park gates. Poppy peeled away from Sid's side and headed to her sister. She didn't notice her blanket fall from her shoulders, and she didn't know that Sid picked it up. She didn't hear the cries of the birds in the trees or the leaves rustling on the gentle breeze. She didn't see the young girl on a horse and cart go by or hear her cry for rag and bones. All she saw was Rose. She walked towards her, arms outstretched, not even trying to hold back her tears. All she wanted was her sister in her arms. Rose was taller now than Poppy, but oh so terribly thin. Poppy flung her arms around her and buried her face in her neck.

How long they stayed like that, she didn't know, but it was Sid who interrupted their reunion. 'Come on, we need to get back to Ryhope as quick as we can,' he said, casting a nervous glance back. 'Once Scurrfield finds out what's happened, who knows what he might do.'

Poppy reluctantly pulled away from Rose and they stood together holding hands, looking into each other's eyes, neither of them needing to speak. She noticed how waxy her sister's skin looked, and how pale she was. The eyes that had once been sparkling with light were now dull and yellowed. There was no trace of the beauty Rose had once had as a child. Poppy pulled her sister to her for another hug.

'Come, now,' Sid urged.

'He's right, we should go. James won't be happy when he finds me missing,' Rose said, stepping away from Poppy.

Those were the first words Poppy had heard her sister speak in over ten years.

'It's really you, isn't it?' she said, threading her arm through Rose's as they walked through the park.

'Yes, it's really me,' Rose smiled.

'Oh Rose, I want to know everything that happened. Everything. Leave no detail out.'

'Don't worry, I'll share it all,' Rose replied, but then she turned her face away and Poppy didn't see the worried look that clouded her expression.

'I've thought about you every day,' Poppy said. 'I even . . . well, I thought you might be dead. And now you're here, walking next to me, and we're taking you home. It feels like a dream, nothing seems real.'

'It's real enough, girls,' Sid said, pointing ahead to the terminus. 'Our tram's just arrived. Poppy, do you feel up to running?'

'I think I'll be all right,' Poppy said. She threaded her free arm through Sid's and the three of them ran as fast as they could to the tram. It was just like old times, and for a moment she was back in Ryhope as a girl, with Rose at her side and Sid as her best friend, and their whole lives ahead of them.

When they reached the terminus, Poppy noticed Rose's clothing for the first time. In their mad dash from Gray Road, she hadn't taken in much more than how ill her sister looked. She'd assumed Rose was employed as a maid for the Scurrfields, but her clothes suggested otherwise. She wore a long, heavy black coat with brass buttons. Her boots were polished and shined, and unlike Poppy's, they had no holes in them. She wore a pale blue scarf at her neck, tucked into her coat, and her hair, instead of falling lank around her face as it had done on the day when Poppy had spied her through the window, was tied up in a neat bun. As she stepped on to the tram, Poppy noticed a pretty ornament at the back of her head, decorated with tiny white stones.

On the journey to Ryhope, Poppy sat next to Rose in a double seat. The two of them held hands, and Rose laid her head on Poppy's shoulder and closed her eyes.

Sid leaned over from the seat behind. 'Don't you want to know how I got her out of the house?' he whispered, looking at Rose's sleeping face.

'Of course I do, but not yet. I just want to get her home and look after her.'

Poppy was struggling to process what had just happened; she couldn't believe that the woman sitting next to her was her little sister. She couldn't find the words to express what she was feeling – the enormity of it overwhelmed her, and she wanted nothing more than to get Rose settled in the barn. Sid had already offered to sleep on the floor and let Rose take his side of the bed. As the tram trundled its way through Grangetown, Poppy thought of what she'd give her to eat, for she needed feeding up. However, she only had two cauliflowers in the pantry, and she'd have to eke the soup out with more water than usual to make enough to feed Rose too.

The first thing she planned to do was set the fire and brew tea. Then they'd sit and talk; discover each other's pasts and make plans for the future. She'd collect the children from Maisie and Bill and introduce Rose to her twin nephews and baby niece. She'd leave her news about expecting another baby until later. She didn't want to bombard Rose with everything at once.

Her thoughts turned to all the fun they'd have in the coming days and weeks. Long walks up Tunstall Hill, picnics . . . maybe Rose could even walk the boys to school each morning come the autumn. With her sister helping around the barn, Poppy might be able to spend more time working at the Trewhitts'. The future was full of possibilities, making her mind race and her heart soar.

Meanwhile, Rose's head lolled against her shoulder; her sister was fast asleep.

She had to be nudged awake when the tram pulled into its stop on Ryhope village green. The three of them climbed down, and Rose looked around in astonishment.

'Why, the village hasn't changed a bit!' she exclaimed. 'The cattle market's still there. And there's the Trewhitts' shop and the Albion Inn. Do Hetty and Jack still run it?'

'Yes, they do,' Poppy replied. 'And they'll be shocked to see you back; everyone will be. But there's time for all of that in the days and weeks ahead.'

Rose breathed deeply as they walked across the green. 'The air smells wonderful, it's smoky from the coal pit and salty from the sea – bracing, exactly as I remember it,' she said.

'You'll not be saying that when you smell the pigs at the barn,' Sid replied.

'The barn?' Rose said, surprised.

'It's our home, Rose. Sid and I are married,' Poppy said.

Rose looked from her sister to Sid, and the skin around her mouth pulled tight as she smiled. 'Of course you are, of course! I always hoped your lives would entwine,' she said.

'Sid and his dad fixed the place up after Nellie died,' Poppy explained.

Rose stopped in her tracks. 'Nellie's dead?'

Poppy nodded. 'Come, there's so much to tell you.'

They walked through the cattle market and into the yard.

'Is Norman still alive?' Rose asked.

'Yes, he is,' Poppy replied. 'But he's recently sold the

farm to—' She stopped mid sentence. Ahead of them, waiting at the barn door, was the farm's new owner, Amos Bird.

'It's all right, Poppy, I'll deal with him.' Sid strode forward. 'You said you wanted a word, sir?' he said. He ran his hand through his hair.

Amos nodded at the barn. 'I won't beat around the bush. I'm a man who, when he's got something on his mind, comes right out and says it . . .'

Poppy wished he'd get to the point. If he was going to raise their rent, she needed to know. Her heart sank at the thought of having to hand over more money – they barely had enough to scrape by as it was. They'd had to leave Dan's chimney brush at the Scurrfields' house, and she knew Dan would be wanting payment if they couldn't retrieve it. That was even more money they'd have to find.

'. . . and so I won't keep you from your business any longer than necessary. I'm a busy man, Mr Lawson, and I'm sure you are too.'

Sid shuffled awkwardly and Poppy stepped forward and reached for his hand.

'What is it, sir?' she asked, unable to take the agony of suspense any longer.

'Why, it's the barn, Mrs Lawson. My barn.'

'Our home,' Poppy said.

Amos Bird puffed his chest out. 'Not any more, I'm afraid. Come the end of the month, I'll be bringing in a new flock of sheep and moving them into the barn.'

'But you can't throw us out!' Poppy cried.

Amos softened a little. 'That's why I'm giving you notice until the end of the month.'

'With all due respect, sir, that's not enough time for us to pack up and find somewhere else,' Sid said.

Amos waved his hand dismissively. 'I'm afraid that's not my concern. Norman tells me you're a pitman, Mr Lawson. Surely you can make use of a colliery house? Now, if you'll excuse me, I've got business to attend to in the farmhouse with Norman. Any rent owing to him should be given to me instead when you move out.'

'But, sir . . .' Poppy pleaded.

It was too late. Amos was walking away. Poppy turned to Sid with tears in her eyes.

'Oh Sid. What on earth are we going to do?'

Chapter Twenty-Seven

'Make a fire, Sid, so I can get the kettle on to make tea,' Poppy said once they were inside the barn.

As Sid busied himself at the fire, Rose looked around, taking it all in. 'Everything looks different and yet somehow the same,' she said softly. 'It smells familiar.'

'That'll be the pigs,' Sid laughed.

Poppy watched as Rose tentatively made her way around the barn. She saw her sister reach out and touch the walls, glance at the ceiling in awe and run her fingers along the banister, looking up the stairs.

'Sid and his dad did all of this?' she asked.

Poppy beamed with pride. 'Yes, they did. They turned it into a real home. But you heard what Amos just said. He wants us out at the end of the month, and we've nowhere else to go.'

'I'll get myself to the Miners' Welfare Hall once I've washed this soot off my face and put our name down for a pit house as soon as one becomes free,' Sid said.

Poppy knew they had no choice, although she was still worried about losing the peace and space of the barn. 'What if a house doesn't become available before the end of the month?' she asked. 'You know the only way to get one is to wait until some miner's carried out to his funeral in a box.'

'If we don't get one straight away, then we move in with Mam and Dad,' Sid said matter-of-factly. He looked at Rose. 'You too, Rose. It won't be easy, we'll be cramped in one room, three of us and the bairns, but it'll have to do for the time being.'

'Bairns?' Rose said, looking from Poppy to Sid.

'Twin boys, Harry and Sonny – they're three years old – and we've also got a six-month-old baby girl. I called her Emily Rose; Emily after Mam and Rose after you.'

'You gave your baby my name? I'm honoured,' Rose said. Her cheeks flushed and tears sprang to her eyes. 'Where are your bairns now?'

'They're with Sid's mam, Maisie, she dotes on them. I can't wait for you to meet them.'

Rose gripped tight to the banister. 'May I go up?' she asked.

'Of course, I'll come with you,' Poppy replied.

She followed Rose to the landing that had once been their room. Rose gasped when she saw the double bed with its eiderdown and blankets.

'You've got a real bed up here. How on earth did you manage that?'

'Sid and his dad hoisted it up, they worked really hard. They even fixed the holes in the roof and made the barn safe from the wind and rain.'

Rose pointed to a corner of the room. 'We slept there, on straw. Remember?'

'How could I forget?' Poppy replied. 'I still wake in

the night, you know, when I hear St Paul's bells chime, and the first thing that goes through my mind is . . .'

'. . . waking up Nellie the knocker-upper,' Rose finished.

Poppy walked to her sister and took her again in her arms. 'Oh Rose, I've missed you so much. I still can't believe you're here.'

'We've got so much catching-up to do. But I must ask something of you,' Rose said softly.

Poppy looked deep into her sister's eyes. 'You know you can ask me anything.'

'When I tell you what happened to me in the years I've been away, don't rush me, please.'

'I wouldn't dream of it,' Poppy said gently, holding her sister's hand. Then she remembered something. She dropped Rose's hand and walked to the corner of the room, where she knelt down and rummaged behind the bed. When she found what she was after, she held it tight in her hand, then sat on the bed and patted the eiderdown.

'Please, Rose, sit with me a while.'

Rose sank down and wrapped one long, thin arm around Poppy's waist. Poppy unfurled her hand to reveal a silver sixpence.

'I kept it all these years. I couldn't bear to spend it, or part with it.' She looked at her sister; tears were streaming down Rose's face. 'I'm sorry, Rose. I didn't mean to upset you.'

Rose squeezed Poppy's waist and kissed her on her cheek. 'I'm not upset. I'm stronger than I look, and when you get to know me again, you'll realise that,' she said. 'But today's been overwhelming, my head's spinning, and now this . . . Is it really the same sixpence that Scurrfield gave me, the one I handed to you to buy your boots the day I was taken away?'

'Yes, it is,' Poppy breathed.

Rose took the coin in her hand and turned it over, looking at the King's head and the coat of arms.

'I blamed myself every day for Scurrfield splitting us up,' Poppy said. 'If only I'd kept quiet, we might never have been parted. He would never have thrown this coin to decide which one of us to take. We could have been spared ten years of sorrow.'

Rose returned the coin gently to Poppy's hand. 'Listen to me, Poppy. You must never blame yourself. The only thing that matters is that we're together now. I'm shocked that you still have the coin, though. I hoped you'd buy boots so you could go to school. And with any money left over, I imagined you and Sid buying jam tarts at the Trewhitts' shop.'

'There were days I was so hungry I almost did spend it on food,' Poppy said. 'And there were days when I walked past the boot mender's shop and knew I could buy a second-hand pair of boots. But by then I was so behind at school, I didn't see the point of going back, and Nellie didn't care enough to send me. Besides, she needed me at her beck and call after you'd left. Of course, she hunted high and low for the sixpence – she wanted it for herself – but I was always one step ahead. I couldn't bear to lose it. It was my only link to you, and I had to keep it.'

The sisters embraced for a long time, until finally Rose pulled away.

'I'm dying for a cup of tea,' she said.

Poppy stood and placed the coin back under the bed. 'Come, let's go down to sit by the fire.'

Sid was putting his jacket on as the sisters walked downstairs. His face was now clean, and he'd even combed his hair.

'How do I look?' he asked. 'Think I'll pass muster when I go to ask for a house?'

Poppy walked to him and straightened his collar. 'You look fine,' she said. She gave him a kiss on the cheek. 'And good luck.'

'I'll be back later,' he said. 'Do you want me to collect the bairns from Mam and Dad's house on the way home?'

'No, I'll do it. Rose and I will go together. I want to have a word with your mam about Emily and find out how she's been. I'm worried sick about her.'

'Is something wrong with your baby?' Rose asked.

'Nothing for you to worry about. You've enough on your plate,' Poppy said.

Rose walked towards Poppy and Sid and took their hands in hers. 'I can't thank you both enough for what you've done for me today. Especially you, Sid, getting me out of that dreadful house. Fortunately James was out visiting a friend. If he'd been at home, he would've fought you. With his temper, I'm afraid you would have come off worse. You did well to distract the housekeeper, she always falls for flattery. On a more serious note, though, I want to say something to you both, and it's this: if your baby is ill, and you have a problem, then it's now my problem too. I'll do all I can to help. You've taken me into your home, welcomed me without question, and I'm here for you both whatever comes your way . . . *our* way. We're family.' She dropped their hands and took a step back. 'And I promise I'll never get in your way.'

Sid smiled at Rose. 'You always knew when to do and

say the right thing, even when we were kids.' Then he kissed Poppy on the cheek, before heading out of the barn. Poppy and Rose stood together at the door, as they'd done many times in the past. Poppy slid her arm around Rose's thin waist as they watched him go.

'And remember to ask for a house with a garden if you're given a choice. We need somewhere the boys can play,' Poppy called.

Sid turned and waved. 'I'll do my best, love.'

Poppy turned her face to the sun, then looked around the yard. Chickens pecked at her feet, and one tried to make its way into the barn.

'Shoo, chicken!' Rose said, stamping her foot to scare the bird. She looked at Poppy and rolled her eyes. 'Some things haven't changed while I've been away.'

Poppy felt her throat constrict and knew she was in danger of crying. Instead, she swallowed hard and guided Rose to a chair by the fire, then busied herself brewing a pot of strong tea. Pouring it into two mugs, she handed one to Rose.

'Do you have sugar?' Rose asked.

Poppy shook her head. 'No, we don't have much, I'm afraid.'

She took her own mug of tea and sat opposite her sister. Rose had removed her long, black coat now, and Poppy saw that she was wearing a pretty blue velvet dress. It looked too big for her skinny body, though. She wondered if it had once been a good fit. Its sleeves came all the way down to Rose's thin wrists, and the high neckline accentuated her shrunken face. But there could be no denying that it must have been expensive.

'I don't know where to begin,' Rose said softly, turning

her face away, looking instead at the dancing flames of the fire.

'Start at the beginning,' Poppy said.

Rose gripped her mug tightly, then slowly and hesitantly, she began to tell her tale.

Chapter Twenty-Eight

'You said earlier that you thought I'd died,' Rose began.

'We've all lived through a war, Rose. I know bombs were dropped on Sunderland, and I assumed the worst.'

'Did you keep up with the war news in the *Sunderland Echo*?'

Poppy shook her head. 'I still can't read,' she said sadly. 'I've heard of an evening class that's starting in a few weeks' time in the hall above the Co-op. It'll teach lasses like me how to read and write, but . . .' She shrugged. 'What do I need that for when Sid reads to me? He read your letter when it arrived at the church.'

'I hope Reverend Daye didn't pry too much. Or maybe there's a new vicar at the church now. I wasn't sure, you see. I didn't know if you'd still be at the barn, or where you'd be living. There was only one place I trusted to send the letter to, and that was St Paul's. I'm glad it found you. I don't know what I'd have done if it hadn't.'

Poppy decided to keep quiet about the stone she'd called Rose's grave for the last ten years, as she knew it would upset both of them too much.

'Yes, Reverend Daye is still our vicar, and he handed

me the letter last week. It was right to send it to the church; it found me as intended. You . . . you can read and write, yes?'

'Yes, I had a tutor who came to the house.'

'A tutor?' Poppy was astonished to hear this. 'You didn't go to school?'

'No. I wasn't allowed out of the house on my own. I took a risk posting the letter. It was the day of Malcolm Scurrfield's funeral, and Mrs Hutchins was with me. But while her back was turned, I slipped the envelope into the postbox and she never noticed a thing.'

Both girls broke into smiles.

'Oh Rose. All these years and I never knew where you were. I didn't hear a peep from you, not one single word. Nellie never told me anything about Scurrfield, although I pleaded and cried until I was hoarse. So yes, I thought you were dead. It was easier for me to think that way, to imagine you at peace.' She looked at Rose's long, bony fingers cradling her mug. 'Can I say something?'

'Since when did you need to ask? I'm your sister and I love you.' Rose's hand flew to her heart. 'Ask me anything you like, and I'll always be honest. There's no need for things to change.'

Poppy nodded. 'Then . . . are you well, Rose? Because if you don't mind me saying so, you don't look well at all. You're so thin, and your face . . .'

Rose dropped her gaze to the floor.

'I'm sorry, I didn't mean to upset you,' Poppy said quickly.

'I'm as well as can be,' Rose replied.

'What's that supposed to mean?'

She held her mug out. 'Pour me more tea, please. I

need to tell you everything that happened, right from the start.'

And so, as the bells of St Paul's chimed another hour away, Rose told Poppy what had happened after she'd been taken by Malcolm Scurrfield.

'Scurrfield and his wife treated me badly from the moment I stepped over the threshold of the house on Gray Road. The only decent thing they did for me was to arrange a tutor, who taught me to read and write. They made me memorise poetry to perform to their friends at dinner parties, and pretended to be proud of me, but once their friends had left, they didn't show me any affection at all. They gave me my own room in the house, but it was little more than a prison cell. I cried myself to sleep every night for a year because I missed you so much.'

'I did the same,' Poppy replied. 'What was Mrs Scurrfield like? I remember that on the day Scurrfield came to take you, he said something about you being a welcome Christmas gift for his wife. What was really going on?'

Rose took a sip of tea. 'Mrs Scurrfield's greatest wish had been to have a daughter, but she couldn't conceive any more children after her son was born. She tried for many years. Finally, in desperation, Mr Scurrfield replied to Nellie's advertisement in the *Sunderland Echo* offering us both for sale.'

'Do you really think she wanted both of us? I've often wondered about that, you know.'

Rose shrugged. 'I have no way of telling. I did ask her, many times, but she refused to answer. She always deferred to her husband, who spent a lot of time away. They didn't share a bed, and lived in separate rooms – it couldn't have been much of a marriage. Mrs Scurrfield died when I turned sixteen. I heard Mrs Hutchins gossiping with the cook one day, and I gathered that it was women's problems that took her, something to do with her womb. The Scurrfields were a cold couple in private, but when they held dinners and parties at Gray Road, I heard them talking brightly to their friends. On the surface, in public, they appeared the perfect couple, and as far as their friends knew, I was the chosen child they liked to show off.'

'Because of your beauty,' Poppy said. 'Not like me with my freckles and my hair that curls any way it wants.'

Rose tutted loudly. 'Oh, you and your freckles and curls. You're beautiful, Poppy, you always have been.'

Poppy waved her hand dismissively. 'Sorry, I've stopped you from telling your tale.'

Rose took another sip of tea, then continued. 'As I've said, the Scurrfields didn't show me any affection. I was ignored, left to my studies with my tutor, who came each day to the house. I was nothing more than a pretty party piece for them, a decoration to be wheeled out in front of their friends to help their standing in society circles.'

'What about James, their son?'

Rose faltered slightly before she carried on. 'He was sent away to school, returning home at Christmas and each summer. When the war began, he enlisted and was posted overseas. He was shipped home from the front in 1915 with an injury to his leg. Since he returned, he hasn't been in his right mind. He suffers terrible anger and frustration. But it's what he does with that anger . . .' Her eyes flickered to Poppy's face. 'He . . . takes it out on me.'

Poppy gasped. 'No!'

'After Mr Scurrfield died, James and I were the only people living in the house apart from Mrs Hutchins and Bertie, the cook. And they locked themselves away in the kitchen when his mood took a turn for the worse. I had no lock on the inside of my door, no way to defend myself, and I couldn't fight him off. And so I had no choice but to suffer.' Tears began to roll down Rose's face.

'You're safe, Rose, he can't hurt you again,' Poppy said. 'Me and Sid will look after you now. James will never find you.'

Rose raised her tear-stained face. 'I hope you're right,' she replied. 'You see, it wasn't just the beatings and bruises. James Scurrfield is a cruel man, Poppy. He deprived me of my freedom and locked me in the house. He humiliated me and punished me for speaking out against him. He deprived me of my basic needs, even controlled how much food I was allowed to eat, and he repeatedly put me down, saying I was worthless. And do you know what the worst thing was? I was beginning to believe he was right. So in answer to your question asking if I'm well, all I can say is that now I'm here in your home with you by my side, I hope to be well again in both body and mind.'

She pulled at the sleeve of her blue velvet dress. 'I wasn't always so thin, but James told Mrs Hutchins I was running to fat. She was so terrified of him, she did what he asked, pandering to his whims, afraid that if she went against him, he'd beat her the way he beat me.'

'She never offered to help you escape, not once?' Poppy asked.

'She's weak-willed, and anyway, we never got along. She puts up with the situation because he provides her with a roof over her head.'

'What about the cook you mentioned, Bertie? Couldn't he have helped you?'

'No. He's a drunk and a womaniser – he used to sneak women into his room in the basement. It suited him to keep his mouth shut about what went on in that house.'

'You suffered all of this for so long. It's unthinkable, so cruel.'

Rose took a deep breath before she continued. 'When I was taken from here, I was treated by Mrs Scurrfield like a new doll she'd won at the fair. She dressed me in fine clothes to parade me around Mowbray Park, and we took tea with her society friends. I saw parts of Sunderland I'd never heard of before, such as Ashbrooke and Roker. I was told to keep silent and only speak when I was spoken to, but I . . .' she faltered, 'I was rarely spoken to. I was lonely, Poppy, you can't imagine what it was like.

'After she died, I lived alone with Mr Scurrfield. I did try to escape, you know. I was always planning and thinking of ways to come back to you. I tried a couple of times to head to the tram stop when the side door was left open after deliveries were made. One time the fish man didn't close it properly and Mrs Hutchins was distracted. But somehow Mr Scurrfield always seemed to be one step ahead of me, and he found me and dragged me back. I think it made him feel less lonely knowing I was about. But I can only go on what I overheard Mrs Hutchins tell Bertie. I have no idea of the real reasons he kept me there after his wife died.'

'Oh Rose. How I wish you'd never had to suffer a minute of this.'

Rose sighed heavily. 'It's over now. I'm here and I'm safe and I couldn't be more grateful to you and Sid for getting me away.'

'How did Sid manage to get you out of the house?' Poppy asked. 'We haven't had time to talk about it.'

Rose set her mug on the hearth. 'Oh, he was wonderful, Poppy. He reminded me so much of the cheeky young Sid I once knew. Fortunately, James was away. I wouldn't be sitting here now if he'd been at home. Sid charmed the pants off Mrs Hutchins, flattering her so that she'd leave him alone to get on with his work. Of course, he had to make it sound as if he knew what he was doing, and he asked for dust sheets to put down around the fireplace in each room before he began. She helped him, of course, all the while lapping up his compliments. When he came into my room, I got the shock of my life, as you might imagine. He explained what was going on, but I didn't recognise him until he gave our secret wave. Anyway, I crept down the stairs once he gave me the nod that the coast was clear. He'd made sure he left the front door open – he'd placed a stone there to stop it closing – and I ran out. I don't know how I'll repay you for the kindness you've shown. Somehow, some day, I'll make it up to you both, I swear.'

'Oh Rose, I still can't believe you're here,' Poppy said. She got up and walked over to Rose, and once again they embraced. When she finally pulled away, she offered her sister more tea, but Rose declined.

'Do you know what I would really like?' she said, wiping her tears away.

Poppy gave a wry smile. 'I hope you're not going to

ask for cake, as we haven't any.'

'I'd love to meet your bairns.'

Poppy gathered up the mugs and placed them on the table. 'Are you sure you feel up to it after the day you've had? It's only a short walk to Maisie's house on Scotland Street, but you're bound to meet folk on the way. You'll attract comments if anyone recognises you.'

Rose threaded her bony arms into her coat sleeves. 'I want to see Ryhope again and feel at home as soon as I can,' she said. 'I can take whatever gossip comes my way. There's more to me now than meets the eye.'

'What's that supposed to mean?' Poppy asked, curious.

'It means that I'm not the same girl who left here ten years ago, Poppy. Our mam always said she named me Rose because of my beauty, but after everything I've been through in the last ten years, I know my looks have faded. This rose has grown thorns. I'm different now . . . I'm angry, if you must know. Angry at the Scurrfield men. It's going to take a long time for my burning toward them to subside.'

'Oh Rose, I want nothing more than to keep you from harm. You're my little sister. I only ever wanted the best for you, and now I feel it more than ever. Thank you for being so honest with me about everything.'

Rose looked away, unable to meet Poppy's trusting eyes.

Chapter Twenty-Nine

Poppy linked arms with Rose as they headed from the barn. There was no one in the yard, as the cattle market was closed, and the pens where Norman's pigs were offered for sale stood empty. Her stomach turned as she walked, thinking about what Amos had said. She crossed her fingers and hoped they wouldn't have to wait long for a pit house. Moving on to the colliery wasn't ideal, and certainly not what she wanted, but at least it would save them money on the rent.

When they reached the road, she turned right, the quickest way to reach Scotland Street.

'Could we go this way instead?' Rose asked, pointing left. 'I'd love to see our old school, for old times' sake.'

Poppy happily obliged, and they were soon standing at the gates, peering in at the stone building where they'd spent their school days.

'I always knew you and Sid would end up together, you know,' Rose said. 'You were inseparable when we were bairns. How did he propose?'

'He didn't; I did,' Poppy replied, smiling at the memory. 'Oh, he wanted to ask me – I knew he'd been trying to pluck up the courage to say the words for days – but you know Sid, he's no good at talking about his feelings. Or at least he wasn't back then; he's better now. Since we had the bairns, he's opened up more. So I asked him to marry me, he said yes, and here we are, with the twins and Emily and another on the way.'

'Another?' Rose cried, glancing at Poppy's stomach. 'Oh Poppy, that's wonderful news. You and Sid seem so happy together.'

'We are,' Poppy beamed.

Rose turned away.

'Rose, what is it?'

She turned back with tears in her eyes. 'I was never allowed outside of Gray Road without a chaperone,' she explained. There was a catch in her voice, and she kept her gaze on the ground as she spoke. 'There was never any chance of me meeting a boy who'd love me like Sid loves you. There was only . . .'

'James?' Poppy dared to ask.

Rose nodded. 'I'll tell you everything about him, but in my own time. However, I have to warn you that you'll learn harsh things, things you might not want to hear.'

Poppy was puzzled by this cryptic remark. She was about to press for more, but Rose was already striding away from the school.

'Come on, I want to meet your bairns,' she said.

Poppy decided there and then to let her sister tell her all about their years apart in her own time, as she'd promised she would.

'You mentioned Emily was poorly,' Rose said.

'She's not eating well or taking much milk. She's underweight, thin, and seems listless. Sid wants her seen by the doctor, but we haven't got the money.'

'Can't Sid's mam and dad loan you the cash?'

'No, they're as poor as we are. There's not much we can do apart from keep on trying to feed her, keep her warm and give her love.'

'I can't wait to meet her and the boys,' Rose said, squeezing Poppy's arm.

'Prepare yourself. The boys can be boisterous. As for Sid's mam, well, don't worry, she won't pry into where you've been all these years, and she's definitely not a gossip, not like some Ryhope women. There's a woman called Lil Mahone, up on the colliery bank, who goes out of her way to know everyone's business. She's always spreading gossip and tittle-tattle. If we ever see her, I'll point her out so you don't inadvertently tell her something you don't want shared around.'

'She sounds awful,' Rose said.

'Oh, she is, and best avoided.' Poppy pointed ahead. 'Here we are, Scotland Street. Maisie's house is the one at the end.'

Rose slowed her pace and looked around. 'Oh! I remember this street. I remember the trains that used to pass and all the smoke in the air.'

'They still run south to Durham and north to Newcastle. And then there are the trains from the pit carrying coal to the docks. It's a busy line. When a train rumbles past, Maisie's house seems to shake. I don't know how she puts up with it.'

When Poppy knocked at the door, it was Sid's dad Bill who opened it. Sonny was on his back, clinging on to him like a baby monkey, with his legs wrapped around his waist and his arms around his neck.

'Oh Sonny, get down from Grandad's back,' Poppy chided.

'Ah, he's all right, lass. We're just playing, aren't we, Sonny?'

Bill stepped to one side to allow them to enter. 'Is this her?' he said abruptly, eyeing Rose. 'Maisie said you were off to find your sister.'

Sonny jumped down from Bill's back and ran along the hall.

'Yes, this is Rose,' Poppy replied.

'Nice to meet you, Mr Lawson,' Rose said politely.

'Can't say I remember you from when you were a girl,' Bill said, eyeing her cautiously. 'I knew Poppy, of course, she was all our Sid used to talk about. Come in, please, both of you. I'll leave you with Maisie, she'll put the kettle on. I'm off out. I can't be doing with women's talk, and I dare say you three will have a lot of talking to do.'

As Poppy and Rose made their way along the hall into the small kitchen, they heard the front door close as Bill left the house.

'Come on, let me introduce you to Maisie. Do you remember her?'

But before Rose could reply, Harry came running along the hall, followed by Sonny.

'Mam! Mam!'

Poppy bent down and kissed both boys on the cheek, then straightened up and stepped into the kitchen.

Maisie was sitting at the table with Emily in her arms. A man was sitting next to her, someone Poppy didn't recognise.

'This is a friend of Bill's, Arthur Mason,' Maisie said,

introducing him. 'He called in for a word with Bill.'

Arthur was a good-looking man, Poppy noticed. He was slim, with fair hair and a pleasant, open face. He shot his hand out towards her and she shook it, noting his firm grip.

'Arthur, this is Poppy, our Sid's wife,' Maisie said.

'Good to meet you,' Arthur said.

Then Maisie's gaze flickered to Rose and she stopped dead, her mouth hanging open in shock.

'Rose? Is that really you?'

'It's her all right,' Poppy said proudly. She gently placed her hand in the small of her sister's back, nudging her to take a step forward.

'Yes, it's me, Mrs Lawson. I'm pleased to meet you.'

Maisie snapped her mouth shut. 'My word, lass. If you don't mind me saying so, you could do with feeding up. Sorry . . . I forgot my manners there, but I don't know when I've seen such a thin face before.' She turned to Poppy. 'Is she all right?'

It was Rose who replied. 'Yes, I'm just a little under-weight, that's all,' she said quickly. 'I'm afraid I can't remember you, Mrs Lawson. It's been a very long time, as you know. I was just a child when I left Ryhope. I remember Sid, of course. And I can't tell you how wonderful it is to find out that he's my brother-in-law.'

'Call me Maisie, lass,' Maisie replied. 'There's no need for Mrs Lawson, you're part of our family now.'

When Maisie finally took her eyes off Rose, she turned to Arthur. 'Arthur, this is Poppy's sister, Rose. She's returned to the village after living away. You won't know her from when she was here before, as you're a relative newcomer to Ryhope.'

Poppy watched Rose and Arthur make eye contact, and saw Arthur take in the sight of her sister. Instead of being repulsed by Rose's thin face and jutting cheekbones, he seemed entranced by the way she looked. Rose held out her hand, and Arthur held it in his for a few seconds longer than necessary. He kept his eyes firmly on her as he replied to Maisie's comment. 'You're right, I don't remember her. For if we had met before, I don't think I'd have ever forgotten such a unique face.'

Poppy looked at Rose and saw her pale, waxy cheeks blush pink.

'Arthur was just about to leave,' Maisie said tersely. Poppy noticed the change in her tone and wondered if she'd also noticed how the pair had reacted to one other in their brief exchange. 'He's got to get back home to his wife.'

He was married. That was settled then, Poppy thought. Whatever attraction had passed between Arthur and Rose couldn't go any further.

Arthur stood, doffed his cap and headed out of the door, but not before he turned to look at Rose. And in that instant, Poppy saw that her sister was smiling shyly. She silently implored Rose not to have her head turned by a married man, and was relieved when she heard the front door close behind him.

'May I hold your baby?' Rose asked.

Poppy nodded, and watched with a lump in her throat as Rose sat next to her mother-in-law, who transferred Emily to her.

'Rose, meet your niece, Emily,' she said. 'And these two little horrors are Harry and Sonny. Boys, say hello to your aunt Rose.'

Harry and Sonny were hiding behind her, peeping shyly out from either side of her skirt.

'They're confused, poor loves,' Poppy said. 'The boys have been visiting the churchyard with me each week where we sat beside the stone I called your grave. I'm going to have to do some explaining to them both later.'

Rose looked from one boy to the other and back again, taking in their identical features.

'Oh my word, it's like looking at Sid as a boy, twice over!' she exclaimed, her face breaking into a smile. 'You must have handled the same teapot as another woman while you were pregnant.'

Poppy gave her a quizzical look. 'What on earth are you talking about?'

Rose tutted. 'Oh, you must remember, it was one of Mam's old wives' tales. She always said that if two women handled the same teapot, one of them would give birth to twins.'

'Mam quoted a lot of old wives' tales and none of them made sense,' Poppy laughed, remembering the mustard she'd once spread on her freckles. She gently pulled her boys from behind her skirt to face Rose. 'They're not usually so quiet and shy,' she explained.

'I expect I'll take some getting used to,' Rose said.

Poppy watched her sister cradle Emily. There was a look of pure joy on her face; her eyes came alive and her expression softened. And in that moment, Poppy saw something she hadn't seen all day. She saw the old Rose, the pretty girl she'd once been. Her beauty was hidden under taut, waxy skin, but it was definitely there. The old Rose was there in the light in her eyes, in the way that love and affection poured from her to the child. And then

Emily began to wriggle, kicking her feet, and a smile made its way to her tiny mouth.

'That's the most animated she's been all day,' Maisie said approvingly. 'It might be a good time to try feeding her again.'

'I'll get the milk and warm it by the fire,' Poppy said.

Once the milk was heated and the bottle filled, Harry and Sonny crept forward and sat on the floor at Rose's feet, staring up at her.

'Could I feed her?' Rose asked.

Poppy had been ready to feed Emily herself, wanting nothing more than to make the most of this moment with her child so animated and happy. But she didn't want to refuse Rose, for her sister looked radiant with the baby in her arms.

'Please?' Rose said.

Poppy handed the bottle over. 'Do you know what to do?' she said.

But she needn't have worried, for Rose seemed to know instinctively. Holding the child correctly, she gently raised the bottle, and Emily began to drink.

Chapter Thirty

Poppy gaped in astonishment. 'Well, would you just look at that,' she exclaimed. 'I've not seen Emily take so much milk in weeks. I hope it's the start of a turnaround for her. The poor thing needs feeding up.'

Rose looked up at her. 'Both Emily . . . and me,' she said.

Poppy laid her hand on her sister's shoulder. 'I'll look after you, Rose.'

'Where's our Sid got to?' Maisie asked.

Poppy filled her in on Amos Bird wanting them out of the barn at the end of the month.

'But he can't throw you out, you've got the bairns to think about,' Maisie cried.

'It's all right, I'm sure Sid will be doing his best trying to get us a pit house.'

'It all depends on whether there's one free,' Maisie said cautiously, glancing around her small kitchen. 'If you have to wait, you could always move in with me and Bill for a while.' Maisie scratched her head. 'Mind you, I've got no idea where you'd all sleep. There's the box room upstairs, but you wouldn't all fit. The bairns could sleep

211

down here with Rose, and you and Sid could sleep upstairs.'

'Thanks for the offer, Maisie, but I'm hoping it won't come to that. I've told Sid to ask for a house with a garden, but to be honest, we'll have to take what's offered.'

Maisie tapped her fingers on her chin, thinking. 'Sally Winter moved out of her house on Tunstall Street not long ago. As far as I know, no one's moved in there yet.'

'Why did she move out? Did her husband retire?'

'No, lass, he died underground, had a heart attack at work while hewing coal. Ryhope Coal Company let Sally stay on while she mourned and arranged his funeral, but after that they turned her out with a small compensation. The last I heard was that she'd gone to live with her sister in Seaham.'

'That's a bit harsh, forcing her out of her home,' Poppy said.

Maisie shrugged. 'It's the way the coal company works. Those pit houses were built for miners to live in, you know the rules. If you do get a house, at least you'll not need to pay rent. That'll give you and Sid a few extra bob.'

Poppy sat opposite Rose, pleased to see that Emily had drunk almost all of the milk. She gently stroked Rose's arm. 'Thank you, my sister,' she said.

Rose looked at her. 'Do you know how good it feels to be called that again?'

Poppy felt tears prick her eyes. 'It feels good to say it. Come, we should get home to the barn. Sid might be waiting for us with news, and I'll need to start cooking tea. It's just cauliflower soup and bread.'

Rose laid a bony hand on Poppy's arm. 'I can't think

of anything better than to sit down to eat with you, Sid and the bairns. I've dreamed of days like this so many times over the last ten years.'

'We're a family now. Today's the first of many we'll eat together.'

Poppy pulled her blanket around her and reached down to take Emily from Rose.

'Could I carry her?' Rose asked.

Poppy was heartened by this. 'Of course you can. Keep her tight to your chest inside your coat. She needs to stay warm.'

Rose stood, and with Poppy's help positioned the baby correctly for the short walk back to the barn.

'Sonny, Harry, come on,' Poppy called. The boys kissed Maisie goodbye and walked ahead of Poppy and Rose to the street.

On the short walk to the farm, they passed folk who stared at Rose and whispered.

'It can't be Poppy's sister, can it? I thought she was dead,' they said.

'She's so thin, she looks as if she might be dying,' others murmured.

Poppy's stomach rumbled with hunger. She was desperate to return to Sid and was in no mood to stop and tell folk what had happened to Rose. Besides, it was Rose's business and only she should decide how much she wanted to share of her past. She knew that folk would talk, as Ryhope was a small village where news travelled fast. The gossip about Rose's return, and how emaciated she looked, was bound to spread like wildfire.

'I'm sorry that people are whispering about you already,' she said.

'I'm just going to have to get used to it, aren't I?' Rose replied with a wry smile. 'In fact, there's a couple of people I'd love to talk to right now, if it's all right with you.'

Poppy looked at her. 'Who?' she asked, puzzled.

Rose nodded across the green to the Trewhitts' shop. 'Ella and Ambrose. Are they still alive?'

'Just about,' Poppy laughed. 'You might give old Ambrose a scare when he sees you, though, so be gentle. Ella's got problems with her hands – she can't hold things as well as she could. Ambrose does all the work these days while she sits on a stool behind the counter, talking to their customers.'

'Could we go and see them now?' Rose asked.

'Now? But Sid will be waiting at the barn . . . I need to know what's happening about a pit house.'

'Go and talk to him, then. I'm sure the two of you will need to speak in private about your living arrangements now you've got me to accommodate. Or I could always move in with . . .' Rose thought for a moment. 'Wasn't there a home in Ryhope for girls with nowhere to go? It was run by a woman . . . Mrs Gilson?'

'Miss Gilbey,' Poppy replied. 'I was always terrified of her when we were younger. But I soon found out that she's not as scary as she looks, although she still dresses from head to toe in black and rarely cracks a smile. Her home is still there, you know. I lived with her after Nellie died, before I married Sid. It wasn't a bad life. I made friends there, girls who've moved away from the village now. I used to wonder how our lives might have turned out if we'd been taken in by Miss Gilbey instead of Nellie. But I wouldn't dream of letting you live anywhere other than with us now. I never want to let you out of my sight again.'

'Look, Poppy. Go and speak to Sid while I reunite with the Trewhitts. I'll not be long talking to them. Here, do you want to take Emily?'

Poppy took the baby, but the moment Emily was in her arms, she began to wail. Poppy tried shushing her and gently rocking her, but nothing seemed to work.

'I think she likes being with you more than me,' she said with concern.

'Then please let me take her. I'll calm her down and you can walk back to the barn.'

Poppy had been ready to take Emily home, knowing she could quieten her once she was there. But while she'd been speaking to Rose, Harry and Sonny had been chasing each other around an oak tree on the green. Harry had fallen and grazed his knee and was now sobbing his heart out. Poppy looked from her sobbing boy to her crying baby.

'Are you sure you don't mind?' she said. 'You've just arrived back here and now I feel that I'm taking you for granted, asking you to look after the baby. But you can see how I'm fixed. You're an extra pair of hands sent from heaven above. I'll get the boys home and bathe Harry's knee.'

She handed Emily back to Rose, who cooed at the baby, gently rocking her to sleep.

'How on earth do you do that?' Poppy said, amazed. 'You're a calming influence on her. Promise me that you won't be long at the Trewhitts'. I want you back in the barn so we can talk tonight with Sid once the boys have gone to bed.'

'I'll be half an hour, tops,' Rose said. She cradled Emily to her chest, then walked in the direction of the shop.

Poppy held hands with her boys as she headed back to the barn. As she'd guessed, Sid was there already. 'Harry, sit at the table and I'll mend your poorly knee,' she ordered.

As she busied herself getting water and a cloth to clean her son's wound, she looked at Sid. 'What happened at the Miners' Welfare Hall, what did they say?'

Sid looked up. 'They've given us Bob Winter's old house, on Tunstall Street,' he said. 'We can move in the same day we leave here. Bob died after a heart attack at the pit, poor fella.'

'Your mam told me about him earlier,' Poppy replied. 'Give me a minute while I sort Harry's knee – he fell over and scraped it. He'll be all right, he's just making a mountain out of a molehill. You know what he's like.'

'Where's Rose? And the baby?' Sid asked.

'Rose has taken Emily to see the Trewhitts. Oh, you should have seen it, Sid. She got Emily to drink almost a full bottle of milk at your mam's house. And Emily was kicking her legs and smiling and gurgling.'

Sid sighed with relief. 'I'm pleased to hear it. Has Rose said much about her life at Gray Road?'

'She's said little so far. We need to let her settle in with us before we start asking questions. I don't want her to feel like we're prying.'

Poppy tended to Harry's knee, then sat opposite Sid by the fire. 'Well, come on then, tell me. What's the house on Tunstall Street like? Did you see it?'

Sid's face dropped. 'Oh, I saw it,' he said glumly. 'Tunstall Street's as bad as all the other pit lanes. Limestone houses squashed together in tight rows. It'll be noisy up there from the pit and the trains. Noisy and dirty and . . .' he glanced at the twins, 'there's nowhere for our bairns to run free.'

'No garden?' Poppy said, dismayed.

'There's a patch of earth at the front that looks as if it hasn't been turned over in years. Some of the miners have got vegetables growing. I reckon if I ask Dad for help we might be able to do the same, although it's going to be hard work.'

'Can we refuse the house and wait for something better?' she asked, but Sid shook his head.

'No, it's either take this one or move in with Mam and Dad until who knows when. I say we take it and make the best of it.'

'We've got no choice, have we?' Poppy said.

Sid's shoulders dropped and he looked around the barn. 'I never thought for one minute I'd miss this old place. It's just a barn on a farm with pigs at the front and chickens at the door. Mind you, we had fresh eggs any time we wanted them although we had to pay for them, fresh veg from Norman, sometimes free if he was feeling generous, and each Christmas he offered us a nice piece of ham. The farm might stink to high heaven, but it's home. Our home. And I'm going to miss it a lot.'

Poppy felt a pain in her stomach and gasped.

'What is it?' Sid asked, concerned.

'Just a twinge from the baby, making itself felt. Anyway, listen to us, getting sentimental about an old barn. It's nothing more than wooden beams and stone floors. At least we'll have our own netty on Tunstall Street.'

Sid shook his head. 'I'm afraid not, Pops. The netty's

in the back lane. There are two netties behind Tunstall Street, and they're shared by everyone who lives there. The women take turns to clean them after the night-soil men take the worst away.'

'No, Sid, I can't clean up other people's muck; I won't.'

'You're going to have to, love. We're going to have to grit our teeth and get on with it.'

'What about water taps?'

'They're in the back lane too. The fella I spoke to in the Miners' Welfare Hall told me that lasses like to talk at the taps, it's somewhere for them to gather. You might make new friends there.'

'Well, I'll have Rose to talk to, but I'll do what I can. I'll make the house nice, I'll keep it clean, and with the little extra money we'll have because of not paying rent, we should be able to manage. Mind you, we'll have this one to feed,' Poppy patted her stomach, 'and Rose too. Although I'm sure she'll go looking for a job as soon as she settles in.'

Poppy and Sid talked for over an hour about the house, planning their new life and how they'd include Rose. They were lost in their plans for the future, and the sound of the bells of St Paul's took them both by surprise. They hadn't realised they'd been talking so long.

'What time's Rose coming back with the bairn, Pops? I'm starving for my tea.'

A worried look clouded Poppy's face. 'She said she'd only be half an hour. She must have got talking to the Trewhitts and time's run away with her, just like it's done to us. Why don't you go and fetch her, and I'll start making the soup.'

Sid sauntered from the barn with his hands in his

pockets. Poppy tore the cauliflowers into florets, using the leaves too, and added more water than usual to eke the soup out so there was enough to feed Rose. When she heard the barn door, she swung around, fully expecting to see Sid with Rose and Emily. But Sid was on his own, puffing and panting and red in the face.

'What's happened?' she asked.

He sank into a chair at the table. 'I went to the Trewhitts' to get her, just like you said.' He raised his eyes to Poppy. 'But they said they hadn't seen her. She didn't go to their shop, Pops. Rose has gone missing, and she's taken Emily with her.'

Chapter Thirty-One

'When I couldn't find Rose at the Trewhitts', I ran all the way to St Paul's,' Sid explained. 'I thought she might be there, but the church was closed and there was no one in the churchyard. Then I ran to the school, and even halfway down the beach road, but there was no sign of her anywhere.'

Poppy's heart was beating wildly as she tried to make sense of it. 'But she can't just have disappeared. She must be somewhere. Why would she disappear when she's only just returned?' And then for one awful moment, she had a dreadful thought. 'You don't think . . . No, it can't be possible . . . can it?'

'What, love?'

'What if James Scurrfield has come for her and taken her? And Emily too. Oh Sid. What if he's got them and he's taking them back to Gray Road?'

Sid laid his hands squarely on Poppy's shoulders. 'Don't be daft, lass. Scurrfield can't possibly know where she is. You're not thinking straight. This has come as a shock. We've got to work out where she might be, where she would have gone.'

Poppy stepped away from him and began pacing the floor. 'I can't believe she's done this to us, Sid. I don't know what to say.'

'Think, Poppy, think,' Sid urged. 'Did she say anything to you today about somewhere she's been longing to visit in all the time she's lived away?'

Poppy racked her brains but couldn't for the life of her remember Rose saying such a thing.

'Come on, Pops, there must be somewhere you know that she loves above all other places in Ryhope.'

And then it came to her in an instant. She knew exactly where Rose would be. She tore her pinny off and handed the wooden spoon to Sid. 'Here, stir the soup until it boils, then feed yourself and the boys. I'll eat when I come back.'

She ran from the barn, leaving Sid in shock. 'Poppy, where are you going?' he yelled, but Poppy was already in the yard and his question disappeared behind her.

She ran as fast as she could, past the village green, the school and the church. Past the Grand Electric cinema and the police station, up the colliery bank to the pit. A stitch in her side slowed her down and she ended up gasping for breath. She knew that if Sid was with her, he'd be telling her to take it easy, to think of the baby inside her, but all she could think about was Emily and Rose.

By the time she reached her destination, the evening sky was beginning to turn pink from the sunset behind Tunstall Hill. She crossed her fingers as she climbed. For if she was wrong, if Rose wasn't there, she didn't know what she would do. But when she reached the peak, she saw the back of a woman's head, her body wrapped in a black coat, and knew in an instant that she'd guessed her sister's place of refuge correctly.

Rose was sitting with her back against a tree, looking out over Ryhope, down to the sea. And there in her arms was Emily. A rush of relief went through Poppy, so overwhelming that she thought she might faint. She pressed her feet hard against the ground and took a deep breath. Then she slowly walked towards her sister. When she reached her, she sank to the grass at her side. She knew that whatever Rose's reasons were for running off with the child, she had to handle the situation carefully. She wondered how much more there was to Rose's story than she'd so far revealed, and her earlier cryptic remarks went through her mind.

The sisters sat together under the tree without speaking, looking out over the village, where street lights were being lit, creating a gentle glow.

'We always loved it up here when we were girls,' Poppy said eventually.

Rose shifted a little, as if realising for the first time that she wasn't alone. 'It was always my favourite place,' she replied softly.

'Do you remember the picnics we had with Mam and Dad when we were little?' Poppy asked. When Rose didn't answer, Poppy turned towards her and saw tears streaming down her face. 'Rose, may I take my baby?' she asked.

Rose handed Emily over without hesitation.

'Rose . . .' Poppy tried again. 'What is it that drove you here with my child? What is it you're not telling me?'

Rose turned her tear-stained face to her sister. 'You always knew when I was holding something back,' she said. 'I'm sorry, Poppy. I couldn't help it. When I held

Emily in my arms today, when I saw her tiny face, it brought such an intense reaction, a powerful emotion, I don't know how to explain it.'

'Please try,' Poppy said.

Rose sniffed back her tears, then slowly began to speak.

'James . . .' She swallowed and closed her eyes, as if the words were too difficult. 'He and I . . . had a child.'

Poppy gasped. Above them, the sky began to darken. There was silence for a few moments before Rose spoke again.

'The baby died two weeks after he was born.'

Poppy closed her eyes and felt tears threaten to fall. They sat in silence for a while.

'I'm so sorry, Rose,' she said at last. 'I can't imagine . . .'

'James forced himself on me,' Rose continued flatly. Tears streamed down her face and she buried her head in her hands.

Poppy laid her free arm around her sister's shoulders. When Rose's tears were no more, she sat up straight and looked Poppy in the eye.

'That's what I meant when I told you that I'm stronger than I look. I've suffered the loss of my child. I've suffered . . .' she faltered before she spat the name out, 'James. I'm not the same innocent girl I was when I lived here before. My heart has been hardened. Your little sister isn't the person you thought you knew.'

'Oh Rose, you're still my sister. I still love you, now more than ever, after everything you've been through.'

Rose gazed out to sea as she continued. 'Holding Emily and seeing her eyes looking up into mine, feeling a rush of love towards her, it was all-consuming. I didn't know what I was doing or feeling, I wasn't in my right mind. I needed to get away. I'm sorry, Poppy. Will you ever forgive me?'

Poppy opened her mouth to say something, but snapped it closed when Rose spoke again.

'I'm scared that James will come looking for me. When I wrote my letter to you, I was desperate to escape. He was cruel and abusive, my captor. He kept me as a possession in that house and forced me to sleep with him. But I always longed to be free. I was entirely terrified of him, and now I'll always be looking over my shoulder. You see, Poppy, I know that if he finds me, he'll hurt me or take me by force back to that prison of a house.'

'Listen to me, Rose. Sid and I will keep you safe,' Poppy said firmly. 'And of course I forgive you for taking Emily. As for James, how would he even find out where you've gone? Did he know you came from Ryhope when you were a child? Does he have the address of the barn?'

'He has his father's papers, and Malcolm Scurrfield never threw anything away. They'll still be in his study.'

Poppy thought this over. If proof existed, something that connected Rose to Ryhope, there was every possibility that James would be able to find her. All he had to do was turn up in Ryhope and ask the first person he saw. And if that person couldn't help, he'd simply need to ask the next person, then the next. Ryhope was a tight-knit community where everyone knew everyone's business and gossip was spread by busybodies like Lil Mahone. Rose's return to the village after ten years away was news that would spread like wildfire now she'd been seen with Poppy. James would soon find someone who knew Rose's story and would point him in her direction. However,

Poppy kept this to herself, for she didn't want to cause her sister more distress.

'Will you come back to the barn, Rose? I've left Sid in charge of the soup. Heaven knows what it'll be like. He's no cook, that's for sure.'

A wry smile made its way to Rose's lips. 'Yes, and I promise I'll never run away again. Today has been overwhelming. My emotions got the better of me.'

'Emily's safe, and you will be too,' Poppy replied. 'But please, never take her again.'

'I promise,' Rose replied.

Rose stood, then helped Poppy up as she held tight to her daughter. And then together the sisters walked back down Tunstall Hill.

In bed that night, Poppy snuggled up to Sid and told him all about Rose and James and the child they'd had who had died.

'She's worried he'll come looking for her. There's a possibility he might find her, if he's determined enough.'

'We'll be moving to the pit house soon,' Sid said. 'It might make it harder for him if he does come to Ryhope, as no one knows us on the colliery bank.'

'Sid . . . ?'

'Yes, Pops?'

'Are you sure you don't mind Rose living with us in the new house? From what you've told me, it sounds like a small space. There'll be little privacy for us and it's going to be cramped.'

Sid tenderly stroked Poppy's curly hair. 'Of course I don't mind. Rose is family, it's as simple as that, and we must all stick together.'

'You're a good man, Sid Lawson,' Poppy whispered.

'And you're a wonderful woman, Pops.'

Poppy closed her eyes and fell into a troubled sleep as the bells of St Paul's chimed.

As the days went by, Poppy was grateful for the summer warmth, which meant she could leave the barn door open and sit in the yard with her boys playing around her. During those days she kept a watchful eye on Rose. She noticed her sister's face starting to lose its waxy hue as the sun and fresh air worked wonders on her, and her cheeks took on a healthy glow. She was still dreadfully thin, but her features were losing their hardness and her eyes began to sparkle and shine. She wore her long dark hair tied at the nape of her neck with the beautiful ornament with its tiny white stones. She seemed happy to go for long walks around the village on her own, as content in her own company as she was with Poppy at the barn.

The twins had been suspicious of her at first, afraid to speak to her, curious about who she was, where she'd come from and why she was living with them. But after Poppy explained to them, in gentle terms, that Rose had been away but had now returned home it had only taken a few days for Rose to win them round. Even Sid seemed pleased to have her living with them once he'd got over the shock of her disappearing with Emily. Rose had apologised profusely and Sid had listened patiently to her explanation. He seemed to particularly enjoy chatting to her by the fire of an evening, as she and Poppy darned socks or mended clothes. The three of them spent many nights reminiscing about years gone by when they were children at the village school. However, there was still a dark cloud hanging over them all, as Amos Bird often called by to remind Poppy and Sid that he wanted them out of the barn.

When Rose was feeling strong enough and settled after a few days at the barn, she announced to Poppy that she wanted to visit the Trewhitts' shop. Poppy was pleased to hear this and sent her off with her good wishes. When Rose returned later that day, Poppy wanted to know all the details of how Ambrose and Ella had reacted to seeing her again.

'Poor Ambrose went as white as a sheet when I walked through the door,' Rose said. 'He clutched his heart and staggered sideways. Ella sat rigid on her stool behind the counter, with her mouth hanging open. Neither of them could believe it was me, even though they'd already heard the news from Lil Mahone.'

'Did they recognise you straight away?'

'Ella did. I remember she's always been sharp, and she missed little when we were young. Ambrose took more persuading that I was who I said I was, so I told him about the day on the beach when he and Michael rescued you, me and Sid from the sea. Once he knew it was me, he took me in his arms and cried. He and Ella made such a fuss of me, Poppy. Ella sent Ambrose to the back room to brew a pot of tea, and they even fetched a plate of Ambrose's jam tarts, still warm from the oven, and we ate them with the tea. It was like stepping back in time. The Trewhitts and their jam tarts, eh? Some things never change.'

'What did you tell them? I mean, they must have asked where you'd been.'

'I didn't tell them the truth, put it that way,' Rose

explained. 'There's no need for them, or anyone in Ryhope, to know. It'd only upset them if I told them about Malcolm Scurrfield and James. I lied and said I'd lived with a good family and had been treated well. I told them I was back in Ryhope because you needed help with the bairns now you were in the family way again and moving into a new house. Oh, and Ella said I looked like I needed feeding up, and she gave me these . . .' Rose brought a paper bag to the table and opened it. Poppy peered inside and saw five perfectly round, golden jam tarts filled with ruby-red jam.

The following morning, after Sid left for work, Poppy asked Rose if she'd like to walk to Tunstall Street so they could inspect their new home.

'Sid says we can collect the key from the Miners' Welfare Hall and see what's what. The house might need cleaning from top to bottom. And if we have a look now, at least we know what we're letting ourselves in for before we move in.'

As they left the village behind and walked up the colliery bank, Rose held hands with Harry and Sonny, while Poppy carried the baby. When they reached the Miners' Welfare Hall, Poppy went inside, leaving Rose and the boys by the door. For a split second – and Poppy hated herself for thinking it – a dreadful thought passed through her mind that when she returned to the street, her sister would have disappeared again. She shook her head to dismiss it, but was surprised how relieved she was when she headed outside to find Rose and the twins still there.

She jangled the key for everyone to see. 'Come on, let's go and see our new house.'

Chapter Thirty-Two

Poppy handed Emily to Rose, then slid the key into the lock and swung the door open. The first thing that hit her was the rotten, pungent smell. She put her hand over her nose to block out the stench. The dark, gloomy room was dominated by a large black hearth and fireplace. The walls were bare, and there were no floor coverings, no curtains at the window, nothing to make the house feel like a home.

'Mrs Winter made sure she took everything when she left,' she muttered under her breath.

'Get the window open. It needs airing out,' Rose called.

Poppy went to the window, which looked out over a dirty cobbled lane at the back. There were no trees around the house, not like at the barn, which was close to the green. The view from the window was made up of hard angles of walls and rooftops.

'What on earth is that dreadful smell?' Poppy said, looking around. She kicked against the stone floor, where clods of earth had dried. 'Whatever it is, it stinks,' she moaned. 'Cover Emily's nose to keep the worst of it away.'

Rose did as Poppy instructed. Meanwhile, Harry and Sonny looked around, holding hands, unsure. Poppy beamed at them with the brightest smile she could manage. 'Well, what do you think of your new home?'

Sonny's bottom lip began to tremble, and Harry dropped his gaze to the floor. Poppy and Rose exchanged a worried look.

'Is this all there is to the downstairs, just this kitchen?' Poppy wondered.

She headed to a wooden door in the corner of the room and pulled it open. Beyond was a small room with another window. A further door led out to a yard, where a large rusty hook was attached to the wall. This was where their tin bath would hang. The tiny yard was their only outside space, the place where her boys would play, where she and Rose would sit on a summer's day, where her washing would dry in the sun. She spun around and looked at Rose, who seemed surprised and disappointed at how small the house was.

'Perhaps it's better upstairs,' she suggested hopefully.

Poppy headed to the bottom of the stairs and looked up. Then, with a deep breath, she gripped the handrail and started to climb, noticing as she went that it was pitted with woodworm. Harry and Sonny followed, still holding hands, and Rose brought up the rear, cradling Emily. At the top of the stairs was a small landing, with two doors leading off. Poppy pushed the first door and let it swing open. She dreaded entering, unsure of what she would find. But when she stepped inside, she was pleased to see that the room was filled with sunlight, struggling in through a grimy window. The floor was bare, laid with boards, but the space was bigger than she'd expected. 'It's all right, come in,' she called.

'Not as bad as downstairs,' Rose agreed, looking around.

Poppy returned to the landing and opened the door to the second room. This one overlooked the back lane and was smaller, with a square window. She walked to the window and looked left and right along the cobbled lane. She spotted one of the water taps that Sid had told her about. This was where she'd collect water to feed and bath her family, wash clothes and pots and pans. Further along she saw a dilapidated outhouse, one of the dreaded shared netties, and a shiver ran down her spine. She wasn't looking forward to cleaning up other folks' muck. Life was going to be different living on the pit lane.

A noise behind her pulled her from her reverie. She turned to see Rose walking into the room. Across the landing, she saw Harry and Sonny sitting on the floor of the front bedroom, drawing patterns with their fingers in the dust.

'What do you think?' Rose asked.

'I think I haven't any choice but to make the most of it,' Poppy said. She reached for Emily, and Rose handed her over. 'I'm going to clean every inch of it before we move in. I've got to get rid of that smell.' She beckoned Rose to the window. 'Just look at this dreadful view.'

Rose edged to the window and looked down on the cobbled lane.

'Not as pretty as the village green, is it?' Poppy asked.

Rose was silent for a moment, and when she spoke, her voice was low, and she sounded distant and sad. 'It's better than looking out at Belle Vue.'

Her words broke Poppy's heart. She laid her arm around Rose's shoulder and gently kissed her on her cheek.

'It'll be a fresh start for us all,' she said softly.

They stood in silence a while, looking out of the window, taking in the weeds, the water taps and the netties.

'Sid reckons he might be able to get a garden going at the front, with his dad's help, like,' Poppy said with forced brightness.

Rose raised her eyebrows in mock surprise. 'What? He'll have more luck prospecting for gold than turning that piece of barren land into a garden.'

Poppy laughed out loud, then turned to Rose as past memories began to surface. 'Do you remember our garden when we were girls? Dad used to grow raspberry bushes.'

Rose shook her head. 'No, I don't remember raspberries, but I remember the roses Dad grew for Mam. That's how she gave me my name; she always told me I was as beautiful as her favourite flower.'

'I was named after the poppies that grew wild in the fields. Mam never told me that poppies were pretty, and I've never felt that I *was* pretty, not once,' Poppy said sadly.

Rose tutted loudly. 'You're a beautiful woman, Poppy Lawson. You shouldn't be so hard on yourself.' Her attention was drawn back to the window. 'Who's that?' she asked, pointing along the back lane.

Poppy leaned forward to see a black horse pulling a cart. Sitting on the cart was a pretty young woman with long brown hair.

'Rag and bone!' she called. 'Any rag and bone!'

'A girl doing a rag and bone round – why, that's a man's job!' Rose exclaimed. 'It's unheard of for a woman to do such a thing.'

'She's called Meg Sutcliffe,' Poppy explained. 'She took on her dad's rag and bone round after he died. Her horse is called Stella and they're out in all weathers. I hear she even goes to the market at Hendon to buy and sell goods.'

'Hendon?' Rose sounded horrified. 'A girl as bonny as her goes down to the docks on her own? I used to hear Mrs Hutchins talk about the market by the docks, and what she said about the fellas there made my skin crawl. It's a dangerous place, from what I know.'

'She's a tough lass, Meg. I'm sure she can handle it.'

'What type of goods does she deal in?' Rose asked, suddenly curious.

'Clothes mainly, but she'll buy anything she thinks she can get a good price for at market.'

'Rag and bone!' Meg called as she carried on along the cobbles.

Poppy and Rose walked across the landing into the front room, where Harry and Sonny were still sitting on the floor.

'Me and Sid will take this room and have Emily's cot with us,' Poppy decided, turning to Rose. 'As for you . . . you can either sleep in the small room upstairs, though you'd have to share with the boys, or if you'd like your own room and some privacy, you could take the room downstairs off the kitchen.'

'The room downstairs will be fine. I'll help you clean the house up; we'll have it shipshape in no time, you'll see.'

Emily began to cry, and Poppy called the boys to her. 'Come on, everyone, let's go back to the barn.'

Harry and Sonny ran from the room, down the stairs and on to the street.

'They can't wait to get out,' Poppy mused. 'Mind you, I feel the same.'

By now, Emily's cries were getting louder and more insistent, but no matter how many times Poppy tried to shush her, she wouldn't settle. She locked the door and dropped the key in her pocket. Glancing up at the dirty windows, she knew she would have her work cut out to get the place clean.

'Oh Rose, I can't help feeling that bringing my child to live in this awful house will do her no good. It stinks to high heaven,' she moaned.

'We'll sort it out. I've told you I'll help,' Rose said firmly. 'Now, let's return the key to the Miners' Welfare Hall and head back to the barn. We'll gather as many buckets, brushes and cloths as we can, and we'll beg the Trewhitts for soap to clean the floors and walls. We'll speak to Sid's mam – she'll look after the bairns, won't she, while we get to work?'

Emily's crying ramped up, and soon she was bawling.

'Shush, little one, please,' Poppy cooed.

They were about to set off when she saw a man she recognised walking towards them. It took her a few moments to remember his name. It was Arthur Mason, the man she and Rose had met at Maisie's house.

'Hello, ladies,' he said.

Poppy nodded at him, concentrating all the while on Emily, wondering what could be causing her so much distress. When she looked up, she was perturbed to see

Rose exchange another shy smile with Arthur, before he tipped his cap and walked on.

'Listen, why don't you return the key and I'll take the boys back to the barn,' Rose said quickly.

'Don't you want to wait for me and we'll walk together?' Poppy asked, confused.

But Rose shook her head. 'There's something I need to do,' she said, and she began to walk away, holding hands with Harry and Sonny. Was Poppy mistaken, or was she hurrying after Arthur, as if she wanted to catch up with him?

'Rose . . .' she called.

Rose turned. 'Don't worry, I won't disappear again. I promised you I'd never do that, and I meant every word.'

Poppy let her go. Emily had finally begun to quieten, and Poppy took one last look at the small terraced house that would soon become her home, then turned to walk away, intent on heading to the Miners' Welfare Hall. At that moment, though, she saw a woman walking towards her, and her heart sank. Bumping into local gossip Lil Mahone was something she hadn't expected.

'That's a bloody noisy bairn you've got there!' Lil said grumpily. 'I could hear it crying all the way along the lane.'

Poppy stood her ground, pressing her boots against the cobbles and pulling Emily to her as she glared at Lil, who'd now stopped in front of her. The older woman was short and thin. She wore a black coat and a green knitted hat, and held a shopping basket over her arm. Her dark, beady eyes searched Poppy's face.

'Well, got nothing to say for yourself, girl?' she sniffed.

Poppy lifted her chin defiantly. 'I don't see what concern it is of yours,' she said.

'Oh, it's my concern all right,' Lil said, pointing to the door of the house next to Poppy's. 'Because that's my house, and the last thing I want is a crying baby to keep me awake.'

Poppy looked at the door. No, she thought, please say this isn't true. Her mouth went dry.

'You live there?'

Lil marched to the door and pushed it open, then turned back to Poppy. 'Yes, I do, so it looks like you and me will be neighbours,' she said. 'Just remember what I said about keeping the noise down. These houses have very thin walls.'

Chapter Thirty-Three

Poppy walked home with a heavy heart. Of all the people in Ryhope, why did it have to be Lil Mahone who was their next-door neighbour? She cursed the unfairness of it. She knew she'd have to tell Rose the minute she saw her, to warn her not to say anything confidential that could carry to Lil's ears. Rose's baby being born out of wedlock; Scurrfield and the sixpence . . . all of it would come out if Lil Mahone knew the truth.

When she returned to the barn, she was astonished to find Rose cooking by the fire. Her long hair, normally so tidy and neat, kept in place by the pretty ornament, hung loose around her shoulders.

She turned when Poppy walked in. 'Carrot soup all right?' she said.

'That sounds perfect, but there's no need for you to cook.'

Rose paused in her work and held the wooden spoon in mid-air. 'I'd like to make dinner tonight – it's the least I can do for you and Sid and the boys after all you've done for me.'

Poppy sniffed the air. 'How did you learn to cook?

237

You had a housekeeper at Gray Road.'

'I used to read recipe books when James locked me up in my room. My culinary skills don't extend very far, though, so don't get too excited,' Rose said.

'Well, it smells wonderful, thank you.'

Harry and Sonny ran towards Poppy, and she told them both to slow down.

'There's bread, but it's not great. I guess I need more practice making that,' Rose said. 'And there's ham and potatoes roasting in the oven to eat after the soup.'

Poppy was about to place Emily in her cot when she stopped what she was doing.

'Sorry? What? For one silly moment I thought you said there was ham in the oven.'

'There is,' Rose said lightly, turning back to stirring the soup.

Poppy laid the baby down and covered her with a blanket, then walked towards Rose. Rose took a cloth and pulled a large roasting pan from the bottom of the oven. Inside was a good-sized piece of ham with potatoes turning crisp and brown.

'How on earth . . . ?' Poppy cried.

Rose slid the pan back, then continued stirring the soup. Poppy put her hands on her hips and looked at her sister. 'Where did the money come from to buy ham?'

'I sold something to pay for it,' Rose replied.

Poppy was puzzled. 'What?'

'When I left you at Tunstall Street, I told you I had some business to attend to, and that's exactly what I did.'

Poppy gave an exasperated sigh. 'I hope this doesn't have anything to do with Arthur Mason. I saw the way you two looked at each other.'

'Arthur Mason?' Rose tutted and rolled her eyes. 'We shared a smile, that's all.'

'I just want to protect you, Rose. Can't you understand? Are you going to tell me what happened?'

'We saw the horse,' Harry piped up.

Poppy looked from her boys to Rose. 'What horse? Will someone tell me what's going on?'

'I found the rag and bone girl, Meg Sutcliffe,' Rose explained. 'I sold my hair ornament to her. She reckons she can get a decent price for it from a lady she knows. She said it was too good to sell at the market.'

'Oh Rose. You sold your hair ornament to buy food for us all?' Poppy sank into a chair by the fire. 'You shouldn't have, really.'

Rose shrugged. 'I have no use for ornaments and trinkets,' she said. 'And guess what? Meg said she often has material for sale. Perhaps we could afford to buy some in the coming weeks to make curtains for the new house.'

In all the excitement of having ham and potatoes for tea and knowing how happy Sid would be when he got home, Poppy had forgotten for a moment about Lil Mahone. But with Rose's mention of the pit house, Lil's thin face came to her mind.

'About the new house,' she began, choosing her words carefully, as Harry and Sonny were sitting close by and she knew how much they liked to listen to her conversations. She didn't want them overhearing something only for them to blurt it out at the wrong moment, within earshot of Lil Mahone. She beckoned Rose to her as she delivered the news, in a whisper, about who their new neighbour would be.

A noise at the barn door caused Harry and Sonny to jump up and run to greet Sid.

'Leave your dad alone, boys,' Poppy warned them. 'You know he likes to get settled in first.'

Rose untied her pinny and took the boys by the hand. 'I'll take them for a walk while Sid has his bath,' she said. 'We'll be back in half an hour, by which time the ham should be ready.' Poppy thought her heart would explode with gratitude.

After Rose had left with the boys, promising them a walk to the beach to find pebbles, Sid slowly undressed by the fire, while Poppy moved the pan of carrot soup from the coals and boiled a pan of water to top up the bathwater. Sid slid into the bath, and so began their evening ritual. Poppy started by washing the coal dust from his back. Then she massaged soap into his hair and scrubbed away the dirt and grime. His head dropped forward and he moved his neck from side to side, letting her massage his shoulders. He held his arms out as she soaped his long limbs, then she handed him the soap so he could wash his legs and feet.

'I'm ever so tired, love,' he said at last. 'It's been a tough day at work. Do you know, I'm so worn out that I think I've started to hear things. I could have sworn I heard Rose say that we're having ham for tea.'

Chapter Thirty-Four

Early the next day, Poppy headed to Scotland Street carrying Emily. Harry and Sonny walked behind, holding hands. 'Come on, boys, keep up,' she said, marching at a brisk pace.

The boys were still sleepy after she had woken them earlier than usual. Harry rubbed his eyes and yawned loudly. 'Mam?' he asked. 'Why do we have to go to Granny Maisie's?'

'Because your aunt Rose and I are cleaning our new house. We're going to get it ready for moving in at the end of the week.'

When they reached Maisie's door, Poppy knocked three times. Maisie answered the door in her dressing gown. She'd clearly not been out of bed long, as her hair was unkempt, sticking up on one side. She looked at Poppy and the children through sleepy eyes. Then her hand flew to her heart.

'What's wrong?' she asked, sounding panicked. 'Is it Sid? What's happened to Sid?'

'Nothing's wrong. Sid's at work,' Poppy said calmly.

Maisie's face clouded over. 'Then what the devil are

you doing here at this unearthly hour? I haven't even had breakfast yet.' She pushed a hand through her thick hair and glanced out into the street before beckoning Poppy and the children into the house.

Once indoors, Poppy explained about the pit house and the state it was in. 'It needs cleaning from top to bottom before we move in. Rose and I are going to tackle it today.'

'But isn't it your day for working at the Trewhitts'?' Maisie asked.

'Not today. Ambrose sent word to the barn that he doesn't need me – he said he's not well. I don't know what's wrong, but I know he hasn't been looking good lately. He and Ella are getting old. I don't know where they find the energy to keep the shop on, if I'm honest.'

Maisie sank into a chair, and Sonny clambered on to her knee and threw his arms around her neck. 'I suppose this is my grandson's way of buttering me up to look after him while you're working at Tunstall Street today,' she laughed.

'Would you mind, Maisie?' Poppy asked. 'Rose and I are going straight there.'

'Course I don't mind. What else am I to do if I don't have this lot to look after? Leave the bairns with me, and you and Rose get your new home ready. Speaking of your sister, how is she? Has she settled in all right? Is she eating? My word, I got a shock when I saw her after all those years.'

'Yes, she's eating, and even putting on a little weight around her face. She's great with the lads . . .'

'We love Aunt Rose,' Harry piped up.

'She brings us ham,' Sonny added.

Poppy smiled. '. . . and she knows when to leave me and Sid alone. She's never in our way. She's going to start looking for a job once we move. It's going to be hard living on the colliery, though, after the freedom and space of the barn.'

'You'll manage, love,' Maisie said, then she dropped her voice to a whisper. 'I heard that Rose and Arthur Mason are getting friendly, by the way.'

Poppy started at the news. 'No, surely not,' she whispered back.

Maisie gave her a knowing look. 'Thought it best to tell you. Arthur's a friend of Bill's, but he's no friend of mine. He's a rogue, and if I were you, I'd warn your sister to be careful.'

Poppy felt a sting of pain at the thought that Rose was carrying on with a married man. But then she remembered the cruel things her sister had told her about James. After his bullying and beatings, a touch of kindness from another man, even a married one like Arthur, would mean a lot to her. She wondered where the two of them had been seen, and guessed that Rose must have met Arthur on her walks around the village when she'd gone off on her own. She felt uneasy about what her mother-in-law had said.

'Now then, who'd like oats for breakfast?' Maisie asked the boys.

Harry and Sonny's hands shot into the air as Maisie stood from her chair and took Emily from Poppy. 'Go on, get your work done, lass,' she said.

'Emily's still a little unsettled. I thought I should mention it in case she acts up today. She's still not taking as much milk as she should. As soon as she was in the new house on Tunstall Street, she was crying and bawling her lungs out.'

'I'll take good care of her, love.'

'Thanks, Maisie. I don't know what we'd do without you.' Poppy kissed Maisie on the cheek, but Maisie wiped it off with her fingers.

'Don't be soft, lass,' she huffed.

As Poppy returned to the barn to collect her sister and as many cloths, brushes and buckets as they could carry, Maisie's words about Rose and Arthur Mason rattled around in her mind, and she tried to find the right words to ask her about it when the time felt right.

She and Rose walked to the Miners' Welfare Hall, where Poppy collected the key, and this time there was no need to return it.

'I'm still not sure how we'll get the furniture moved from the barn,' she said. 'There's the table and chairs, beds, pots and pans. Sid said he'd ask the lads at the pit if they know anyone with a cart who can help us.'

'What about asking the rag and bone girl? She's got a horse and cart,' Rose suggested.

'Meg Sutcliffe?' Poppy mulled the idea over. 'I don't think so. The cart is her livelihood. If she's not out earning money, buying and selling, she might want us to pay for her time. Let's wait to see what Sid says.'

Soon the tiny house on Tunstall Street was in front of them.

'Which house does Lil Mahone live in?' Rose whispered.

Poppy nodded to Lil's front door. 'In there. She says the walls are thin, so we should be careful what we talk about if we don't want her to know.' She glanced at Rose. 'Your business is yours, Rose. It's up to you what you tell folk about your past, or whether you tell them at all. If Lil Mahone gets wind of any gossip about either of us, I can guarantee she won't have heard it from me.'

She laid her cloths and buckets on the ground, slid the heavy iron key into the lock and turned it. The door swung open, and she was greeted again by the stench from within. She squared her shoulders, picked up the cleaning equipment and marched into the house.

The sisters worked hard, carrying buckets of water from the tap in the back lane. They swilled floors, washed walls and cleaned windows. When it was all done, they swilled and scrubbed the kitchen floor again until Poppy was certain that all the muck had gone. When the exertion of the work became too much for her, they emptied their tin buckets, turned them upside down and took them outside.

'Let's sit in the sunshine by the front door,' Poppy said. 'I can't bring myself to sit in the back yard, it makes me feel hemmed in.'

They perched on the buckets and leaned their backs against the wall at the front of the house. Poppy turned her face to the sun.

'This pregnancy's tiring me out. I was never so tired while I was pregnant with the boys, and there were two of them inside me, although I had no clue at the time,' she said.

'Moving house while you're expecting can't do you any good,' Rose said. 'And you've already got a lot on your plate, what with me turning up. Plus you've got bairns to look after and your husband to care for. It's no wonder you're tired. But I'm here for you now. I'll help.'

Poppy looked up and down the lane to ensure no one was about. Then she glanced behind her to check that Lil Mahone wasn't hovering by the window before she decided to ask the question that had been plaguing her all day. She kept her voice low, just in case Lil was listening behind her front door. 'Rose, I heard something this morning from Sid's mam. She said that you and Arthur Mason had been seen together. Is it true?'

Rose stiffened, giving Poppy the answer she'd dreaded.

'Well, what have you got to say for yourself?' she went on.

Rose tilted her chin defiantly. 'I'm a grown woman, Poppy, and I can see who I want. I'll always be younger than you, but I'm not your little sister any more. You can't tell me what to do and it's about time you realised that.'

Poppy felt as if she'd been slapped by her sister's harsh words. They'd never argued or fought as children, and she didn't know how to respond. They sat in silence for a while, with only one thing turning over in Poppy's mind: the fact that Arthur Mason was married.

'I won't have shame brought on my family,' she said at last.

'It's too late for that,' Rose said quietly. 'I've already told you what James did to me.'

Poppy swallowed hard. 'I want to keep you safe, Rose,' she said.

Rose laid her hand gently on Poppy's arm. 'I need to learn to cope on my own.'

As much as it hurt, Poppy knew she was right. What Rose did now she was back in Ryhope was her own business; Poppy couldn't keep protecting her like she'd done when they were small. Rose was old enough to make her own decisions – and her own mistakes. They fell silent again.

'Do you think we've done enough to get rid of the smell?' Rose asked at last. Poppy was grateful that their difficult words about Arthur had been put to one side, for now.

'I hope so. The air up here on the colliery is bad enough as it is, what with the pit and the trains. But it's not all bad. At least we're close to the Co-op.'

'It's more expensive than the Trewhitts' shop, though,' Rose sighed. 'Still, I might be better placed to get work up here. There are a lot more pubs on the colliery than in the village. Mining's thirsty work and the pubs are busier. I'll look for a job as soon as we've moved in. I'll start in that poky little pub at the top of the bank . . .'

'The Colliery Inn?'

'That's the one, then I'll work my way down, asking in every pub, and I won't stop until I find something. You're lucky that you've got a job with the Trewhitts. They pay you fairly and it's easy work.'

'I'll keep on there for as long as I can. Mind you, Ambrose telling me not to come in today was most unlike him. He and Ella are normally sticklers for routine, and today was one of my cleaning days. Still, I dare say I've done enough cleaning for one day.' Poppy stood and collected her bucket. 'Come on, let's get back to the barn and start packing up.'

Rose stood too and linked arms with her sister. They stood side by side, looking at the front of their new home. The windows that had been streaked with dirt hours before were now sparkling clean. The front door had been brushed clean too. They'd left the windows open to air the house overnight.

'I think we did a good job,' Rose said, admiring their work.

'And I want us to be happy here,' Poppy said decisively. 'All of us. Me, Sid, the boys and Emily . . .' she pulled Rose tight to her, 'and you. We're a family again, Rose, we'll always look out for each other.'

She stepped forward and took the key from her pocket, ready to lock the front door. Rose stayed where she was, eyes fixed on the cramped terraced house.

'Penny for your thoughts,' Poppy said when she saw the look of concentration on her sister's face.

'I was thinking . . .' Rose began. 'I was worrying, really. I know I shouldn't, but I can't help it. It's James. What if he finds me? I'm scared he'll drag me back to Gray Road . . .'

Poppy held up her hand. 'James won't find you. It's as simple as that. There's no way in the world that he will. Haven't you already told me you're a grown woman, harder now, someone who can cope with life? Well, now's your chance to put your words to the test. But please, don't use married men like Arthur Mason as your emotional crutch. You're worth ten of someone like him.'

In silence they gathered up their cloths, buckets and brushes, preparing to return to the barn. As they walked away, next door, at Lil Mahone's house, a curtain twitched at the front window and Lil's pinched face appeared.

Chapter Thirty-Five

On the morning of the move, all of Poppy and Sid's belongings were packed into tea chests and boxes. Not that they had much, of course. Their possessions consisted of a few sticks of furniture, pots and pans, clothes and blankets. Harry and Sonny had been warned to be on their best behaviour, but they couldn't seem to settle and were running around excitedly. In the distance, the bells of St Paul's chimed the hour. Poppy glanced at Sid.

'What time's your mate Freddy coming with his horse and cart?' she asked.

'He should be here any time,' Sid replied. 'I'll walk out to the village green to see if he's on his way.'

'Take the boys with you, would you? A walk might work off some of their energy. I don't want them running around and making a noise at the new house. They're going to have to get used to living more quietly there. We'll have neighbours to consider, for the first time.'

Sid laid his arm around Poppy's shoulders. 'Aye, that's true. And from what you've told me about Mrs Mahone, it sounds like we're already in her bad books before we even move in.'

Poppy looked around the barn and saw Rose sweeping dust around the hearth. 'Leave that, Rose. There's no need to clean up. Amos is moving sheep in, not people. I don't think they'll mind the dust.'

Rose leaned the brush against a tea chest and walked towards her. 'I suppose you're right. I was just thinking of what Mam would have wanted us to do. She'd have expected us to leave the barn tidy and clean.'

'Do you still think of Mam a lot?'

'Every day. And you?'

'I think of her and Dad each morning when I wake and every night before I sleep.' Poppy slid her arm around her sister's tiny waist and pulled her close. 'I'm going to miss this old barn,' she said, looking around. 'Despite the reason we were first brought here, to live with Nellie when Mam died, it's not been such a bad place.'

Rose gave a wry smile. 'Apart from mice nibbling our toes in the dead of night,' she said.

Poppy shivered at the memory. 'But it was always warm in here, and for that I was grateful, even though Nellie never loved us . . .'

'She didn't care a jot,' Rose chipped in.

'. . . and we went hungry a lot of the time.'

The sisters stood together for a few moments, lost in memories of the past.

'The day Scurrfield came to take you is a day I will never forget,' Poppy said sadly. 'I tried to erase it from my memory so many times. I tried to pretend it'd just been a dream and that you'd walk through the barn door as if you'd just returned from school . . .' Her voice started to break.

'Hey there,' Rose said. 'I won't allow you to get

maudlin. Not today of all days. Today is a fresh start. You're moving to your new house and a new life.'

'With new neighbours on either side, one of whom will be asking constant questions. Lil Mahone will want to know everything about us; she's not shy about coming forward.'

'But that doesn't mean we have to tell her everything she wants to know,' Rose said firmly. 'Besides, I've nothing to hide. I've done nothing wrong. Old Scurrfield is dead and buried now, and as for James, well . . .'

'Consider him dead and buried too,' Poppy implored. 'Anyway, listen to me carrying on like this. This pregnancy is making me emotional when I need to keep a level head.'

A noise at the door made them both turn to look.

'Poppy! Freddy's here with the cart!' Sid called excitedly.

Poppy walked into the yard and saw a large black horse clip-clopping its way towards her. Harry and Sonny were sitting in the back of the cart with cheeky grins on their faces, loving every minute of the adventure.

'Morning, Freddy,' she called.

She liked Sid's friend Freddy; he was a no-nonsense kind of bloke, direct, to the point and trustworthy. He was also good-looking and single.

'Have you met my sister, Rose?' she asked.

Rose looked up at the mention of her name. 'Morning,' she said, and a tentative smile made its way to her lips.

Freddy raised his cap politely, then stuck his hand out and greeted her cheerfully. 'Morning!' he said. 'I've heard a lot about you from Sid.'

Poppy watched Rose take his hand and shake it. How wonderful it would be, she thought, if Rose and Freddy became friends, maybe more. Then she chided herself for wishing her sister's life away. Still, she felt heartened by the friendly exchange. Perhaps Freddy might even take Rose's mind off Arthur Mason.

Freddy began to lift boxes on to the cart. When everything was loaded, he clambered up and took the horse's reins. As he manoeuvred the animal, Poppy took a moment to say a final goodbye to the barn. She looked at Sid and took his hand, then took Rose's hand too. The three of them stood in silence as a chicken strutted past.

'You can stay this time, chicken, I don't need to shoo you out,' Poppy said. 'I'm sure the sheep won't mind.'

Then they turned their backs on the barn, walked out of the door and headed to the cart. Sid helped Poppy clamber up, then he gave Rose a leg-up before jumping up himself.

'Right you are, Freddy, we're all aboard,' he called.

Freddy geed up the horse and it made its way from the farm. Poppy's legs dangled over the back of the cart as it headed through the cattle market. At the village green, she peered through the windows of the farmhouse, wondering if Amos Bird was watching, but he was nowhere to be seen.

Sid noticed her looking. 'Amos Bird is a businessman, love, and that barn's a valuable asset,' he said. 'He's running the place more efficiently than Norman. Selling sheep is more profitable for him than we ever were. We've still got to pay him the rent we owe. He'll not be happy that we're leaving still in debt, but there's nothing I can do. We haven't got the money to pay him; we spent most of it on tram fares to and from Gray Road.'

Behind them, Harry and Sonny began arguing, and Poppy spun around to see what was going on.

'Mam! Tell him to put it back!' Sonny cried.

'What's got into you two?' she said crossly. And then she saw the chicken in Harry's lap. 'Harry! You can't steal a chicken!' she said. 'Sid, put it back, would you? We can't take it with us. There's not enough room for us lot at Tunstall Street, never mind chickens.'

Sid took the chicken, leapt off the cart and ran back to the farm, where he let it go free. Then he ran to catch the cart and jumped back on, sitting next to Poppy. He put his arm around her shoulders, and she rested her head against his broad chest. As they trundled along, something caught her eye on the village green.

'Look, the Trewhitts' shop is still closed. Ambrose has normally opened up by now. Should we call on him to make sure he's all right?'

'He's probably having a lie-in,' Sid said. 'And I wouldn't blame him. He's getting on. He and Ella deserve to take things easy. They've worked hard all their lives.'

But his words did little to dispel Poppy's fears. 'I worry about them, Sid. Ambrose and Ella have been good to me all my life, and I've always felt close to them. Something's up, I can tell. You know how much of a stickler for routine Ambrose is. Not to have the shop open isn't like him. I already know he's not been well, and I'm very concerned. I'll call on them later, once we've unpacked.'

The cart lumbered past the school and the church, the police station and the Grand Electric cinema. On it went past the row of pubs and inns that lined the colliery bank all the way up to the pit. It was a short journey, no more than ten minutes, but the air up here was filled with smoke from the pit and its trains. In Poppy's arms, Emily began to cough, and she turned the baby's face to protect her from the smog.

'We're here!' Freddy called as he pulled the horse to a stop outside the house on Tunstall Street. Sid helped

Poppy and Rose from the cart, then Harry and Sonny leapt into his arms and he swung them down to the ground.

'You and Rose go inside, love. Me and Freddy will bring everything in,' he said.

Poppy unlocked the door with her heavy key and walked into the kitchen with Rose.

'It smells better after the cleaning we did,' she said, relieved. 'Once we get the coal fire going, that might improve things too. I'll need to find somewhere for Emily to sleep. She can go down by the hearth for now, once Sid brings her cot in.'

Rose took her coat off, folded it and laid it outside by the door. Then she rolled up the sleeves of her blue velvet dress and helped Sid and Freddy bring the boxes inside. When everything was off the cart, the two men carried Poppy and Sid's bed upstairs and into pride of place in the sunny front bedroom. Then Freddy waved goodbye and called out cheerily to Rose. She patted the horse and thanked Freddy for all his help.

Poppy watched them with interest, wishing again that Rose would take up with a handsome, honest single man like Freddy, instead of married Arthur, who was deceiving his wife. However, she realised again that what she wanted for Rose and what Rose wanted for herself were different things, and she was going to have to get used to it.

Inside the house, Sid and Rose went back and forth, opening boxes, lifting out blankets, pots and pans.

'Where do you want this, Pops?' Sid called, holding a box of knives and forks.

'Put it on the table for now,' she replied.

'Poppy? Would you like these blankets taken to the bedroom?' Rose asked.

'Yes, please, Rose.'

However, there were still no curtains at the windows and no rugs on the floors. Poppy knew there was a lot of demanding work to be done in order to make the house feel like their home.

Sid hauled a sack of coal into the back yard, then took a shovelful to the hearth. 'It'll feel better once the fire's going,' he said cheerfully. Oh, how Poppy wanted to believe him. 'Where's Rose?' he asked, looking around.

'She's setting up the boys' bed in their room. I'll make tea for us as soon as the fire gets going.'

A clatter of footsteps on the stairs announced Rose and the boys coming down.

'I never realised this place would be so noisy,' Poppy said, adding another problem about the house to her growing list.

The boys bounded into the kitchen, almost knocking Sid sideways. 'Steady on, lads,' he warned. 'You can't run around in here like you used to do in the barn.'

Harry and Sonny collapsed sulkily to the floor at Poppy's feet just as Rose walked into the room.

'Did anyone bring my coat in from outside?' she asked.

'No, I didn't. Did you, Sid?'

Sid shook his head.

'Boys, have you seen Aunt Rose's coat?'

Harry and Sonny shook their heads too.

'Perhaps Freddy took it by mistake?' Poppy offered, but Rose was certain the coat had been there after Freddy had left. Her face clouded over.

'It's been stolen!' she cried.

Chapter Thirty-Six

Poppy handed Emily to Sid. 'Here, take the baby. I'm going to sort this out,' she said firmly. 'If anyone out there thinks the Lawsons are a soft touch, I'll make them think again.'

'Poppy, wait!' Sid called, but she was already marching out of the door.

Outside, she looked up and down Tunstall Street, but there was no one about. She pursed her lips. 'Someone's taking us for fools,' she muttered. 'Well, I won't have it. I'm going to get to the bottom of this. If anyone saw who stole your coat, Rose, it'll be her next door. She's always got her beady eye on the street. She misses nowt; that's what everyone says about her.'

She rapped her knuckles on Lil's door. Rose stood by her side, Sid and the children behind. The door opened immediately, as if Lil Mahone had been waiting. Lil was wearing a blue pinny over her skirt, tied around her thin waist. The green knitted hat that she always wore when she was out and about was still on her head. Poppy wondered if she ever took it off. Lil crossed her arms and straightened her back.

'What do you want?' she said. Her tone was less than friendly.

'My sister's coat, that's what I want,' Poppy replied. 'Did you see who stole it?'

Lil puffed out her chest. 'I hope you're not suggesting that *I* took it,' she said defensively.

'I never said that.'

'No, but that's what you're implying. You think we're all liars and thieves in these pit houses, don't you? I bet you think living on the colliery bank's beneath you.'

Poppy felt every single one of Lil's sharp words cut straight into her. 'No, that's not what I meant. I was just—'

'What my sister's trying to say,' Rose chipped in politely, 'is that my coat has gone missing, and we wondered if you'd seen anyone who might have taken it, that's all.'

Lil tutted loudly. 'If you'll take my advice, you'll leave nothing of value where you can't see it. Lock it away indoors or chances are that a passing beggar will steal it.' She eyed Rose keenly, then looked at Poppy and back to Rose again. 'Why, you're the orphan girls, aren't you?' she cried. 'I wasn't sure of it before, but I'm certain of it now. You lived with Nellie Harper at the cattle market after your parents died.' She peered closely at Rose. 'You . . . you're the one who disappeared for ten years. Oh, I've heard all the gossip about you, Rose Harper. Returning to the village without an explanation as to where you've been.'

'It's no one's business where my sister's been,' Poppy said firmly. 'All you need to know, Mrs Mahone, is that we've moved in next door. We'd appreciate our privacy and ask not to be gossiped about.'

Rose stepped forward. 'Mrs Mahone, we'd be grateful if you'd treat us as you would any neighbour. Yes, I've been away for ten years, but as Poppy says, it's no one's business but mine. And my name is Rose Thomas, not Harper.'

'Circumstances have forced us out of the barn in the village, Mrs Mahone,' Sid piped up from the back. 'But I can vouch for my family, and you've no need to worry about us living next door. My name's Sidney Lawson. I'm a hard-working miner, a hewer at the pit. My wife works for the Trewhitts in the village and my sister-in-law will be working as soon as she can. The lads start at the village school in the autumn and our baby is usually as good as gold. I promise we'll do our best to keep the noise down. We're decent people, Mrs Mahone. You might know my parents, Maisie and Bill Lawson, they live on Scotland Street. I'm sure we can all get along.'

Lil looked at Sid, who was holding the baby, and her face seemed to soften. Then she glanced down at Harry and Sonny. 'My word, what bonny little lads. Twins, eh?' She returned her gaze to Sid. 'Yes, I know Maisie Lawson. We went to school together. She was called Maisie Smith back then. My husband's a hewer too, you might know him from the pit. His name's Bob Mahone.'

'I know Bob by sight, but not to speak to,' Sid said respectfully. 'I hope he and I can be friends. Maybe I could ask his advice about turning this patch of earth at the front into a garden to grow vegetables, just like he's done at your house.'

Lil nodded sharply, then unfolded her arms. 'Well,

I can't stand here chatting. As for your missing coat, I didn't see a soul. I've got my husband to look after and a house to run. Now if you don't mind, I've got to get Bob's bait ready. He's about to start work and I don't want you lot making him late, or I'll be holding you accountable for lost wages.' And with that, she slammed the door.

'Well, really!' Poppy exclaimed.

'What a rude woman,' Rose muttered.

'Come on, everyone, back indoors,' Sid said.

They all trudged into their new home.

'I'm going to have to find the rag and bone girl again to ask if she's got a cheap coat I can buy once I get a job,' Rose sighed.

Poppy sank into a chair by the fire and put her head in her hands. Sid sat opposite, holding Emily, who seemed to be developing a cough. Poppy glanced at her child with concern.

'She's getting worse, Sid.'

'I know, lass, she sounds bad. I'm as worried about her as you are,' Sid said, casting an anxious glance at Emily.

Poppy shook her head with despair. 'If it's not one thing it's another. Rose has her coat stolen, our next-door neighbour's the most unfriendly woman I've ever met, and there's not enough space to swing a flaming cat in here, never mind bring up my family.'

Emily began coughing again.

'Hand her over,' Poppy said, and when the child was in her arms, she tried to quieten her with soothing words, gently rocking her. However, Emily's breathing was becoming strained. Poppy shook her head. 'I don't like the sound of this. It started the first time we came here;

259

she was never like this in the village or the barn. Before we moved, she wasn't taking as much milk as she should, but her chest didn't sound like this.'

After a while, Emily fell asleep, and Poppy laid her in her cot. Then she sat up straight in her seat and looked around the kitchen, where boxes and tea chests were strewn.

'Right, everyone. Let's finish unpacking.'

She busied herself around the small room, placing pots and pans in a row, and with Rose's help moved the table to a spot underneath the window.

'We're going to need to buy curtains and rugs,' she said. 'And I have no idea where the money will come from.'

'I've still got a little money left from the sale of my hairpin,' Rose offered. 'It's not much, but it might buy cheap material.'

Sid bustled past with another shovelful of coal, and soon the flames were roaring, warming the small room, making it feel cosy. He laid his arm around Poppy's shoulders.

'This place will be all right, love, you'll see. You and Rose will have it feeling like home in no time.'

Poppy gently put her hand on her stomach. 'Thanks, Sid. I guess I'm out of sorts after my run-in with Lil. And I'm still feeling sick with this one growing inside me.'

'Then what we need is a mug of tea,' Rose said cheerfully, putting the kettle on the flames to boil. 'I'm sure I saw the box with the mugs in somewhere. Harry? Sonny? Come and help me find them.'

* * *

After tea had been drunk and boxes unpacked, Poppy and Rose laid blankets and pillows on Poppy and Sid's bed upstairs.

'You should rest, you're looking done in,' Rose said when they headed downstairs. But Poppy shook her head.

'I can't rest, not when I know things aren't right at the Trewhitts'. I need to go back to the village to see if they've opened the shop.'

'Let me go instead,' Rose offered. 'You stay here, get to know your new home. The boys are playing in the yard and seem happy.'

But Poppy had made up her mind. 'I need to go. I have to see them.'

'Would you like me to come with you?'

'No, you stay here with the boys. Sid's having a nap, then he'll get ready for work. His boots and work clothes are in the yard. I'll take Emily with me, I want to keep my eye on her. I think she's struggling with the coal dust up here. These pit lanes are no place for a baby.'

'Plenty of other women have brought up their bairns on pit lanes,' Rose said sagely. 'Emily will get used to the air here; we all will.'

But Poppy looked at her baby's pale face and listened to her breathing, which had now turned into a worrying wheeze.

Chapter Thirty-Seven

Poppy hurried from Tunstall Street with Emily. She had to see Ambrose and Ella with her own eyes. She needed to know what was going on. All through her life, ever since she'd been a child, the Trewhitts had been there for her. It often felt to Poppy that they were as much a part of her family as Sid's parents were. They were the only friends she had, the only people apart from Sid and his parents, and now Rose, who she trusted. The thought that something was wrong with either of them was of great concern, and she wanted to do what she could. For there must be something wrong, she reasoned, otherwise why hadn't they opened the shop? Ambrose and Ella worked long hours and dedicated themselves to their work and each other. For many years, their shop had provided groceries and bread for those who lived and worked in the village.

She hurried past St Paul's church and saw the welcoming village green with its oak trees and horse trough. In her arms, Emily began to writhe. 'It's all right, little one, we'll be there soon,' she said soothingly.

As she walked past the village school, she thought of

Rose selling her hair ornament to buy food for them all. She was beyond grateful to her sister. She recalled their childhood, when they'd taken turns to wear their one pair of boots. She glanced down at her boots now, to where her toes poked through. She was a mother to two boys and a baby girl, and she was pregnant with another child. She was a wife to Sid, who she loved with all her heart. 'But I still can't afford decent boots,' she muttered under her breath. Maybe now, she thought, now that they'd moved to the pit house and after they'd paid Amos their rent arrears, she could afford to have her boots patched up by the cobbler.

Her mind turned to what Rose had said about asking Meg, the rag and bone girl, to find her a decent coat, and curtains and rugs for the house. And if she saved up enough money, after buying goods for the house and fitting Harry and Sonny out in warm clothes for school that would see them through autumn and winter, maybe she could even afford new boots.

As the Trewhitts' shop came into view, Emily started coughing again.

'The coal dust in the pit lanes is no good for your lungs, little one,' Poppy said softly.

The shutters on the shop were still closed, and an uneasy feeling settled in the pit of her stomach. She knocked loudly at the door. When there was no reply, she rattled the handle, trying to force the door open, but she should have known better, for there was no way that Ambrose would ever have left his beloved shop unlocked. She stood back from the door, shielded her eyes from the sun and looked up at the windows of the Trewhitts' rooms above, but there was no sign of life there either.

A tall, slim woman with auburn hair piled messily on her head was walking towards her carrying a wicker basket. When she reached her, she stopped. It was Hetty Burdon, landlady of the Albion Inn.

'It's like trying to raise the dead, trying to get Ambrose to open up recently,' Hetty said. 'I hope you have better luck than I had this morning. I tried knocking for ages, but no one stirred.'

'You haven't seen Ambrose or Ella at all?' Poppy asked. Her stomach was in knots. She didn't know whether it was the nausea of her pregnancy or anxiety over her friends.

'No, love,' Hetty said, glancing up at the window.

Poppy reached a decision. 'I'm going to go round to the back of the shop to see if I can see anything through the window there.'

'Good luck, lass,' Hetty said. 'Oh, by the way, am I right in thinking you and your family have moved out of the barn now? My husband Jack said he saw you all on the back of a cart this morning with furniture and boxes.'

Poppy took a moment to reply. Nothing went unnoticed in Ryhope. Try as she might to live a private life, it was almost impossible in such a small village.

'We were offered a pit house and we've moved in today,' was all she said.

Hetty gently patted her arm and leaned towards her to look at Emily.

'Such a beautiful bairn. But she sounds a bit chesty, if you don't mind me saying.'

Poppy pulled her baby to her. 'She'll be fine.'

Hetty stepped back. 'I'm sorry, lass. I didn't mean to suggest you weren't looking after her. I know you've got a lot on your plate with your sister turning up out of the blue.' She narrowed her eyes. 'Ambrose told me she was living with a good family . . .'

'She was, yes,' Poppy said quickly.

'Well, that's all that needs to be said.' Hetty turned as if to walk away. But then she stopped and turned back, standing closer to Poppy than before. Poppy was con-fused. What on earth did the woman want now?

'There's something I should tell you, lass. There was a fella in our pub last night, asking about Rose.'

Poppy's stomach lurched. 'What fella?'

Hetty shrugged. 'He wasn't a Ryhope man. Me and Jack had never seen him before.'

Poppy's heart began to beat wildly. 'What did he look like?'

'Tall, wide, dark hair, stern face. He wore a good coat, I remember that, because I was wondering what a man with such fancy clothes was doing in Ryhope.'

Poppy felt like she was going to faint. She moved to stand beside the shop window and leaned against it, terrified she was going to drop Emily. Breathing deeply, she tried to pull herself together.

'Are you all right, love? You've gone as white as a sheet. Do you need to sit down? I could take you to the Albion Inn and pour you a brandy.'

'No . . . no, I'm fine,' Poppy said, although she felt anything but. 'This man who asked about Rose, what did he say?'

Hetty thought for a moment. 'He asked me and Jack if we knew anyone in the village called Rose. He didn't mention a surname, so I can't be certain he meant your sister.'

'And what did you tell him?' Poppy asked. 'Please, Hetty, think . . . it's important.'

'Well, you know me and Jack, love. We've run the Albion Inn for over twenty years. Our customers know they can trust us not to gossip or spread news. As a pub landlady, I hear all kinds of things. But I keep my mouth shut, and so does Jack. What we hear inside that pub stays inside our four walls. We didn't tell him anything.'

'Nothing at all?'

'Nothing,' Hetty said firmly. 'I've known you and Rose since you were girls – I knew you before your mam and dad, heaven help their poor souls, passed away. Rest assured, lass, if this fella comes back, he'll get nothing from us a second time, or a third.'

'Do you think he'll come back?' Poppy asked. 'I mean, did he say he would? Did he say anything else?'

'No, love. He simply asked about Rose, and me and Jack told him there's many women in the village with that name. He had a drink, a pint of stout if I remember correctly. And then he left.'

'I appreciate your silence, Hetty,' Poppy said.

'My lips are sealed. But I'm pleased I bumped into you, as it reminded me to tell you about him. I hope Rose isn't in any trouble?'

'No . . . of course not,' Poppy said quickly. 'Anyway, it might have been a different Rose he was looking for.'

'Well, there's always that possibility, of course,' Hetty said, all the while keeping her gaze on Poppy's face. 'But if you need to talk any time, you know where to find me,' she said, nodding at the Albion Inn.

'I'm grateful to you and Jack. Please give him my best

wishes. I must go, Hetty. I've got to check on Ambrose and Ella.'

'I'll leave you to it,' Hetty said as she took one last look at Emily. 'Such a beautiful bairn. I hope you don't think I'm interfering, love, but can I offer you a word of advice?' She continued without waiting for Poppy's reply. 'Have her looked at by Dr Anderson; her chest shouldn't sound that bad.'

Chapter Thirty-Eight

With Hetty's warning ringing in her ears, Poppy held Emily close. They had no money to pay the doctor. They had no money at all until Sid picked his wages up at the end of the week. Even then, they had their final rent at the barn to pay. Poppy knew there wouldn't be anything spare, and certainly not enough to pay a doctor, unless they saved up for weeks. She sent up a silent prayer that Emily would be all right, but Hetty's words had shaken her. She knew in her heart that there was something wrong with her child. She looked at Emily's face. She couldn't remember Harry or Sonny being so pale, and neither of them had suffered bad chests.

She watched Hetty walk away, reeling from the news about the man at the Albion Inn. It had to be James Scurrfield, she felt sure of it. Ryhope was a close community, and the folk who drank in its pubs lived in the village and worked at the coal mine or on the farms. Outsiders were uncommon, so when a stranger arrived, their presence was noted and gossiped about. While there were two other women called Rose that Poppy knew of in the village, it seemed too much of a coincidence that this stranger, this outsider, was asking for someone of that name. From the description Hetty had given, he sounded very much like the same man Poppy had run into when she'd tried to rescue Rose from Gray Road.

She closed her eyes and tried to push the image of James Scurrfield away. Rose had been worried that he would come looking for her. Well, he could try, Poppy thought, he could try all he wanted, but she was determined he wouldn't take her sister away. She had suffered enough being separated from Rose once by the Scurrfields, and she would make certain it didn't happen again. She decided she'd talk to Sid as soon as she could to ask him what they should do. She also decided not to tell Rose about the man in the Albion Inn; she didn't want to upset her when she was still finding her feet. No, she wouldn't give her cause for concern.

By now Poppy was at the back of the Trewhitts' shop, where there was a yard with a wooden gate. She expected this to be locked, just as the shop door had been, and so was surprised when the sneck lifted with ease. The gate swung open, and she stepped into the yard, where wooden crates were stacked along the walls. She walked to the back door and knocked hard, calling out for Ambrose. A noise above caught her attention, and she looked up to see a window slide open and Ambrose's pale face poke out. He looked dishevelled, still in his nightgown, his hair sticking up on end.

'Ambrose? The shop's locked. I wanted to make sure you and Ella were all right,' Poppy called.

Ambrose nodded and slid the window closed. A few moments later, the back door opened. He was wearing a jacket over his nightgown. 'You'd better come in,' he said.

His voice was raspy and he walked with a stoop. He looked more tired than Poppy had ever seen him. 'Come up to our living room,' he said.

Poppy followed him upstairs and couldn't fail to notice how out of breath he was with each step. She followed him to the front room, which was in darkness.

'Would you like me to open the curtains?' she said, looking around.

'Aye, lass, please do,' Ambrose said.

She laid Emily on an armchair, then pulled the curtains open, letting in the sunlight of the summer day. 'It's glorious outside,' she said. 'A smashing day.'

When she turned, Ambrose had collapsed into an armchair with his hands crossed on his stomach. Poppy flew to his side. 'What is it? Are you in pain?' She looked into his watery, bloodshot eyes.

'Me and Ella suffered a strong dose of the flu and it's knocked us both for six. We didn't want you in here cleaning in case you caught it and gave it to Sid and the bairns.'

'Is Ella still in bed?'

Ambrose nodded slowly. 'Aye, she's taking a bit longer than me to recover. We had to close the shop, as neither of us felt well enough to work and the last thing we wanted was to pass the flu to our customers.' He struggled to stand. 'But I'll open up today.'

Poppy steadied him, placing her hand under his arm to help him. 'You'll do no such thing. You're in no fit state. You need to stay here, build your strength up and look after Ella.'

'But the shop . . .' Ambrose protested.

'The shop can wait until you're both well,' she said

firmly. 'I'm not letting you go downstairs. Look at the state of you. You can hardly stand on your own, never mind get dressed and work.'

'Customers depend on us. We can't keep the shop closed. Every minute we're not open, we lose money.'

Poppy helped Ambrose back into the chair, where he leaned his head back and began to breathe deeply.

'What if . . .' she said, thinking fast, 'what if I opened the shop? It'd just be while you're recovering.'

'No, lass, I couldn't ask you to do that.'

'You're not asking, I'm offering,' Poppy said, then she paused. 'Although . . . I'll need Rose's help. You know I'm no good with numbers and money, and I won't be able to read the packets and tins.'

Ambrose closed his eyes and gently nodded his head. 'Let me go and ask Ella. I've never made a business decision without her in all the years we've run the shop, and I don't intend to start now.'

Poppy helped him to stand again, and once he was steady on his feet, he disappeared from the room. She picked up Emily, who seemed restless and was still coughing. When Ambrose reappeared, he didn't come into the room, but stayed by the door, holding on to the door frame as if to keep him upright.

'Ella's agreed, and we'll pay you both.' He handed Poppy the key to the shop. 'Do what needs to be done to keep the place ticking over. I asked Michael and his wife Doris if they could look after the place for a few days, but Michael's got work at the pit and Doris cares for her ailing parents. You know our business well enough after all these years – just do what you can, lass. We'd be grateful.'

'What about up here? Would you like me to set the fire for you? I could boil up some beef tea for you both.'

'Aye, that'd be grand,' Ambrose said, struggling for breath.

'I'll have to go up the colliery to get Rose first, and I'll need to bring the boys here as Sid's off to the pit,' she said. 'But they'll keep quiet, I promise. I'll send them to play on the green if they get too noisy.'

'Thanks, lass,' Ambrose said as he shuffled back to his bed.

Poppy gathered up Emily, locked the back door and headed up the colliery bank. Her mind whirled with anxious thoughts about James Scurrfield seeking Rose, and about Ambrose and Ella in their sickbed. Above all, she was worried about Emily's cough. She walked quickly to Tunstall Street and explained to Rose what had happened at the Trewhitts', but kept quiet about what Hetty had said. If she told her and then it turned out the fella had been looking for someone else, she'd feel a fool and Rose would've been upset for no reason.

She waited while Rose called Harry and Sonny from the yard, where they were throwing stones at the wall. As they left the house, Lil Mahone poked her face out of her front door.

'Where are you all off to now?' she demanded.

Poppy sighed and shook her head. 'Do you have to know everything we do?' she said.

Lil crossed her arms. 'There's no need to be rude. I was just being neighbourly. Besides, I heard the baby coughing, and I was concerned. Such a young bairn shouldn't be coughing like that.'

'My baby's fine,' Poppy said defensively. 'And if you must know, we're going to work in the Trewhitts' shop. Ambrose and Ella are taking a break and me and Rose are helping them out. So if you're looking for news to spread today, Mrs Mahone, you can tell everyone you meet that the shop is back in business.'

'Oh, is that right now? The Trewhitts are open – well, that's good to hear. My husband Bob's a big fan of Ambrose's jam tarts.'

'There's no baking been done. There are no jam tarts, I'm sorry.'

Lil's face sank. Poppy and Rose began to walk away with the children.

'Oh, Poppy?' Lil called.

Poppy turned around. 'What now, Mrs Mahone?' she said impatiently. 'I'm in a hurry.'

Lil bristled. 'Well, since we're neighbours, there's no need to keep calling me Mrs Mahone. You can call me Lil from now on if you like.'

'Thank you . . . Lil,' Poppy replied.

With Rose holding hands with Harry and Sonny, and Poppy carrying Emily, who was now asleep, they made their way down the bank. Poppy kept glancing at her sister, wondering whether she was doing the right thing keeping the news from her about the man at the Albion Inn. She felt anxious and chewed up inside, not helped by the nausea from her pregnancy.

When they reached the shop, she unlocked the door, and gave Rose instructions to open the shutters and leave the door ajar to let passers-by know they were open for business. Upstairs, she set the coal fire in the living room, and once it was burning, she boiled beef tea and filled mugs, which she took into the bedroom for Ambrose and Ella. Ella was fast asleep, but Ambrose was sitting with a pillow propped at his back, and he thanked her for all she had done.

The afternoon passed quickly, giving Poppy little time to dwell on what Hetty had told her about the stranger in the Albion Inn. Harry and Sonny sat quietly behind the counter for all of half an hour before they started acting up. When they became too boisterous to stay indoors, she sent them out to play on the green, and kept her eye on them through the shop window. She laid Emily on a blanket she'd found in the back room and put her behind the counter in an empty box that had once held eggs from the farm. The baby slept as Poppy and Rose served customers. Poppy had to let Rose take charge of the money, adding up and giving change, and together they worked hard through the day. Each time the shop was quiet, Poppy headed upstairs to give Ambrose more tea, although Ella didn't wake from her sleep.

At the end of the day, when the bells from St Paul's chimed the closing hour, Poppy pulled the shutters closed and locked up. She took the money from the till upstairs, and was happy to see that Ambrose was up and dressed, sitting on the sofa by the fire.

'Are you feeling a little better?' she asked. 'You've got more colour in your face than before.'

'Aye, lass, I think I'm on the mend, which is more than can be said for Ella. She's still not well enough to get out of bed. I think I'll be all right to return to work tomorrow.'

Poppy handed him the bag of money.

'Thanks, lass,' he said. 'And thank your sister too. The

pair of you have worked wonders today.' He took coins from the bag and handed them to her in payment.

'Thank you, Ambrose. We did what we could, but if you need me again, just send word up the colliery bank and I'll be only too happy to help. We're living on Tunstall Street now.'

'Bit of a change from the barn, I'll bet,' he noted.

'The pit house is small and poky and there's no outside space for the boys to run around. But the worst of it is the coal dust and the noise of the trains. The air's affecting the baby already.'

'Take loving care of her,' Ambrose said. 'And take good care of yourself, Poppy. You're so busy with your bairns and your husband, and now your sister too, you need someone to look after you.'

'Fat chance of that,' Poppy laughed. 'We'll manage, you'll see.'

'Aye, lass, you're nowt if not capable. You always have been, even when you were a bairn. I dare say you can cope with anything life chucks at you.'

A vision of James Scurrfield came to her mind, and a shiver ran down her spine.

Chapter Thirty-Nine

In the days that followed, Poppy tried to settle in to her new home. Sid was working night shifts, and when he was home during the day, he slept. Poppy worked around his shifts, preparing the tin bath for him when she'd scrub the coal dust from his skin. A fire roared constantly in the hearth, even on the warmest days, for it was needed to boil water for bathing and washing, and for cooking the food that Poppy prepared for them all. As for Rose, she left the house each morning seeking work but always came home dejected.

'Don't they need a barmaid in any of the pubs?' Poppy asked one afternoon. 'Surely there must be jobs going somewhere, perhaps at the Co-op?'

But Rose shook her head. 'I keep coming up against the same problem at every place I ask. I don't have experience.' She sank into a chair at the table. 'I've never worked in a pub before, and I haven't done any work at all apart from the time I spent with you at the Trewhitts'.'

Poppy brewed a pot of tea and handed a mug to Rose as she continued her lament. 'The pubs want barmaids who know how to pull a pint and can provide a character reference. I haven't got anyone who can do that for me. I've never had to work before. But I was thinking about Hetty and Jack at the Albion Inn . . .'

Poppy's blood ran cold at the mention of the pub, and the thought of the man matching James Scurrfield's description.

'. . . Hetty Burdon's a good woman. She might take me on without a reference. Do you think it'd be worth me asking her for a job?'

'No!' Poppy snapped, then turned her face away.

There was silence between them for a few moments. She knew she'd gone too far.

'Poppy, are you all right?'

She was about to reply when the sound of Emily's cough reached her from the bedroom. She stood to head upstairs to her child.

'She doesn't sound well,' Rose said softly.

'She isn't,' Poppy replied. 'She needs the doctor, but we don't have the money. The little Ambrose paid us is certainly nowhere near enough for that.'

'I have a little left from selling the hairpin. And I could always offer to sell this dress to the rag and bone girl. Course, it'd mean I'd have to share your clothes. If I sell it, I'd have nothing else to wear.'

'I wouldn't let you do that,' Poppy said.

'Can't Sid get an advance on his wages?'

She shook her head. 'He asked, but they turned him down.'

Flying up the stairs, she picked Emily up out of her cot and brought her down to the kitchen, but the child still wouldn't settle. Poppy's soothing words, which had always worked their charm on her beloved daughter when they'd lived in the barn, had no effect now.

'She's burning up, poor thing. I'll take her out to the yard; it's shaded there, the air will be cool. I wish I knew what to do. The boys were never like this as babies. If I don't get her some help, who knows what might happen?'

Rose stood and began pacing the small kitchen from the fire to the back door. 'We need money for the doctor,' she muttered as she walked, deep in thought.

'And we need it fast,' Poppy added. 'Sid asked the lads at work in case any of them might have been able to lend us the cash. One lad said he knew someone who loaned money, but we'd have to pay it back threefold, and if the debt's not settled on time, he comes into your house and takes what he likes by way of repayment.'

She squeezed past Rose and walked into the small yard, with its walls that hemmed her in like a pig locked in a pen. With Emily coughing, and her own constant nausea as her pregnancy developed, she was starting to feel very sorry for herself.

'Come on, Poppy, pull yourself together,' she whispered to the four walls. The cool air seemed to ease Emily's breathing a little. Just then, Rose appeared at her side.

'Well, have you come up with a grand plan that'll save us?' Poppy said sarcastically, then stopped short and looked at her sister. 'I'm sorry, Rose, you didn't deserve that. I'm on edge.'

Rose laid her hand on Poppy's shoulder. 'Actually, I have got an idea,' she said.

Poppy stared at her. 'You do? What?'

Rose took a deep breath. 'You're not going to like it.'

Poppy tilted her chin. 'Try me.'

'I've got . . .' Rose began, then faltered before she

continued. 'I've got a friend I could ask to help find me a job . . .'

There was something about the way she emphasised the word *friend* that Poppy didn't like. 'A friend? You mean Arthur Mason, don't you?'

Rose's cheeks coloured and Poppy knew she'd hit the spot. When her sister didn't deny it, Poppy tutted loudly, disapproving.

'Oh Rose, he's married! I won't let you ask him, no, it'd be wrong. Anyway, why are you going after a married man? You've never explained it to me.'

'Arthur listens to me, Poppy, and he doesn't judge or ask where I've been in the last ten years. He's one of the few people in Ryhope who doesn't care about my past. All he's interested in is how I am now . . . no, more than that, he's interested in *who* I am now. You expect me to act like the girl I was before, not the twenty-year-old woman I am now! Anyway, me and Arthur aren't carrying on with each other, as you seem to imagine. I've only met him a few times. We bumped into each other on the village green, and now we sit and talk. We've only kissed once. That's all. I've done nothing else with him, not in the way you mean. But so what if I had? I've lost years of my life being controlled by the Scurrfields. At least it would be my choice this time.'

'What about his wife? Does she know what's going on? I bet she doesn't, does she?' Poppy said harshly. 'If I found out that my Sid was sitting on a bench on the village green with another woman, I'd chuck him out on the street and never let him see his bairns again.'

Rose was silent for a while. 'His wife's bad with her nerves and she doesn't leave the house,' she said.

'Oh, listen to yourself, Rose. I bet you've only got Arthur's word for that, haven't you? You'll be telling me next that his wife doesn't understand him, or they've fallen out of love, or you're the apple of his eye and the girl he should have wed. He's spinning you lies. Maisie says he's a rogue.'

Rose put her hands on her hips. 'So he's married and he's a rogue . . . so what?' she yelled.

Poppy looked up at the sky, for she couldn't bear to look at her sister. 'I thought I knew you, Rose. I thought I could trust you. And now you're telling me you've been kissing a married man. I'm disappointed in you.'

Rose's face flushed red with anger. 'Well, I'm not sorry and I won't apologise for having Arthur as a friend. Have you any idea what it's like to feel lonely? Well, have you?' Poppy stared open-mouthed as her sister continued. 'You've got Sid and the boys and the baby and another on its way, and I've got no one. I've got nothing, Poppy. Nothing.'

'You've got me and Sid and the bairns. You're part of our family,' Poppy cried.

'It's not the same. Do you know how lucky you are to have Sid? I haven't got anyone to cuddle up to at night, no one to whisper my thoughts to, no one to help me make sense of being back in Ryhope. I'm lost, Poppy, lost. That's why I turned to Arthur. He doesn't judge me, and he shows me compassion. If I want to see him, I will.'

Rose turned her back on Poppy and headed indoors. By the time Poppy had calmed down enough to follow her, her sister had already left.

Poppy sat by the fire going over what Rose had said, trying to make sense of it. Oh, Arthur Mason was a good-looking man, strong and tall with sparkling blue eyes, and she could understand what Rose saw in him. But he was married. Married! How could Rose be stupid enough to get involved with him? But even as Poppy tried to make sense of it, her sister's words about treating her as an adult, and about being lonely, cut her to the bone.

Chapter Forty

Poppy waited anxiously for Rose to return, but when the afternoon turned into evening and there was still no sign of her, she guessed there was only one place she would be: with Arthur. If that was the case, there was nothing she could do. Sid returned from his day shift, relieved to no longer be working nights, for now. He had his bath, and Poppy cooked cabbage soup. She set a place at the table for Rose, but still her sister didn't appear.

Once the boys were in bed and Emily was settled in her cot, Poppy and Sid sat either side of the hearth. Sid cradled a mug of tea while Poppy began unpicking stitches in Harry and Sonny's trousers.

'The boys are growing so quickly,' she sighed. 'I'll speak to Meg Sutcliffe the next time I see her on the pit lane. She might have bairns' clothes for sale on her rag and bone cart.'

'It's hardly the life I wanted for you all,' Sid said quietly. 'My family shouldn't need to wear other people's old clothes. I should be able to provide for you and the twins and pay for the doctor's care that Emily needs. It sounds as if her cough is getting worse.'

'Is it worth asking again for an advance on your wages?' Poppy wondered.

'Oh, I've asked a second time, but I was given the same reply. I even asked in the Miners' Welfare Hall if anyone knew a fella who might loan us cash, but . . .' Sid shook his head, 'the only name that gets mentioned is the fella who charges three times what he loans and then threatens folks who can't repay on time.'

Poppy looked hard at her husband. 'Some days I worry that Emily's bad chest means she mightn't last even another day.'

A look of horror passed over Sid's face. 'Does her cough really get that bad while I'm out at work?' he asked.

'Sometimes it does, yes,' Poppy said. 'If we don't get her to the doctor soon, Sid, I'm afraid we'll lose her.'

Whenever Poppy and Rose had been poorly as children, their mam had eased their ills with hot drinks of infused herbs or crushed leaves from the raspberry bush in their garden. But Poppy knew in her heart that no herbs or leaves would cure Emily, and no old wives' tales would help. She dropped her gaze to her sewing.

'You know, Rose said something earlier,' she began cautiously.

'Where is she, anyway?' Sid said. 'It's not like her to miss tea. Is she out looking for work again?'

'No,' Poppy said.

Sid looked at her, puzzled. 'Then where is she? What's going on, Pops?'

Poppy laid her sewing down. 'We argued and she stormed out. I've no idea where she's gone.'

Sid laughed. 'Don't be daft, Pops. You and Rose have

never argued in your life. What's happened?'

Tears sprang to Poppy's eyes. 'She suggested asking Arthur Mason to help her find a job.'

Sid struggled to understand what he was being told. 'Arthur Mason? My dad's mate? What's he got to do with Rose?'

Poppy raised her eyebrows at him. 'Oh!' Sid exclaimed as the penny dropped. 'But he's married!'

'I know; that's what we argued about.'

'Are Rose and Arthur carrying on?' Sid asked.

Poppy shrugged. 'I thought they just went out for walks together, but when I pressed her, she admitted they'd kissed. She said something else too: that she's lonely and wants someone to love. Me, you and the bairns aren't enough for her, she said. She wants a fella and a life of her own.'

Sid leaned back in his chair. 'My word, I had no idea. I thought she was happy living with us.'

'I thought so too, but the more I think about what she said, the more I realise how alone she must be feeling. I'm so wrapped up with you, the boys and the baby that I took Rose into my heart as if she'd never been away. I realise now that I've been treating her as though she's still my little sister. And there's something else you don't know, something I've been keeping from you.'

'Go on, I'm listening,' Sid said.

Poppy told him the full extent of James's bad behaviour to Rose. She told him things she had kept from him before as she'd been unsure whether to tell him, in case he judged Rose badly. Sid took the news stoically.

'You're not angry with Rose, are you?' Poppy asked.

'Of course not, my love,' Sid replied.

'There's more bad news, I'm afraid,' she continued.

Poppy told him what Hetty had said about the man matching James Scurrfield's description in the Albion Inn. 'He was asking for someone called Rose. Now it could've been anyone, I know. My sister's not the only one in Ryhope by that name. But it seems too much of a coincidence.' She sighed heavily. 'I'm struggling, Sid. It's not easy running the family and tending to everyone's needs. And sometimes I forget where I am in all of this. I'm being sick every day; our baby inside me is making me tired and ill. I worry for Emily all the time, and then there's Ambrose and Ella . . .'

Sid walked towards her and knelt down in front of her, resting his hands on hers. 'I love you, Pops. I love you with all my heart. We'll look after Rose for as long as she needs us. But I can't help feeling uneasy to learn that James Scurrfield might be looking for her. What do you think he wants?'

'He's an evil man,' Poppy said. 'We need to keep Rose safe.'

Sid kissed her on the lips, then stood and returned to his seat as Poppy continued.

'Have I failed her, Sid? Have I done the wrong thing keeping her close to me on such a short leash? I thought I was shielding her from being gossiped about, but maybe she's feeling as hemmed in as I am within the four walls of this house. Maybe palling up with Arthur Mason was her way to escape; perhaps she felt I was too controlling.'

Sid sipped his tea, then slowly raised his gaze. 'Rose isn't a girl any more and you're no longer bairns. The two of you have grown up and apart in the years she was away. She's different now, she's been through a lot. But my goodness . . . learning she's friendly with Arthur has come as a shock. Does his wife know about it?'

'Rose said his wife is bad with her nerves and doesn't leave the house. It could be a line that Arthur's spun her to ease his conscience, or it might be the truth. Either way, he's married and that's the end of it. What he and Rose are doing is wrong.'

'But he offered to find her a job, is that right?' Sid asked.

'I don't think he offered. It sounded as if Rose was willing to ask him. That's when we argued and she left the house, and I haven't seen her since.'

Sid had opened his mouth to reply when there was a knock at the door. He and Poppy looked at each other.

'That might be Rose now, coming home with her tail between her legs,' he said.

Poppy laid her sewing on the hearth. She doubted very much it would be Rose, as the door was unlocked and she would have simply walked in. She headed along the hallway and was surprised to find Lil Mahone on the doorstep, dressed in her black coat and green hat with her handbag over her arm.

'Evening, Lil. What can I do for you?' she asked.

Lil glanced up and down the pit lane, then leaned towards Poppy. 'I've got something to tell you,' she whispered. 'It's probably best if I come inside.' Without waiting to be invited, she stepped into the hallway.

Poppy was slowly getting used to the strange behaviour of her neighbour. She turned and walked to the kitchen with Lil following.

'Sid, Lil says she's got news,' she announced.

Sid sat up straight in his seat. 'Evening, Lil,' he said politely.

'I won't stay long; I'll just say my piece and go.' Lil's eyes darted from Poppy to Sid. 'It's about your sister. I thought you should know that I've just seen her in the Guide Post Inn.'

'She's in a pub? See, I told you she'd get herself a job,' Sid said.

Poppy shot him a look, then turned back to their neighbour. 'Go on, Lil,' she urged.

'Your sister isn't working in the pub. She's drinking with Arthur Mason, and they're both as drunk as lords. I came straight here to tell you. I'd only called in for a small glass of stout with Bob when I heard an awful noise coming from the back room at the bar. There was yelling and carrying-on and so I had to see who was causing it. I'm afraid it was Rose and Arthur, both the worse for wear, shouting at each other, screaming blue murder.'

Poppy couldn't speak. She looked at Sid for support, and without being asked, he knew what to do. Stepping forward, he took Lil by the arm and escorted her along the hallway.

'Thank you, Lil, we appreciate you telling us, and we'd be obliged if you'd keep the news to yourself.' Before the woman knew what was happening, he had opened the front door and was encouraging her to leave.

Once she had stepped outside on to the pit lane, Sid closed the door and headed back to the kitchen. 'I'll go and get Rose and bring her home immediately,' he said. He thrust his arms into his jacket and prepared to leave, but Poppy grabbed hold of him.

'No, Sid, leave her be. She'll not thank us for stopping

her from doing what she wants. I think we should let her relationship with Arthur run its course, let her get him out of her system. She'll come back when she's ready.' She sank into her seat.

Sid stared at her. 'Are you sure? Because once gossip spreads about her drinking with a married man . . . well, it's the sort of news that will stick. It won't do her any good, especially when she's looking for a job with decent folk. Let me have a word with her and make sure she's all right. For all we know, Arthur might be plying her with drink and planning to take advantage. And if she's as lonely as she claims, who knows what she might do?'

Poppy relented and Sid left the house.

Left alone by the fire, she put her head in her hands, taking long, deep breaths and trying to calm her racing heart. She thought of herself and Rose as girls, always together, and then as orphans, supporting each other while they lived with Nellie Harper. Sharing the one pair of boots for school. All Poppy had ever wanted was to keep her little sister safe. But Sid was right: they were women now, not girls. Rose knew her own mind, and nothing Poppy could say or do could influence her. She knew she had to take a step back and allow her sister to live her own life.

She was still sitting by the fire, worried thoughts turning over in her mind, when she heard the door open. She sat up straight in her seat. 'Sid?' she called.

There was no reply, just a scuffling noise, and then she heard Rose's slurred voice, pleading and cajoling. 'Come on, Sid, just a little kiss?'

Her blood ran cold. She stood and walked to the hallway, where the sight that met her eyes made her stop dead. Her sister was kissing Sid full on the lips. As for Sid, he was trying to prop Rose up as best he could, for she could barely stand on her own.

'She's drunk, Pops,' he said when he pulled himself away. 'I can't get her off me. She was like this all the way up the bank, begging for kisses and cuddles.'

'I know you like me, Sid. I was always your favourite,' Rose slurred, then she looked up and saw Poppy. 'Oh, and here's my sensible sister. The woman who keeps her beady eye on me. Well, not for much longer. As soon as I get a job, I'm moving out of this dump and I'm going to live with Arthur.'

'Help me, Pops,' Sid begged. 'I can't hold her. She's sliding down the wall.'

Poppy helped Sid carry Rose to her room and lay her down on her bed. The minute her head hit the pillow, her eyes closed and she began snoring.

Poppy laid her head on Sid's chest. 'I want to keep her safe, Sid . . . but I don't know what to do.'

Chapter Forty-One

The next morning when Poppy woke, her first thought was Emily. She bathed her daughter while Harry and Sonny played in the yard, throwing stones against the walls. They'd become fractious with each other since moving to the pit house. Poppy couldn't blame them, however, as the space available for playing out was constrained. Even she and Sid, who'd never had cross words in all their years of marriage, were beginning to get tetchy with each other, snappy over the smallest thing. They always seemed to be in each other's way around the house when Sid was at home.

As she bent over Emily in the tin bath, she noticed that the baby's breathing was weak. A noise at the door made her look up, and she saw Rose, her hair unkempt and clothes crumpled.

'Morning,' Poppy said.

Rose put her hand to the table to steady herself, then flopped down on to a chair. She sank her head into her hands and moaned softly.

'Got a bad head from drinking too much beer last night?' Poppy snipped, then stopped herself. Now that she knew a little of how her sister was really feeling, she decided to choose her words carefully. She would try to remember to treat Rose as a grown woman, not as the child she'd once known.

'How did I get back here?' Rose asked. Poppy looked at her carefully and saw how pale her skin was, her eyes red and watering.

'You really don't remember?'

Rose shook her head.

'Sid brought you. Lil Mahone told us where you were. She said you'd had a lot to drink and you were with your, er, friend Arthur.'

'Oh, him . . .' Rose groaned.

'Are you two still courting?'

'We're not courting, we never were. Why won't you believe me?' Rose muttered. 'I don't remember Sid coming for me.'

Poppy straightened up and gave her sister a hard stare. 'Oh, you were in a bonny state. You were kissing Sid on the lips, trying to cuddle him. You even told him he was better off with you than with me.'

'No!' Rose cried, her eyes wide.

'I'm afraid so,' Poppy replied. 'I'm sure he will be embarrassed when you see him. It's probably best if you apologise to him.'

'Oh, I will, of course,' Rose said quickly, 'and I want to apologise to you too.' She laid her head on the table on top of her arms. 'My head hurts something terrible.'

Poppy thought for a moment. 'What was it that Mam used to give Dad for his headaches? Can you remember? She used to go to the field and pick a plant . . . Was it mint?'

'Mint and sage,' Rose said, raising her head. 'She'd put them in boiled water, then bathe Dad's head with the liquid. Or did she make him drink it? I can't remember. But it was definitely mint and sage.'

'You'll find both growing in the field at the back of the store,' Poppy said. 'They might do your hangover good.'

'I'm never going to drink again as long as I live,' Rose declared. She seemed to notice Emily for the first time. 'How is she this morning?'

'Still not breathing as well as she should, and still coughing a lot.' Poppy gazed at the baby with concern. 'Her chest's tight and she needs a hot poultice, but I've never made one before and I don't want to get it wrong. I might end up doing more harm than good. She was never this bad before we moved.'

'What about Lil next door? She might know how to make one. Go and ask her, you never know.'

Poppy dried Emily, then wrapped her in a warm blanket and laid her in her cot. 'All right, I'll go and ask,' she said.

She made her way next door and knocked long and hard at the door, but there was no reply.

Much later that day, at the Trewhitts' shop, Ambrose was struggling to open the shutters. The flu had left him weak, exhausted and suffering pains in his chest.

'I've got them open, Ella,' he said softly. He wasn't expecting a reply, as Ella was still upstairs in bed, too ill with the flu to even get up. She'd stopped eating during the last few days, and had drunk little. Ambrose was so worried about her that he'd asked their neighbour to request Dr Anderson to call that evening. Still, he was determined to open the shop for a few hours before going back to bed.

'I'm opening the door now, love,' he said under his breath. The bell above the door tinkled, as it had done almost every day since he and Ella had taken the shop on, and Ambrose stood looking out at the village green. He spotted Amos Bird, the man who'd taken on Norman's farm, but he didn't have the strength to raise his hand in a friendly wave. As he stood there, he could hear birds singing in the oak trees on the green. In the distance, a dog barked and the bells of St Paul's church chimed the hour.

He headed to his spot behind the counter and flopped down on Ella's stool, getting his breath back. No sooner had he done so than two customers walked in. The first one he recognised, and he greeted her with a welcoming smile.

'Ah, Lil. How's your Bob doing? Is he still working hard?' he managed to say.

'Bob's fine, thanks for asking. I heard you and Ella had the flu, is that right? If you don't mind me saying so, you're not looking well. But I'm pleased you've opened up, I've been hoping you would – you know I only like to shop here. Now then, I'd like half a dozen brown eggs and two jam tarts.'

Ambrose forced himself off the stool. 'No jam tarts today,' he said. 'I haven't felt well enough to bake them.' All the while he was aware of his other customer waiting by the door, a man he hadn't seen before.

As Ambrose fetched the eggs, Lil rummaged in her handbag and the man stepped forward. He was heavy-set, with dark hair, dark eyes and a stern expression on his face.

'Excuse me, sir,' he said politely to Ambrose.

Both Ambrose and Lil turned to look at him. The man removed his top hat.

'I'm sorry to bother you,' he continued, 'but I'm looking for, um, a friend of mine. A lady friend named Rose. I understand she recently returned to live in Ryhope.'

'Oh, you'll mean Rose Thomas; she's just come back after living away,' Lil said.

Ambrose shot her a warning look. She really was indiscreet, and it annoyed him that she was sharing personal information about Poppy's sister with the stranger.

'Do you know where I might find her?' the man asked.

'Do I know where to find her?' Lil laughed out loud. 'Why, she lives next door to me on Tunstall Street.'

'Lil!' Ambrose said sternly. The effort of getting the word out seemed to knock the wind from his sails, and he had to rest with both hands on the counter. When he finally got his breath back, he glared at her.

The gentleman put his hat on and headed out of the door. Ambrose watched him walk away towards the Albion Inn, then turned back to Lil. 'You can't go telling folk other people's business,' he said, wagging a finger.

But his words were like water off a duck's back. 'Oh Ambrose, don't get yourself worked up. It's no secret who lives where on the pit lanes. We all know each other up there.'

Ambrose put the eggs in a small box, which Lil placed in her basket. Once she had paid, she walked from the shop, tutting loudly. As she left, a shadowy figure emerged from the doorway of the Albion Inn and began to follow her.

Meanwhile, inside the shop, Ambrose sat down on Ella's stool again. Serving Lil had taken its toll, and his heart was jumping from the exertion. 'I tried, Ella. At least I tried,' he muttered under his breath.

After a while, he stood, closed the shutters, locked the door and began climbing the stairs to their bedroom.

'How are you feeling, Ella?' he called as he puffed and panted his way upstairs. 'Are you able to face a cup of tea yet?'

But Ella never replied, for while Ambrose had been working downstairs, she had taken her very last breath.

Chapter Forty-Two

James Scurrfield stayed a respectable distance behind Lil so that she wouldn't spot him if she turned. His walk from the Trewhitts' shop to Tunstall Street was a slow, arduous one, for Lil stopped to talk to passers-by on numerous occasions. At last, though, she crossed the road by the Miners' Welfare Hall and headed towards the rows of limewashed pit cottages.

James felt his breath quicken. He looked around at the dilapidated houses, at the festering muck on the cobbles. This wasn't where he'd expected Rose to be living; he'd imagined something grander. Had this little woman he'd been following given him false information? Was he about to find the wrong woman, another Rose?

He saw Lil disappear through a front door. There were houses either side of the one she'd entered, and he had no idea which was the one where Rose lived. He pushed his shoulders back and knocked at the door to the left. When there was no answer, he knocked again, but still the door didn't open. Shrugging, he went to the door of the house on the right and rapped hard, three times. As he waited for it to open, he heard the sound of a baby's cry. He took a step back and was about to knock again when the door was flung wide. In front of him stood two small boys. James did a double-take as he looked from one round, chubby face to the other. They were identical in every way. He shook his head, trying to clear his mind. Was he seeing things? Going mad?

'Harry? Sonny? Who's at the door?' a woman's voice called.

'There's a man here, Mam,' one of the boys shouted. Neither of them showed any sign of moving; they simply glared at him. And then, all of a sudden, Rose came into his line of sight.

Rose moved quickly towards him, a look of stunned disbelief on her face. Her heart pounded under her blue velvet dress and her legs felt like jelly. She forced herself to take a long, deep breath before she addressed him. But first she had to shoo the twins away. She pulled the door closed and stepped outside to the pit lane.

'What do you want?' she said quickly, looking up and down the colliery bank. All the while her heart was beating wildly. She was confused and scared.

'I want you back at Gray Road. You seem to have forgotten that you belong to the Scurrfields,' James snarled.

Rose swallowed hard, then cast a nervous glance at the door. She knew Poppy would be wondering what was going on. Her sister had her hands full with Emily and the twins; she didn't want to alarm her by calling for help. She braced herself and met James's dark eyes. 'I'm staying here, where I belong, with my family,' she said firmly.

She was about to say more when the front door swung open and Poppy appeared. Her eyes widened in shock, and she caught Rose by the arm and tried to yank her indoors, but James stuck his boot against the door so that it couldn't close.

'She's coming with me,' he said, grabbing Rose's free arm.

'No, she's not,' Poppy said, trying to pull Rose further into the house.

'Stop it, both of you! I'm not a rag doll to be torn apart!' Rose shouted, shaking herself free.

Poppy kicked at James's foot, trying to get him to move it so that she could force the door shut, but her efforts proved futile. She was no match for the man, and he shouldered his way indoors.

In the kitchen, Emily was lying in her cot, coughing and wheezing. Poppy flew to her and picked her up, attempting to calm her, but it was no use.

'She needs the doctor,' she cried, pacing the stuffy kitchen from the hearth to the back door, cradling Emily in her arms.

James indicated a chair at the table. 'May I sit?' he asked.

'No!' Rose said sharply. 'Say what you've come to say and then leave. We've got a poorly bairn here. How dare you turn up demanding to see me? How did you find me?'

Poppy noticed her sister's harsh tone and thought of what she had said before about having grown thorns. In that moment, she detested James Scurrfield for what he'd done to Rose at Gray Road.

'Don't question me, girl,' James snapped. 'I'm here to take you home.'

'Home?' Rose exploded. 'That place was never home,

it was a prison.' She rocked back on her heels and took a deep breath, then continued in almost a whisper, trying to contain her anger. 'You controlled me and beat me. And there was worse . . . You know what you did to me, and I will never forgive you for that! You locked me in my room, told Mrs Hutchins not to feed me. Look at me, I'm skin and bones even now. I had no life with you on Gray Road. I saw no one but you, I wasn't allowed out without you. You even chose the clothes I wore. I had no say in my own life. What makes you think I'd ever go back there?'

James took a step forward. 'Don't tell me you're happy living here in this hovel? Just look at the state of your clothes and your hair. You were never so unkempt when you lived at Gray Road.'

Poppy stopped pacing the floor and shot him a dark look. 'A hovel? How dare you be so rude about my home!'

Emily began coughing again, gasping for breath, and Poppy turned to Rose.

'I need to get her to the doctor, right now. I don't care about paying three times over the odds to Sid's workmate. I'd rather lose all my belongings than lose my child. I must go. I don't know how much breath she has left.' She looked at James again. 'Get out of my house,' she said coldly. 'I said get out! I need to take my child to the doctor immediately.'

Rose laid a gentle finger against Emily's cheek, then she stepped forward and held her hand out to James. Poppy couldn't believe what she was seeing.

'No . . . don't tell me you're thinking about going with this monster,' she gasped. 'He beat you, Rose. You begged us to rescue you. How can you consider going back?'

Rose tilted her chin defiantly. 'We need money for the doctor, it's as simple as that,' she said calmly, then she turned her gaze to James. 'I will go back, but I have one condition.'

'Name it,' he said.

'That I stay with you for one night only, and that this time you pay for the privilege of sharing my bed.'

Poppy gasped in horror. 'Rose! No!'

Rose kept her eyes fixed on James's face as she continued. 'If you want me as badly as you say you do, you will pay for my company. I will only leave here with you if you agree to hand over the money now.'

Poppy felt anger building inside her. 'Don't be ridiculous, Rose,' she hissed.

Rose stood tall and pushed her shoulders back. 'Pay my sister. Now,' she ordered James.

'I haven't any money with me,' he replied.

She stepped forward and breathed into his face. 'I know you go nowhere without your velvet purse. Pay her now or you'll never see me again.'

Defeated, James rummaged inside his thick coat and pulled out a black velvet purse. He flung it on the kitchen table, where it landed with a thud. Poppy looked at Rose.

'Sister, take it.'

Poppy couldn't breathe, she couldn't think. She wanted to scream at them both, to say she wouldn't take the filthy cash. But in her arms, Emily's head lolled back. She was incandescent with shame over what Rose was suggesting, but more than that, more than anything, she had to save her daughter. Unable to take any more, she picked up the purse, heavy with coins, pushed her way past Rose and James and hurried outside. All she could think about was getting Emily to the doctor's house as fast as she could. Harry and Sonny ran behind her, holding hands.

After she'd gone, Rose and James stepped on to the street. Next door at Lil Mahone's house, a curtain twitched at the window as the pair walked away.

Ambrose was paralysed by sorrow and grief. He sat on the bed next to the lifeless form of his beloved wife and kissed her softly on her cheek. Then he lay down beside her and held her cold hand. 'You're not going anywhere without me,' he whispered.

He closed his eyes. He was fatigued from the flu, nowhere near as well as he should have been when he'd opened the shop. It had been a mistake to think he had the strength in him to return to work. Climbing the stairs had done him in, his heart going like the clappers, and now the shock of seeing Ella had proved too much for it to take.

It was the Trewhitts' daughter-in-law, Doris, who found them that evening. She'd gone to the shop to check on them, as she knew the doctor was due to attend Ella. She stood at the threshold of their bedroom and respectfully bowed her head, offering a silent prayer for the souls of the much-loved couple. Then, slowly and carefully, she closed the bedroom door and returned downstairs, locking the shop with the key that Michael had given her. As she walked away, the last sound she heard was the tinkle of the bell at the door.

She went straight to Dr Anderson's house to report

what had happened. Afterwards, holding back tears, she walked to St Paul's, where she sat in a pew at the back of the church. She bowed her head and made the sign of the cross, shedding silent tears for the loss of the loving couple. Then she stood, dried her eyes on her handkerchief, and walked briskly home to break the devastating news to her husband.

Chapter Forty-Three

Poppy ran down the colliery bank. Her heart was beating wildly and she couldn't think straight. All she could focus on was getting Emily to the doctor as quickly as possible. She flew past the Co-op, past the rhubarb field and the Miners' Welfare Hall. Folk stared at her as if she was mad, running with a baby in her arms and the twins chasing after her.

'Slow down, lass, you'll fall if you're not careful,' a woman called out, but her words were lost on the breeze.

Poppy passed the Duke of Wellington pub, the Guide Post Inn, the cinema and the police station. When she reached St Paul's church, she was forced to slow down by the pain of the stitch in her side. She leaned against the stone wall to get her breath back. Reverend Daye was waiting by the church door, and when he noticed that she was panting and red in the face, he invited her to sit for a while in the church.

'I can't, Vicar, I'm sorry. I must get to the doctor. It's the baby, she can't breathe properly.'

'Then you must go, my child,' Reverend Daye replied kindly. 'Would you like me to look after your boys while you're with the doctor? They could sit quietly in the church until you return.'

The thought of Harry and Sonny trying to sit quietly made Poppy shake her head. 'Thank you for your generous offer, but I'll take them with me. I need to keep them close.'

'And how is your sister?' the vicar asked, but Poppy had already started hurrying away.

She had too much on her mind. She was still reeling with shock over what had just happened at Tunstall Street. Rose offering to sell herself to evil James for a night proved too hard to comprehend. As she hurried past the church and the village school, she didn't dare take a peek at Emily's face, terrified in case her beloved child had already breathed her last. She swallowed hard, crossed the road at the school and headed to Stockton Road.

She arrived at the doctor's house panting and gasping for breath. When she knocked on the door, it was opened by Sylvia, the doctor's daughter, an attractive young woman with long fair hair and sparkling blue eyes.

'I need to see Dr Anderson. It's my bairn, she's not breathing right,' Poppy gasped.

Sylvia led her into a small, square room. Poppy hadn't been inside the doctor's house before. The room was cold and bare and felt sterile; it wasn't what she'd expected from the home of a man as wealthy as the doctor.

Sylvia glanced at Emily, and what she saw clearly alarmed her. 'Please, take a seat, I'll call my father,' she said.

Poppy thrust the velvet purse at her. She had no idea how much money was inside, but it felt heavy with coins; surely there had to be enough.

Sylvia shook her head slightly. 'My father will examine the child first, to see what can be done,' she said, then she disappeared through a large wooden door.

Poppy slid the purse into her pocket and looked around the room. A hard wooden bench ran along three sides of it.

'Sit down, boys,' she ordered, and the twins obediently climbed on to the bench, holding hands, their legs dangling. Poppy couldn't sit, she was too worried about Emily. And each time she thought of Rose, her stomach turned at what her sister had offered to do in exchange for James's money. Rose had made the ultimate sacrifice for her, offering herself to a man she hated in order to save Emily.

Poppy's heart pounded and her thoughts whirled. She dared herself to peek inside the blanket that Emily was wrapped in, and when she saw her daughter, she gasped aloud in shock. She marched to the door Sylvia had walked through and pulled the handle, but it was locked. She banged on it as loudly as she could. 'Please help me, my baby . . . !'

The door was flung open and the looming presence of Dr Anderson filled the room. He was a tall man, with broad shoulders and a thatch of dark hair. He wore brown trousers and a matching waistcoat over a white shirt with the sleeves rolled up to his elbows. Sylvia hovered behind him.

'Let me see the child,' he said, and Poppy offered Emily into his capable hands. He turned back through the doorway.

Poppy looked sternly at Harry and Sonny. 'Stay there. Don't touch anything. Don't run around and don't leave. Got it?'

'Yes, Mam,' they chorused.

Then she ran to the doctor's side as he carefully laid Emily on a table covered with a white cloth. 'She's not been breathing properly for a while,' she said urgently. 'Her name is Emily Rose Lawson. Just look at her, Doctor, she's gone an awful colour.'

Dr Anderson snapped into action, turning Emily this way and that, rubbing her back and her limbs.

Poppy watched in horror; she couldn't bear it. She sank into a chair and covered her face with her hands. 'I'm going to lose her, aren't I?'

Sylvia put an arm around her shoulders. 'Father will do everything he can. It seems you brought her to him in the nick of time. Look . . .'

Poppy opened her eyes to see the faintest blush of pink making its way to Emily's cheeks.

'She's going to be all right,' Sylvia said gently. 'But she will need to stay here overnight so we can watch her, just in case.'

'My daughter's right,' agreed Dr Anderson. 'We'll need to observe her. You can stay if you wish. It won't be a comfortable night, but there's a chair to sit in.'

'Yes, I will, of course,' Poppy said.

She stood and walked to the table. Emily was still struggling for breath, her chest wheezing, but she was no longer the dreadful colour she'd been just moments before.

'She'll need medication to overcome the infection,' Dr Anderson said warily.

Poppy took the velvet purse from her pocket. 'I can pay,' she said. She handed the purse to Sylvia, who peered inside.

'Why, there's too much here. The medication and my father's fee won't cost this much.'

'Take what you need,' Poppy said.

'Don't you want to count it first?'

She shook her head. 'I can't,' she admitted.

Sylvia laid the purse carefully on her father's desk. 'We'll settle the bill tomorrow.'

Dr Anderson listened to Emily's chest and lungs, then ordered Sylvia to bring medication.

'Will she be all right, Doctor?' Poppy begged.

Dr Anderson looked at her gravely. 'The night will tell,' he said darkly. Then he pulled himself up to his full height. 'I apologise for my tone, Mrs Lawson. But I am concerned about Emily. If she survives the next few hours, she'll need all your love and care. I am not expecting any patients for the rest of the night; my colleague Dr Hill is on duty, as it's my evening of rest. I only agreed to see you because Sylvia told me how ill your child was. You won't be disturbed, I assure you. Sylvia will bring you a cup of tea while you settle. Your baby will sleep once she has the medicine inside her. But I need you to alert me if she worsens in the night.' He pointed to the door that Sylvia had walked through. 'Through there is my home. This end of the house is where I see patients. If anything happens, if Emily's condition worsens, knock loudly for my attention.'

A rush of gratitude and relief flooded through Poppy. 'May I pick her up?' she asked.

Dr Anderson shook his head. 'Not yet. Let's wait for Sylvia to return with the medicine and see how Emily responds. Then you can hold her, in fact I recommend that you do. The child needs to be kept warm.'

'Thank you, Doctor. I can't express how grateful I am. But . . .'

'What is it?' he asked.

'My sons are in your waiting room; they're just small boys and I can't expect them to walk home on their own. Besides, there's no one there. My husband works at the pit, and he's not due home for hours. He wasn't supposed to be working the night shift tonight, but he got called in at the last minute. The pit needed more men and Sid needed the money . . .'

Dr Anderson rubbed his chin. 'I see,' he said, thinking this through. 'If only Miss Marchmont was still with us. She could have helped, taken your boys home and stayed with them until your husband arrived. Damn that woman for leaving us in the lurch!'

Poppy started at his outburst.

'I'm sorry, Mrs Lawson,' he said contritely. 'Miss Marchmont was the surgery assistant, and very good at her job. But she left us last week and we've been struggling since. My daughter does what she can, but we need a new member of staff. I've tried asking in the village for a replacement, but we can't find anyone suitable.' He gave a wry smile. 'Apologies, I'm sure you don't need to hear my woes when your heart is full of worry for your child.' He paused for a second as if deciding whether to carry on, and when he did, his words took Poppy by surprise. 'I don't suppose you know anyone who might be interested in the position, Mrs Lawson? Perhaps even yourself?'

She looked at him, confused. 'Me, sir? No, I . . .' She was about to admit that she couldn't read or write, then thought better of it. 'I have a job already, working at the Trewhitts' shop.'

Dr Anderson visibly blanched. 'The Trewhitts? Ambrose and Ella?' he said.

She nodded. 'I clean their shop and their living quarters.'

'Oh, my dear child. You haven't heard the news?' he said softly.

'What news?'

Dr Anderson pulled a chair across to sit opposite Poppy. Gently he broke the news to her that Ambrose and Ella had passed. Each word hit her hard, and she struggled to take in the enormity of it all. Tears rolled down her face. The doctor patted her hand and expressed his condolences on the loss of her friends. Then he walked to the door that led to the waiting room and opened it wide. Harry and Sonny were sitting in exactly the same spot where Poppy had left them. Harry was biting his lip, and Sonny was staring straight ahead.

'Twins!' Dr Anderson remarked. 'Now then, would you boys like a ginger snap and a cup of milk?'

Harry and Sonny looked at Poppy, unsure of how to reply.

'That's very kind, thank you,' Poppy replied, wiping her tears away.

'I'll ask Sylvia to bring blankets for your overnight stay,' Dr Anderson said. 'And she'll set the coal fire in the waiting room. Emily will need bodily warmth from you, Mrs Lawson. And once again, I'm deeply sorry for the loss of your friends.'

'Thank you, Doctor,' Poppy replied.

Once Emily had been given medicine to help her breathe and control her wheezing, Poppy took her in her arms and sat in a hard-backed chair. Through the open door that led to the waiting room, she kept her eye on Harry and Sonny, who were lying on the wooden bench, covered with blankets. Soon, both the boys and her baby were asleep.

Poppy's troubled thoughts turned to Ambrose and Ella. The news that they'd died . . . well, it didn't seem real. She found their passing as hard and as difficult as anything she'd suffered before. And there was Rose to worry about too. Despite the efforts she and Sid had gone to to rescue Rose from Gray Road, was there a chance James might imprison her again? Please no, she whispered. She thought about Sid, who'd be returning from work expecting to sink into his bath in front of the fire, expecting his dinner on the table, his children in bed, his wife waiting for him. Instead, he'd return to an empty house with no idea where his family had gone.

She closed her eyes, pressed her tears away, and sent up a silent prayer for the souls of Ambrose and Ella. Then she prayed for Emily to be kept safe in the hours ahead. And so began one of the darkest nights of her life. The last time she'd felt so lost and alone was the night when Rose had been taken. She prayed that her baby would survive.

Chapter Forty-Four

Poppy woke in the dead of night. She didn't know where she was, and it took her a few moments to remember the dreadful situation she was in. She thought she'd heard a noise, and sat up straight, listening, but it didn't come again. In her arms, Emily was asleep, breathing easier now, and Poppy rested her head against the back of the chair, relief rushing through her. It was cold in the room, as the fire had burned itself out, and there was just a little light left in the lamp. She turned her head to look through the open door to the room where Harry and Sonny were sleeping, oblivious to all that was happening.

The sound that had woken her reached her again. Some-one was knocking at the door that opened to Stockton Road. Carefully, slowly, she stood up and walked across the waiting room.

'Who is it?' she said softly.

'It's me, Pops. Lil Mahone told me you were here.'

Poppy slid the bolt and opened the door with her free hand, and Sid stepped inside. Even though she couldn't see him properly in the darkness, she knew he'd come straight from work. His eyes shone white from his coal-blackened face, and he stank of the pit and cold earth.

'How's the bairn?' he asked.

'Come through to the other room so we don't wake the lads,' Poppy whispered.

Sid followed her to the room where she'd spent the last hours cradling Emily, waiting with fingers crossed for her to recover. He sat in the chair where Dr Anderson had sat earlier when he'd delivered the awful news about the Trewhitts. Poppy returned to her own chair.

'Emily turned an awful colour, Sid. I had no choice but to come here. I know you said we couldn't afford the doctor's fee, but something happened at home, something involving Rose. I don't know where to begin to tell you about it.'

He cut her short. 'I know.'

'You do? How?'

'Our next-door neighbour heard everything,' he said.

'Oh, that dreadful woman!' Poppy said angrily, but Sid was more charitable in his reply.

'Without Lil listening in, I wouldn't be here now, love. She waited up all night, waiting for me to come home, so she could tell me where you were and what had happened to Emily. She wasn't prying, love, don't be angry. She was worried sick about the bairn and said she wanted to help. I came straight away. I didn't even get into the house; Lil met me at the end of Tunstall Street.'

'And she knows about Rose, too?'

Sid nodded. 'I can't believe Rose has gone back to James. What was she thinking?'

Poppy gazed at the baby. 'She was thinking of us, Sid. She was thinking of Emily and getting her well. She's sacrificed herself to that beast to get us the money for the medication Emily so desperately needs. Without Rose, our daughter might not have made it through the night. She could have died.'

Sid leaned across to her and kissed her lips. When he pulled away, Poppy saw tears streaming down his face, streaking the coal dust on his skin.

She took a few moments before she continued. 'I'm not sure I understand Rose any more, but I will always be in her debt for saving Emily's life. I'm just the sixpenny orphan who stayed in Ryhope. I have my family, I have you, but Rose . . . well, she carries a heartache inside her. All I ever wanted to do was protect her, but it turns out I can't even do that.'

'She knows her own mind, love. We have to let her do what she wants. Besides, James is aware that we know where he lives, and he's probably aware that we know what he did to Rose. He might be in fear of us telling the police if he doesn't let her go free in the morning.' Sid straightened in his seat. 'Oh, but Lil told me something else. It's going to break your heart, so I need you to be strong when I tell you what's happened. It's about the Trewhitts.'

Tears sprang again to Poppy's eyes. 'I already know. Dr Anderson told me. I still can't take it in. What'll I do without them, Sid?'

'Oh love, I'm so sorry.' He took her hands. 'I know how close you were to them.'

'They were like family to me. And now Rose has gone again, and Emily . . . We almost lost her last night, and she might not be out of danger yet.'

'Hey, come on,' Sid said soothingly when Poppy began crying again. 'Dr Anderson will look at her in the morning, he'll tell us what's what. As for the Trewhitts, Lil says she'll let us know when their funeral will be held just as soon as she finds out. I know you'll miss them, love. But we've got a baby on the way; we've got to be positive and look to the future – *our* future.'

Poppy wiped the back of her hand across her eyes. 'If it's a boy, I'll call him Ambrose,' she said decisively.

'And if it's a girl, we'll call her Ella,' Sid added.

'And if it's twins again and there's one of each?' she asked, forcing a smile.

'I don't think my poor heart could take twins again,' Sid said wryly. 'Speaking of the boys, should I take them home with me now? I need to sleep, Poppy, or else I'll not make it into work for my next shift, and we can't afford to lose money.'

'Yes, take them both, please. Wake them carefully; they're going to get a shock when they see your coal-covered face, and they'll not know where they are.'

'I'll turn it into a big adventure for them, walking through Ryhope in the dead of night,' Sid said.

He walked into the waiting room and gently shook the boys awake. Sonny began crying, and Sid shushed him and calmed him. He brought the boys to Poppy, who kissed both of them on the cheek, then Sid kissed Poppy, leaving another smudge of black coal on her face. She rubbed it off with her hand before seeing the three of them out, then she returned to her chair and sat by the oil lamp cradling Emily until the morning's soft light crept into the room.

Early morning it was Sylvia who bustled into the room. She lifted the baby from Poppy's arms, unwrapped her from her blanket and laid her on the table covered with the white cloth. Poppy watched, holding her breath.

'How is she? Has she recovered? Is she going to be all right? Please, Sylvia, tell me,' she urged.

Sylvia moved Emily's limbs one by one, then massaged her chest and her back as Dr Anderson had done the previous day.

'Do you know what you're doing?' Poppy asked, then realised how her words must have sounded. 'Sorry, I didn't mean to cast doubt on you, but it's your father who is the doctor, after all.'

'And I'm a student nurse,' Sylvia said kindly. 'I'm studying at the Royal Infirmary in town, and when I'm not studying, I learn all I can from my father.' She returned to examining the child. 'She looks to be a little improved,' she said.

Poppy thought she was going to be sick as relief flooded through her.

'Father is on his way; he'll give you medication to take home with instructions on how to administer it until your baby improves.'

Poppy forced herself out of the chair to stand next to Sylvia, and together they looked down on Emily. A rush of love went through her as she gazed at her darling daughter. Emily's skin was still pale, her breathing uneven, but she was certainly in a better condition than she'd been the night before.

'Thank you, Sylvia,' Poppy said gratefully.

The door behind them was flung open and Dr Anderson strode in.

'Sylvia, where is my black notepad? I can't find the blasted thing! Miss Marchmont used to keep it on my desk, but it seems to have disappeared.'

'I'll find it for you, Father,' Sylvia said as she disappeared through the door.

The doctor walked to Emily and inspected her in the same way that Sylvia had done minutes before.

'Will she be all right, Doctor?' Poppy asked.

He turned to her, laid a hand on her shoulder and looked into her eyes. 'Yes, she will. She's survived the night. She's a fighter, a determined little child. And what about you, Mrs Lawson? How are you after spending the night in that uncomfortable chair?'

Poppy stretched out her back. 'A little achy, that's all. And I feel sick too, but I think that's my pregnancy developing.'

'Another child on the way? I trust you will be well,' Dr Anderson said. 'But I'm afraid I must leave you, as I have patients to prepare for. Sylvia will give you the medication and my bill. Wait here, she won't be too long.'

'Thank you again, for all that you've done,' Poppy said.

She sank back into the seat and waited. A few moments later, Sylvia wafted into the room carrying a mug of tea, an envelope and a small paper bag. 'I thought you might appreciate hot tea before your walk to the colliery,' she said.

Poppy took the tea gratefully.

Sylvia held up the envelope. 'Father's bill, I'm afraid,' she said apologetically. 'And this is the medication with his instructions written inside.'

When Poppy didn't open the envelope to read the bill or look at the medication, Sylvia understood immediately. Mrs Lawson wasn't the first of her father's patients in

Ryhope who couldn't read or write, and she made no fuss about it. She simply explained the instructions on the medication, then opened the bill and pointed to the numbers at the bottom of the page while reading out the total.

The figures made no sense to Poppy; they were nothing more than marks on the page. 'Take whatever money's needed from the purse,' she said.

Sylvia picked up the velvet purse and counted out most of the coins. When she handed it back, it felt much lighter in Poppy's hand. Then she opened a black ledger on the desk and wrote something inside. 'Miss Marchmont used to keep our books in order, I really don't have time for this,' she muttered under her breath. She turned to Poppy. 'I must go and help Father prepare,' she said. 'Please, stay a while and finish your tea, and when you let yourself out, leave the door unlocked. Father's surgery will be open to patients this morning; his first appointment should be arriving quite soon.'

Left alone with her baby, Poppy finished her mug of tea, then wrapped Emily in her blanket and cradled the baby to her heart. She picked up the purse and medication and stuffed them into her skirt pockets, leaving the doctor's house on Stockton Road as the sun rose over the sea. And as she began the slow walk home, she prayed and hoped that Rose would return that day.

Chapter Forty-Five

When she reached the pit house, she paused at the door and crossed her fingers. 'Please let her be inside,' she whispered to the morning air. But when she pushed the door open and walked into the kitchen, it was only Sid who was sitting by the fire. The coal dust had been washed from his skin, and Poppy saw splashes of water from his bath on the floor.

'How's the bairn?' he asked immediately, rising to walk to his child.

'Much better,' Poppy replied. 'Dr Anderson has given us medicine for her, we're to give it to her three times a day for a week. If she's no better by the end of it, I'm to take her back. Where are the boys?'

'Upstairs, sleeping.'

'And Rose?'

Sid shook his head. 'She hasn't come home, love.'

Poppy gently laid Emily in her cot. She pulled the doctor's bill and the velvet purse from her pockets and handed both to Sid. He opened the envelope first and sucked air through his teeth when he saw how much the doctor had charged.

'There's no way we could have afforded this without Rose's help,' he said. 'I dread to think what might have happened if James hadn't arrived when he did.'

'Don't look upon him as a hero,' Poppy warned. 'That man . . . who knows what wickedness he's up to with Rose.'

Sid opened the purse and counted the money that was left. 'Why, there's enough in here to last us to the end of the week until I get paid,' he exclaimed. 'We can finally give Amos the rent we owe and pay Dan for the missing chimney brush.'

'Put the purse on the mantelpiece, Sid,' Poppy instructed as she collapsed into a chair. She gazed down at Emily, relieved that her baby was breathing more easily. 'Dr Anderson's medicine seems to be having an effect already,' she said softly before turning her gaze back to her husband. 'Do you really think Rose will return?'

'Yes, I do,' he said firmly.

'But what if James won't let her leave? He's controlled her before in that house.'

'Poppy, give your sister some credit. She wouldn't have left here with him if she didn't know what she was doing.' He laid his hand gently on Poppy's arm. 'You've got to trust her, Pops. Did she sound in control of herself yesterday when she agreed to go with him?'

'Yes . . .' she said, thinking back, calming down a little now. 'Yes, she did, very much so, in fact.'

'Then we have to assume she knows how to play him to her advantage. He left the purse of money at her request, didn't he?'

'Yes, but—'

'No buts, Poppy. It sounds to me as if an arrangement was made.'

Poppy sighed deeply. 'Let's hope he keeps his part of the bargain. I couldn't bear to lose her again.'

Sid's stomach rumbled loudly, and she glanced at him. 'Oh Sid, you must be starved. I haven't given a thought to breakfast. Did the boys eat anything when you brought them home?'

'No, it was still dark out and I put them straight to bed. But you're right, Pops, I'm hungry. I could eat an old pit pony the way I feel. I had a look in the pantry, but all I could find was carrots, potatoes and tea. There wasn't any bread.'

Poppy stood and picked up the purse from the mantelpiece. 'Then I'll take this and go to the store for bacon and eggs. We deserve something in our bellies after the drama of last night. I keep thinking about Ambrose and Ella. I still can't believe they've gone. I'm not thinking straight, Sid. This whole thing has knocked me for six. It'll do the baby inside me no good either. I need to rest.'

'Then let me go to the store,' he said, reaching for the purse. Poppy gladly handed it over.

'Buy bread too,' she said, as Sid put his jacket on and headed out of the door.

Left alone by the fire, Poppy found her head drooping forward. Unable to keep her eyes open, she let them close, her shoulders slumped, and she soon fell asleep in the chair. When she opened her eyes again, she couldn't believe what she saw. Not only was Rose standing in front of her, but Lil Mahone was there too, wearing her black coat and green knitted hat. She shook her head and swallowed hard. 'I must be dreaming,' she muttered.

Rose ran to her side, then looked into the cot to check on Emily. 'You're not dreaming. I'm back. Is the baby all right? Oh Poppy, I've been so worried about her.'

Poppy was so surprised at Rose being in the room that she could barely speak. And what on earth was Lil Mahone doing there? She couldn't make sense of it. She looked from Rose to Lil and back again. She had to touch Rose's arm to convince herself she was real.

'Is it really you?' she asked her.

Rose threw her arms around her and kissed her on the cheek. 'It's really me,' she smiled.

'But how did you get away? I mean . . .' Poppy stopped and turned to Lil. 'And what are you doing here? This is a private matter between me and my sister.'

'Lil's the reason I'm here, Poppy,' Rose said, smiling sweetly at Lil Mahone.

'What do you mean?'

Lil nodded sharply. 'I heard you arguing last night. I told you these walls were thin. That's how I was able to get hold of Sid when he came home from work and send him down to the doctor's house.'

'Yes . . . but what's this got to do with Rose?' Poppy asked, wishing Lil would get to the point. She pinched her leg to make sure again she wasn't dreaming, but the pain she felt was real. She focused on Lil as she began to explain.

'I heard a house on Gray Road mentioned while you were arguing. I know that area of town – it's where Bob's sister lives. She worships at St Michael's church and I know there's only one house on Gray Road, so I knew exactly where Rose was headed, and it sounded to me as though you were concerned she might not return.'

'My word, you really can hear everything through these walls,' Poppy said.

Lil straightened her back as she went on. 'After Sid came home from work and I told him where you were, I headed to Bob's sister's house.'

'In the dead of night?' Poppy exclaimed.

'Bob came with me; it was the least he could do. He's been in my bad books for a couple of weeks – too much drinking in the Colliery Inn after a hard day's work – so I made sure he made it up to me last night. He walked with me all the way to Gray Road. It took us a couple of hours, and I was exhausted when we got there. We stopped on the way at the house of a friend of mine. She fed us and helped us on our way.'

Poppy's mouth opened in shock. Lil Mahone was turning out to be quite the surprise.

'Bob's sister let us into the church, and we stayed there keeping watch on the house. This morning at first light, we knocked on the door and demanded to see Rose.'

Rose squeezed Poppy's hand as she took up the story. 'James didn't try to stop me leaving,' she said. 'Once he realised I have family who love me and friends like Lil and Bob who care about my welfare, he knew he couldn't keep me locked up any more. He had to let me go, he had no choice.' She lifted Poppy's hand to her lips and gently kissed it. 'I'm back, dear sister, and this time it's for good.' The front door opened and Sid walked in. When he saw Rose and Lil, his mouth hung open in shock. Then he swung his bag of groceries to Rose.

'Well, since you're here, you can make yourself useful,'

he said, giving her a cheeky smile. 'Put the kettle on and we'll have some bacon and eggs.'

Poppy looked at her neighbour, who was still standing with her arms crossed. 'Will you stay for breakfast, Lil?' she asked.

Lil tutted loudly. 'I thought you'd never ask.'

Chapter Forty-Six

Inside St Paul's church, Reverend Daye was presiding over not one, but two funerals. Ambrose and Ella would be buried in the churchyard together, in death as they had been in life. Poppy sat in a pew with Sid on one side and Rose on the other. They bowed their heads to pray, they stood to sing hymns, and they listened with tears in their eyes as Reverend Daye gave eulogies. When the service ended, Poppy shuffled along the pew, her heart grieving for the loss of her friends.

As she made her way to the church door, she saw Ambrose and Ella's son Michael shaking hands with the mourners, thanking them for coming and inviting them to the wake at the Albion Inn. The crowd moved slowly forward, and then finally it was Sid and Rose's turn. Sid shook Michael's hand and told him how sorry he was about the passing of his parents. Rose planted a kiss on Michael's cheek and said she would raise a glass to Ambrose and Ella at the Albion Inn. Poppy stepped forward last.

'And you, Poppy? Will you come to the Albion Inn to take a drink for Mam and Dad?' Michael asked.

'Yes, I'm heading there now,' she said softly.

She kissed Michael on the cheek, and as her lips brushed his tear-stained face, he gently held her hand and whispered to her, 'I need to speak to you, in private.'

She pulled back and looked into his eyes, and saw Ambrose looking back at her, for Michael was the double of his dad. She didn't know him well, as he lived in the next village and she'd only met him a handful of times when she'd bumped into him and Doris at the shop. She was confused about what he had to say.

'We'll talk at the Albion Inn. I'll be there soon,' he said.

She nodded politely and stepped out of the church, to where Sid and Rose were waiting.

'What was all that about?' Sid asked suspiciously. 'It looked like Michael Trewhitt was having a private word with you.'

Poppy hooked her right arm through Sid's and her left arm through Rose's and they began walking down the church path. 'He says he needs to talk to me about something,' she said softly, so that none of the mourners milling outside the church could hear. 'But I haven't a clue what it is.'

'Must be something to do with Ambrose and Ella – perhaps they left you something in their will?' Rose suggested, but Poppy shook her head.

'They were as poor as church mice. I cleaned upstairs in their rooms, remember? I saw how they lived hand to mouth. Their furnishings were sparse. All they owned in the world was their shop and the rooms above. No, I don't want or expect anything from them, but I'm intrigued to know what Michael has to say.'

Sid began to walk faster as they left the church path. 'Come on, let's get to the Albion Inn, I'm gasping for a pint. Might as well make the most of it while Mam and Dad are looking after the bairns.'

'I just hope Emily stays well,' Poppy said.

'She will, love,' he assured her, 'thanks to Rose's sacrifice. Emily's responded well to Dr Anderson's medication; there's no reason to think she won't continue to improve.'

Poppy smiled at him, then picked up her pace as the three of them headed arm in arm to the wake. When they rounded the corner where the village school stood, however, Rose began to slow down.

'I'd like to take another look at our school again. I know I've walked past it a few times already since I returned, but I'd like to see it properly, Poppy, with you,' she said.

'Aw, Rose, but the pub's just down there,' Sid teased.

'You go on, Sid. Buy me a glass of lemonade. Me and Rose will catch you up,' Poppy said.

Sid stuffed his hands into his pockets and set off for the pub on his own while Poppy and Rose stood together looking through the iron railings in front of the school. Rose ran her hand across a honey-coloured stone.

'The Trewhitts' funeral gave me a few things to think about,' she said. Poppy looked at her.

'What sort of things?'

'Things about love and friendship, about Ambrose and Ella being so close. It seems fitting that they went together, doesn't it?'

'I can't imagine it any other way,' Poppy said with a catch in her voice.

'Theirs was a true love, a real love, just like the one that you and Sid share.' Rose turned to Poppy with tears in her eyes. 'I want that too. I want to find someone of my own who'll love me like Ambrose loved Ella. I want someone who'll love me like Sid has always loved you.'

Poppy slid her arm around her sister's slim waist. Rose had begun eating more, and was putting on a little weight. Her body felt less bony and sharp than when she'd first returned to Ryhope.

'You'll find someone,' she said softly. 'He's out there for you. And if you don't mind me saying so, it isn't Arthur.'

Rose gripped the railings with both hands. 'The funeral made me realise that what I had with Arthur wasn't even friendship. It was loneliness on my part, and he was desperately looking for someone to help him leave his wife.'

Poppy dropped her hand from Rose's waist and looked down at her boots, choosing her words carefully. 'You never . . . That night when you returned to James, you've never spoken of it,' she said.

'No, and I won't speak of it ever,' Rose said bitterly, before softening her tone as she turned to Poppy. 'The only joy I'll take from it is that Emily is well. That's the reason I did it.'

'And I'll always be grateful. Sid and I will never forget what you did. But . . . what if James returns, Rose? What if —'

Rose raised a hand to stop her saying more. 'It's over. I'll never go back to him, and I dare say after the dressing-down I gave him on the night I spent there, he'll never seek me out again. Finally I can stop looking over my shoulder. As for Arthur Mason, I don't intend to see him again. I was so confused when I escaped from James – I couldn't imagine being worthy of any decent man. Now I want to believe I am. I don't know if I'm ready yet, but perhaps one day you and Sid might introduce me properly to his friend Freddy. He and I . . . Well, he seemed kind and friendly when we met that day you moved house. I'd like to talk to him again. That's if he's single, of course.'

Poppy's heart leapt with joy. 'I'm proud of you, Rose, and if they were still here, I know Mam and Dad would be proud of you too.' A beat passed before she dared ask another question. 'You and Lil Mahone seem to be getting friendly. Are you sure you can trust her not to spread everything she knows?'

'I'm sure,' Rose said, gazing ahead. 'The reason Lil helped me that night on Gray Road was because she's led a hard life too, harder than you can imagine. She told me a little of it, enough for me to know that behind her harsh exterior lies a sad and broken soul. Her dad beat her. She suffered cruelly at his hands as a girl. That's why when she heard our argument through the walls, she wanted to help in any way she could.'

She turned away from the school, smiling weakly, and threaded her arm through Poppy's. 'I think it's about time we joined Sid in the pub to raise a glass to Ambrose and Ella.'

They walked past the Trewhitts' shop, where the wooden shutters were pulled back and black crêpe paper lined the windows. When they reached the Albion Inn, the door was propped open. They walked inside and Poppy saw Sid sitting at a small table by the window with three glasses in front of him. She sat next to him, surprised to see that the glasses contained brandy, rather than beer for him and Rose and lemonade for her as expected.

'I didn't need to buy these – they're on the house, all paid for in advance by Ambrose,' he explained.

A tap on Poppy's shoulder made her spin around.

'Sid, Rose.' Michael nodded politely. 'Would you mind if I took Poppy away for a quiet word? It's in confidence, like.'

Sid raised his glass. 'As long as you bring her back in one piece.'

Poppy stood and followed Michael to a quiet corner of the pub, away from people reminiscing about Ambrose and Ella. He pulled a chair out and indicated for her to sit. She was feeling anxious and confused. Why was he being so secretive? What could he possibly have to say that he couldn't say in front of her husband and sister? He gave a little cough and sat up straight in his seat.

'My parents thought the world of you,' he began.

'And I them, Michael. My condolences to you and Doris.'

'Thank you,' he said. He laid his flat cap on the table, then stared at it for a few seconds as if trying to gather his thoughts.

'Go on, please,' Poppy said kindly.

'Ah yes, sorry, forgive me,' Michael said. 'What I have to tell you is of some importance.'

He delved into his pocket and brought out a long white envelope, which he slid across the table towards her. There was writing on the front of it, a sprawl of large, looping letters in black ink.

'Everything you need to know is in here,' he said.

Poppy's heart dropped. She stared at the envelope,

then reached out to touch it and run her fingers over it. Remembering Rose's words about the possibility of being left something in Ambrose and Ella's will, she pushed the envelope back towards Michael.

'I can't take whatever's in here,' she said.

'Of course you can, lass, it's what Mam and Dad wanted. They always thought of you as the daughter they never had.'

Poppy felt tears prick her eyes.

'Open it and read it,' Michael urged.

She shook her head. 'I can't, Michael. I can't read.'

He sat back in his seat. 'Ah, I see. Then would you like me to read it to you?'

She looked across the room to where Sid and Rose were chatting. Whatever was inside the envelope was of some importance, Michael had said. There was someone else she wanted to share this moment with.

'Would you mind if I asked my husband to read it to me?'

'I wasn't sure if you wanted anyone else to know, Poppy. That's why I spoke to you in confidence outside of the church.'

'I tell my husband everything,' Poppy said.

'Then I'll get him.'

Michael walked across the pub and Poppy picked up the envelope. It felt heavy in her hand, quality paper by the feel of it. Not for the first time, she wished she was able to read. The feeling of shame she sometimes carried at her lack of ability to do so now hardened to anger. Was it too late to learn?

Sid appeared at the table, carrying his glass of brandy.

'I'll leave you to it,' Michael said. 'And if you have any

questions, if you need to clarify anything, just come and ask. I'll be here with Doris for the rest of the day. I'm going to the bar now, as I could do with a drink.'

'Thanks, Michael,' Poppy said.

As Michael walked away, Sid slid into his chair and Poppy gave him the envelope. 'Read it to me, please.'

He looked into her eyes, took a deep breath, then slid his finger under the flap at one end and pulled out a sheet of paper, which he unfolded and laid on the table. Poppy could see lines of handwriting, neat as a pin.

'What does it say?' she whispered.

Sid took a moment to take it all in, and then a huge smile spread across his face. 'It's the recipe for jam tarts,' he said, his face lighting up and his eyes twinkling. 'Ambrose and Ella have given you their secret family recipe for jam tarts!'

He and Poppy grinned at each other. 'How generous,' she said. 'You or Rose will need to read it to me when I make them at home.'

Sid folded the sheet with the recipe on and began to return it to the envelope, but it wouldn't go back in. He tried again, but it still wouldn't go in as smoothly as it had come out.

'Hang on, there's something else in here,' he said, peering inside the envelope. 'Why, there's another sheet.'

He laid the recipe down, pulled out the second sheet of paper and smoothed it out on the table. Poppy stared at it, desperate to know what it said. This sheet was typewritten, not handwritten like the recipe. There was a large, impressive stamp at the top of the page, but she had no clue what it meant. She looked at Sid, who was concentrating hard.

'Sid?' she asked.

He reached for his brandy glass and drained it in a single gulp.

'What is it? What does it say?' she urged.

'It says . . .' he looked up, eyes wide, 'it says that Ambrose and Ella have left you their shop.'

Chapter Forty-Seven

Poppy's jaw dropped, her head spun, and if she hadn't already been sitting down, she would have fallen to the floor in shock.

'The shop?' she said when she found the power of speech.

Sid tapped the letter on the tabletop. 'That's the gist of it, Pops. It's all in legal writing, I can't make head nor tail of some of it, but that's what I'm able to glean from the parts I understand.'

'The shop?' she repeated, dumbstruck.

Michael appeared at their table with a pint of Vaux stout in his hand and sat down between Poppy and Sid. 'Well, lass? What do you think?' he asked.

Poppy looked into his serious face. 'I can't take the shop,' she said. 'It's yours, Michael. Your mam and dad should have left it to you. You're their son and heir.'

'Dad offered it to me and Doris many times over the years, but we always turned him down. And when he knew that he and Mam weren't well, he offered it again, but we still turned him down.'

'Why?' Sid asked.

'Because I'm getting on a bit, lad, and I don't know anything but work at the pit. Besides, me and Doris don't want to run a shop. It's too far from home, which means we'd have to move house, and we're not prepared to do that. We're settled where we are and we like it. I know how much the shop means to the people of Ryhope – it's more than just somewhere for them to buy groceries . . .' he tapped the envelope, 'and jam tarts. It's a place folk rely on. It'd mean the world to me if you took it on. And I know it'd mean the world to Mam and Dad, too.'

'Don't you want to sell it? It's your inheritance, Michael,' Poppy said.

'Me and Doris have been over this many times,' Michael explained. 'What do we need the money for? We weren't blessed with bairns, so there's just the two of us, and we're doing all right as we are. Please, the best thing for us would be for you to take the shop on, if you're willing.'

Poppy's head was whirring, still reeling from shock. She glanced at Sid, before dropping her gaze to the envelope. Then slowly she looked up again. 'Michael, it's an honour to be offered the shop . . .' she began.

'And the rooms above, remember,' he chipped in. 'Your family will have plenty of space to live up there.'

'. . . but it's an offer I can't accept.'

'Pops?' Sid whispered.

'No, Sid,' she said sadly, shaking her head. 'You know how I am, both of you know I can't read and write, and as for adding up numbers, well . . . how can someone like me manage a shop? Accounts will need doing, orders will need to be checked . . . I can't do it, Michael. I'm sorry, but I can't.'

Michael sat back in his seat and took a long drink from his pint. 'Dad told me you'd say that,' he said gently. 'And do you know what his advice to me was?'

Poppy looked at him, waiting to hear.

'He said to offer you whatever it takes to put you behind the counter. He wanted the shop kept in the family, Poppy, and he thought of you as one of us, he always did.'

Poppy looked from Michael's trusting face to Sid's, and an idea began to form in her mind. 'Well . . . there's Rose, of course, I could ask her to help me. She is in need of a job.'

'The Thomas girls running the shop together. Oh, I'm sure Mam and Dad would be pleased.' Michael glanced at Sid. 'I'll leave you to talk things over. I expect you'll have a lot to think about. I know you've just moved up to Tunstall Street. Let's meet here a week today to talk it through, get the paperwork signed and sealed and . . .' He paused and shifted uncomfortably in his seat. 'Of course, I'll need your signature, Poppy, on the documents.'

Sid laid his hand over hers. 'I'll help you,' he said. 'Don't worry.'

Pub landlady Hetty Burdon approached the table to collect empty glasses. She bent low to Michael and kissed him on the cheek.

'I'm sorry for your loss, Michael. Your mam and dad will be missed by us all.'

Michael stood and excused himself, then headed to the bar with Hetty. Poppy looked across the room. Rose had been chatting to Lil Mahone, but now she was sitting alone.

'Do you think Rose would want to work with me?' she asked Sid.

'There's only one way to find out. Why not put it to her right now? Might as well strike while the iron's hot,' he said.

'I've got some news!' Rose said excitedly when Poppy and Sid sat down opposite her. Poppy had never seen her so animated. 'Lil Mahone told me last week there was a job going at Dr Anderson's house for a general assistant. She put a word in for me, and I met Dr Anderson yesterday. I didn't say anything to you, Poppy, in case I didn't get the job – I didn't want you disappointed. See, it's a live-in position. And guess what? Lil's just told me she's seen the doctor today and he asked her to tell me that the job's mine. Oh Poppy, isn't it wonderful? I'm so excited. It'll be a new life for me, a new chance, a new start. I'll be able to stand on my own two feet for the very first time in my life. This job will be the making of me, I can feel it in my bones.'

Poppy knew in that instant that she couldn't – wouldn't – puncture her sister's happiness. Rose needed her own life, her independence, and the job as Miss Marchmont's replacement sounded ideal. But where did that leave Poppy with taking on and running the shop? She couldn't do it on her own. She needed someone by her side, someone reliable. She needed someone she could trust with all her heart as Ambrose and Ella had trusted each other. She looked at Sid, and they exchanged a knowing smile.

'Are you thinking what I'm thinking, Mr Lawson?' she said.

Sid gave a cheeky smile. 'Why yes, Mrs Lawson, I do believe I am.' He cleared his throat. 'Actually, Rose, we've got some news for you. I'm going to give up work at the pit, and we're moving back to the village.'

Poppy looked at him and thought her heart would burst with love. 'Are you sure about this?' she said.

'Surer than I've ever been about anything. You know I've had enough of working underground, Pops. It's a hard, dangerous job that leaves me no time to spend with you and the bairns. Almost losing Emily . . . well, it's given me a jolt. I'm putting family above everything now. When the new baby comes, I don't want to miss out on seeing little Ambrose growing up.'

Poppy patted her stomach. 'Or little Ella,' she smiled.

Rose raised her eyebrows. 'What's going on?'

Sid slid his arm around Poppy's shoulders. 'Do you want to tell her, or should I?' he said with a mischievous grin.

'Tell me what? Oh, you two, you're always so secretive, always in cahoots,' Rose teased.

Poppy sat up straight in her seat and looked her sister in the eye. 'Me and Sid . . .' she began, then she paused. The words about to come out of her mouth were going to change their lives. The first thing she'd need to do once she left the Albion Inn was head to the Co-op to sign up for their evening class to learn to read and write. 'Me and Sid . . .' she started again, 'we're taking on the Trewhitts' shop!'

Epilogue

Nine months later

'Harry, Sonny, put those jam tarts down, now!' Poppy called. 'You know they're not for eating, they're to sell downstairs in the shop.'

'Aw, Mam, can't we have one?' Sonny pleaded.

Poppy looked at her sons and smiled. It would be too easy to give in to them, again. 'Sorry, lads. If there's any left at the end of the day when you come home from school, you can have those.' She kissed Harry on the cheek, then did the same to Sonny. 'Be good for your teacher at school today.'

'We always are, Mam,' Harry replied.

She watched as the twins walked hand in hand down the stairs, heading out to the village school, which was just a minute's walk away. With the boys gone, she had Emily and baby Ambrose to see to, before she carried both children downstairs to the shop. Ambrose was a contented, happy baby who slept on a blanket in an old egg box behind the counter while Poppy and Sid worked.

Emily, however, was different altogether. She liked to see who was coming and going in the shop, and enjoyed the attention from customers, who declared her the happiest, bonniest bairn they knew. Poppy's heart always swelled with pride at such compliments.

She worked hard, with four children and Sid to look after and the shop to keep running too. In addition, there was her class at the Co-op, something she'd never once missed. For a couple of hours each Wednesday after work and every Saturday morning, she attended the lesson in the hall upstairs at the store. Learning to read and write was proving just as difficult as she'd expected, but she was determined to master it.

As she was dressing Emily and Ambrose, Sid walked into the room. 'Think we'll need more jam tarts, Pops? I've baked two batches, but you know how well they sell.'

'Two batches ought to be fine,' she said, and then she remembered what she'd promised her sister. 'Oh, but Rose and Freddy are coming to us for tea tonight. I invited them last week. Freddy will be wanting his jam tart; we'd better keep a few back for their visit.'

'It's good to see them getting on so well, isn't it?' Sid said.

'She's got a good man in your pal. And she's loving her job with Dr Anderson too. Everyone who comes into the shop speaks well of her.'

A noise from downstairs stopped them both in their tracks.

'What on earth was that?' Sid said. 'There shouldn't be anyone down there, we're not open yet.'

'Harry and Sonny must've left the back door open on

their way out to school,' Poppy replied. 'I've told them loads of times to close it behind them, but you know what they're like. It's in one ear and out the other with those two.' She handed Emily to Sid. 'Here, look after the bairns. I'm going downstairs to find out what the noise was. It might be a stray dog. I'll use Ella's old broom to chase it away.'

'No, let me go,' Sid said, but Poppy was already striding across the room.

When she reached the bottom of the stairs, she saw the back door standing wide open. 'I'll be having words with those two when they come home from school,' she tutted.

Just then, there was another noise, and this time she froze. Then she picked up Ella's broom and gripped it with both hands as she walked into the shop. 'Who is it? Who's there?' she called.

In front of her, a tall, gangly lad was helping himself to a tin from a shelf. Poppy propped the broom against the wall and took a step towards the lad, who turned and looked at her guiltily.

'Henry Donnelly, I should've known it'd be you. What do you think you're doing? I'm going to have a word with your mam and tell her you've been in stealing again.'

Henry took a step back. 'No, don't tell my mam, please, Mrs Lawson. She'll have my guts for garters if she finds out.'

'Empty your pockets,' Poppy demanded.

Henry cast his gaze to the floor, then put his hand into his trouser pocket. Poppy had to bite her tongue to stop herself from laughing when he brought out a tin of mustard powder.

'Put it on the counter,' she ordered.

He did as he was told.

'Now listen to me,' Poppy said firmly. 'If I catch you stealing again, it won't be your mam I'll tell, it'll be the police. You could lose your job at the pit if the coal company find out.'

'Aw, Mrs Lawson, please don't tell them,' Henry pleaded. 'It's my mam, like, she's not well and there's not been much money coming into our house.'

'And you thought a tin of mustard powder might help her?' Poppy shook her head. 'Don't give me your lies, Henry. I know your mam's perfectly well because I was talking to her yesterday on the colliery bank. Now get out and don't let me see you in here again unless you've got money in your pocket and you want to buy something. Got it?'

Henry shuffled his feet and nodded his head.

'Go on, scram,' Poppy said. She moved so that he could squeeze past her, then she followed him to the back door and locked it.

Walking to the front of the shop, she stood a moment gazing out over the village green. She and Sid had long ago taken down the old wooden shutters that Ambrose and Ella had installed. She liked the way the morning light filled the shop. She opened one of the windows, and the sound of birds singing in the oak trees on the green flooded in. She saw a tram trundle past, then waved to Hetty Burdon, who was cleaning windows at the Albion Inn. Upstairs, Sid was singing to the bairns, and his deep voice floated down to reach her. She smiled, and a feeling of contentment bloomed in her heart.

Just as she was about to head up to help him and get

ready for another day of work, something on the ground caught her eye. It was a tiny silver coin, glittering in the sunlight. She bent down and picked it up.

'Why, it's a sixpence!' she exclaimed. She put it in her skirt pocket and patted it twice, for good luck.

The *Sixpenny* Orphan

Bonus Material

All About Ryhope

Ryhope is a village on the northeastern coast, south of the city of Sunderland in Tyne and Wear. The first mention of Ryhope was in 930AD when the Saxon King Athelstan gave the parish of South Wearmouth to the See of Durham. King Athelstan's name lives on in Ryhope with a street named after him – Athelstan Rigg.

The name Ryhope is an Old English name which means 'rugged valley'. Originally Ryhope is recorded as being called *Rive hope* and has also been recorded as *Refhoppa*, *Reshop* and *Riopp*.

Ryhope developed as a farming community and was popular as a sea bathing resort. However, in 1856 sinking operations reached coal seams deep beneath the magnesian limestone and Ryhope grew as a coal mining village. Ryhope had two separate railways with their own train stations, putting Ryhope within easy commuting distance of Sunderland. By 1905 electric trams also reached Ryhope from Sunderland. The coal mine closed in 1966, marking the end of an era for Ryhope.

For more on Ryhope's past, present and future, Sunderland City Council have a very interesting planning document showing historic pictures. You can find it at http://bit.ly/RyhopeHistory.

And if you'd like to know more about the village of Ryhope, here are some good websites you might like to explore for historic maps, guided walks and a visit to the ever-popular Pumping Station at Ryhope Engines Museum.

A guided walk around Ryhope – From agriculture to coal
http://bit.ly/RyhopeWalks

Historic map of Ryhope
http://bit.ly/RyhopeMap

Ryhope Engines Museum
http://www.ryhopeengines.org.uk/

Chapter 1

Helen Dexter was sitting on the window seat at the Seaview Hotel, looking out over the sea. The Seaview was her home, a three-storey, ten-room hotel on Scarborough's North Bay. She'd been sitting there all night, gazing out of the window, a bottle of whisky by her side.

It wasn't something she made a habit of, sitting up all night drinking. But then it wasn't every day that she held a memorial service for her late husband, who'd been the love of her life. Helen and Tom had known each other for over thirty years: attended the same schools, gone to the same youth clubs, hung around with the same friends. But it wasn't until their late teens that they finally started dating and became inseparable. Everyone said they were made for each other. They married on a warm July day when she was twenty-one and Tom twenty-three. On their wedding day, Helen pledged her love for Tom in front of their families and friends, vowing to love him and cherish him 'till death us do part'.

How the years had flown by since. Helen was forty-eight now and Tom would have been celebrating his fiftieth birthday in April, a milestone that would now go unmarked.

After Tom's memorial, Helen had invited close friends and family to the Seaview for a bite to eat as a way to say a final farewell to the man they'd all adored. Around her now lay the detritus of half-eaten sausage rolls and glasses stained by wine and beer. Her best friend, Marie, had offered to clean up before she left, but Helen wouldn't hear of it. As the afternoon had dissolved into evening, she had tried hard to disguise how relieved she was when everyone started to leave. She wanted to be on her own, for she had a lot on her mind.

She slid her legs along the window seat and noticed a ladder in her stockings above her right knee. Her calves shone in sheer black nylon seven-denier, smooth as silk and now ruined. She pushed her bobbed hair behind her ears and caught a reflection of herself in the window. Her big brown eyes stared back at her; she was surprised that she didn't look as tired as she felt. Her black jacket hung on a chair and her black shoes lay at the end of the window seat. She'd kicked them off after everyone had left, but when Suki had padded into the lounge, she'd had to lift them from the floor. Suki had a thing about shoes; she liked to chew them and Helen had to be careful about what she left lying around. Suki was sprawled on the floor like a pool of liquid caramel. She was a retired racing greyhound, all long limbs and soulful eyes.

Helen turned back to look out of the window. The sun was beginning to rise now, turning the sky milky blue.

Tom had been ill for months, cancer eating away at him at a cruel, relentless pace. When Helen could no longer manage his pain and care, he'd been moved to St Paul's Hospice. She'd visited daily, sometimes taking Suki so that Tom could see the dog through the floor-to-ceiling window by his bed. Suki would stand outside, cocking her head, staring in at him. As he'd neared the end of his life, Helen had promised him she'd carry on running the

Seaview, but he'd been too ill to notice her cross her fingers when the words slipped from her lips.

The small, family-only funeral at St Mary's Church that had marked the end of Tom's life had done him proud. Afterwards, at the crematorium, his favourite hymn had been sung, hugs given and tears wiped away. When his coffin had disappeared behind the curtains, the first soulful notes of his favourite Elvis ballad had played, his only request. He had been an Elvis fan all his life. On the wall of the lounge in the Seaview was a jukebox filled entirely with Elvis songs, but it hadn't been touched since the day Tom was moved to the hospice. Now, more than three months after the funeral, Helen still couldn't bring herself to play it for fear of the emotions that would overwhelm her if she did.

She took a sip of whisky. After the funeral, she had felt unable to cope with her grief. So when Tom's sister Tina had invited her to stay with her and her family on their farm in a remote part of Scotland, she had jumped at the chance. The farm was in the middle of nowhere, far from Scarborough, far from the sea, far from everything that reminded her of Tom. She'd locked up the hotel, bundled Suki into her car, packed a suitcase, put her foot to the accelerator and driven like a woman possessed. She couldn't get away quickly enough.

She'd told Tina she'd only stay a few days, but those days became weeks and ended up turning into three months. Tina had insisted she stay for Christmas, and Helen gratefully accepted her invitation; she couldn't face returning home to spend Christmas on her own. Being on the farm proved restorative for her. She'd helped feed the chickens, and walked the dogs through fields and along streams each morning. Being around Tina's teenage sons, with their energy and vitality, had helped bring her out of herself.

When she'd finally felt strong enough to return to Scarborough, she'd decided to hold a memorial service for her beloved husband, a chance to fully celebrate his life now that she was about to face her future alone. However, something at the back of her mind was troubling her now as she remembered the guests arriving at the Seaview for drinks. It took her a few moments to remember what it was. Two of her best friends, Sue and Bev, had seemed distant with each other and she couldn't figure out why. Had she imagined it, or did Sue make a deliberate show of walking out of the lounge each time Bev walked in? She shook her head to dismiss the thought. She had more pressing things on her mind.

She set her glass on the table and ran her hands over her face. She still had her make-up on, her mask from the day before. But there was no one here to see how crumpled she knew she must look, no matter what her reflection in the window said. In front of a mirror in the harsh light of day, she knew her soft, round face would be pale, and the skin under her eyes dark from lack of sleep. Her plan was to take Suki for a walk, then head to bed to sleep. The Seaview had no guests booked in. Once Tom had taken ill, Helen hadn't the heart or the energy to run the place; it became too difficult even with the help of her staff. She had cancelled all the bookings, emailing the news that due to a family situation the Seaview was taking a break.

Now it was early March, the Easter holidays were around the corner and the holiday season was about to begin, but for the first time in decades, the Seaview was quiet. When asked by disappointed guests, whose holidays she'd had to cancel, if she could recommend somewhere else for them to stay, she gave them the number of the hotel next door. This was the four-star Vista del Mar, run by Miriam Jones, a woman who thought herself and her hotel a cut above Helen and Tom's three-star Seaview. But it wasn't Helen and Tom's now; it was just Helen's, and that scared her more than she dared admit. Because despite the promise she'd given Tom on his deathbed, she wasn't sure she wanted to keep it. What kind of life waited for her on her own in a hotel that catered for families and fun?

She glanced out of the window again. The tide was rolling in, frothy waves breaking. Early-morning surfers, clad head to toe in black to keep out the worst of the North Sea's icy chill, were making their way to the beach.

Helen often felt as if her heart would never recover from losing Tom. He'd been her husband, lover, soulmate and best friend. He had been her life, her everything, for decades. In the early days of their marriage, she'd fallen pregnant twice, but hadn't been able to carry her babies, first a daughter and then a son, to full term. The raw pain never left her, and she and Tom agreed they wouldn't put themselves through more agony by trying again. That was when they'd bought the Seaview. Now, with Tom gone, could she carry on running it alone? Did she even want to?

Don't miss Glenda Young's page-turning Helen Dexter
cosy mystery series!

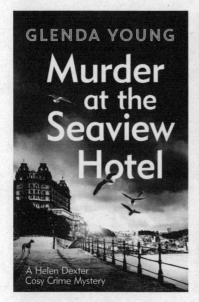

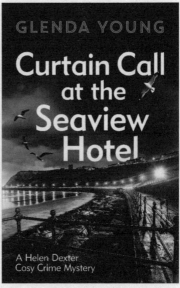

'I loved this warm, humorous and involving whodunnit
with its host of engaging characters and atmospheric
Scarborough setting' Clare Chase

You'll love Glenda's heartwarming festive saga
of family, love and sacrifice!

Will her
dream come
true this
year?

A
Mother's
Christmas
Wish

GLENDA YOUNG

'All the ingredients for a perfect saga'
Emma Hornby

HEADLINE

Don't miss the other enthralling sagas from Glenda Young!

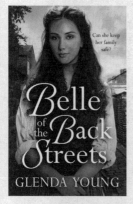

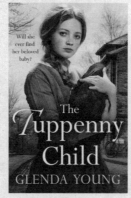

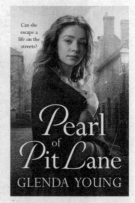

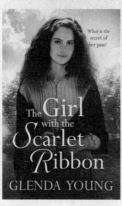

'Real sagas with female characters right at the heart'
Woman's Hour

© Les Mann

Glenda Young credits her local library in the village of Ryhope, where she grew up, for giving her a love of books. She still lives close by in Sunderland and often gets her ideas for her stories on long bike rides along the coast. A life-long fan of *Coronation Street*, she runs two hugely popular fan websites.

For updates on what Glenda is working on, visit her website **glendayoungbooks.com** and to find out more find her on Facebook/**GlendaYoungAuthor** and Twitter **@flaming_nora**.